DOG MYSTERIES

DOG MYSTERIES

The Scent of a Stranger
and
Murder in the Garden

Edna M. Collins

Follow your dreams!

Edna M. Collins

Edna's daughter
works @ K.O.A.
in Wilmington
gave this to
me

iUniverse, Inc.

New York Lincoln Shanghai

DOG MYSTERIES
The Scent of a Stranger and Murder in the Garden

iUniverse books may be ordered through booksellers or by contacting:

iUniverse
2021 Pine Lake Road, Suite 100
Lincoln, NE 68512
www.iuniverse.com
1-800-Authors (1-800-288-4677)

This is a work of fiction. All of the characters, names, incidents, places, organizations, and dialogue in this novel are either the products of the author's imagination or are used fictitiously.

ISBN-13: 978-0-595-42168-8 (pbk)
ISBN-13: 978-0-595-86507-9 (ebk)
ISBN-10: 0-595-42168-7 (pbk)
ISBN-10: 0-595-86507-0 (ebk)

Printed in the United States of America

Acknowledgments

I would like to dedicate this book to Amelia Reynolds Long who encouraged my first book. I would like to thank many who have encouraged me along the way to achieve this impossible dream.

There are too many to name them all but I want to thank some friends such as Julie Paine who read the first draft and liked it. I also want to thank Nancy Dewhurst and Marjie Bassett who encouraged me so very, very much.

I am very indebted to many family members including, of course, my father, William James McKeon. Known as Bill McKeon, he called himself the "Boy Wonder." I don't know if he was but one day, Dad told me to jump and he'd catch me. He didn't. Then he said, "You've just learned the most important lesson in life. Don't trust everybody."

More recently and more importantly, I am grateful to my daughters Dee Christenson, Peggy Dean, and Nancy Vincent.

I am so fortunate to have had the extremely valuable help of my dear Carol Gonzales, who typed, edited, and placed on CD my two mysteries.

I want to especially thank Dr. Diane Holloway for guiding and editing this project through to completion and iUniverse.com for their excellent publishing staff and production crew.

Edna (Eddie) Collins
November, 2006

THE SCENT OF A STRANGER

Edna Collins

CHAPTER 1

▼

The shot rang out loud and clear as the furry mutt rolled against the drifted snow bank.

"What the hell are you doing, Dr. Ralph called out?" Not a question but a demand.

"Just another mutt that thinks he is a sled dog." Jacko returned. "He's followed us for the past four hours. I can't use him. He's too damn big. Better being shot than freezing to death." Jacko and his sled dogs left at the sound of a whip.

The doctor didn't hear Jacko leave as he picked up the over-sized pup from the blood stained snow. "See what I can do for you," the doctor mumbled into the snow and blood-covered shaggy dog. "No, not quite dead!"

He laid the animal in the back of his rusty old truck. He removed his old fur-covered parka to protect the dog from the freezing wind. The doctor patted the bundle saying, "My place isn't too far."

He turned into the Alaskan howling wind and jumped into his truck. "I hope it starts." He said that every time, and every time it did. Snow was flying fast to the point of headlights in daytime. "Frankly, I'm pleased to get home."

The dog was still alive, as he placed the bundle on his kitchen table. The kitchen was his office, where he saw his patients; most were Eskimos. These people had little or no money and Dr. Ralph asked for such in kind.

He unwrapped the dog from the parka. The pup made no movement. His eyes were closed but the man could find a pulse. "Poor thing. He's in shock. Blood loss would account for that, too." He was talking to himself.

The young dog took up most of the table. "What a whopper he is going to be. That is if he pulls through this."

Blood was everywhere; on the white porcelain top table and all over the dog and man.

"Let's get started here," he spoke to the dog. "First, I've got to find the bullet in all this wet and bloody coat of yours."

The bullet was not hard to find. It was in his head, but fortunately not in a serious place. "Damn it! I didn't have to knock him out so badly."

The bullet was out and so was the dog.

"Why all this blood?" Dr. Ralph asked aloud, as he turned the mutt over in search. There was the answer. The dog's four feet were raw and bleeding. Most of his toenails had been pulled out.

"So, you followed that sled for about thirty miles over ice and snow? Why?" He asked the sleeping dog. "Was one of the dogs your mother? It couldn't be for love of Jacko, I hope. Okay, little big boy. Sleep it off. We will talk later. Right now I've got to get both of us cleaned up."

The doctor turned to his desk. He took out a sheet of white writing paper and wrote a letter. The letter began "Dear"—no name. It ended "All my love"—but no signature. Then the man placed the letter in a white envelope and dropped it in a waiting shoebox along with all the others that had never been mailed.

At this point, the dog began to move.

"Oh no," said the doctor. "Those feet are not ready to stand on right now."

The doctor picked up a paw to try to examine it, but the paw was pulled away. It was a huge paw for such a young dog. The dog gave a shiver and tried to get up.

"I'm not going to try to wrestle you," the man warned the mutt. "So, just a little more of the same while I try to put some kind of pen together."

The animal went limp and for some reason, the doctor placed something soft under the dog's head. Then he tried to put a pen together.

Dr. Ralph found some chicken wire. While the dog slept, he wrapped the wire around the four legs of the table. He knew he would have to go around the four legs a second time. He had to hurry because his charge was coming to. He found an old blanket. He quickly removed the dog from the table. He laid the sleeping dog on the blanket. He lifted the heavy table, whose legs were wrapped in wire. Then he carefully placed the homemade cage over the drugged dog.

Dr. Ralph sat down hard on a chair. He was huffing and puffing. He was not a young man. He was a short, red-faced man of 45.

"I hope this holds you until I can build something better."

The man sat in the kitchen with the dog and waited. First, the mutt began to stir; then he opened his eyes.

"How are you doing?" the doctor asked the sleepy dog.

"Grrrr," and his head dropped in pain. He lifted his head again. Now his eyes were open and he fixed them on Dr. Ralph. The dog knew he was caged without looking around. First one raw paw tore at the wire enclosure. He cried like a puppy and lay down on the soft blanket to lick his sore foot. The pen was tall enough that he could stand or lie down. The dog tried to rise.

"Are you hungry?" the doctor asked like he was asking a child. The dog didn't move. He just stared.

"Do you want some water?" The dog got up on his sore feet and began to rock the pen.

"Okay. Steady fellow—just a minute." The doctor tried to steady the wired table.

"Forget it!" The dog was free and the cage was upside down. And a large bowl of water was waiting. The pup drank and drank. Now he was ready for food. Fed and watered, the dog's eye was on the outside kitchen door.

"Hey dog, don't even think of escape. Your paws won't carry you very far. Keep on licking them. That seems to keep you busy and your paws are getting better. Then, I'll let you go."

Days passed and the dog still didn't have a name. He had been the first company Dr. Ralph had had since he arrived in this place of ice cold, snow, and solitude. The man had run away to try to save his sanity. He wanted to be alone with his thoughts, pride, and peace.

The dog had moved the soft blanket closer to the kitchen door. "Come here, you mutt," the doctor moved his chair closer to the dog. "You have to have a name," he said in a kindly tone while he patted his knee. "Come here sport." To the man's total surprise, the dog responded.

"Let's see, what shall we call you? Your nose is long and too heavy to have any Boxer in your line." Dr. Ralph laughed and the dog cocked his head to the side trying to figure out why the laughter.

"Okay, seriously, we will try to figure this out." The dog lay on the blanket as the doctor spoke aloud. "Hmmm. German Shepherd? Chow—coat and jaw? Wolf—for sure? Husky? Well, young man," he addressed the dog. "Your name is Heinze. We have to do this right. Come over here to the sink."

The dog pulled back and showed his teeth. "Have it your way," the doctor agreed. "But your name now is Heinze. Heinze," he addressed the dog as he sat on the kitchen chair. "Did you ever hear the story of *The Lion and the Mouse*?"

Heinze was seated leaning against the door. He appeared to be listening as Dr. Ralph related the proverb.

It took a day or two later to feel a bond developing. Kindness, food, water, and warmth were doing the trick. One morning after Dr. Ralph had shared his breakfast sausage with the dog, the man felt the dog's cold nose on his lap. "Can I trust you to ride in the back of the truck?" he asked the dog.

"Truck?" the dog heard that word before. His long bushy tail began to wag.

"I know I couldn't drive with you in the front. I can't leave you alone. You might decide to wreck the place."

The chicken wire cage was useless. "Come on, Heinze. I gotta get the mail and dog food. The dog followed to the truck. The doctor paused. "Now run away if that is still on your mind."

He dropped the rusty tailgate of the truck. In a leap, the dog was in and down. Heinze seemed right at home.

The village was only five miles away. By driving in the frozen ruts in the road, the ride didn't seem too far. It was a beautiful day. The sun was shining and there were signs of spring. It was almost the middle of May.

The dog and man entered the general store. They bought gas here, the post office was in the store, and so was the gossip mill. The women in the store wanted to pet the dog. They didn't pay much attention to Dr. Ralph. There were plenty of good-looking men in Alaska. Dr. Ralph was well aware. He was surprised that the dog liked the ladies.

"Heinze, I am going to find the thickest collar and the strongest leash they have here. Then I can take you out of the house," the doctor promised.

"It's starting to smell like shit in the kitchen." The doctor laughed and held his nose as he spoke to the clerk and the dog. The dog made a sound.

The doctor reached down and patted the dog. "You're a great dog. We are going to be good friends, ol fellow. I'll even let you pick your collar and leash."

It was no favor for Heinze, who had decided he didn't want anything around his neck.

CHAPTER 2

▼

Dr. Ralph had a brother, five years his junior. It was like a star had been born when he arrived on earth. The mother, father, and son had never known such happiness. From the beginning, the child was deceptive, mean, calculating, demanding, and a first class louse. His name was Bob or "Brother Bob." Like many families, an older son is solid, salt of the earth, and then comes a second son who just wants to rock the earth—and does.

This is the man who wrote Dr. Ralph. The letter was mixed with the other mail, bills, and junk. Dr. Ralph pulled the letter out of the batch of mail. He looked at the return address and remarked "Pennsylvania! By gosh! Bob must have moved!"

Brother Bob was now a doctor, himself. He had two passions—very old things and very young things. He was handsome, tall, and charm just oozed out of him. He could make the people who disliked him purr at his feet. Dr. Ralph recalled with a smile at all the auctions and antique shows his mother had dragged his young brother to.

"Glad it wasn't me," he laughed as he tapped the envelope on the top of Heinze's nose. The dog took a deep breath and turned his head away.

Dr. Ralph went on. "You know he got an education. He learned early what was good and what it was worth; Mother knew and so did he. What he didn't learn from Mom but learned somewhere else was how to slip an expensive piece into his pocket when no one was looking. Something like a "Shimmel," a small woodcarving or a Mountz carving of a dog. Small things to be sure. He would hide his treasures under the bed. No one found them or looked for them because who would ever think he would do a thing like that. As he grew older, his taste for hidden things enveloped him like a cloak.

The long white paper was torn open. A letter fell to the floor. Heinze seized it. "No, no please." Dr. Ralph reached for the letter.

"Good boy, good boy," he repeated. He was out of breath as he grabbed for the letter for fear the dog might tear any word about "her" in the letter. Dr. Ralph's eyes raced across the pages. There was no word about Mariella. Dear Mariella was his brother's wife. She was the reason Dr. Ralph had left Washington, D.C. She was the love of his life.

Dr. Ralph had handed his successful practice over to his brother to run. Dr. Bob's practice was almost nil. He claimed its address was the reason. Address—nothing! The other occupants of the office building were doing fine. Dr. Bob had been on "pot" for twenty years. Now he was progressing to other things that a medical man could get his hands on. Of course, it was another secret for a man who had long hidden many things.

Dr. Ralph sank back into his soft leather chair.

Heinze moved away from the fireplace where he had a puppy-dog dream. All four healing paws were going at the same time as he acted out a dream about running or something.

Dr. Ralph had fallen asleep thinking about Mariella. He recalled the time he first saw her. He was upstairs when his brother Bob came bursting into the house in Georgetown where the brothers and mother lived. He remembered the younger man shouting to one and all "Where is everybody? Come meet my bride, my darling new wife."

They all knew instinctively that she'd be a looker, but Mariella, or Ella as she wanted to be called, was the most beautiful creature Dr. Ralph had ever seen. She was amazing, standing there with her small overnight bag in her hand. Her huge brown eyes sparkled with excitement. She had shoulder-length hair—almost red, but mostly brown. Her teeth and smile were like a movie star. Her figure was visible in a knit suit that followed every curve.

Dr. Ralph enjoyed remembering how his brother pointed all these things out like he had just bought a great prize—"and don't miss those beautiful velvet apples." Bob made a fake move to eat one.

"Does this precious child have a name?" his mother asked.

"She sure does. Meet Mrs. Robert Benson."

Everything was always his. Dr. Ralph offered Mariella a chair and took the bag from her hand. He had to sit down himself. He'd never seen anyone so beautiful.

His knees could hardly hold him and his heart was racing. No woman ever affected him so strongly before.

"That brother of mine does not deserve anyone like her," he thought. Dr. Ralph excused himself and went to the pantry for a shot of Scotch. "Maybe this time he will know how to treat a wife," he silently concluded.

Bob had been married before. She was nice, too nice, for him. She had run off in the middle of the night and never returned. There had been some talk of foul play.

The fire in the fireplace was burning down. Now it was time for bed. Dr. Ralph looked at his new friend and companion.

As he started up the stairs, he said, "If you promise to behave yourself, I'll let you stay in my bedroom tonight."

The dog was up the stairs of the old Georgian mansion before his master as if he understood.

The doctor was downhearted, however. No mention of Mariella. His brother needed money. He wanted to move their office to Roseville, Pennsylvania. Roseville is in the center of Pennsylvania close to Harrisburg, the capital of Pennsylvania. Mother and sons had lived in the beautiful pre-Revolutionary town. All three of them knew the area well. They had lived at the War College, where their father had been stationed.

Their mother was ready for the move at once. She offered to pay all expenses. She had written to Ralph, "So why did he need money from me?"

He asked the dog. The dog answered by cocking one ear and dropping his head. "Thinking back," he told the dog, "my brother has pulled off a few stunts I knew of and some I don't want to know."

A lot of people have a skeleton in their closet but Bob had so many that he couldn't close the door if he tried. Ralph couldn't get to sleep. He dropped his hand at the edge of the bed only to feel a cold nose and licked fingers. This pleased him.

He spoke to Heinze in the dark. "I needed that," he told his new friend. "I really needed that." Dr. Ralph turned in bed and fell asleep.

"Up, up, Heinze! Time for our walk." Heinze was ready to go. He noticed the change in his master.

Late May is a beautiful time in Alaska. All things seem to come alive. The temperature begins to moderate. The snow is melting, causing waterfalls everywhere. Some are small, some large, and others thunderous as they tumble down the mountainsides. To see them in the bright sunshine is to refresh the soul. Dr. Ralph put on his dark glasses to behold the brilliant rainbows.

"Look Heinze," he turned the dog's head to make him take it all in. "Look," he said, pulling the dog's head upright. "Look over there. Where did that large flock of small white birds come from? Look, there goes a small rabbit."

That interested Heinze, but most of all, the dog wanted to walk on the soft moist soil. Heinze felt his master's enthusiasm. He watched the man scoop up some melting snow. He had never seen a snowball and when the doctor threw it, Heinze decided to run after it. But there was nothing to pick up. The snowball was smashed.

Talking out loud, Ralph remarked, "I sure hate to leave this place at this time of the year. But if Bob needs us," he included the dog, "guess we should think about going back. Besides, the cruise ships will be arriving. Ugh."

Brother Bob wasn't at all crazy to have his brother return. It was the money he had asked for. Bob had added gambling to his cocaine habit and chasing young broads and fast expensive cars. At forty, his life was a self-created mess. Roseville would soon recall the number of times he had been picked up by the police as a teenager. Dr. Ralph knew only the half of it. Their mother and father overlooked what they were aware of. Neither one ever asked to see the police records, because they really didn't want to know.

Mothers are not blind but they argue with themselves. They say things like you're only young once, it was the fault of the other driver, he's a good boy, she deliberately got pregnant, or I'd rather he drank and didn't use pot. On and on.

That wasn't all. Dr. Ralph was his brother's enabler. He covered for him all the time, and even sometimes took the blame himself.

CHAPTER 3

▼

"Mariella, dear."

The "dear" dripped with ice.

"Let's talk."

"Oh, here we go again," Mariella thought. She knew without a doubt that her mother-in-law was going to cause her some unpleasantness.

"Honey, sit next to me." Dr. Bob's mother patted the sofa. "Right here, next to me."

She began, "You and Bob have been living with me in my Georgetown house for about two years—right?"

"She's about to ask us or me to move," the young woman thought. But she was wrong.

"Don't you think it is about time you two start a family?" The older woman asked.

"Of course," Mariella replied. "We are trying. Been trying for a long time."

"In that case," the mother-in-law took over, "I know a very good doctor. Maybe you should see him."

"Mother," the young woman choked on the word, "I am seeing a doctor, a fine doctor in New York. And I'm married to a doctor."

She didn't add that she was also seeing her mother. Both were spending time together frequently since her mother was widowed once again. Her mother wasn't happy in the deserts and suburbs of Arizona, longed for the big city, so she had moved east again.

Mariella, a pretty name, never liked her name. She asked everyone to call her Ella. Her own mother tried to call her Mariella but found it difficult to do.

Neither Ella nor her new mother-in-law knew that Bob had had "that operation." Ella thought all naked men looked the same. While it was none of his mother's business, his vasectomy was the reason his wife couldn't conceive. Bob never wanted children and adoption was out of the question. This way, Dr. Bob could "bang" anyone willing and a lot had been ready and willing. He was a handsome devil—great teeth, wonderful smile, nice height—and he knew it.

All the while, the two women tried to communicate but it was going nowhere. Ella changed the subject. "Is it true Bob's brother, Ralph, may be coming home from Alaska?"

"Coming home? Not to this house. Especially not with that dog they tell me about. No, not here! He will have to make other plans. I don't think they would let a dog like that in Georgetown, anyway. Half wolf I've heard. Not here."

"What a mother," Ella thought to herself. "If I have children, I'd love them all the same. This woman has ruined my husband's life," she mused. "She doesn't love him. She just wants to possess him." All this was going through Ella's mind.

Ralph was just as bad. He has always protected his brother. Now he was probably going to do it all over again.

"I can't wait to see the dog," Ella said as she tried to smile. But there were tears in her eyes as her mother-in-law got up and left the room.

It was a beautiful room. Some said it rivaled the White House in antiquity and style. "God help the wife of a favorite son," Ella sighed as she left the room through a different door. "I just cannot live in the same house with her any longer," she thought as she gritted her teeth. "I'm going to tell Bob two years here in her house is too much."

Bob took the news in stride. "Come on Ella, she isn't so bad. For your information," he added, "she's my mother and don't forget it!" He hesitated, "Let me tell you something else. She has offered to help me start a new practice in Roseville."

"With strings attached, I'm sure." Ella said, making a face. Returning to her original thought, she cooed, "Bob, Darling, while you look for a suitable office in Roseville, why don't I look for a place for us? I think it's time to think of "us."

"Forget you," she said under her breath when she realized he hadn't heard a word and was ignoring her. "Damn you," she added.

"No," he started, because he had been listening. "We won't have the money for two places." Bob added, "My thought is to find an office where we can live." He saw the frown on her face at that idea.

He, and she, knew that many offices were on the first floor and living quarters upstairs. "Oh no, not me," she said. "You hear me! For God's sake, no!" Ella really meant it. "I'll think of something better than that."

So the plan was cast. While Dr. Bob looked for what he wanted, Ella covered the Roseville area because she was not going to go along with his idea—"No way."

Weekends were almost happy for both of them. Bob and Ella would drive up from D.C. to Roseville, each with their hopes and ideas of a new way of life.

Dr. Bob really had to get out of Washington. His lifestyle was ruining his practice. The favorite son had long ago lost his taste for pot and his gambling losses caused a change in the office books, and his D.C. mistress had loaned him money.

She said it was "payback time," time for a "tuck here and a tuck there." She wasn't getting any younger, she said, and there was a U.S. Senator calling her. "Time to pay up," she told her lover.

As Dr. Bob summed it up, he thought, "I hope that brother of mine has a buck or two stashed away. Never knew why he left in the first place. There were times that I thought that brother dear had the 'hots' for my wife. Oh, well," he paused, "too damn decent. I'll bet to this day, Ralph never had a 'piece.'"

The handsome man of forty got off his office chair and stretched. Got a lot of stuff to move. He let his eye wonder around the office at the shelves of books and his collection of METTLACK beer steins. He silently recalled, "The first one I paid only $50.00 for and the last one cost me $500.00. Things like that go with me."

He sat down again, and muttered to himself, "Just about an hour more dressing these books. Then I'd better call Lu. Lu was his mistress, the one he couldn't repay, yet didn't want to make her mad. Dr. Bob shook his head, "Can't have any trouble with Lu or her friends, especially the New York ones."

"This could be the beginning of a new life," Ella thought, as she viewed herself in the dressing room in the full-length mirror. She looked a little closer. Can that be a small line at the side of her eye? "No, no, I want a child while I'm still young." She examined her face closer.

"I'm only 24. If luck will have it, I'll be a mother within the year. I've got to get out of this house. I can hear that old pill giving orders to someone in this house right now. I swear I hate her. I caught her going through my mail and I'll bet she opened more than one letter, especially the one from my mother. I have never hated anyone before. Something terrible is going to happen. I can feel it in my bones." Ella shuddered.

It was bedtime and time to wonder where her husband was tonight. Washington was held in a heavy fog. Ella walked to the window. She could hardly see the streetlight. Ella thought it looked like London in the heavy mist—people on the street were mere shadows. She was startled when the bedside phone rang. She looked at the clock. It was rather late for a phone call.

The voice on the other end said, as he often did, "Can't make it, honey. I'll stay here at the office tonight." Dr. Bob pulled Lu closer to him.

He told Ella "Good night, sweetheart."

Lu thought to herself, "This man is a louse. He's even too rotten for my taste."

Ella had made special plans for tonight; her newest most revealing and tempting nightwear. Tears forming in her eyes she thought, "Same old same old. No, he isn't alone. Sometimes I think I hate that man." She looked at his picture on the dressing table. Then she picked it up and threw it at the window.

The morning papers pictured one of the results of the night before. Ella scanned the front page and the picture. Lying on its side was a smashed convertible. Dr. and Mrs. Robert Benson had survived the crash, printed in headlines.

"That bastard," Ella screamed. "Now I know I don't want his child."

Choking with sobs and tears, Ella tore off the new lingerie. "I wish he was dead."

There was a pounding on the bedroom door. Ella swung the door open. She was stark naked. The old woman, with newspaper in hand, demanded, "What are you doing home? Why aren't you dressed?"

"Mother, shut up! I wasn't in the car. How do you think I feel?"

"Go put something on. You're all naked," the older woman ordered.

"Who was the woman? That is your business to know. A woman who loves her husband keeps him home. This is your fault!" Bob's mother was getting hysterical.

"You never loved him," and yelled as she added more reasons. "If you had had a child Bob would be different."

"Get out of my room," Ella pushed.

"Get out of my house," the mother countered.

"It won't take long you old hag!" Ella shoved her mother-in-law out into the hall.

Later in the day, Dr. Bob came home and went into their bedroom to find Ella packing.

He tore into Ella, "How in the name of God? Why did you make this happen? Mother is on the verge of a stroke."

Her husband grabbed Ella by the shoulders. "You and your God darn temper have caused all of this."

Ella stood in awe at her accuser. "You bastard! How dare you talk to me like that after what you did? Get out of my way. I don't want to ever see you or her again. I could kill both of you. And you," she glanced at her husband, "You are nothing but uptown trash." Ella was on a roll. After two years of this crap, she was free.

"Where will you go?" her husband sneered. "You have no family. You'd better think about it. You haven't had it too bad. What's more, you owe Mother an apology."

Ella couldn't believe her ears as she dragged her suitcase down the staircase.

Not a word from anyone. No one offered to call a cab or help with her luggage. Ella sat alone in the large entry hall as she waited for the taxi. A chain of reflections ran through her head.

She went back in time as she recalled her past.

She was young and beautiful, fresh out of college and looking for a job in the D.C. area.

"Becker's Fine Clothing" was advertising in the paper. "A career with a future," read the ad. She bit.

Ella was assigned to the Cosmetic Department. It would do until she found something in her line of study, interior design. Who comes into the store but the handsome Dr. Bob? He was there to pick up the store manager. They are going to lunch. The other girls said her name was Lu.

Dr. Bob came into the store several times before he asked Ella to go out. It was the third time that the two of them had lunch. That did it.

Ella was told by Lu, "You are fired. Get out."

That was the first time Ella didn't have a place to go.

Her mother had remarried and was living in Arizona.

Dr. Bob suggested that he could help to find a flat and offered her a job in his office.

"My office needs a woman's touch."

Ella didn't know then that she would become part of Dr. Bob's network. She had fallen head over heels in love.

CHAPTER 4

▼

"Bank One," Ella told the cabbie. "The one on Pennsylvania Avenue."

When they arrived, she told the driver, "Wait for me. I'll be right out."

Ella walked up to the teller. "I wish to clear my checking account."

She showed her identification and waited and waited, only to be told, "The account was closed earlier in the day."

Ella had a couple of thousand in her savings account. She drew out everything except $500.00.

Back to the cab, she said, "Take me to the Furmont Hotel on 11th Street."

She sat in the cab thinking, "So, I have nobody. I'll show them."

Ella cried for a moment then wiped the tears on her sleeve. Then she thought, "I'll call Ralph up in Alaska tonight. He has always been my friend and then I'll call my mother."

The two guys, one a man, and one a canine were having dinner when the phone rang. The voice startled Dr. Ralph.

"Ella dear, what is wrong?"

"Oh, everything." Ella started to cry. She told her story in great detail.

"Ella, darling, slow up. You know how Bob is; he always has your best at heart." Ralph tried to console as he spoke up reluctantly about his brother.

"No, you don't understand," she insisted. "He had Lu in the car and tried to pass her off as me."

"Now listen to me, sweetheart. Bob knew Lu long before he met you. They are only friends. If she was in the car, it would have been because she was afraid to drive in the fog. I'm sure she had called for help."

"Oh, damn!" she thought. "I should have known he'd say something like that." However, after a pause, she began to think, "Maybe Ralph could be right. I have to think about all this. Could I have jumped to conclusions? I really didn't let him explain."

Therefore, Dr. Bob was saved again by his enabler, his own brother.

"Women!" Dr. Ralph exclaimed to the dog. "No wonder I never married. Why should a woman who has so much to live for be so unhappy? The thoughts were to himself but the dog cocked his head from side to side. The shaggy dog tried to understand. He knew something had made his friend sad.

Heinze scooped up his collar and leash. Then he walked over to his master and placed it on Dr. Ralph's lap. "No way, not this time of night, pal." He thought, "Maybe I upset her even more. I hope not." His thoughts were of Ella.

"This does it," he said to the dog. "Now I know we are heading for D.C. I'll call the ferry in the morning. There is one we can take clear to Seattle. They better take dogs or you will be in trouble," he told the dog. "We will have to be lucky to get space this time of year, but it will be worth a try. We just gotta go, old friend." He patted the dog and the dog wagged his long furry tail.

"You see, Heinze, Ella is my first love. You are my second." Darned if the dog didn't seem to understand. "Off to bed Heinze. We are going to be busy tomorrow."

"Hey, I didn't say on the bed." The dog took up his place at the foot of the large Victorian bed while the doctor crawled into bed wearing his "long johns." He fluffed his pillow a bit and tucked the quilt under his chin. "I wonder what I'm going to have to do with the dog."

While at breakfast, a breakfast of pancakes and sausage, there was a hard knock at the double front doors of the large Georgian-style house. Heinze forgot the sausage he was waiting for and charged through the rooms to the doors. He sniffed the crack in the doors and barked a roar.

Dr. Ralph didn't like the way the doors were being pounded upon. Looking through the peephole in the door, he decided to open a small space. "Well what do you want?"

He pretended not to know the large bearded man. The dog knew him and it was all the doctor could do to restrain him. It was Jacko. The dog's teeth revealed what he would like to do. "What do you want?"

"You can give me back my dog!"

"Who are you?" The dog knew the man.

"I am Jacko. You know who I am," he said as he pushed the door open.

Heinze pushed his master aside to charge the intruder. He knocked the enemy down onto his back and was on top of him with every tooth showing!

"Stop, Heinze! Stop!" the doctor shouted. The dog didn't move. This was a personal thing with the dog.

"Get out of here before I let the dog eat you alive," yelled Ralph.

"Heinze," he demanded. "Let the bastard up. Heinze do you hear me?"

The command worked. Heinze stepped back grudgingly. The unwanted intruder crawled to his feet, out the door and ran to his car fast as his feet could take him.

"I hope Heinze didn't draw blood," Ralph muttered. "I'm sure there is wolf in his background."

Heinze beat the doctor back to the kitchen table where the odor of sausage was still strong. "I hope that is the last we see of him. Jacko and his like can be trouble." Dr. Ralph shook his head and shivers ran across his shoulders.

"Buddy," he addressed Heinze. "To think I was wondering what I was going to do with you. Jacko has a small chance of me handing you over to him! Ha!"

After eating a cold breakfast and an attack of indigestion—"Ugh! I should never eat cold sausage and gravy. I still have a lump in my chest. You really did remember Jacko, didn't you? What did that ass do to you before he shot you, Heinze? I wish you could talk to me. The dog put his front legs in Dr. Ralph's lap and licked the man's cheek.

At that point, the phone rang. Ralph thought it was Ella calling again. "Hello, honey."

But it wasn't Ella.

"I want that dog or three thousand dollars by noon tomorrow!" the voice threatened. The doctor knew he meant it. Thoughts raced through his mind. "This is a job for the police. To think he shot the pup. Jacko didn't want him then, said he was too big. The dog is much bigger now. It's blackmail. Maybe I should see a lawyer."

The next day was very busy. Dr. Ralph started for town. Town was not far away. "Heinze, you stay here. Protect the house. I'm going to see Buck."

Heinze hung his head. He wanted to go along in the old red and rusty truck. "Stay," Dr. Ralph commanded. The dog slowly sat, then lay down. He decided to take a nap on the woolen Oriental rug. The sunshine was coming through the large window and it felt warm and comforting. "Didn't want to go anyway" was the dog's attitude. This is better.

Dr. Ralph was on his way to town. "Police first?" he pondered, "Or lawyer first? Or, face Jacko at the Wild and Wooly Bar? That's where he probably spends his time now that the snow is disappearing."

"Pay him," the lawyer said.

"What?" asked the startled doctor.

"The best way—you have the money, don't you?" The lawyer slapped the desk. "Best way unless you want to go to court."

"I'll be damned," the doctor swore.

"We can get it done while you are in town." Michael J. Kelly was all set for business. There was not too much work here for a retired lawyer.

"I'll go get him. I'm sure he is over at the Wooly," growled Ralph, slowly moving. "He spends most of his time there." The lawyer volunteered his services.

"Are you a friend of Jacko's?" the doctor questioned.

"No, I'm not. But I know who he is," the lawyer replied. "But you don't have a chance. Half the crowd at the Wooly Bar would testify against you. Jacko is going to want cash. You go to the bank. I'll go over to the bar. Meet you there."

"One minute," Ralph stopped the lawyer. "I want this entirely legal—papers signed, if the bastard can read and write." Was the lawyer in cahoots he wondered?

"Better get $3,500.00. That would cover my fee," the lawyer called over his shoulder.

Dr. Ralph watched the man cross the street just in time to see Jacko pull up in front of the pub. "He has been somewhere. God, I hope he doesn't have the dog. Instead of going to the bank, as he had been advised, he headed for the bar. It was the wrong thing to do.

The barstools were filled with Jacko's friends. Even the lawyer was lined up with them. He was ordering a drink. Ralph walked over to Jacko at the end of the bar.

"Jacko, why the hell do you want my dog?" the doctor demanded. "You tried to kill him once. You said he was too big as a pup and now that he is older and larger, why do you want him?"

"I got plans," Jacko sneered.

"You going to fight my dog?"

"No, that isn't my plan. But fights may be a good plan, too," the half-breed replied.

Dr. Ralph's face was blazing red. It was a good thing that his Colt revolver was safe in his desk drawer at home.

"Boy," said Jacko, "he sure is a big son of a bitch peon. I'd have him trimmed like a lion, bushy head, and neck with some left on the end of his tail. I'd hitch him up to a wagon and sell kid rides to the tourists."

"Good idea! Smart! You'd make a lot of money, Jacko," came the replies from some of the drunks in the crowd. The rest clapped their hands. "You are one smart guy, Jacko," said another.

The thought made Ralph sick. He began to think that bastard would beat Heinze until he broke his will. "You don't know that dog. He's a killer, thanks to you." The doctor wanted some wiggle room. "And don't forget he remembers you. One word from me and he'd be at your throat, you bastard."

The lawyer was at the doctor's side. "Careful, now! You are not on your own turf." The lawyer saw Jacko slip off his stool. "Careful. Come on, Jacko," the lawyer changed the scene. "Let's get down to business. Come see me in my office."

"I think I should up the price," Jacko retorted.

"None of that," answered the lawyer. "A deal is a deal."

"And cash is cash," added Dr. Ralph.

The lawyer took a small tablet out of his inside pocket and wrote up an agreement of sale.

"Make sure it's final because I don't want any further trouble from him," whispered the doctor softly to him. The paper was signed, the deal was done, and the three walked to the bank to get the money!

CHAPTER 5

─────────── ▼ ───────────

The deal finished, Dr. Ralph returned home to find the inside of his house a total wreck. Jacko had, indeed, come to the house to collect while the doctor was in town. Jacko thought the doctor was hiding inside. The dog thought the enemy was trying to break in. As Jacko went from window to window trying to see inside, the dog was leaping and jumping from window to window protecting his property. Drapes and curtains were torn down; so were the rods. Chairs were turned over and lamps lay broken on the floor.

As the doctor pieced together what must have happened, he began to cry. The dog had never seen his master cry before. The dog had been too much.

Ralph turned a chair back up, sat down, and covered his face and head with his hands, as the dog licked the tears from his cheek. The man wiped his face and had to smile at the thought of how Jacko would trim the dog. A lion cut might be fun.

Heinze and the doctor worked until midnight cleaning up the damage downstairs. The large windows with Victorian style hangings were the worst. Broken glass was a problem, too.

"Watch yourself, Heinze," the doctor said as he directed the dog away. "Be careful of the glass." Heinze thought he was helping. The dog's breath smears at each window were forgotten. "Let's go to bed," he said, pointing to the bedroom.

The dog flopped hard on the rug at the foot of the bed and the doctor crawled under the handmade quilt on his bed. "Better day tomorrow, Heinze." Those were his last words before he fell into a deep sleep.

Morning came early at 8:00 a.m. Dr. Ralph couldn't believe he had slept that late. Heinze was downstairs waiting for his two-mile walk. "Heinze," he called. "What did you do with my shoes?"

The dog arrived at the bedroom door. His shoes were hanging from the dog's mouth. "You really are something." He gave a wide smile. "You have added new words to your vocabulary. Gun, ride, truck, eat, go, walk, sit, stay, bed, and now shoes. How I wish you could talk."

After the dog deposited the shoes, he went for his collar and leash.

"Okay, let's go. We will try for three miles this morning. Got to get this weight off both of us!" Winters in Alaska, besides being dark and cold, are stay at home times. The TV and good food become great friends.

Dr. Ralph didn't have many friends. He was not handsome and charming like his brother, and he didn't make out with women. Women actually found him unattractive. He was too heavy, large necked, pigeon-breasted, red-faced and was not very tall. The doctor's features were not fine but large and at 45, he had started to slump a little. He really didn't care. He had a secret love. It was Ella.

Ella stole his heart at first sight. However, she was his brother's wife. That is not in good favor in any society. When he could not stand the pain and longing, Dr. Ralph had headed for Alaska two years ago.

He left his brother and sister-in-law with his mother in their Georgetown home near Washington, D.C. Bob refused to move at the time, so Ella was stuck with her mother-in-law day after day.

Ralph and Bob had shared office space in Washington. They were such successful doctors that they limited their practice to three days a week—"Tuesday, Wednesday, and Thursday." That gave both of them four free days a week; one to play golf and chase women, the other time to hunt and fish.

When Dr. Ralph decided to leave for Alaska, he wanted to try it for two years. As a business arrangement, Bob was supposed to send a check each month. He was as good as promised the first year and now and then the second year. Without big brother, things were going to pot in more ways than one.

Dr. Bob blamed the market and bad investments. He wanted to bail out and head for Roseville, Pennsylvania. The handsome self-centered snob thought he had found the perfect spot. It was an old stone house resting on the sidewalk. No front yard, it was taken when the street was widened. "Charming none the less," he told Ella. "This is it. Just what I want."

"What about Ralph?" Ella questioned. "Shouldn't he have some say?"

"I've heard from him. It's okay," her husband lied.

Ella thought about her phone call to Ralph. He didn't say anything about the new quarters. He only suggested that I was wrong to leave Bob. With little hope of better things, Ella humbled herself and returned to Georgetown.

While the Bensons were busy in the east, things were far from dull in the west.

Heinze loved to lie in the sunshine that shone through a large window in the hallway. Dr. Ralph pushed the dog aside so he wouldn't trip over the hulk. "Bacon is going to be hot this morning," he promised the dog. "That lousy sausage we ate yesterday was enough to kill me, but not you." He teased the dog. "You'll eat anything. I never ever saw you turn anything down. A dog that eats raw potatoes must have an iron gut."

The patient mutt, with strings of drool hanging from his mouth, wished the cook would finish his job. "Let's eat," the doctor invited. He didn't have to repeat that. The dog was beside the table first.

"What the hell is that?" It was the doorbell.

"Now who?" The doctor was pissed.

Heinze didn't leave his food, but ate so fast he still beat his master to the door. Both of them could easily see the intruder. The large bare windows revealed a small man, who was a stranger to both master and dog.

"I'm Billy McVay, the one and only realtor in town. I've come with good news."

"About what?"

"I have a wonderful offer for your place," the pushy man grinned. "Word gets around you know. Heard you were moving on."

"Who told you that?" The doctor had not invited the man to come in and stood with the door ajar.

"It's the word over town."

"Bull. I don't believe you. What's the offer?" His breakfast was getting cold.

"Can I come in and look around?" the realtor wanted to know. "It's getting damn cold standing here."

"No, you can't come in. I don't know you." Heinze joined the doctor's attitude. The dog gave a deep growl.

"The offer is $185,000. That's double what you paid for the property and sight unseen."

"Come in. Now what the hell is this about?" Ralph had his hands full trying to restrain Heinze. "Stand here while I put the dog away." Heinze wasn't cooperating.

"They say that dog is a killer. Is he?"

"No. Get in there," the man commanded the dog as he pushed the dog back into the kitchen.

"That was a struggle," the realtor remarked. "He'd make two dogs. Where did you get him?"

Heinze wasn't too unhappy. The bacon and pancakes were nose high. The doctor had not finished his breakfast. Now it was gone and the dog licked his chops. The realtor was no longer in the hallway. He was surveying the living room.

"What did you take?" the doctor asked.

"What the hell you mean?"

"What is that bulge in your pocket?"

"That's my snot rag, you damn fool. I've got a cold," the realtor said as he pulled out a dirty handkerchief.

"I'm sorry." The doctor felt rotten. "Let's get down to business I'm curious."

"I've got a firm offer of $185,000 'as is.' How much land will you let go?"

"Your offer is for the house, right? The land is different. I have five acres but only one acre with the house at that price."

The realtor had not taken time to look up the original cost. Dr. Ralph paid $45,000.00 for all of it.

"Boy, will I have to pay capital gains. I'll take $195,000 with one acre. You can tell them and $10,000 more if they want the furniture, too."

The furniture was worth a lot more. Overall, it was a great deal.

"Who are these people?"

"A young couple from Pennsylvania. They just want it for summer, they say."

"Couldn't be," he wondered, "Could it be brother Bob? Just a minute," Ralph said as he put up his hand. "I have to make a phone call."

"Thought we made a deal!" The realtor raised his voice.

After the phone call, Ralph returned to business. "I had the wrong idea. Let's finish this up." Dr. Ralph had made a very good deal. The realtor had a check in his hand for $225,000.00.

"Gotta make a living," the slime grinned. "Let's get to the bank. Keep this under your hat. I gotta live here."

"You go home, Billy. Get a bath. You stink." The doctor was annoyed at the rip-off, but on the other hand, he had to laugh at the crust of the dirty, small man.

The doctor came out of the deal smelling like a rose. Where could you go to make a profit like that in two years time, plus he still had four acres in case he ever wanted to return?

"One other thing," Dr. Ralph stopped Billy. "Since you are so rich, you pay the tax."

"Okay" was the answer."

Billy and Ralph met outside the lawyer's office. The lawyer was standing in his office window. He was waiting for his share of the new wealth.

CHAPTER 6

"I've had an amazing two days. I wonder what is going to happen next." Ralph asked Heinze. "Well, sweetheart," he addressed the dog, "the check for the house has cleared and the money is in the bank. All we have to do is pack our duds and head for home. We have thirty days."

Home sounded better than he ever thought. The doctor asked Heinze, "Have you ever loved anyone so badly that it hurt because she was not yours?"

He looked so sad. The dog felt the man's pain. He crossed the room to lick the doctor's hand.

"I think you are starting to like me, ole pal."

Heinze, with tail wagging, felt the union and didn't waste any time going for his collar and leash. He brought both to his friend and placed them in the doctor's lap. It was Heinze's way of saying, "Let's take a walk."

The two of them walked to the water's edge. Late day sun shone on the brilliant, sparkly water. Small white birds were flying in circles as if they were happy, too.

"This is really a beautiful place." It was late May.

Supper over, the two males rested on the back porch to watch the setting sun. Heinze lay on his back while the doctor rubbed the dog's belly with his foot.

"Wonder if I'll ever want to come back here?" The man watched all the colors in the sky change and fade. "Time to go in, Heinze. It's starting to get cold."

Inside, the house did feel better. It was warm and inviting.

"Heinze, who or what did I talk to before you came into my life?" He pulled the dog's head closer to his leg. "Heinze," he said again, "what in hell are we going to do with all this food? We only have thirty days to get out."

The doctor went from cupboard to cupboard. "All this and the freezer is full, too. I guess we eat all we can and then throw out the rest." The dog pushed past his master to get his head into the freezer. He could barely smell the moose and elk meat and it smelled wonderful to the dog.

"I just got a good idea," the doctor laughed and slapped his knee. The dog liked it, too. His tail was wagging back and forth so fast it sounded like a whip. "We'll go to town in the morning and see if Jones' Auto might have a new car we would like. See what we can get for the truck. We will need a big car for the two of us. Me up front and you can be the backseat driver." It had been a good day thought the doctor as they headed for bed.

"The first cruise ships will be in town by Saturday. The whole town will be ready to make their money, for the falling winter prices will be out of sight," he said in the direction of Heinze as they were heading for town in the old, red, and rusty truck. "Wonder what I can get for this piece of junk?"

George Jones, the owner of the car lot saw Dr. Ralph and dog coming across the street. "Here comes a sucker." The car lot owner rubbed his hands. By this time, everyone in town knew that the doctor had sold his house for cash and for how much.

"Welcome, welcome, Doc." The man of money was greeted, "What can I do for you?"

There weren't many to pick from. There were only five cars on the lot.

Ralph's heart sank. None were much better than the truck he drove to town.

"That's some animal you got there. What do you want for him? I could use a dog like that to watch the lot at night."

The doctor pretended not to hear. Jimmy, as he was known, knew as well as all the rest what he had paid Jacko. The doctor felt the hot blood in his neck at the thought of Jacko. The doctor patted a gun he was carrying on his hip. "I could kill him," he thought. "That bastard; I've taken all I ever expect to from that guy. He's a real rat fink."

"I'm disappointed, Jones," he said. "How long would it take to get a new car from Fairbanks?"

"Not so fast. Have you ever thought of a Winnebago RV? You could drive it back and sell it when you got home? I've got a new one out back. Come with me."

The car dealer was at his best. "I haven't shown it to anyone. It's a real beauty."

There it was, 32 feet long, a rolling house. It looked brand new.

"Let's see the inside. The dog has to fit," laughed the doctor.

"It's fully contained. You don't have to do anything but drive."

Jones pointed out all the fine points, while the dog took up the passenger chair right up front.

Everything was to the doctor's liking. "How much?" he asked.

"We have to go over it and clean it up." Jones wanted time to think.

"What's the story?" Dr. Ralph asked. "How did you get this? Where did it come from? What is the mileage?"

"Easy, easy. It belonged to the couple that bought your house. Ain't that the nuts?" the dealer laughed. "They drove it here but they don't need it since they bought your house."

"How much?" the doctor asked again. "Do you own it or do I deal with them?" The car dealer knew to the penny what the young couple had paid for the house. He also knew how McVay had gotten out of the deal. The realtor had spread the story all over town. Now it was the car dealer's turn. A lot of money had changed hands in the last 48 hours.

"I'll take $150,000."

"You'll take $125,000 and I'll take $5,000 for the truck."

"No, you'll take $2,000 for the truck—if it drives," came the reply.

With that, a whole new way of life and living began.

"Who is going to get the dog out of the R.V.?" The car dealer wanted to know.

The dog was seated in the captain's chair.

When the dealer made the seat move, the dog left on his own.

"Maybe I can't use this R.V." The doctor scared the hell out of the dealer.

"Why not?"

"How am I going to get it off this island?"

"The same way it got on the island in the first place," the dealer replied.

"And how is that?"

"The ferry—that's the way I get my cars. The ferry takes large trucks. I don't know why they wouldn't take an R.V. When do you want to leave?"

"Thirty days."

"That might be the tough part. People reserve space a year ahead at this time of the year. The room space wouldn't be needed. You could stay in the R.V. If they don't take dogs, you could just keep him in your R.V. It takes five days because they stop each day on the way to the U.S. You could even eat in the R.V. and walk the dog at each stop. Now the ferry will be in, in two days. I know the captain. Let me talk to him and give me a hundred dollars to sweeten the pot. I'll see him when the ferry comes in. I'll call you."

"Then I'll wait till you know for sure to finish the deal."

"That way, I know he will work over the ferry captain for sure," the doctor told Heinze on the way home in the truck.

As they arrived home, the phone rang. It was the call Ralph was awaiting. He and the dog made a race for the phone.

"Yes."

"George Jones here. Come and get your R.V. Everything is all set. I gave the captain the hundred dollars as a deposit, but you owe twelve hundred. That includes meals. Bring cash and don't ask why. I mean the money for the R.V."

"Why am I so excited?" he asked the dog as the red-faced man danced around. His excitement always transferred to the dog, which was running in circles trying to follow his dancing master.

"I am thrilled to pieces. But, I better learn to drive it if I plan to put that big thing on the barge with cars and trucks."

"Okay," said the man. "We can ride to town and settle this tonight."

He reached for the desk drawer to take out the revolver. Jacko was always on his mind if he was going into town.

"Come on Jones. Give me the keys." He handed the car lot dealer an envelope. "It's all there," the doctor told him.

Heinze made the leap into the R.V. with a lot more ease than his master. The doctor drove the rig with understanding care. He looked over at his companion seated comfortably in the over-sized captain's chair, completely unaware of the doctor's shaky hands on the enormous steering wheel.

"God, this thing is big," chuckled Dr. Ralph. "We will avoid big cities. I'll take country roads till I get the hang of the thing."

As they drove up to the home they were about to vacate, a nice new shiny car was parked in front of the house.

"Company, Heinze? Let's see what this is all about."

The couple in the car had heard about the sale. The car dealer had called to tell them he had sold the R.V. for them.

"We came out as soon as we heard." The young man stretched out his hand. "I'm Jim Willis and this pretty woman is my wife, Mary Pat."

"What a beautiful dog," she exclaimed.

Heinze licked her right away.

Mary Pat spoke first. "May we come in and look around?" she asked.

"Of course. Forgive my manners. Come in, come in," Dr. Ralph invited.

As they entered, Jim said, "We also have some information about the Winnebago and hear you're leaving. We thought you might like maps and such in case you are thinking of driving to D.C."

"What a great idea. I bought a cat in a bag, thus far. However, I sure would like all the information I can get. Thanks much. Can I make you a drink?" Dr. Ralph felt like a host. It had been quite awhile since he had living-room company.

"We were out here the other day looking around. The house is a classic. We are so glad you were ready to sell," said the young man.

CHAPTER 7

▼

"It worked out all the way around didn't it?"

Dr. Ralph smiled and stuck out his hand to the new owner.

"Help yourself. Look around and I'll fix us a drink. The doctor was pleased. "By the way, what can I make for you?"

"Make mine Bourbon on ice."

The doctor looked at Mary Pat. "Make mine wine. Any kind. I'm not a connoisseur."

Ralph allowed them full run of the house. After all, it was theirs, Mr. and Mrs. James Willis. Heinze was happy, too, as he followed them around making sure no one stole his leash.

All were seated around the table drinking their drinks. Even Heinze was looked pleased. Mary Pat had shifted her shoe, so she could rub his belly. "Delicious."

This was new to the dog and Heinze thought she was so nice.

"I heard Heinze was vicious. That can't be true." she questioned as her husband sorted papers out of a large envelope.

Mary Pat was so young and so pretty. It was a pleasure to talk to her. So he told the story to both of his guests.

"And then he demanded money from you? I can't believe it." Jim Willis shook his head.

"You got the best of it," Mary Pat said, and added, "and you still have Heinze."

The dog knew she was talking about him. He wagged his tail and placed a huge paw in her lap.

"It's getting late. We brought these papers for you to look over. They pertain to the Winnebago. If you have any questions, we'll be at La View Vista." Jim Willis rose from his chair.

After closing the door behind them, Dr. Ralph fixed himself another drink. He dumped the contents of the large, white envelope on the table.

"God, it's thirty-five feet long! I knew it was big but that's like a house! Hot damn! I feel like a boy! Yep, I'm like a boy and you, Heinze, are like a full-blown male dog. I saw you trying to ride Mary Pat's leg. If I can find a vet, I think I could take care of that. Doesn't sound like internal medicine," the doctor commented aloud. "It would sure settle you down. I sure don't want you running off to prove your manhood."

So the papers on the desk were forgotten about, as the doctor looked for the skinny phone book for a vet. There wasn't one when he needed one for Heinze months earlier.

"But lookie now—Dr. Victor, vet—cats and dogs only." Right there in the phonebook Dr. Ralph told himself. "Boy, thirty days or is it twenty-nine days? That will go fast."

Heinze was waking up slowly. His pride had been violated. The dog tried to get up but fell back in sleep. Dr. Ralph stroked the head of his friend. "Take it easy ole guy." The doctor petted him and hoped his friend wouldn't hate him.

"Where did you find this dog?" The vet was in awe. "It sure took a big shot to keep him under."

"Do you trim and groom dogs, too?" the owner asked the vet.

"No, but there is a woman who does, but she could never handle him."

"I'd like to get him trimmed lion style."

"What's that?" the vet asked.

"You know, keep his thick coat at the neck and shoulders, and take off the rest with just puffs on his feet and at the end of his tail." Dr. Ralph was laughing at the vet, who was bent over with laughter.

"I'd sure like to see that but don't put him through that for at least another week. He has to heal first. Those testicles were the largest I ever saw, like a stallion, a real 'Bull Durham'."

The vet added, "You should be ashamed. Think what the girl dogs will miss." Both men laughed as the male(less) dog tried to awaken.

It was time to get busy. They had a reservation for the ferry, so that was their deadline.

While Dr. Ralph and his sidekick, Heinze, were busy packing belongings, they were also packing food and necessities for the large R.V. His brother, Bob, his mother and his secret love, Ella, were not letting any time get away either.

Dr. Bob decided on a property he had seen before. He and his mother agreed that it was perfect. The house had a hefty price tag but it was an 18th century home in good condition and they are always sought after. They stay in families and don't come on the market often.

The downstairs had space for the waiting room, office, examining room, bathroom, and water. Upstairs were three bedrooms, all small and livable, plus each bedroom had its own bath, something seldom found. The house was charming. Deep windowsills, some original glass, and a beautiful front door that was original to the house. The back yard was large. Someone had treated it beautifully, shade trees, white picket fence, and flowers everywhere.

"I know Mother likes it but I'm not sure about Ella," wrote Bob to Brother Ralph. "The location is so perfect," he added.

Mrs. Benson, Sr. had her eye on the third bedroom. The second bedroom was going to be a nursery if she had her way. The mother was all set in her thinking. She had friends in Roseville, people she had known when they had lived in Roseville before.

Ella was determined that she was not going to live above the office. She was out everyday scouting the area. The area was new to her. She had not been as lucky. She, too, wanted an old house, but one with some land for dogs and children.

"Maybe today," she thought. "I have an appointment with a new realtor. She told me she had just what I want," Ella told Bob. "She told me it just came on the market and that it won't be on the market long."

"That's what they all say," said Bob.

Ella was getting annoyed with realtors. The realtor drove Ella west toward the pre-revolutionary war town called Newville. It was a sunny and bright day in May. The two of them drove over a small creek, bright and shining in the sunlight. The bridge over the creek, Ella had never seen before. It was not a regular bridge, but an old wooden covered bridge. It was painted in different colors and kept in perfect condition. Ella called out, "Please stop. I must have pictures," she exclaimed, as she took picture after picture.

Wherever the young woman turned, she faced beauty and excitement in her heart. Trees in bloom, wildflowers, plowed fields, birds of many species and the air so pure. Not a factory or mill nearby.

"My God," Ella laughed. "Have you ever seen anything like this all at once?" She turned to the sky with outstretched arms.

The realtor thought she had a sure-fire sale.

"Lucky you drove your jeep," Ella joked as they bumped along on an overgrown path to the two-story pre-revolutionary limestone house.

"Five acres go along with the property and the creek runs through it, but not too close. At the same time, it adds charm and beauty." The realtor watched Ella's mood and expression.

"But the house! My God, who would want to live here?" Ella cried out, "Look, the roof has caved in, not even a front door. What a dump."

The realtor looked at her in utter disgust. With tongue in cheek, the realtor asked, "Do you want to see the inside? There are some nice things inside."

"Is it safe?" Ella didn't hide her disappointment.

"Sure it's safe." The woman, walking through high weeds answered Ella. "This property is a dreamland in disguise." The realtor guided Ella toward the open front entrance. "It only came on the market yesterday. Military from Washington looking for retirement property grab these things fast."

"What do they do with them? I'll bet it comes complete with a ghost. Ugh!" The younger woman thought she was being funny but she wasn't. She had just made an enemy out of Ann Collins, the realtor. She walked alone back to the jeep, all the while she was thinking and thinking.

Then Ann gave her one more chance as she talked. "Mrs. Benson, I know there wasn't any glass in the windows. Time and snowballs took care of that, but did you notice the deep window sills and the ingenious way those 18th century builders insulated the houses? In those days, everybody worked. Wives and kids would gather small stones to be dropped between the walls. I'm sure you noticed a fireplace in every room and the walk-in fireplace in the kitchen."

Ann, the realtor, had a dreamy look on her face and Ella noticed it.

Ann continued, "Then that little button of ivory secured in the center of the new post at the foot of the stairs. They would do that to tell one and all that the house was paid for." No doubt about it, Ann was very informing.

"I'll tell you what I noticed." Ella counted on her fingers. "One, the roof has fallen in. Number two, birds were living in those fireplaces. Number three, the odor was a death odor. Sure, I like old things but not dead things. Now you have ruined my day!"

On the way back to Roseville, Ann lamented, "I'd sure hate to see the wrecking ball come in and level this wonderful place. The price of the property is only

$85,000, including land. Another $85,000 would give you a showplace worth at least $400,000.

About now, Ann didn't care too much about Mrs. Benson's thoughts of the place. Nevertheless, selling it to the state for hunting land really got to her. "I have some other properties. One is late Victorian circa 1912, solid as a rock and it is in Roseville. It's been turned into apartments. It is a money-making thing. We have so many students here at the War College. It could be returned to its original state and that could be fun."

"I'm not looking for work," Ella interrupted. "What is the difference between restored and remodeled?" Ella wanted to know.

"Complete disaster," replied Ann. "When you restore it can take up to three or four years to complete."

"Why don't you buy it?" Ella was being rude and really couldn't have cared less.

"Maybe I will," Ann scolded. "And if I do, when I'm finished it will sell for half a million."

Ella returned to the Hanover Street office with bedrooms upstairs. When she was telling her husband the story of the day, she forgot that this was the man who loved old things. "Oh, what did I do?" Ella bit her lip.

"Where is this place?" He was intrigued and added, "It sounds wonderful."

Ella interrupted. "No, you would not like it. It's terrible. The house is falling down. Birds live in every room. It smells like death. I'll bet there are a few ghosts in the place."

At this point, a third person joined them.

"Mother," Bob asked, "are you free in the morning? Ella was talking to me about an 18th century limestone house that just came on the market."

"Shit!" Ella said under her breath. "I might have known!"

"Wonderful, wonderful! Where is it?" The mother was excited.

CHAPTER 8

▼

"Where is this?"

Bob's mother was interested in the old house near Newville.

"I'll call the realtor in the morning to take a look," she said. Dr. Bob and his mother were off to a new adventure.

"I'd like to go, too." Ella felt like a child asking permission.

Then she thought, "I hope she falls through one of those rotten floor boards that I saw. And a stream runs right through the place!"

Aloud she said, "I'll bet it floods every year."

"Then you really have seen all you want to see, right?" Bob was leaving Ella behind.

"I'm an idiot," Ella scolded herself.

"Good. A stream is so charming," her mother-in-law said as she slapped her hands in delight. "That must be the Cantgoinit Creek."

"Five acres! I could even have a horse in a place like that." Dr. Bob smiled.

"It's not too late in the evening. I'll call the realtor right now."

"Oh, do! Oh, do darling," said his mother excitedly.

No one had asked the price. Bob turned to Ella. "What is the asking price?"

"It's $85, 000," Ella replied.

"She is right." Bob reached for the phone. "That won't be on the market long."

"Ann," he purred in a sexy tone, "About this house my wife was looking at this afternoon? I'd like to take a look at it in the morning."

"Sorry," Dr. Benson. It's off the market. I told your wife these houses go fast."

"Oh, no," he said. Mother and son were plainly disappointed.

Ann continued. "The new owners are the best people in the county line and they work right here. They are the very best. They understand restoration. You'll get another chance at the estate. By then the price may be $600,000, however."

As she tightened the screws, Ella was pleased with herself. "I'll bet she bought it for herself," Ella muttered.

"What are you saying?" asked her mother-in-law in a caustic tone.

"I said," Ella faced the older woman, "I bet she bought the place herself and plans to make a bundle." Ella took double delight.

"Ha! Ha!" She laughed behind her hand. She thought, "They didn't get the place. Great! They didn't get it and now I'm not stuck with having to live there.

"I did love that covered bridge," Ella reflected. "What a beautiful spot."

Days' following, in fact, almost at once, the restoration was under way. Sure enough, there stood Ann talking to one of the men. Ann had bought the old house, lock, stock, and barrel.

Ella realized her place was upstairs, over the doctor's office. Not all bad. The one good thing about it was that the three of them ate most meals out, since the kitchen was now a lab.

"I don't feel like a very nice person right now," Ella told herself. "There is so much to hate around here. I hate this town. I hate this house. I hate my mother-in-law. I don't have anything to love. I want a child, a dog, or even a canary—anything to be my own. I don't even have a husband that I can call my own." Ella began to cry.

Meanwhile, Ralph awaited a transaction that would change his life. He watched Mary Pat drive up to the house and get out of the car. She was such a pretty little thing. He looked at Heinze. The dog agreed, wagging his tail and watching out the large window. He opened the door.

"What brings you out here this morning?" Dr. Ralph called to her.

"Have a proposition." She smiled. Such a pretty smile filled with beautiful snow-white teeth.

"Really? You're an early riser. Come have a cup of coffee with us." Heinze had developed a taste for coffee, too, and it had to have cream and sugar just like his master.

Mary Pat let the doctor remove her jacket.

"I have to tell you, I don't want to spend another night in that flea bag hotel. Not another night. Last night something hit me. I don't know what, but look at the welt the darn thing made." Mary Pat shuddered as she showed Dr. Ralph her shoulder.

So, Ralph already knew what Mary Pat had in mind.

"We'd like an early settlement so we could move in today," she said. "Jim could help you pack and I'd keep house. I'd do all the cooking and we would pay rent to the first."

"Hot dog, young lady. You've got a deal!" Heinze agreed also, as he found his choice ball. The dog tossed the ball around the room in apparent merriment with their attitudes.

By early afternoon, the young coupled were settled. Mary Pat had dinner underway. "What smells so good?" the Ralph exclaimed. "Mmmmm, boy!"

"An old Pennsylvania favorite; ham, green beans with boiled potatoes and homemade apple sauce on the side."

She left the slow-boiling pot on the stove and walked into the dining room where Jim and the doctor were going over maps and places where night parking was available.

"And if you get stuck, you can always park at the Wal-Mart parking lot." Mary Pat added.

"What is Wal-Mart?"

"You'll find out." They laughed. Jim continued to talk about Wal-Mart."

Dinner was delicious. "How could anything taste that good?" Dr. Ralph smacked his lips. "And the biscuits! The pie was so good. Hope I can get off this chair." The doctor meant every word.

"You think this was good. Just you wait until you taste the bean soup I'll make out of the broth. Give me a ham bone and I'll make you a meal, as my mother used to say. Food like this is good for traveling. It freezes well and the Winnebago has a nice freezer.

Heinze looked up at Mary Pat like "Where is my bone?"

"We've got a lot of movies." Dr. Ralph wanted to round out this first evening. Do you like westerns?" Before anyone could answer, the doctor had a John Wayne movie going.

"There is enough ham and green beans for a meal." Mary Pat held up a plastic lidded box. "I'll put it in your freezer."

After the movie, all were ready for bed. It had been a good day.

Dr. Ralph couldn't sleep. He was suffering from indigestion. "I should not have eaten so much," he scolded himself. "It was good food but heavy food." He sat up in bed to burp. He could taste the lemon from the pie he ate. "Oh, that pie. I wonder if there might be a piece left." He tried not to wake the snoring dog and headed for the kitchen.

"It was just what I needed," he said to himself as he pushed the dog out of his bed. "Get out Heinze." The dog moved ahead.

Early morning the sun was up, and so was Mary Pat. She was on the second rung of a ladder.

"What are you doing up there?' The doctor laughed.

"What does it look like?" she answered. "I'm cleaning a cupboard that I don't think has had a good cleaning for awhile."

"But what did you do with my stuff like oatmeal, bread crumbs, and such?" He could have cared less but it was fun to tease Mary Pat. "Bet you threw my stuff away."

"Your things that were fit to use or eat are safe in the Winnebago. I'll show you later."

"Where is your husband this bright and sunny morning?" he asked Mary Pat. "I thought you were seeing the lawyer this morning."

"No, change of plans. To answer your first question, Jim is out with a realtor looking for land and lots of land—big!—big!"

"You people amaze me. What are you up to? Why?"

"Wait till I finish. I'll tell you." She was skilled on the ladder.

Dr. Ralph helped himself to a cup of coffee as he stepped over a sleeping dog. "Let me pour you one, too. Join me. Sounds like I'm about to hear something big." Big it was, too.

"Jim is a quiet man, a good man to keep a secret. But this town knows it now. So, I'll tell you." Mary Pat sipped her coffee. "We are here to build homes."

"What?" the doctor interrupted. "What kind? Not igloos, I hope." he teased.

"No, Doc. We are dead serious. Maybe only a hundred at first."

"But that is a terrible undertaking," he warned.

"We can do it, too." Mary Pat slapped the kitchen table.

"I can't believe it. Two kids. How old are you two?" he asked.

"Jim is 30 and I am 24," Mary Pat informed.

"I'm not the one to question but I am amazed. Most of all, I'm going to miss their wonderful dream." The doctor sat back into his chair.

"It's not a dream. Everything has been worked out. All we need is the land and I bet Jim has that right now. You come back in a year and you won't believe what we have done. We plan to build affordable housing like Del Webb did in Arizona."

"Then you better get started. This is May and winter comes early in these parts." Ralph cautioned.

"We are ready." Mary Pat shook her finger. "We have a crew all set to leave Pennsylvania as soon as the land is settled."

"Settled. You have the land?"

"A man they call Jacko owns what we want and he is driving a hard bargain."

"Jacko! My God, I hope not the one I know. Be careful, be careful." Dr. Ralph warned.

Heinze interrupted. As he came into the kitchen, his heavy leash was hanging from his mouth. With a step, he deposited it in Mary Pat's lap.

"He wants you to take him for a walk. The traitor!" Dr. Ralph laughed. "That's supposed to be my job." He pretended to scold Heinze, adding, "He likes the ladies."

"The dog has reason to trade affection after what you did to him." Mary Pat was referring to the dog's operation.

Jim was home smiling from ear to ear. And Dr. Ralph's heart sank.

"It's all taken care of." Jim picked up his pretty wife. He twirled her around and around. "It's a good deal all around. We settled on 100 acres."

CHAPTER 9

▼

"Have you seen a lawyer? Jim, please tell me, have you seen an attorney? What kind of deal did you make with that horrid man?" Dr. Ralph was upset. "I hope it is legal and binding because some funny things can happen here abouts."

"You told him? Damn, we were going to tell the doc together." Jim wasn't cross, just disappointed.

"Doc, it's the last frontier for a young man. Someone said, 'Go West and here I am.'" Jim let go a cowboy yell. "Yahoo!" Then he calmed down and asked, "Any coffee left in the pot?"

"Where in hell did Jacko get 100 acres?" the doctor wondered.

Then Jim said, "If you nice people will excuse me, I have some calls to make."

Jim's wife, Mary Pat, called after him. "Wait for me. I have an interest in this, too."

Dr. Ralph remained seated in disbelief. He had that far away look that Heinze had seen before. Heinze brought the leash to Dr. Ralph and dropped it in his lap. "Oh, now I'm good enough to walk you? Last time, forget it. Let's go."

When the man and dog returned, the house was lit up like Christmas and the place was reeling with life.

"Our first crew will be here by the first of the week and the heavy equipment is on its way." Jim did a jig in the middle of the large hallway. "My dad will be proud of me now," Jim exclaimed, as he kept time with his hands and feet. Mary Pat joined in and the dog ran around in circles. Heinze could feel the excitement.

But not Ralph. "It's their baby," he thought. "In two weeks I'll be gone. I sure hope they are well-heeled because it will cost a fortune. I mean a hell of a lot of money. Furthermore, how the hell did that louse Jacko ever get his hand on that land? The slippery bastard." Dr. Ralph hated Jacko.

The young couple were hugging and kissing when Dr. Ralph interrupted. "Let's go to town for dinner tonight, my treat."

"Great, good idea." Jim still had his arms around Mary Pat's waist. "Doc, do you want to get in on a really good thing? This is just the start. I could make you rich," Jim invited.

"No thanks. I never wanted to be rich, saw what it did to my family." In spite of himself, his thoughts were of Ella.

Dinner was great, good wine, smoked salmon, good music, the kind that made you want to dance. The other people felt the energy in the restaurant. Someone was celebrating none other than Jacko. The good doctor wished for a moment that Heinze was there. He'd take care of that louse.

Two-week's time had dropped to ten days until settlement. Jim Willis hadn't asked for an extension and every day the scene was changing out at the foothills of Mt. Edgecome. Dr. Ralph had taken Jim and Mary Pat to the Wild and Wooly one last time before he left. They saw Jacko at another table and Ralph's thoughts became more worrisome. "Jacko could not have bought that land with the three thousand he stole from me," thought Dr. Ralph as he became more and more upset. "Why does that bastard make me so mad? But, I don't want to spoil the evening. Land must be cheaper here, but nothing else is. Yes, land must be cheap. Someone bought the whole damn country for two cents an acre back in 1867. That someone was the U.S.A."

It was nearing midnight and a limit was restricting their drinks. Then all hell broke out at Jacko's table. Someone grabbed a waiter, who dropped his tray. Someone slapped Jacko's wife and someone peed on the floor. You just don't do that at the Wild and Wooly. The bartender swung the first fist; after that, it became a scene from an old western movie. Everything was flying through the air. Bottles overturned. Everyone, including Jim Willis got into the fray. Everyone, except Jacko, who was sneaking out the door without his wife.

Dr. Ralph had come in to observe Jacko. He saw Jacko going out the door, got up and reached for his gun on his hip. He had not planned to carry it that night and he wished many times over that he had not.

Jacko was lying flat on his face with blood seeping to the floor. The gunshot wasn't heard above the scene and when Jacko was discovered, Dr. Ralph was back in his chair.

"Let's go before we get involved." It was Mary Pat's voice, who had noticed nothing in particular, as she sat talking to her husband.

Dr. Ralph didn't look in the direction Jacko was being carried out of the restaurant. "I hope to God he isn't dead," he moaned. Nobody in the bar knew he was a doctor so other help was summoned for Jacko.

"I don't think he's dead." Mary Pat was looking that way. "But he is going to lose that leg, I'm sure."

"And I don't want him to die you can bet on that." Jim Willis had too much to lose.

Dr. Ralph remained quiet. The next day the story was all over town. No one knew what culprit tried to kill Jacko.

Jacko swore, "Whoever it was that shot me, he's a dead man walking. And I have my suspicions."

Overnight he had lost his leg because the bone had been shattered. Dr. Ralph went to his own room and wept like a baby. His eyes were covered by his hands. Heinze took his paw and pulled his hands away and licked the tears.

The doctor came out of his room round noon the next day.

"I hope you are hungry," Mary Pat called from the kitchen. "We are having pork and sauerkraut and mashed potatoes. I know it smells terrible but just you wait. And I have an apple pie in the oven."

"She's such a nice person," the doctor thought.

"Guess what?" said Jim, who was reading the paper. "It seems Jacko was shot by a Colt revolver. How about that?"

The doctor knew only too well that it had been a Colt. He had just cleaned his handgun, which was a Colt.

It was only a week short of plans. Dr. Ralph knew it was time to get busy. He started to pack and learn all he could about the big coach and the great Alaskan Highway.

Jim entered the room saying, "Doc, why don't you wait another week and leave on my ferry? It's new and strong."

"You have a what? Your own ferry? You amaze me, Jim." The doctor shook his head.

"How did you expect me to get heavy machinery here? The ferry isn't set up for man and beast but the R.V. is fully contained and no one would resent the dog. No stops. You'd get to Seattle a lot faster."

"Oh, I don't know," the doctor was thinking.

"And I wouldn't charge you a cent."

"That's the best part," the doctor laughed.

"How say you?" Jim waited. "Let's ask Heinze."

"Come here buddy. Do you want to make a trip with no ladies aboard?" Heinze gave a bark followed by a yip.

"Plan on a week from today," added Jim. "The barge will be here in two days. All that stuff has to be unloaded and double checked. Wait till you see this machinery. It's so large that we are bringing in the men that know how to drive them." Jim was gung ho.

"You must be a very rich young man." The doctor was in awe.

"Young, yes. Good credit and a wife who won a hundred million dollar lottery. What do you think of that?"

Dr. Ralph said, "I need a drink. Will you join me?"

When the ferry arrived gleaming in the bright sun, it looked like it was brand new. The doctor, Heinze and Jim watched the unloading from the water's edge. Man and dog were anxious to board and look around.

Jim was gone to look after things. Ralph and Heinze decided to get away from things that were being brought aboard. "It takes a man with a dream and a wife with dough," he muttered. "But, I wish him the best."

The bright colored elephant-like machines were busy clearing the land. Half the town was there to see the elegant machines at work. As the land was cleared, flags went up to indicate new roads and sewer pipes. "I hate to see all the old trees fall," Dr. Ralph told Jim.

"Oh, we are not going to take all of them. This is just to add a line to the golf course," Jim told the doctor with a smile and a twinkle in his eye.

"Then where is the shopping center?" The doctor teased.

"Right over there close to town. We want the course and the houses at the foot of the mountain."

"This would make me crazy. It's good I'm leaving in the morning."

The last person he saw in town was Jacko being wheeled out of the new doctor's office.

"Leavin' early, ain't ya?" Jacko yelled at the pair in the large Winnebago.

"Want to take advantage of the good weather," Dr. Ralph replied. The dog glared but not at Jacko. The gun was burning a hole in the doctor's pocket. "I'll get rid of it as soon as I can," he thought.

"God, this rig is huge. I hope I can handle it." The doctor was almost frightened. "God help me trying to get on the ferry." All they had to do was wait for the barge to settle at the dock.

Most of the ferry was filled with cars and people only going to the other side, all paying people, but he was a freebie. Now it was the doctor's turn to board.

Snot was dropping from his nose and eyes. "Don't move an inch," he ordered the dog.

Jim came alongside and guided him on safely. "God, I thank you my angel," the doctor said. "Jim, I can't thank you enough." The dog remained inside but the doctor got out and hugged Jim. They shook hands and promised to write.

There was a knock at the RV door. The dog barked and Dr. Ralph opened a window. "Jim says you have full run of the place. The dog, too. Just pick up the shit."

They were on their way aboard the ferry. Most of the day was used to reach the other side. "Looks like we are the only passengers left," he commented as he patted Heinze. "No more stops till Seattle." The two walked to the side of the barge. The air over the water seemed so fresh and the setting sun with its myriad of color was an inspiration.

"Now," the doctor spoke to the dog "let's go and cook our first dinner in the R.V." Heinze was busy charming a few seagulls.

A few days later, they could see the Seattle skyline at the shoreline. "Heinze, let's stay here in Seattle a few days till I feel more secure in what and where I really want to go. South to Phoenix or west to Chicago?" The dog came to the doctor with his leash in his mouth. "I'll open the door and you can walk all you want. Just don't jump overboard," the man laughed.

When the time came to leave the ferry, they left in style, waving and barking. They saluted the crew. They were off to a new way of life!

CHAPTER 10

▼

The doctor, with Jim's assistance, had studied maps, routes and towns, etc. So, Dr. Ralph was looking for Route 80 going west. Heinze was no help. He had his eye on the hated gun that was lying on top of the drawers along with the maps. The gun was in easy reach just in case. Even so with traffic so heavy the doctor wouldn't be able to stop the R.V. Dr. Ralph put the weapon in the bottom drawer, closed it, and got down to the business at hand. Heinze fell asleep. He could dream what dogs dream about. Ahead was a sign for the "Friendly Haven Campground." They were the last to enter the grounds for the day. The gate was full behind them and the "Full" tin sign swayed in the sunset.

"Yes," was the reply. "First time anywhere in an R.V.," Dr. Ralph answered. "Didn't know how it's done."

"You better call ahead and make reservations at this time of year," the owner addressed.

Relieved to have a place to park, Ralph said, "Find your leash, Heinze, and we'll take a walk. My legs want to cramp and my arm muscles are sore. I shouldn't hold onto the steering wheel so tightly. Man is that a large wheel." He spoke aloud but no one seemed to notice, as he passed one after another lighted R.V.s, all in their assigned spaces. He could smell the cooking as he walked by. It didn't go unnoticed by Heinze, as the dog smelled the air. Then Heinze spotted a rabbit. It took all Dr. Ralph could do to hold onto the dog. "Heinze, stop it. Calm down, damn it." The dog obeyed.

A neighbor, a fellow traveler, called out, "Who is taking who for a walk?"

"Nice evening." The doctor returned in like manner. Heinze didn't want to return to the R.V. "What's the matter, Pal?" The doctor realized the dog had been cooped up all day, too. With an "Okay," he unhooked the leash. The place was fenced and Dr. Ralph could let Heinze roam free within. They both returned to the Winnebago. It wasn't dark outside, yet. Dr. Ralph opened the drawer and checked to be sure the gun was still resting there.

There was a knock on the screen door. "Would you like to join us for a beer?" the neighbor asked through the screen.

Dr. Ralph quickly pushed the revolver back into the bottom drawer but he didn't close it tightly. "A beer sounds great. Stay here Heinze." He told the dog and he absent-mindedly left the R.V. door ajar and headed for a bit of friendly entertainment.

"What is that dog doing to the rosebush?" A woman looking out of their window asked her husband. "He is trying to bury something."

"They just had dinner, probably a bone." She continued to watch and read the newspaper. Heinze joined the beer drinking threesome. "Where did you come from?" Dr. Ralph was surprised. "How did you get out?"

"A dog as big as that could get out of anything he wanted." the neighbor laughed.

"He's trying to tell me it's time to go home and go to bed. It's been a long day."

Inside the trailer with a light turned on, the doctor yelled. "No! No! Get off the bed. Where did you get all that dirt? What were you doing when I thought you were in the coach? You have tracked dirt everywhere." Dr. Ralph looked at Heinze's dirt-covered nose and paws all covered with brown earth.

"Back away," ordered his master. "What did you do—find a bone? You can't stay in here till you are cleaned up. You are a mess." So, outside with a bucket of sudsy water and a couple of towels Heinze was made fit to return inside.

"I saw him trying to bury the biggest bone I ever saw," an elderly woman passing by offered. "That rosebush has had it," she laughed.

"Where did you get the damn bone? Have you been in someone's trash?" The doctor was huffing and puffing. He wasn't used to bending over a bucket.

The next day, the two were friends again, as doc and the dog walked in the early morning sunshine. Coming toward them was the elderly woman, who spoke to them the night before.

"Howdy, that is some dog."

"He sure is," replied the doctor. "Madame, do you know anything about this huge R.V. camp? I need a haircut. Is there a barber shop here?" Dr. Ralph was certain that the woman would be a walking vocabulary.

"Of course," she replied. "We have a barber shop at the end of the street, next to the restaurant and across the clothing shop."

"Restaurant, right here? I thought you forgot how to eat out when you bought one of these things," the doctor teased.

"Wives are on vacation, too. I mean it. These things are what men dream about. Women would rather stay home."

The three of them parted laughing. Heinze thought she was funny, too. "Heinze, ole fellow, I'll make breakfast today. You guard the door and I'm going shopping. I need some new things and a haircut."

As it turned out, the joke was on the doctor. The shop in the R.V. Park had a nice-looking woman with a pleasant smile who approached him. "Dr. Benson," she addressed him, after learning his name, "we have an exercise pen here for dogs. We really don't like them walking on the paths if you know what I mean. And your dog frightens people, especially children."

"I see." The doctor wondered what she would look like with no clothes on. It had been a long time, and just looking at her, he could tell he didn't need Viagra. He heard himself say, "Would you like to go someplace other than here for dinner tonight?"

"Sorry doctor, but I'm married."

"Oh, shit!"

"What did I hear you say, doctor?"

"Now it's my turn to say I'm sorry." His face was red.

Back in the R.V., the doctor turned to Heinze. "Funny how fast a woman can turn you off."

In the east, it was so very busy. Dr. Bob was setting up offices. Mother Benson was moving into the great bedroom and Ella was trying to find a suitable house for them. Ella knew she wanted some land around her new house. She had fallen in love with the site at the end of the covered bridge. The young woman was told you can't build there because it was too close to the creek, as the bank was soggy. In order to build you had to be at least 100 feet from the creek. That was the distance where the old stone house was situated. Ella didn't want the old house with a passion but at the same time resented it being sold from under her. When she would drive past the old stone house, her attention was drawn to the crews of workmen teaming all over the place.

"There are no more skilled workers available in this area. And she has hogged them all up," she thought. All of a sudden, there stood Ann, the realtor, and by God, her husband.

"What is that all about?" she thought as she considered stopping but thought better of it. Everyone noticed her; workmen as well as her husband and Ann. Ella would have been hard to miss in her fire-engine red two-door Lexus flying up the dirt road at top speed with dust leaving a trail.

Dr. Bob was told in no uncertain terms, "The house and grounds are not for sale. Furthermore, Dr. Benson, I know a great deal more of what to do with the house. Far more than you or your mother. I'm determined that your little wife would have no idea of what to do with it," Ann paused for breath. "Please just stay away," she concluded.

"There's a price for everything. Don't forget, you don't know who you are dealing with," the doctor threatened. "We will see, we will see."

"It will be for sale when I'm finished and I'll pick the buyer and at my price." Ann waved him off.

"How did you get so God-damned smart?" Bob wasn't moving an inch.

Ann reached to the ground, as if she were going to pick up a rock.

Dr. Bob decided to leave but as he left, he called over his shoulder. "You are not finished with me, you son of a bitch."

The next day Ann went to the police and to the Roseville Fire Department and told her story. "I'm afraid he will hire someone to light a match." Everyone knew what she meant. The fire department and local police came to the old stone house to post signs of "Private Property" and "Stay Off."

When Dr. Bob saw what Ann had done, his face alone was so hot he could have set fire to the weeds around the property. But, the weeds where he was forced to stand were the only ones in jeopardy because the weeds around the house had been cleared. The trees had been trimmed and there in the sunshine stood a future treasure.

The builder Ella had selected was very sorry, but now he would be too busy for the best part of a year. "You know my dear," he was trying to be nice; "it's the old McCarthy place." Ella didn't know and did not give a damn. She was determined to get out of the bedroom above the doctor's offices.

The next morning, Ella headed for Billsberg, a nearby town, with a phone book in hand. That last builder couldn't do anything with the plans that Ella had drawn.

"I have a nice home near completion. Be glad to show it to you." The new builder was hoping, and could see Ella was interested.

The houses were nice and Ella was impressed. "I'll think about it. Must talk it over with my husband. Let me give you a call."

His face was red with rage when he stood in the weeds at the McCarthy house, and it was redder still when Ella announced she had found the perfect place.

"I will not drive that far. I will not drive into the sun every morning." He all but yelled at his wife, "That's the last of that! Do you understand? One, find something between here and Newville. Two, something between here and Machinsburg, and three, something between here and Boiling Springs."

Ella left the room while he continued to count on his fingers. She left the house, climbed into her small car, and propped a local map on the steering wheel. "He only thinks I won't find a place. I'll show him." Ella headed for the Newville area again, right about Nockstown. She had seen some large, beautiful homes being built and the creek was nearby. "Funny," she thought. "I'm always drawn to the creek. I have always loved water."

After looking at an incomplete structure, Ella walked along the creek's edge, looked at the lily pads in the creek, and saw her own reflection.

CHAPTER 11

▼

The cell phone rang and Dr. Ralph jumped in surprise. It was his brother, Bob.

"Good to hear your voice. What's up? How's it going?" Bob inquired.

"I'm getting the hang of this vast bus. It's so big and the dog takes up the whole front seat and when he sits up like now, he is blocking my view. Down, Heinze," he yelled at the dog. "I damn near hit that woman. I'll bet she has wet pants. I think I do," Dr. Ralph uttered a nervous laugh.

"Bob, he continued, "I'll call you tonight. Right now I gotta get through this Chicago traffic."

"Sure, sure, I just want to talk. Call me tonight."

Ralph turned toward Heinze. "We are about to go into Chicago. Shit, where did I leave Route 80? Heinze, ole buddy, I think we are lost. Holy shit, where are we now?"

Traffic was bumper to bumper and in the midst of 4:00 p.m. stress. Sweat was pouring down Dr. Ralph's thick neck. "God, Heinze, I just saw a sign. Now we are in Indiana." The doctor was frightening the dog.

"Jim said, you remember Jim Willis, he told me that we could take Route 80 across the country. We just have to pull off the road as soon as we can. I have to look at the map." It was fine with Heinze. He had to "go."

Ahead was a blue sign that read, "Rest Stop." Both were pleased to get out of the R.V. There was a bathroom on board, but not for Heinze, and the dog had been passing gas for miles. Heinze liked the sweet smell of grass.

"Heinze, we will find a place around here for the night. Tomorrow, we can pick up Route 65 that will take us south to Indianapolis. Did you know, ole dog, that the even routes go east and west and the uneven ones go north and south?"

The dog distracted his master with eye contact, and then got off his seat. He carried his empty water dish to his master's lap and dropped it there. "Hey, I'm driving! Sorry, guy," the doctor apologized. "I'm thirsty, too, but I can't stop in the air, you know. Let's start to find a nice R.V. park."

They drove quite a while trying to find a park. Traffic was terrible. Cars to the left and cars to the right, not to mention the cars that jumped from lane to lane and the ones that passed and then slowed down in front of the large R.V. "I got to get off the road," the doctor spoke aloud. And with that, the doctor shot into the free right lane and off the road and made a quick right turn into the most beautiful R.V. Park. And then the entrance light flashed "Field."

After about an hour, they found themselves in a small town. It was so small a town that it harbored only one traffic light and couldn't be more than an hour from where they got lost.

"Pick a field, pick a field. Looks like we found our place to stay. Since we are self-sufficient, we can stay in this field," he thought. It had been a tough day for both man and dog, but it wasn't over yet. "Since we are self-sufficient, we stay where we want unless someone drives us off."

The dog looked around and heard the first sound of thunder. Heinze was gone. He couldn't get under the bed so he hid in the closet. The large Winnebago was lumbering over wet grasses and weeds, slipping and sliding as they came to a halt. The rain began in mothball-size hail. It hit all the windows with hard pellets of ice. Poor Heinze, now he was trying to get on the doctor's lap. Then the rain began in earnest. It poured in silver streaks like the silver strands you put on Christmas trees. Lightening lit up the sky, as it tore up the night. The windows in the R.V. began to fog. Wind picked up and they could feel the pressure against the body of the huge rig. Heinze couldn't stop barking. Between thunder and lightening, there was a pounding on the door.

"Where is my gun? My God," he raised his voice, "Did you see my gun?" he demanded of the dog as Heinze crowded away. Heinze knew the word gun, as well as walk, leash, eat, and pee. Those were pleasurable words. Not gun. People outside were throwing pebbles and small stones at the R.V. windows. The doctor, half-furious and half-afraid opened the door just a peek. Outside stood a man and woman in the soaking rain. They were covered with weeds, mud, and water.

"Please," the man pled. "We need help." He could hear the woman crying and in her arms, she held an infant. Dr. Ralph could hardly believe what he saw. The woman's wet hair was plastered to her face. Her clothes were ripped and torn, while her arms were scratched and bleeding from the thorns and bramble. But, there was not a scratch on the baby.

"This could cause a nightmare. Give me the child first," the doctor suggested, as he tried to help the woman on board. She would have nothing of it, as she held the baby closer to her chest. Her eyes were wild with fear. "What happened?" Dr. Ralph asked the young husband. "Why are you out on a night like this and with a baby?"

Now Heinze forgot the storm. He tried to sniff that noisy wet thing the mother held so tightly. But a bolt of lightening and a clap of thunder that sounded at once sent the dog under the table. The doctor dug into a chest and found a sweatshirt and pants that had been saved for the trip. They were new and warm.

"Take a warm shower and then put these things on. You are shivering." He turned to the girl-like wife. "I'm a doctor. Do as I say. You are welcome and you are soaked. Give me the child and I'll bathe her at the sink, while you get into the clothes," Dr. Ralph persisted.

"Oh, no." She clung to the baby. The girl-wife must have had second thoughts. She gave the baby to her husband and showered and put on the dry clothes the doctor had offered. While the men were having a drink for their health, she bathed her child at the sink.

"I do have blankets if you would like." Dr. Ralph was on his second drink and getting very friendly. He offered hot coffee or hot cocoa. She chose the latter, as she tucked her baby into a chest drawer full of the doctor's new tops and shorts. Their clothes were hung up on hooks or over backs of chairs to dry. The baby had been wrapped papoose-style in a large towel. She was sleeping like a baby should. The storm seemed to have calmed down only to say with a bolt of lightening and a loud clap of thunder, "I'm still the boss."

The doctor asked, "Have you any formula or are you nursing?"

"I'm nursing. I was so afraid I'd never be able to nurse her again. When she is ready, we will all know." The young man laughed, as he well knew.

Ralph said, "I'm going to make some soup." The doctor hadn't questioned anyone at the time. "When the baby wakes up, you use the bedroom. The bed is large and the room is warm. It's yours for the night—I mean for all three of you. In the meantime, I'll warm up some soup for all of us and a hot toddy might just be what we all need at this point," the hospitable doctor offered.

When the young wife went to care for the crying baby, she shut the bedroom door. Heinze couldn't put up with that. The dog scratched the door with his paw as he heard the bed springs. "What was that noisy thing she had in there? He wasn't allowed on the bed. What was that thing in the bed?" He scratched twice more.

Everybody warm and content, including the silent child, their story began. "Doc," the thin young man began, "hope you don't mind I called you Doc. You have been so friendly since you introduced yourself." Once again he started. "We don't live far from here. I take this road everyday. That gully has been here forever, but I never saw it flooded."

CHAPTER 12

▼

"There are no street lights out here. This is country and it was dark as blind. I was in that little dip in the road before I knew it." He paused.

"Go on," the doctor encouraged.

"Well, we jumped out of the car when it began to move with the current of water where we had been stuck. Christ," the young father exclaimed, "we dragged ourselves up the muddy bank of what had become a lifesaver. We saw your lights and hoped for the best. Thank God for your help."

Dr. Ralph said a silent prayer. "Thank you, Lord, that I didn't find the gun. Who knows what might have happened."

It was a day to be remembered. The couple and child took the bedroom in the trailer, while Dr. Ralph opened the second bed that had been a sofa earlier. It was wet! He looked up thinking the roof was leaking. Then he remembered his soaking wet guests had sat there. "Now, where the hell is Heinze?"

The baby was asleep in the bottom drawer of a piece of furniture. The man and woman were sound asleep when Dr. Ralph opened the door just a peek. Heinze was lying next to the smelly, sleeping thing and he wouldn't move. The doctor backed noiselessly away.

The sun shone warmly on the new day. Someone was banging on the screen door with a long, thick stick. That brought a roaring "woof" out of Heinze. He woke everyone up at that point. It was the farmer, whose land they were on.

"What's the big idea? You ran over my peas and onions. You crazy nut. My things were ready for market, you son of a bitch." His face was red and so were his eyes. "That your car down in the dip?" The farmer continued. "This is gonna cost you a pretty penny."

Dr. Ralph shook his head in bewilderment. "Let's take a look." The large rolling R.V. had run over rows of peas, onions, flowers and a fence.

"This man," said the young husband pointing to the doctor, "saved our lives last night. I don't live too far from here. I promise you I'll come out to your farm the next two Saturdays and Sundays. I'll work all day, any way I can to help. I'm a farmer's son. I've plowed many a row and I can haul to market. I'll work free. I can fix that fence."

"What the hell does that have to do with what has happened here?" the farmer wanted to know. "Did I say I came here to make trouble? I just want to get the car out of the middle of the road so I can get to market with what's left."

"Was this man for real?" thought the doctor. "What calmed him down? Was it the baby he had been watching in its mother's arms out of the corner of his eye?" Whatever it was, the three of them were grateful and Heinze licked the farmer's boots.

"Amy, that's the Mrs., will want to see that baby. By the way, she sent me out to tell you sausage gravy and biscuits are ready for breakfast." None could believe their ears. What a wonderful man. They could smell the good food the closer they got to the man's house. Heinze was running ahead, baby forgotten. He could smell the food also.

After breakfast, the dog, Amy, and the young mother were busy in the flower garden taking turns with the baby. First Amy held the baby and cooed. Next, the mother breastfed the baby. And Heinze barked and barked at what he saw as strange. The men were around the kitchen table. Maps were strewn every which way. The farmer showed where they were on the map.

"Boy, did I get lost," the doctor said with amazement.

"We are just outside of Cleveland, Ohio," the farmer explained. The men agreed that the best route to take was 70 if the doctor wanted to head for Washington, D.C.

"I'm gonna sell that damn rig just as soon as I get home," said Ralph. The doctor blamed the floating hotel for his error.

"If that's the case, Amy," the farmer called as they came through the kitchen doorway, "get me a piece of paper. The nice doctor and I might make a deal. You go down and take a look at that runabout, doc, and tell me what you think. Cosmos Miller, cell phone 608 214-858. Now that's me. Remember, I get first choice."

Amy had her look. Returning to the kitchen, she was all smiles. "Cosmos," she addressed her husband, "it's just perfect."

Heinze kept trying to get a better look at the baby. The young mother relented, no longer afraid of the large dog. Heinze looked, sniffed and was about to lick the baby. The mother stopped that in a hurry. Amy packed a lunch for Dr. Ralph and a bone for the dog while the men were getting the car out of the ditch where the young couple had ditched it.

Everyone was on their way, the farmer back to the kitchen for a beer, the young couple and baby heading home and the doctor and dog were searching for Route 70 East.

"Heinze," the doctor addressed his friend and companion, "what stories we will have to tell when we get home. Aren't they just the nicest people in the world?" Heinze sort of agreed except his interest lay in the brown bag the woman had handed the doctor.

He read aloud the directions he was given. "Take Route 70. It will take you right onto the Pennsylvania Turnpike. Stay on 70 till you see the Hagerstown exit. That will take you to Frederick, Maryland. You'll be in Washington in no time. If, as you said, you might need to go to Roseville first, do this. At the Hagerstown exit, you will take 81 north." Cosmos had written all this down. "That 81 Route north will take you right into Roseville."

While reading these instructions, the doctor missed Route 70. "Shit!" he cried out and slammed on the brakes. There was the 70 East he wanted. Heinze had landed on the floor and the look he gave the doctor made the man laugh. He got up from the driver's seat, walked back, and replaced things that had fallen, and put some information in the drawer where the gun had been.

"Wonder where I put the thing?" he asked himself.

The dog got off his co-pilot chair and walked back to the bedroom to join his master. Heinze tried to get under the bed, as he had at home. But the bed was nailed to the floor. The big R.V. floated up the ramp and now all were on Route 70.

"Never figured out what happened to Route 80. We traveled that route from Seattle and then it disappeared. I must have done something stupid," the doctor mused. "Getting old, I guess. Old at 45.Rest stop ahead. Just what we need, old boy." And with that, Heinze was back in his co-pilot chair.

After things at the rest stop were taken care of for both, Dr. Ralph bought two cans of Coke and two candy bars. They sat under a shady tree and fed themselves. Both man and dog enjoyed the ham and egg sandwich that Amy made. Heinze was getting bigger and fatter each day on the road. He liked soft drinks as much as his master. One was poured into his pan. The dog hadn't taken his eye off the candy, either.

Stretching his legs and leaning back against the tree, allowing the summer breeze to part his hair, the doctor took two handwritten notes out of his plaid shirt pocket. Johnny Parker and his wife, Martha, asked that the baby girl be named Mary Benson Parker, when she is baptized. "We will tell her how you saved our lives that night."

"Good people," he told Heinze. They had had another long day. By this time, they knew it was smart to find a place to stay by 4:00 p.m. The doctor drove in the far right lane and slowed down a bit, as he watched for R.V. park signs. "Gate Way Park ahead."

As they pulled into their allotted space, both travelers were pleased. It was the nicest one so far. "Wake up, Heinze. We've hit the Ritz. It will cost a lot more than we have paid, but look out the windows."

A large and beautiful lake in front of them, there was grass everywhere and a restaurant flashing a sign "Home Cooking." There was also a store, where the doctor could replace some clothing he had dished out. "This is great. I'll eat at the restaurant in style tonight."

The waitresses must have been chosen by her chest measurements. Brains were off limits. They talked to all the customers with their asses on the corners of the tables. The food was cold when they served it. Most unnerving of all, they took the dinner bill out of their bosoms.

Dr. Ralph had not had a woman for a long time but things looked very promising here. "Maybe I'll get lucky this time. I'm tired of my four queens. But not tonight. I'm pooped."

Viagra was available at the store and the doctor secured a pack just in case. "I think we should stay here a couple of days," he thought but didn't share that thought with his friend Heinze. Ralph was getting horny. The dog made eye contact with the doctor, who was embarrassed. "I swear, Heinze, you can read my thoughts."

He was looking at the map. "Not far from Roseville and not too far from D.C. I think I should call my brother," he mumbled. He called D.C. first and his mother answered.

"Where are you?" she asked. Before Ralph could answer, she stated, "Don't come here. You can't park that thing anywhere in Georgetown. And that dog! What are you going to do with him?"

Her older son replied to none of her questions. "I see Bob briefed on what I'm doing. Is he there?"

"No, he is in Roseville for the weekend." She gave Ralph her younger son's phone number and they hung up.

"Hi, Bob! This is your wandering brother."

"What is taking you so long? We thought you'd be here a week ago. Sure you're not walking the dog?"

"Is that your big brother, Ralph?" a laughing voice came from the background. "Let me talk, let me talk," Ella exclaimed.

C H A P T E R   13

His heart was on fire and the sweat sprang out of his neck. Dr. Ralph heard Ella talk. He could hardly speak.

"Is it really you? I thought you had decided to jump off a cliff or something."

She laughed. "Where are you right now? Why are you not here by now? Talk to me."

"You didn't give me a chance, you chatterbox." He could hear his heart pounding.

"Good to hear your voice," she replied. "You sound so young."

"I am young. Are you still as beautiful as I remember?" he asked hoping his voice didn't carry his passion.

"Of course, why not? I'll see you soon." She handed the phone back to her husband.

"Should I go to Roseville?" he asked his brother.

"Hold on and I'll give you the address and the phone number," which he did.

"Now you come here," his brother invited. "We have a fenced yard and a guest room. I'll tell Mother you'll be here for awhile, so she should make her own arrangements if she wants to come to Roseville."

"I can hear her now," Ella laughed into the phone. "She won't like that."

After the call, Dr. Ralph relaxed a bit in his chair. Nothing has changed. Ella could break his heart and Mother is still *Mother*. "I wonder if I'm doing the right thing." He asked himself.

This is a beautiful place. "Heinze, let's stay here a couple of days. I'm not anxious to see her again. I feel the old pain. Get your leash. We'll take a walk before it gets too warm." Heinze was only too glad to comply. He opened the drawer where the gun had been. He used his long nose and front teeth, as he had before. The leash was deposited in the doctor's lap.

Outside the compound was a large fenced property where dogs could meet each other, run, and play. When the doctor opened the gate, Heinze was the only dog there. Heinze chased rabbits and even brought one home for dinner.

"If you don't want that bunny," a woman in the trailer next to his called out, "Just give it to me. That will make a good dinner for both of us if you want to come."

"You mean you and me?" The doctor was surprised. "Great, what time?"

"About 6:00 will be fine," she smiled. What beautiful teeth, the doctor noticed. "She looks about my age," he thought. "Nice." Then he remembered his appearance. He thought, "I've got to get a haircut."

On the way, a stranger remarked, "Your dog needs to have some of that hair cut off. Look at him panting. It's too hot for all that coat."

"Thank you. We are on our way to the barber shop right now."

"Barbers don't trim dogs, not here at least. Take him to the trimming parlor for dogs. Some people!" the stranger remarked. Then the stranger stopped in the path. "I saw the dog running through all that undergrowth. This is tick season and flea season, too. Those critters get on people, too."

"What a busy body," Dr. Ralph thought as he shook his head and rolled his eyes.

"You first." The doctor almost had to drag the dog into the parlor, which was part of someone's house. "What was that smell? What is that shiny toothy thing in the pretty girl's house?" Heinze probably thought as he headed for the door. The blonde blocked the door. She stopped to pet Heinze and baby-talked as she stroked the dog. In that position, she showed Dr. Ralph she had nothing on under her short skirt. Heinze calmed down to the point that the two of them could get Heinze on the grooming table. He even let her drop the holding noose around his neck.

"Don't try to take his collar off. He won't put up with that," the doctor offered, while trying to conceal his sexual arousal.

She put the clippers to Heinze's face. "See, nice doggy. They won't hurt you. I'll be very, very careful." Dr. Ralph couldn't believe the dog's good behavior. Heinze even kissed her.

"The lucky buck," Ralph uttered aloud and she heard him. Then she smiled at the doctor and blew him a kiss. "That little sexy lady is looking to be laid," he thought.

"Before you start," the doctor instructed her, "I want him trimmed like a lion, but save some hair on his head and neck. Trim his body close and leave a tuft on his tail. Okay?"

"Sure, whatever you want." She smiled again. "They tell me you are a doctor." "What kind, are you a vet?"

"No, I'm an M.D."

"Gosh, she is gorgeous," he thought. And when she bent over the dog, her cleavage revealed breasts the size of grapefruits. Her top was cut low and she took time to use Kleenex to mop her brow and then dab her cleavage. Her hair was streaked blonde and red. And when she bent over in that short skirt, the doctor was getting excited. From where he was sitting, he thought, "Glory Hallelujah!"

"This coat is going to ruin my clippers," she baby-talked to the dog.

"I'll buy you all the new clippers you need." At the sound of his master's voice, Heinze wanted to turn around. Ralph said, "I'll help you hold me, I mean him."

"Get that thing back in its sack." The groomer told Heinze, who was trying to ride her arm. "I do men, not dogs."

"What did she say?" the doctor wondered. "I must be wrong." But he wasn't wrong. The beautiful young woman had the doctor in the sack before he left the shop.

"We don't have to fool around here in the shop. Come, I have a room out back."

Dr. Ralph was trying to undress the girl. "Not in front of Heinze. He's got the hots, too." The doctor excused himself for a moment and Heinze was quickly returned to the trailer.

When the groomer opened the door behind the shop, she greeted the doctor almost naked. Dr. Ralph shot his bolt then and there. The girl reached for his penis through his pants. "Take this pill and take me. I'll take you Doc, any way you like it," she whispered in his ear. Dr. Ralph stroked her long hair gently at first and as passion rose, he kissed her eyes, throat and sought her mouth with kisses of desire. She climbed onto his now naked body and began to slide down slowly bringing him ecstasy.

"You can clean up here if you like," as she asked for help with her bra. The doctor was pleased with his sex. He had lost it earlier but the second one in less than an hour was a tribute. He forgot he had taken a pill.

The girl startled the doctor. "That will be one hundred bucks, Daddy. Fifty for the dog and fifty for the screw. Forget about dinner. I have a date."

The doctor was mortified, "Unprotected sex with a whore," he said going back to Heinze. "Old Charlie worked. She was the first woman in two years, since he had set his eyes on Ella." He felt a little guilty but not enough to chase the smile off his face.

As he reached for the latch on his screen door, he heard a voice. "Dinner at six. Don't forget doctor, the rabbit."

"Oh, I almost forgot," Ralph said, less enthusiastically than earlier when the invitation was issued.

The more the doctor thought about the afternoon, the more it pleased him. Even more, it scared him. "I've forgotten her name or did she tell me her name? I paid in cash," he reflected. "What a great lady. I'd have been willing to pay a hundred just for me."

The doctor was getting hot again. "I'm a dirty old man," he told Heinze, as he danced his way into the cold shower.

He looked at his watch. "Five o'clock. Wonder what rabbit will taste like? Our family was never hunters. I really didn't take a good look at this rabbit woman. But I will tonight." He ruffed his knuckles against his wet chest. "Just call me Casanova!"

The lady next door came to the van with a dinner bell in her hand. "Ding-a-ling! Cocktail time!" She was very pretty and she looked like Betty White. Her front and back were hidden by an apron. Her smile was nice and her teeth were beautiful.

"Oh Ella, dear Ella, maybe it's best that I can find other women attractive."

The drink was strong, the music was low, and the candles were burning with a soft glow. "Set up." He thought.

"The rabbit was very good. How did you make it?" He thought he better keep talking because the "lady" across the table was using her shoeless big toe to run it up his trousers. "You told me your name was Bette with an "e" but you remind me of Betty White, the actress."

"Well, thank you, sir. What a nice thing to say. That breaks the ice." It also broke the idea the doctor was receiving. "Why don't you watch the news while I clean up here?" Bette suggested.

"Better still, let me help, and you can tell me how you cooked the rabbit."

"Well," she paused, "I'm from Pennsylvania."

"So am I," the doctor revealed.

"Where?" she asked.

"You first," he teased.

"Ever heard of Intercourse?"

"Sure did, right next to Paradise." They both laughed.

"Where did they get those names?" The newly discovered lover spun Bette around and kissed her soundly on the mouth. They both sat down on the sofa. He pulled her closer.

She asked, "How long are you staying here?"

"It depends," he whispered.

"On what?"

"On why you asked, sweet lady."

"I like you so much, and you liked my cooking. I was wondering, first, can you dance?"

"Not well," was his answer.

"They have a Saturday dance here. Would you take me?"

"I'd like to take her right now," he thought. "Sure, what's another day," he said. "I'd be proud to take you." With that, he kissed her again. This time his hand was on her leg.

"Your dog is having a fit. I can see him in your R.V. going from window to window. I think maybe you should leave," she teased.

"I didn't have that in mind," the doctor pushed.

"Tomorrow, pull up your blinds when you wake up. I'll make you breakfast."

The doctor was whistling as he left and Bette was laughing.

The dance band was rotten. Every instrument was doing its own thing. Besides, Dr. Ralph couldn't dance. They decided it would be more fun to walk under the full moon and talk.

She was a widow of three years, married once to a man who died of a heart attack. "I'm an antique dealer, have been all my life. I have been house-taught by my mother, my father, my aunts, and my uncles. They owned the best of early Pennsylvania antiques. Wonderful things have passed through my hands."

"Why did you sell them?" the doctor asked. "My mother could have made you rich."

"I couldn't afford to keep them," she explained. They reached her trailer.

"You seem to be doing well." Dr. Ralph pointed to her traveling home.

"I sold my house to buy it." They were inside.

"What are you going to make me for breakfast?" The doctor grinned.

CHAPTER 14

▼

As the smiling doctor readied to break camp, he found her card tucked in the pocket of the shirt he had been wearing the night before.

"Antiques You Can Be Proud To Own—Bette Shultz. Intercourse, Pennsylvania, Phone 707-1234."

The doctor studied it for a moment and then he placed the card in his wallet. "You never can tell," he said to himself as he went on with his plans.

"Must call my brother." He picked up his cell phone. Sunday was a good time to call.

"Hi," his mother answered.

"Oh shit!" He turned off the phone.

"I'll find a drugstore."

Heinze looked great with his new haircut and the doctor felt great as they backed out of their allotted space in the R.V. Park. As he turned onto the highway, Dr. Ralph realized he hadn't said farewell to Bette. "Rotten of me, really rotten of me. Well, I have her number. I'll call. Heinze, it looks like everybody is in Roseville for the weekend. Guess that's the way to go."

As he drove along, his thoughts were of the past 24 hours. The first one, he didn't even know her name. She was a Las Vegas beauty type, everything made to order. "Why was she hidden away? I'll bet there is some worthless guy behind that girl."

"Now take the other one. Bette, she is a lady, a little horny. She told me I was her first in three years. Her husband had died of a heart attack. She is a looker. Some lucky guy will find her."

Traffic was picking up as they approached the Pennsylvania Turnpike. "God help us. No one had mentioned the long, dark tunnels. Not just one, but two, or were there three?" The doctor's feet were sweating, not to mention the palms of his hands and the prickly sweat under his arms.

"Heinze, we can do it." Dr. Ralph was a new man. "And I'm getting closer to Ella everyday." He scolded himself. "I can't think of her this way. She belongs to Bob."

Hanover Street in Roseville looked the same as it did when Dr. Ralph lived there as a kid. Ralph, with Heinze seated next to him, drove to the old courthouse at the square in the charming tree lined streets of Roseville. "No place to park," he mumbled. A left-hand turn took him through the quiet old college town. "Still no place to park."

"Now we are on Route 41 and as memory serves, we are on our way to Newville," he told Heinze, at which point he recognized his mother's car at the Cross Roads Restaurant. "What would her car be doing here?" he wondered. Heinze could smell the good food and hopped around as Dr. Ralph pulled into the small parking space. "Everybody must eat out," was his remark.

Right then, the three most important people in his life came out of the restaurant to see if what they thought was true. Greetings from all directions. "When did you get in town?" "You look wonderful." "Is that a dog?" There were hugs and kisses all around.

Heinze watched people big and small enter and leave the popular restaurant. All was okay until some teenagers decided to tease the animal inside the R.V. They started to throw pebbles against the windows. Heinze began to leap and jump from window to chair, to bed causing the van to move ever so slightly. The emergency brake was not engaged and the doctor had parked on a slight dip.

The diners inside the small restaurant left plates and dishes as they flew to safety. Not everyone could run fast enough as the motor coach came through the plate glass front window of the restaurant. Safety glass or not, glass was everywhere. Some people were cut, others mostly frightened. Heinze was thrown to the floor of the coach, where he decided it best to remain.

Ralph's mother was okay, just mad. "Ralph, why is it that you always do something stupid?" She spat out the words. Ella had gotten out of the way of the flying glass but Bob was badly cut. Roseville was the nearest hospital. Wife and mother followed the ambulance.

Dr. Ralph remained to face the police, fire department, a town doctor, and a lot of angry customers. "Where are you going?" A large fireman stopped him.

"I want to see if my dog is okay."

"Your dog?"

"Yes, my dog. Do you mind?"

The fireman blocked the exit. "I understand you are a doctor. Look after these people until more medical help arrives!"

"It's just cuts. Nothing serious, but they will make the most of it, I'm sure."

"Officer," the fireman called to a local cop. "Arrest this man. His motor van wrecked this place."

"Let me get my first aid kit out of the van so I can be of help." The doctor pushed ahead to the van. That way he saw that Heinze was okay. The owner of the restaurant, upon arrival, was more understanding. He was fully insured.

Ralph's mother stayed at the hospital while her favorite son, Bob, was being treated. Ella returned to the scene to find the R.V. had been removed from the entrance of the restaurant. Dr. Ralph and Heinze were inside watching TV.

"Are you okay, Ralph?" she wanted to know, as he let her enter the van. "What a rotten welcome home."

"How is Bob?" the brother asked even before he kissed her hello. Or, was it a way to avoid the kiss?

"Your hand is wrapped. Are you hurt?"

"No," he replied. "Just cut my hand getting a piece of glass off the floor."

There was no way Ella could overlook the dog. "Good doggie." She patted Heinze's head briefly while trying to get past. "Does he bite?'

"Only if your name is Jacko." He laughed as the dog gave the girl a second look at the word Jacko. Heinze insisted on sniffing the new guest.

"Go away! I want to see my big brother," Ella pushed.

"It has been a day." Ralph looked tired and worried. Could she hear his heart racing and pounding? "It has been a day," he repeated like he had not said it before.

"Me, too," Ella offered but went no further to explain.

"Sorry, Ella, that you had to run out here tonight. Heinze and I plan to stay right here tonight. I will have people to see in the morning."

Ella bent over and kissed the doctor on the cheek. "If I can't do anything here, I had better go back to the hospital. Mother is acting like she is going to have a heart problem." "Don't I wish?" she added silently. "Ralph, I'm sure Bob is okay; just a bad cut or two. Wish it had been his head."

"Now, now, no way to talk, dear. That's your husband," he scolded.

"Don't I know it?" The remark was cold.

Ella returned to face her mother-in-law and the husband she considered an enemy.

Dr. Ralph gave Heinze an aspirin and took one himself. All evening and half the night, people were driving by to see what had happened. There hadn't been anything like that since some kids shot a hole in the display window of the local furniture store. One shot had caused that window to collapse. Poor Heinze was in the doghouse. He drew closer to Dr. Ralph. He tried to lick the small cut on the doctor's hand. When Heinze tried to say he was sorry, he would utter a sound that was only used at those times. It was something between a growl and a whimper. Both man and dog knew what it meant.

At 3:00 a.m., Ralph called the police. Someone was trying to pry the spare tire off the back of the coach. By the time the police arrived, the culprit had given up. But the officers did walk around to see what other damage there might be.

It was coffee time. No use trying to go back to bed. The sun was more awake than he was.

Not knowing just where his brother might be, Ralph used his cell phone. As he waited for an answer, he asked himself again, "What could I have done with that gun? Oh, well, I hope it's lost forever. I'm not sane to have a gun. Take last night, for example. I could have shot someone."

"So early?" was the question on the other side of the telephone.

"Yeah, I want to get out of here before the parade of people are up going to work."

"Take the bus over to Wal-Mart. You can park it there. It's just a short walk over to the office. Do you have the house number?"

"Yes, I do."

"OK, then I'll have the coffee ready, dear brother." No one else could say those words and exude charm like brother Bob.

Dr. Ralph turned to Heinze. "I didn't mention you old friend. I remember someone mentioned a fenced yard."

Roseville was close by and so was Wal-Mart, where Ralph was told to park the Winnebago. Instructions were followed and Heinze and the doctor set out on foot for Hanover Street and the new offices.

It was a beautiful morning as the two males, both pretty shaggy, heard the fruit vendors calling up and down the streets, "Strawberries, York County berries, strawberries!" It was a sound of the doctor's youth. They had to buy a quart to take along for breakfast. As he reached for 85 cents, he could taste the berries. The doctor had forgotten smells of his childhood. Now he decided to buy two boxes.

"Make it a dollar and a half total."

"Good." The doctor liked a bargain. So did Heinze and began to wag his tail.

"Big dog," the vendor said as he made change. "Does he bite? Where did you find the lion?" the street merchant wanted to know.

"In the jungle. Where else?" he replied trying to hold the dog's leash and balance the strawberry boxes. "Heinze, damn it. Be still and sit." The dog sat.

"A regular circus dog, eh? Let me find a 'tut' for the boxes. These strawberries are the best—a wet spring, ya know!"

Dr. Ralph smiled at the word "tut," sometimes called a "poke." These were Pennsylvania words, which meant bags.

CHAPTER 15

▼

Off they went, man, dog and strawberries. The morning was so fresh and the strawberries smelled heavenly. Dr. Ralph was home.

Ella met them at the door. She was so beautiful. Her eyes sparkled and her teeth gleamed in the sunlight. When she threw her arms around Ralph, her hair touched his face. It was all he could stand. He dropped the "tut" at his feet so he could embrace this beautiful person with both arms.

"Brother, dear." She kissed him once more on this cheek. "And, look at the pooch. What a handsome pair. Come in. Don't stand there for God's sake, come in."

Ralph's mother entered the hall. "That's not a dog. That's a beast!" Heinze knew from her tone that she wasn't his friend. The dog sat down and offered his paw. When she reached for it, Heinze pulled the paw away. Everybody laughed except Mother and Heinze.

"By the way, Ralph, there is a box here for you from the police department," said Bob.

They all, including Heinze, had strawberries, coffee, and Danish buns. Then the box was brought out.

"It's a heavy box with a letter also." Bob explained.

Dr. Ralph shook the box before he opened it. The dog knew what was inside the box.

"It's a gun!" Someone said at all at once, everyone had a look of stunned disbelief.

"What were you doing with a gun for God's sake?" Mother's astonishment set the tone.

"This is the damnedest thing. I thought the gun had been stolen," uttered Ralph.

"Read the letter," said Bob. "Maybe you are a wanted man?"

The thought amused him. "What could he ever do to be wanted by anyone?" He read the letter aloud.

"Dear Dr. Benson." It told the story. A rose bush had to be replaced. In doing so, the gun was found. The I.D. was checked and the owner was traced. Dr. Ralph had used his brother's address when he checked into the Friendly Haven Motor Court.

"What were you doing with a gun?" asked his mother. "Your father would not allow one in the house."

"I know why," Dr. Bob thought with a shy smile. "We are looking for a place to live. Ella thinks she has found something. Do come along. We can put the dog in the basement."

Then Ralph suggested, "Here's a better idea. Give us an hour. I'll pick you up with the R.V. It's 8:30 now so make it 9:30." All the while, Dr. Ralph was thinking to himself, "No one puts my dog in the basement."

"I thought we might go to the Club for lunch," Bob offered, seeming upset with the new plan.

"I'll make lunch. We can eat on the bus," said Ralph. The others were finally getting the idea that the dog came first.

They picked up the building and went on along the way. They passed the disaster of the night before. Someone asked, "Was your dog hurt last night?"

No answer. Ralph was wondering why there was so much traffic on a county road. Repairmen were busy at the restaurant.

"The owner must know someone," Bob mentioned. "Workers are hard to find right now."

"They are really lucky. Miss Somebody has all the best construction people tied up. I heard she is paying special wages for special people."

"It's the old Murphy place down the road a piece." Dr. Bob was resentful and it showed in his tone.

As they rolled along, Ralph was told the whole story including what they thought of the realtor. "I think her name is Ann."

"You and Mother always liked old things," he added.

"You mean dead things," Ella interrupted. "I like charm and cozy things. I'll bet the Murphy place comes with a ghost.

Ella's dream house suited all but Mother. "I'll stay in Georgetown," was her phrase. That suited Ella fine.

"Keep the one bedroom for me in Roseville. That would be handy for when I want to come to see old friends." No one paid attention to the old woman's ramblings.

Heinze had made his decision. He thought she smelled like pee.

"As you can see, there are five bedrooms. We will have a bedroom for Brother Ralph." Ella was showing the almost completed house of her dreams. "I want bedrooms for children and one bedroom for a play room. I never had a place to play," Ella continued. "When I was a child, I was raised in hotels and apartments. I also want play places where I can play with the kids, too, like dress up, reading stories and making noise. I don't know why I can't get pregnant."

"You are trying too hard. That's what Dr. Isadore told me," said Bob. Not a head turned her direction.

"How much land goes with this place?" Ralph asked, trying to change the subject.

"It's a half-acre. That's enough and the land goes to the creek. Not too many regulations. You can have a house, but not pigs and no peacocks." Ella was showing the last word in kitchens.

"It even has a walk-in fireplace, just like the old Murphy place," her mother-in-law pointed out.

"What about travel trailers?" Ralph asked.

"Oh, no," answered the building. "No trailers of any kind." The builder wanted to make a new house sale. "Now, I have some land back of my place where you could park. I won't charge very much and you'd have a good view of the Murphy place. That girl is something to watch, too."

The builder had a dirty little laugh. "By the way, what kind of dog is that?" He pointed to Heinze. "Let him out. I like dogs." The builder wanted to size up Heinze. "Just so he doesn't kill chickens. He could have the run of the place. Course you have to watch out for ticks. Lots of brush and trees on vacant land." Heinze ran right up to the man, sat down, and offered his paw. Old Mrs. Benson saw the act, too.

"Pew!" she offered.

"We all lucked out. That damn Ann can't do anything about our watching. You can get a good view from this hilltop. Keep a good view on her. She's a devil." Brother Bob didn't like the lady.

"And, she can just piss up a tree." Ella laughed.

When Ella's house was finished, it was a very pretty place. The house was filled with charm. Mostly country and almost everything was reproduction. That was fine with Ella. Her new old things were just what she wanted.

"I love all the windows," Ella said turning around in the large family room with the huge limestone fireplace. The view of the mountains and the creek was only 200 feet away. "It's the first thing I see in the morning." she exclaimed. "Somehow it always seems to glisten. But I'm afraid my husband doesn't like it."

"But I do," said Bob. "You have worked so hard and you have a lovely house." "But you know where my heart is?"

"Yes." Ella thought of Lu. He thought of the old Murphy place.

"I think your house is charming and just the right size for a family," the mother remarked.

"Here, here," added Dr. Ralph. "I thought the house was near completion. This place is ready to move into."

"It's a surprise," Ella laughed. "I pushed and pushed this dear man." She indicated the builder. "I wanted it finished before you got here." Ella turned to Ralph, "Don't forget, you have not seen your room. Come with me." She took her brother-in-law's hand.

"Now, you have seen what I like. There is a place for a pool and a triple garage. And the area is limited to five houses."

"Glad you are happy," said Bob. "There will be times when I can't make it home. I told you from the start. It is a little out of my range but this is what you wanted," he warned.

Ralph thought it was time to change the subject. "Is it okay if we park here?" he asked the builder. "We would like to have lunch here and you are invited to join us."

Ella was as happy as a child with a new toy. The smell in the house was new paint, not dead birds and dead people.

"What you have done, my dear, is very nice. But, if you plan on any changes, I'd be glad to help you," her mother-in-law suggested, as only a mother-in-law could.

"No way!" Ella was just as rude and didn't care at all. "This house is ME all the way."

Heinze was banished to the bedroom in the R.V. because he took up so much space. The insulted dog got up on the bed and peed. It was a deliberate act.

Ella's dollhouse only needed curtains and shutters and they were on order. All were impressed. Ella loved to hear the accolades. In the glow of the moon Ella announced, "This house is for children, many children, dogs, cats, plus their friends and anything they want. But, no snakes. I couldn't stand snakes."

Days were spent watching the old Murphy house come alive. Dr. Ralph had a front row seat. He watched with admiration as Ann ran the reconstruction. "Boy, that woman is really in charge. She's rough and respected by her crew." Dr. Ralph was impressed. Ann was in jeans and boots, with her golden hair in a wide, long braid hanging from under a man's baseball cap.

"Over here. Put that here. Get off your ass!" These were becoming frequent comments. Under Ann's tutelage, the old stone house began to regain its original splendor.

Before leaving for Georgetown, the older Mrs. Benson took Ella aside. "For every child you have, I'll leave one million in the child's name and one million to you, Ella. So, get busy!"

When Ella related the story to her husband, it gave him reason to think. "Could the operation be changed or was it too late?" He also realized that no member of the family knew about the vasectomy he had had. "Remember, honey, you will have to give me half for services rendered."

CHAPTER 16

▼

Bob phoned his mother to ask if adoption was an option. "If it is an infant and a male to carry the Benson name," was her reply.

"Ella and I have to have a talk," he responded. Inside he thought, "I'll tell her I had the mumps when I was a kid and they went down on me to my testicles." He lied.

When Ella was told about his "condition," she understood why they had not been able to have a child after two years of marriage. "Let's keep trying for awhile and if I don't get pregnant, we will seek aid for adoption."

"I'd want a boy," Bob interrupted. "That would go well with Mother."

"You selfish bastard." Ella wanted to wring his neck. "Remember, I said try. You don't get an 'A' for your homework." Ella didn't mean it as a joke. She knew where he spent his free time. Her name was Lu. In fact, he had spent so much time away from their new home that Ella found other things to do.

Ella liked to visit her brother-in-law, Dr. Ralph. She and the huge dog had become friends.

"I wonder where he goes." Ella asked Dr. Ralph.

"Honey, take it easy. You know he has office hours twice a week. He still goes to D.C. to clear things up there. He called me to come back because he needed help. I've been lazy," Ralph confessed. "Tomorrow, I'll go down to the office in Roseville and see what I can do to help."

Watching Ella standing in the sunlight, Ralph thought to himself, "She is so beautiful and so sad." That old feeling was still there. How could Bob neglect her? He thought, "Why didn't I meet her first?" Dr. Ralph reached for her hand just to hold it for a moment.

While Ralph loved Ella, Ann and her project stirred the manhood within him. Ann called and waved to Dr. Ralph each morning when she came on the job. He looked forward to watching her. Ella was a girl, a lovely young thing. Ann was a woman in every way. A female isn't truly beautiful until she reached 40. There is so much more development from 20 to 40. Ann was not young, but she was handsome. She carried a long, wide braid of blonde hair down her back. Her eyes were brown and they held a spark of life, wit, and sexual desire. There was the other side of Ann, all business leaving no doubt about who was in charge. The woman was still a lady.

She was excellent in a man's job. She knew what and why and how to restore the house to its original beauty. The home had been built in 1751. The cornerstone on the chimney said so.

Ann had never been married. "By choice," she said. She was no youngster, well past 40. While Dr. Ralph loved Ella, Ann and her independence stirred him. Why did he want her?

Ralph watched Ann arrive at the job each day at daybreak. "Time for a cup of coffee," he called after her.

"No time, but maybe sometime." Ann returned his call with a smile and a wave.

"She is so different from Ella in every way," Dr. Ralph Benson thought, as he watched her climb over rocks and boards, giving orders and getting things done by workers, who respected her and her knowledge. Heinze had grown to like her, too. To prove it, he found a garter snake in the weeds and brought it to her.

"Good boy." Ann took the trophy and tossed it back into the weeds.

"What a gal!" Dr. Ralph exclaimed from his perch next to the R.V., where the view was getting better and better. "What beautiful teeth she has. Some men are tit men, others are tush men! I think I'm a tooth man." Dr. Ralph laughed out loud at himself.

It was an especially lovely morning when Ann went out of her way to stop at Dr. Ralph's place. "What about a cup of coffee?"

"Black, no sugar and no cream." She smiled and her beautiful teeth just glistened.

Dr. Ralph asked her to sit as he handed her the cup of brew. About 150 pounds he measured with his eyes. Her blouse was open at the neck; boots on her feet and blue jeans covered her ass.

"Want to see what we have done so far? It's coming together beautifully."

Dr. Ralph was off his lawn chair and they took off downhill. Ann let the doctor assist her over rough ground. He was amused because she hadn't broken her stride when she approached him earlier. "Women," he thought. "Aren't they wonderful?" At that point, Dr. Ralph stumbled.

"Watch out!" she cried, as she tried to steady him before he fell. The house was about 200 feet downhill from where Dr. Ralph was parked. "You do keep the emergency brake on all the time, don't you?" She laughed remembering the accident at the restaurant.

"Looking good—real good." He could only see the rear of the house from his perch.

Once inside, Dr. Ralph was impressed. "Ann, you are something else. I'm amazed at what you are doing. It's just great. I've been waiting for an invitation." He put his arm around her. Both smiled and looked into each other's eyes for a second. Then he dropped his arm. He didn't turn and run. Instead, he asked, "What do you do for fun? All work and no play, they say." This time, the short, stocky, thick-necked man felt 6 feet tall.

"How about dinner?" It was a statement. In the next statement, he remembered the woman in the northwest who had turned him down. He prepared himself for Ann's negative answer.

"I'd love to go," was the delighted answer. "What's more, I'd like to stay for breakfast," Ann teased.

Where did I hear that line before? He remembered the antique dealer. "Hot dog!" He recovered quickly. "Looks like I've found a real woman," he said as he took her in his arms without hesitation.

"About 7:00 p.m., no make it 5:00 p.m. By the way, you will have to drive. I get my new car tomorrow." Dr. Ralph said. He had put off buying a new car. His brother had two cars and Ella had one. However, under the budding circumstances, he decided he better get his own.

He was looking forward to the evening. Heinze could pose a problem. Maybe she will suggest her place. "I hope, I hope." Thinking and not looking, he tripped over a long piece of limestone in the field of work. "Have I grown fickle or am I having a mid-life crisis or what? That woman is going to drive me nuts."

He recollected, "I was thinking of staying another day and paying that whore twice what she asked, but I didn't. I wanted to stay another day with Bette, the antique dealer, but I didn't, and she was very nice. Now what am I going to do about Ann? Ella is the love of my life or maybe she isn't?" Dr. Ralph whistled while he showered.

They went to Mt. Holly, a town nearby for a long, long dinner. Both talked and talked. She dated but never married by choice. He had never married, had been in love but it was of no use. Talk like that was part of their conversation.

"Tell me about Alaska." Ann was interested.

When Ralph thought he had told her enough about Alaska, he asked if she was ready to leave.

"You have told me just what I wanted to hear. I know it would be a wonderful place." There was more than a spark going on when they decided to stop at Ann's place. Heinze would have been in the way.

The next morning, she dropped him off at the Cadillac agency to pick up his new car. Then he stopped off at the Roseville office, first, to show off his car and second, to see if he could be of any help. As the doctor stepped up to the door of the office, he hoped the glow he was feeling wouldn't show. He would blame it on the new car. The front door of the office was unlocked. In fact, it was standing slightly open. That's strange.

"Hello," he called as he entered. His brother appeared at the head of the stairs that led to the bedrooms. "Did I come at a bad time?" Dr. Ralph apologized, as his brother stuffed his shirt into his open pants.

Dr. Bob laughed. "That million for each child looks good, don't you think?'

At first Dr. Ralph didn't understand. And then it dawned on him that his brother was talking about what their mother had offered. With that, a woman appeared at the top of the stairs. It wasn't Ella. It was Lu.

"For Christ's sake," was all Dr. Ralph could say as he reached for the door. "Better keep your door locked, you son of a bitch. What a let down. I thought that was over a long time ago." He kicked a stone into the door of his new car. He recalled the auto accident and Lu was with him at that time.

"Poor Ella, I think she really loves that bastard. My brother, the 'family louse.' Men will be men. Why can't they change that to man can be man."

Dr. Ralph thought of his own escapades of the night before. "I wasn't hurting anyone, not even myself or Ann." He made excuses. Ann told the doctor that she had a wonderful, romantic time. Her admission pleased him because he had a ball. Ralph overlooked another sin of his brother, as he headed for home and the sight of Ann bossing the crew.

There was a call waiting for Dr. Ralph when he arrived home. The call was from Ella. "Dear Brother Ralph, Ella here. I have to talk to you. Please call."

He said hello to Heinze and felt guilty until the master patted the bedspread. "Heinze, you are jealous and this peeing has got to stop. Damn it!" Heinze crawled away.

CHAPTER 17

▼

"Ella, Ella." I must call but that dog has got to change his ways. I'll not put up with this action. The doctor scolded, but at the same time, he felt sorry. It really was his fault. The dog was locked in the motor home for a night and half a day. "Come here, Heinze." The dog refused. "Go ahead and be mad." The dog ignored Dr. Ralph.

"Guess I'll have to tell Ann if she wants my company we come as a team, you and me Heinze." The dog seemed pleased. He wagged his tail and made that funny noise in his throat when he would like to bark but should not. "Heinze, you made me forget to call Ella."

"What's the problem, Kiddo?"

"Kiddo, who is kiddo," asked Ella.

"You are at the moment," Ralph joked. "What's up?"

"I've made plans to go to New York."

"Why?" he asked.

"To see my mother," she stated.

Dr. Ralph wondered at the sudden warmth Ella had with her own mother. She never mentioned her before. Was Ella up to something, he thought. Why had she not mentioned it before? Why the secret way?

"Wouldn't surprise me," he imagined, "if Ella were going to New York to locate an investigator or a detective." Dr. Bob was gone too many nights leaving Ella alone. More than once, Ella had asked if Heinze could spend the night. Dr. Ralph thought himself clever as he had said, "Not to Heinze's liking, but I'd always say yes."

It was just a bit past 9:00 p.m. Ralph had kissed and hugged Ann goodnight. He wasn't tired. With nothing to do and too early for bed, he called to Heinze. "Let's take a ride." As usual, those were happy words to the dog. He loved to go, go, and go. The dog even knew where Ella had hidden her door key. Happy ears and wagging tail were his way of saying, "Let's go."

Ella's dollhouse had such appeal. The blue and white colors were soothing. The seating was for comfort and conversation. There were hooked rugs, braided rugs, and planked floors with touches of brick red here and there. "I think she did a great job." And, then he remembered hearing that was her major in college. "It really is a place for kids. Maybe that is why she went to New York, to find a surrogate mother."

The doctor's rambling thoughts were abruptly interrupted by a low growl from Heinze. The dog moved slowly at first and then he dashed at the dark window. Then the dog moved in a low crawl and then sprang against the rear door with such force the door almost lost its hinges. Someone, or something, had scared the hero out of Dr. Ralph. He moved slowly to the phone to call 911. The dog kept sniffing at the door. He had gotten a good scent. The stranger had been on the back patio.

The police arrived quickly. They seemed to be more afraid of the huge dog than an intruder.

"I know he was right here at the door. The dog knew someone was there."

"Let's let him out. If that dog picks up his trail, he won't be back." One officer laughed. Heinze picked up the trail. It had been someone. Heinze followed the footsteps to where the intruder's car had been parked.

"Good dog, good dog! Where did you ever find a dog like that?" one policeman wanted to know. "Let's go over the trail one more time. Probably just a Peeping Tom, but you never know. We could pick up something. Go," he ordered the dog. The dog obeyed.

Ella had told her mother that she thought someone was watching the house. After the police left, Dr. Ralph went to the laundry of the house. He found a dirty sock that belonged to his brother. The dog smelled the sock and showed no interest. "Thank God," whispered Ralph as he gave thanks in his heart. He was afraid it could be his brother. It could be a way to drive Ella away. At least, the police are aware of something going on. He wiped the sweat off the back of his short, red neck.

"Ella must get a gun," he concluded as he and Heinze rode home. "You are a hero. Good dog," the doctor praised his friend.

The incident was almost forgotten until Ella phoned for help. Someone had shot Dr. Bob, as he was getting out of his car. It was a figure all in black, head covered. All Ella had seen was the figure disappearing into the night. Dr. Ralph lost no time getting to his brother's house.

"The bastard got me in the shoulder. I think it's broken. It hurts like hell," Bob moaned. The ambulance and the police were arriving at the same time.

Ella stepped back in horror. "That could have been me."

Ella had received a handwritten note. "Get back to New York." She hadn't even told Ralph. Instead, she had torn the threat into small pieces in the shredder.

"Somebody has your number," Ralph remarked to her when he learned of the note. There was no answer. Voices were low as Bob was placed in the ambulance.

"Lord God, I hope I don't lose the baby." Ella was bent over in pain.

"Baby, what baby?" her husband called from his gurney.

"Steady, doctor. Take it easy. Don't pull out that I.V." the helping paramedic warned.

The Newville Police had been called. Once Bob was in the hospital, it was decided to call the Roseville Police. Dr. Ralph thought it had been an attempt to murder his brother.

"Something is very wrong around here," thought Ralph. "Bob had many enemies, the kind you really don't want, the boys from the Syndicate, for example. Who were they really? Maybe that was why Bob went to New York so often." Ralph sighed, "I always thought those weekends were to be with Lu."

He continued his thoughts. "Why did Ella go to New York? To see her mother or is she having an affair hoping to get pregnant? She had returned about a week ago. Where is Ella? She must have stayed at the hospital with her husband."

Ella drove Bob home from the hospital to find a message on the phone from the local police. "The gun was found and it belongs to Dr. Ralph Benson." the police related.

"My God." Ella muffled a cry. "It can't be. No, no, it's the money. That damn money. It just can't be, not Ralph."

When Dr. Ralph was told, he quickly recalled that he had not taken the gun home. It had been left in the office in Roseville. "Who found it? Who took it?"

Surely, Bob hadn't shot himself, or maybe he did. "I think I'm going to get sick." Ralph headed for the bathroom.

Everybody was suspicious of the other guy. Only Heinze was free and clear.

"I'm glad your lousy brother didn't die." It was Ann on the phone. "The police even questioned me. You can't keep a secret in this town. I bet that smart-ass brother of yours shot himself by mistake."

"No, he wouldn't take a chance like that," said Ralph, defending his brother once again.

"I hope no one called Mother." Dr. Ralph wanted to protect her also. Mrs. Benson, Sr. was getting up in years. She was hard as nails about most things, but it was very difficult if it pertained to her precious son.

Ralph could not fall asleep. "Why this and why that?" He turned over, pounded his pillow, and then invited Heinze to join him in the bed. His last thoughts were, "Why did Ella cry out, 'oh my baby?'"

Dr. Bob couldn't sleep either. "What did Ella mean about 'my baby'? God knows it isn't mine. Could she have persuaded Ralph to sleep with her? No, I'd want a better looking kid than that. I think she would do anything for that kind of do. It's been twenty years since I had the vasectomy." He continued, "Maybe it leaked." He laughed, as he fell asleep. He dreamed how thrilled his mother would be to learn she was a "Grandma."

So far, the police were not threatening anyone, but they did ask Dr. Ralph to retell his story about the gun. Whoever had taken the gun had worn gloves. The only prints were Ralph's. They were made when he had taken the gun from the shipping box.

"Are you going to arrest me?" he asked the officers, who just arrived at the office where Ralph was going over the books that Dr. Bob had tried to cover.

The officer reached across the desk to shake the doctor's hand and assure him that no arrest was being made at this time. He added, "We might want to take a look at these ledgers."

Even Ella was giving Ralph a hard time. She spoke to him and said, "If Bob was gone, if he had died, you would get the golden calf. Right?"

The words burnt a hole in his heart. "How could you say anything like that to me?" In anger, Ralph blurted out. A wife always gets her husband's money. "And by the way, whose baby are you having?"

"Yours, of course!" The laughter was cruel.

Could this be the woman he had loved so much for such a long time, the bewildered doctor wondered.

"That's not funny Ella. You could create a lot of trouble if overheard."

"I'm not being funny," Ella returned. "Someone has to take the blame if Bob denies he got me pregnant. I'll say I was raped and you did it!"

"Could she be serious?" At a time like this, the doctor was overwhelmed. "The little bitch," he thought. His love for her was in sudden jeopardy.

"Oh, come on, a joke is a joke." She looked hard. "I wish it were true. You are such a nice guy, but I think it's his." And that wasn't followed by a laugh.

The local policeman was still in the hallway. He heard every word Ella had said. After Ella left, the officer surrendered the gun to Dr. Ralph. "Just don't leave town. We might need you."

It sent a shiver up the doctor's spine. "God, don't tell me I could get involved in this mess." It was said as a prayer. "When they look at these records, the police are going to see how things were covered up. But, I had no hand in it. Why do I sweat in my neck?" Dr. Ralph thought. "I hate that. No wonder my brother never wanted any office help. Not to save money, but to be able to save his neck. Worst of all, he is mixed up with some big city gamblers, names I have heard about and names I have read about. No wonder he was shot," Ralph said in a whisper, as though someone was listening. "That was a warning shot. These goons don't miss if they want you dead." All this was running through the doctor's head.

"Poor Ella, poor Bob," he thought. "There will be hell to pay if Mother gets the rotten news." Dr. Ralph was still concerned about his brother and Ella. His mother did find out and very quickly. Ella had delivered the news in a gleeful manner. Her mother-in-law was shaken to her knees.

"People like us never get mixed up in scandal like this," she blurted out. "It's Ralph's fault. Ralph always looked after him but then he ran off to Alaska and brought that damn dog to look after."

Meanwhile, Ann tried to reach Ralph at his R.V. Having no luck, her next step was to go to the office of the Ralph's brother. After ringing the doorbell and pounding on the door, Dr. Ralph finally came to the door. "What do you want?" he asked Ann in a dead tone.

"Can we be overheard here?" Ann pushed her way in.

"Not that I know of. Why?" The big dog was rubbing the side of his back against Ann.

"Don't knock me down, big guy."

"Let's go out into the backyard to talk," Ralph suggested.

They sat down close to each other on the swing. "Listen," Ann said softly. "The police called me again and I told them you had been with me when Bob was shot. I know you and Heinze were home at the time. The dog couldn't say so, but I did."

"Ann, I appreciate your kindness, but I am not starting to lie early in this mess. Lies are too hard to remember."

"Bless your heart, Ralph. I offered because I love you." Their eyes made contact in the soft glow of sunset.

"Strange as it sounds to me, I have feelings for you, too, Ann." They embraced and swung into a deep meaningful kiss. "What am I going to do?" he asked the woman in his arms. The swing was an impossible place for their next move so they went inside to the bedroom.

"Listen to me. I know in these whereabouts that people don't like outlanders. But they will listen to me. As I've already told you, you were with me." Then she addressed the dog, "Move over, that's my place." Ann gave Heinze a push. "This bed is for two people." Heinze knew by this time he would wind up in the spare bedroom over the office. Instead, he was allowed space on the floor at the foot of the bed. Heinze liked Ann. He felt no fear around her. However, Ella was different. Around her, he felt a natural caution.

After the loving, Dr. Ralph made a drink for both of them. He smiled to himself. "Thanks to the whore who gave me back my manhood."

The next morning, Mrs. Benson, Sr. was at Bob's office. In she came with a swish! The older woman stopped dead in her tracks when she spotted Ann. The younger woman's hair was messed up and there were other signs of a satisfied woman. "And who are you?" as if she didn't know. Mrs. Benson made it her business to know everyone else's business.

"We have not met." Ann extended her hand. "I'm here to try to save the skin of your bull-headed son," Ann informed. The two women marked off their territory. No love would be lost here.

"Well, you can step aside, young woman. This is where I take over," the matriarch glared. Even Heinze got out of her way. "First, that damn dog. Before I fall over him, he has got to go."

"Grrrr," came out the side of his mouth.

"See." The mother pointed at the dog. "That dog is vicious."

"I'll take him home with me," Ann offered.

"If he will go, it would be the best."

Dr. Ralph came into the room from the bathroom, having heard some of the icy stand-off. He didn't need to spend any more time with the two women in the same room.

"Did you know Ella is pregnant?" he asked his mother to clear the air.

"You can bet it isn't Bob's." Ann showed her dislike of Ella.

"Who are you to make a report like that?" the mother-in-law demanded.

"Ask around." Ann wasn't afraid of the woman. Heinze not only pulled his leash off the nail in the office hall, but he carried it to Ann. "Let's go." He didn't know why his master let those two women fight.

"By the way," Mrs. Benson said, changing the subject, as Ann and the dog were leaving, "when did you get the new Caddie? And what's this about Ella? I hope you two are not having an affair. She is trash."

Ann talked to the dog seated next to her in the pick-up truck. "Heinze, ole boy, no one should be out at Dr. Bob's right now. Let's go and see if you can retrace those tracks from the other night."

They did and to her great surprise, Ann found some money that could have fallen out of a pocket, a ten dollar bill, two quarters, and a dime partly covered by a clump of weeds. Heinze found them very interesting.

"Don't like them." Ann pulled them away. "Here," she offered. "Smell them, though." Ann spoke softly to Heinze. "Try to recall if you can."

Heinze amazed her. She watched as the dog sniffed around and picked up the scent once more. "Let's go," Ann ordered as she released the leash so that the dog was free. Having running in a nearly straight line for a few feet, he came to an abrupt halt, having no more scent to follow.

Now she hooked it up again and he reflected, as she did. The collar Heinze wore was just what you would expect on a large dog, but the leash was inches wide and a half-inch thick. "Why so strong?" Ann thought. Ann had been told nothing about Jacko and the hate he and his master had for that one. The scent was not Jacko. If it had been, she would not have been able to hold the dog. The scent was that of a stranger to the dog.

Ralph and his mother were driving toward Bob's house. "What's with you and that Amazon?" she almost sneered.

"You don't mean Ann, Mother. She has become very important to me."

CHAPTER 18

▼

"I wouldn't expect anything more of you," she insulted Ralph. "Two homely people, for God's sake. Don't have any children. I can do without ugly grandchildren."

"You are terrible, Mother. Try to be kind to me. If I am so ugly, Mother, start with yourself. The genes had to come from someone."

They never spoke again. His mother died of a heart attack less than an hour later. The heart attack followed the announcement Ella made. "I'm pregnant and it isn't Bob's child. I've been implanted with the genes of a handsome Rhodes Scholar."

Ella never told anyone else besides her mother-in-law, but her secret was overheard by someone hiding in the hallway. That person slipped away easily as Ella tried to help her dying mother-in-law. The culprit got away unnoticed, without the sound of a car starting, by letting it the car coast down, brake off, until it finished a slight decline.

The funeral was a real parade. People came from everywhere, especially those who thought they were entitled to a share of the family wealth.

The police contacted doctors Ralph and Bob. "We don't wish to further your pain at this time, but again, don't either one of you leave town. We know your mother died a natural death but we have a lot of loose ends and will contact you both later."

Ralph decided it was time to call his lawyer.

After the funeral in Washington, D.C., the deceased Mrs. Benson's attorney asked certain people to come for a meeting in his office. At this time, the lawyer read the will. He explained in advance, "There is only one recipient of this large fortune. Only Ella, who is with child. If it is a female child, it is to carry her name, Gertrude Lauck Benson. That child shall share the estate with mother, Ella Pike Benson. If the child is a male child, it is left the entire fortune with a ten thousand dollars a month sum to the mother, Ella Pike Benson, until said male child reaches the age of 21 years. The fortune is seven million dollars, not counting her house, cars, furniture, jewels, etc."

"She can't do that!" screamed Bob. Then he turned to his wife. "Who is the father of that child?"

"Not you, honey. She never said it had to be yours."

Bob crossed the room and slapped his wife's face in front of everyone, and no one objected. It was not a very pleasant place to be.

"You bitch!" Dr. Bob sneered.

"A bastard child!" Ralph began to laugh. "Well, brother, looks like we have to go back to work."

"I'm not finished." The attorney from D.C. asked for everyone's attention. "There is a codicil. If the child is born dead, the estate goes three ways, Dr. Robert Benson, Dr. Ralph Benson, and Ella Benson."

"I wouldn't like to be that child," Dr. Ralph offered aloud to himself. He wondered if his brother could be trusted. Ella will have to be careful, he thought. He was ashamed to think he could have had such a thought.

The Murphy house that Ann was restoring was coming along beautifully. People were starting to take notice. Ann had accepted a $500,000.00 offer for the property. The peculiar turn of events left Dr. Bob in no position to buy his dream property.

When his mother's house was sold in Georgetown, it brought a pretty penny. The furniture was sold at the finest auction house in New York. It realized 3 million dollars and her jewels another 3 million dollars. The estate was now worth another 6 million dollars.

There were things in five different bank boxes, Russian enamels. One contained an egg nestled in a nest of gold wire. When a button was pushed on the rose quartz egg, it opened to a golden yoke. When another button was pushed, there lay a tiny diamond rosary. Another item was a Tiffany 2-inch clock in silver and bits of glass. None of it was going to the two sons.

Dr. Bob got drunk and Dr. Ralph felt sorry for Ella. "What is she going to do to take care of all this wealth? Who will take care of her?" Ralph was really concerned.

"I don't like her," Ann told Ralph. "But, she had better get a bodyguard with that husband."

There were no stipulations in the will. As long as she was pregnant, Ella could leave her husband, so she could live elsewhere and do whatever pleased her. She still had to produce a live child to get the entire fortune. There was no mention of an adopted child in the will.

Ella feared for her life. She was sure someone would try "foul play." Ralph offered Heinze to protect her and Ella was glad to have the dog nearby.

Heinze sensed her fear and it was transferred to him. The dog became aware of the sound of a cricket. He, in turn, wasn't fearful as long as a gun wasn't in sight. Heinze hated the look of a gun, which he associated with ear-splitting noise and pain from his own gun shot wound.

The doorbell rang. Ella jumped and looked at the door. "Who is there?" she yelled.

"Just me, Ralph. Are you alone?" he asked as she opened the door a crack.

"Why did he ask that?" She trusted no one. "Are you alone?" she countered. The dog knew who it was. His long tail was whacking in air.

"Are you going to let me in?" Dr. Ralph was aware of her hesitation.

"Oh, alright." Ella unlocked the three locks she had added to the door. "I've got to get a gun," she thought to herself.

"I came to make sure you are okay and to visit my dog." The dog was so glad to see his master that Ralph had trouble getting past the dog and his wagging tail. "Move, you old hound! I missed him, too," said Ralph as he smiled at Ella.

"Just one more day. Then I'll let him out," said Ella. "He knows his way home. The dog has come here in the past to visit me on his own."

"I've wondered about that," the doctor spoke aloud. "I hope he will always return."

Ella spoke. "One thing, he seems to have a fascination about some smells around here. At first, I thought Heinze was eating grass—he walks with his nose so close to the ground."

Dr. Ralph changed the subject. "You know Heinze is becoming very social. People I've never met wave to him when we are walking together." He noticed that Ella was jumpy and scared and decided to stay awhile. "Honey, do you have any coffee?" he asked.

"Sure, but it's from breakfast. I could make another pot."

"Good idea. I'll just stay awhile longer." Dr. Ralph patted his beloved dog. Then he got off his seat and followed Ella to the kitchen.

"That's where he was," she pointed out the kitchen window.

"Who?" as if he didn't know.

"The thing, man or woman. I have to get out of here for awhile." Ella was crying.

"You could stay with me. I've got a gun."

"No, there would be talk," Ella sighed. "Oh, did you hear that?" Ella stepped back in fear.

"Your garage door was open when I drove up," Ralph said in a low voice. Heinze added to the situation with a low growl followed by a dash to the back door.

Dr. Ralph's heart was in his mouth. "I'll take a look." He saw Bob's car going at full speed down the country road. "Only Bob. He must have forgotten something."

The telephone rang. They both jumped.

"Ella," said Bob, "I'm sending someone to pick up some of last year's records that I have stored in the garage. See you, Hon." Her husband hung up abruptly before she could say anything else. Neither asked who was driving Dr. Bob's car.

"Can I make you a drink? Your coffee is cold." Ella had to be doing something. "I think I need one," she added.

"No thanks Honey. I had dinner with Ann. Just wanted to see how the two of you were doing." Heinze was doing better than Ella to be sure, but Ralph left anyway.

The drink wasn't enough. Ella had a feeling of fear to the point of choking on her own breath. Her heart wouldn't stop pounding. The palms of her hands were wet and a chill swept across her shoulders. "That's it, that's it!"

Ella flew up the stairs turning off lights behind her for fear she was being watched. She stopped at the top of the stairs. It felt good to stand in darkness. Heinze followed and stood close to her, "like I'm here."

Ella turned the light on in the closet with the door closed behind her so she couldn't be seen. "It's the money. It's the damn money," she thought as she pulled down a suitcase from the shelf and began to pack. She opened the closet door just wide enough to let Heinze enter. The dog was frantically scratching on the door. It was his duty to be with her. Both sat on the floor amidst shoes, pocket books and a hanger. Ella wished she had her cell phone. She should call her husband. No, he would just laugh at her. "I don't really trust anyone but you, old dog." Ella wiped her tears. Heinze gave a little "woof" and tried to wipe her tears with his big rough tongue. He woofed again to say, "Don't be alarmed. I'm here."

Packed and ready, Ella carried her suitcase downstairs and entered the garage through the kitchen door. She realized the garage door was still open. It was the last thing she ever saw. A masked figure lunged for Heinze who was trying to attack, wielding a huge knife into his thick hairy shoulders. Ella had not been the challenge this beast was, but the job was finished. Both lay on the garage floor. The villain, dressed and masked in black, plunged the knife once more into the large dog's throat, just to get even for the fight the dog had put up.

Ella lay dead. The dog was bleeding profusely from the slash in his throat. The assassin removed the thick, heavy collar from the dog's neck. It was calmly placed around the dead woman's ankles. Then her body was dragged to the close by Cantgoinit Creek. That accomplished, the murderer returned for the travel bag and picked it up. Heinze wasn't dead. He waited and wanted the killer to bend over. It didn't happen. Instead, the assailant took off on foot, leaving Dr. Bob's car behind.

Heinze tried to lift his head to see where the killer had gone. It was too painful. It had started to rain. Heinze tried to stand, but couldn't. His front leg was broken. He crawled from the garage out to the driveway. He tried to bark but his throat wound prevented that. He passed out lying in the soaking rain.

It rained and flashed lightning all night long. Storm after storm raged. The roads were flooded and the creek was overflowing. Over two inches of rain had fallen in just a few hours.

Dr. Bob had not returned home. He had spent the night in the bedroom over the office. And, he had spent the night alone.

Dr. Ralph awakened to the thunder and flashing lightening. His first thoughts were of Ella. "She must be disturbed. Poor Heinze will be under the bed." The storm raised such a clatter of thunder. Ralph started to count the seconds between thunder and flashes of light across the midnight sky to estimate how far away the lightning was. Bang, crash, flash. "Boy, that one was close." After more time passed, Ralph disturbed Ann to make sure she was all right.

"Why in the hell did you have to call? This is one morning I could have slept. Can't work in this weather."

"Just worried," Ralph said. "Couldn't sleep."

"I'll bet!" she mumbled, as she turned over. The storm didn't bother her.

Under the circumstances, he thought, "Better wait till 7:00 a.m. before I call Ella. She should be okay with Bob there." He didn't know that Bob had spent the night in Roseville.

"Boy, I'm glad I bought that car." Ralph was looking at the Caddie from the safety and dryness of the motor home. "I'd have a time trying to get out of the mud in this thing."

At 6:30 a.m., Ralph called his brother's house. There was no answer. "They must have spent the night in Roseville." Dr. Ralph called the office. "I called to see how Ella was doing, but there was no answer at the house. She was alone when I saw her last."

"She's probably in the shower. Go back to bed," Bob ordered.

Ralph tried Ella's phone once more. When there was no answer, he took off into the storm. Summer storms tend to level off in the early morning, but not this one. The rain hit the car windows with such force it sounded as if the car was being bombarded with nails. Next, it was hail, like mothballs. The windshield wipers gave up. They were caught in rain and ice. "I can't believe this and in the middle of summer." The windows were clouding up and he could not see. He was forced to open his window in order to see ahead. "Thank God, this is a country road with only creeping traffic," he thought. He opened the window further because he was contending with fog. Now, with the window opened wide, he was getting soaked. "Whoever said it didn't rain in fog? He was an ass, whoever he was!"

There were no lights on at Ella's house and the garage doors were still open when Dr. Ralph arrived. Getting out of the car, he almost fell over what looked like a large stone in the driveway. It was hard to see in the heavy fog. The stone moved only slightly and Heinze uttered a weak cry. The dog knew who it was.

CHAPTER 19

▼

"My God, oh my God. Heinze, is that you?" The lump tried to move in silence. Dr. Ralph was on his knees with the rain battering his head and stinging his eyes with rain and tears. "What happened to your collar?" His hand was covered with Heinze's blood. "Stay here, I'll get help. I have to see Ella." Thinking the door from the garage was locked, Dr. Ralph headed for the front of the house, missing Ella's suitcase lying on the floor of the garage.

The good man ran from room to room calling her name. "Ella, Ella." Not finding her, he tried to calm down, but his heart was racing and he couldn't get his breath. Not finding her in the house, he ran into the garage and out the door to his beloved dog.

"What happened? My God, what happened to you?" He cried into the blood soaked coat of Heinze. "Where is your collar?" Dr. Ralph felt around in the rain-soaked fog. He tried to pick up his dog. Heinze had been stabbed twice, but what hurt the most was his left front leg which had been broken in the fight. Heinze's cuts and bruises had been well cleaned by the torrent of rain that had fallen upon the dog all night long. He was very cold; the rain was cold even if it was July.

Dr. Bob arrived home expecting breakfast. He found instead, his brother, Ralph, the dog, and a missing wife. Neither man had noticed the luggage, still closed, over to one side of the garage. "We had better call the police." Bob entered the house. He seemed too nonchalant to suit Ralph.

"Call a vet, too." If he had noticed Heinze, Bob didn't mention it. "Come on, man, she could be out there hurt like Heinze. If you don't want to look for your wife, I will." Ralph said in disgust.

"You always had a crush on Ella. I've even wondered if you aren't the father of the brat." With that remark, Ralph hit Bob whose front teeth flew out and lay beside him as he hit the floor.

"My God, look what you have done," groaned Bob, laying on one elbow and staring at two front teeth he had in his hand.

"You are a disgusting man. Someone should have knocked your block off long ago." Ralph left the house to look for the woman he once loved. He buttoned his raincoat to try to stay dry and the rain made a little waterfall at the tip of his hat. "My God." He said again, "It's Cain and Abel all over again. What a truly rotten man that brother of mine has become. Of course, it's the money. Mother set us against each other," Ralph thought as he still tried to make an excuse for his brother.

"Heinze, my buddy, how could I forget you?" The rain had subsided; the fog was lifting and a bit of blue was appearing in the sky. "Let's see what we can do about you." The doctor examined his dog. He found cuts and stab wounds, but nothing too deep. There was a bad slash across the dog's throat. It looked like it would mend. Things would have been worse for Heinze, except for the dog's lion cut. The massive hair at his head and chest was a saver. Heinze held his broken leg in the air as his master got him into the garage. He made Heinze comfortable, even found something in the garage to rest the dog's head upon while he assembled items to set his broken leg.

Mud and runoff rain were everywhere. The sun was peeking through the morning clouds. With a heavy sigh, Dr. Ralph took off knee deep in slush, after making his dog comfortable. He lost his shoes in the first heavy steps. As he went looking for them, he found drag marks in the weeds and mud. He said a silent prayer and followed the path to the creek. He forgot he was leaving a deeper trail of his own. In 75 years, the small creek had never flooded its banks. This time, it changed local history. The creek waters were rushing toward a 12-foot dam. Ralph watched young tree parts, jugs, cans and all sorts of debris rush by. He saw something pink caught on a branch. He stood frozen in his tracks. Could it be Ella's clothing?

"Mother of God," part prayer and part disbelief. "How could this happen?" The kind man had tears flooding down his cheeks.

After searching in vain, he backtracked thinking, "I must call the vet for poor Heinze." The doctor wiped his eyes and face with both hands. He returned to the House of Horrors. The distance from creek to house was only 500 feet or less. Dr. Ralph felt like a beaten man. "What could I have done to prevent this? Look what money can do? No, I can't think that, not even him. I won't believe that." He still wanted to think the best of his brother.

When Ralph approached his brother's house, he found it circled with people. Someone had thought they had seen a body in a pink dress going down creek. People watched Ralph as he entered the house, shoeless and covered with mud. Even his face was bleeding from the thorn-covered brush.

"He did it," someone in the crowd hollered as they pushed forward.

"This is like in the papers," someone else offered. "She was pregnant, too."

Dr. Ralph ignored them for the moment and went over to his dog that someone had just tripped over, because he was too weak to move.

Another voice entered the crowd. "What the hell did you do to the dog? He's all bloody."

Ralph slid to sitting position, lifted his dog's head, and placed it on his lap. In a broken voice, he said, "Someone call the police."

"I did," a rough-looking man announced proudly to the enlarging crowd. "He ain't gonna get away with this!"

To the doctor's relief, he heard police approaching. The crowd was getting nasty.

Bob pushed through the crowd. Pulling out a piece of torn pink clothing sticking out of Ralph's coat pocket, he yelled, "Why did you do it? Why? Answer me. I thought you loved her."

The dye had been cast. It was Cain and Abel. This time, it was a large amount of money. The crowd was getting larger and larger. A state trooper approached. He went over to the exhausted man.

"Doctor, come with me. I've called a vet to pick up the dog." The two men walked into the garage to talk and Heinze gave out a cry, a sound like a wolf. The officer saw the group all set to follow and told them, "You people go home and mind your own problems."

One voice was heard. "You can't do that. This is my home." It was Bob's voice.

"Who was that?" The officer asked.

"My brother." Dr. Ralph cried for the second time that day. "This must be the worst day of my life."

"We found a lady's body with knife wounds. It's on its way to the morgue." The trooper was kind, not rough. The trooper knew that you could get more out of a suspect at a time like this if you didn't push.

Someone pounded on the garage door. "Open up!" The patrolman unsnapped his weapon and opened the door with his hand on his revolver.

It was Ann and a lawyer. "I could hear the damn fools clear over to my house. Heinze is going to be okay," she assured Ralph. "I talked to the vet." She was trying to console the doctor, the man she had fallen in love with. "Don't talk, don't say a word," Ann warned. "You haven't said anything, have you," she questioned and then turned to the lawyer. "Take over." She stepped aside adding, "Do your job!"

Ann was perfect. With her, the old saying "What you see is what you get" was true. The blonde Swede, about 5'9" or 5'10" was tanned by the sun and her outside work. She was as honest as the day was long and expected the respect and honesty of others. People either liked her very much or couldn't stand her. The men who worked for Ann admired her and respected her knowledge. She had her enemies; some thought she was too direct, taking a man's job. However, if the word went out that Ann Minton was looking for workers, they were on their way to find her. She paid a good wage. One other thing, Ann had never been in love before.

"I'm going to have to take you in," the doctor heard the trooper say, while also addressing the lawyer. "For two reasons. One is investigate a murder but also that crowd outside is getting nasty. I heard one woman call you an Outlander?" The state police had been called and they were there to make sure the crowd disbursed.

"Hang the bastard!" someone shouted as the officer escorted Ralph to a waiting vehicle. "Leave him here. We'll take care of him."

"You sons of bitches," Ann yelled back. "Go home, the party is over." Then she turned to another policeman. "Keep these locals out of the house before they steal it blind."

The doctor was handcuffed and placed into a patrol car. Ann tried to enter, but she was stopped. "He can call you later," she was informed. "He has one phone call you know."

Ann looked at the silent lawyer, who was wondering, "How the hell did I get into this?"

She told him, "Stay with the doctor and make sure he gets justice." She learned that as just his girlfriend, she had no rights as far as the police were concerned. A wife would have been treated with respect.

Dr. Ralph posted bond in his own name and though it would be $5000.00.

"No, in your case, they decided to set it at a million," said the presiding bail officer.

"You got that much?" the hay shaker lawyer wanted to know. "Might as well spend it," the lawyer whispered with a laugh.

An unexpected enemy was entering. Bob arrived and said, "I'll call Bill Williams, mother's lawyer in D.C."

"Had Bob changed his mind about things? Was he going to help? I hope so," Dr. Ralph wished. But, no, his brother was planning to tie the noose even tighter.

Bob was dreaming away, "Think of all that money and it will all be mine." He knew he was a rat, but he had to get that New York crowd off his back. "It should be easy; Ralph is in very deep do do."

Dr. Ralph spent the night in jail. He was going over events in his mind. "Bob thinks the baby is mine. I was the last person to see Ella alive. Ella was running away from someone because they found her suitcase in the garage. Someone set this up. Who?"

"I just called Bill Williams. He won't take the case. He claimed, can't win that one." Dr. Bob tried to look sad. The liar never even tried to call D.C.

The case had reached unexpected proportions by coverage on T.V., radio and most of the newspapers. They were all ready to hang the doctor. Things were looking very bad for Ralph. People across the country had made up their minds. The locals were furious to think a stink like this could come to their town. A jury could not be picked there, not now. The brutal act reminded people of another heinous crime, where a young wife and child had been killed.

A handsome man was reading a paper. He was spending his retirement in Scottsdale, Arizona. This famous lawyer, who had never lost a case, took the phone his wife handed him. "It's Jim," she said, "our son."

"Hi Jim, what's up? Need money?"

"Listen Dad, this is very important."

"Okay, shoot," the father said.

"This Dr. Benson that the papers are full of, he is the one whose house I bought and he bought my Winnebago. Remember, I told you what a great guy he is?"

"Yes!"

"He needs help, Dad. Please call his lawyer and see what you can do. Do it for Mary Pat and me. We are sure he is being framed."

"Okay," the father murmured. "Let me think. Hey, honey, want to go to a small town in Pennsylvania?"

"I was listening," she confessed. "I'll pack our suitcases."

"Oh, Dad, Mary Pat and I can't thank you enough."

It was decided. The lawyer and his wife were packed and ready to travel. Jim's father explained his trip to his law firm partner saying, "My kid says this guy is okay and I can see he is being ram-rodded. Shows what too much money can do. There is a rat in the nest somewhere."

Jim's father, Zack Willis, was as well-known as F. Lee Bailey or Melvin Belli and his fame was spread far and wide.

CHAPTER 20

▼

Dressed in a cowboy jacket, hat, silver buckle, not to mention the rattlesnake leather boots, Zack Willis was a handsome sight. Many people in the airport recognized him. He could hear their speculations.

"He's off to a big case." A man whispered to his wife, "I'll bet he is off to Pennsylvania."

Zack Willis contacted the original attorney, who was more than glad to assist the great Zack Willis. When Ralph was told of the changes, he fell to his knees and thanked God. It was agreed, the trial would have a change of venue to be held in Harrisburg, Pennsylvania. Zack Willis' influence was at work.

Dr. Ralph was released in the company of his two lawyers. The three men drove back to the doctor's motor home, where Heinze and Ann were waiting. She had drinks ready for them. The sight of Ann and his dog made the doctor smile for the first time in three days.

"What a dog!" Zack Willis exclaimed. "Where did you ever find a dog like that? I swear, he's the size of a lion." Heinze had a new friend.

Ann extended her hand and introduced herself. "I'm Ann."

The doctor spoke, "I want Ann to stay. At this moment, I think she and the dog are my only friends."

"That is where you are wrong," Zack Willis reminded him. "My son and I are your friends. We not only like you, but best of all, we believe in you."

Ann crossed the room and planted a kiss on the doctor's cheek. "The phone has been ringing constantly."

"Time is wasting," Willis stated, as he finished his drink. "Start from the beginning." Now he sounded like a lawyer as got out his pen and paper.

Dr. Ralph related his past history from the time of his arrival in Roseville while both lawyers made notes.

"Just as I thought," the famous man expressed his feelings. "Where do I find that brother of yours?"

"He has nothing to do with this! We saw someone spooking around for a couple of weeks. Each time we knew where Bob was. That creep all dressed in black was a lot shorter than Bob. My brother is tall," Ralph explained.

"I left my lady antiquing," said Zack. "She is probably back at the hotel. I've got enough information for a start. I'll see you tomorrow." As he stood up to leave, Zack extended his huge hand. The other lawyer waited a bit.

Ann was impressed. She turned to Ralph, "Boy, are we lucky. That man is famous and what a handsome man—whew! They say he has never lost a case."

"Maybe this will be his first." The doctor felt his goose was cooked.

"I wonder what his wife looks like." Ann added.

"Watch it," the doctor teased.

The small town lawyer finished his drink. He announced to his Ralph and Ann, "The great man has asked me to be his assistant. He must have asked around about me."

He was so proud. I told them, "My name is Bert Miller and that name will be known coast to coast." With that, he left Dr. Ralph, Ann, and Heinze alone or so they thought.

The great man had purposely stayed behind the R.V. and now was knocking at the door. "I don't have the car and I can't reach my wife on the cell phone. Who can take me back to my hotel?"

"I will, I will." Ann offered. "My car is right here." Off they went as Ann seemed excited to carry off the handsome hunk.

"Women!" Dr. Ralph felt ditched.

"Fill me in, Ann. I need to talk to you. Tell me about his brother. Money can do funny things to people."

"I know," Ann advised. "The brother is a spoiled louse. He is a womanizer."

"Right there, tell me about his women." Zack Willis interrupted.

"There is one in particular. She has been in his life since high school when the family used to live here before."

"And who is that?" he asked.

"Her name is Lu Arthur. She lives in town," Ann offered.

"Anyone else?"

"Oh, there are others but I don't know them."

"Your friend gave me something to think about."

"What was that?" Ann asked.

"Later," the lawyer responded secretively.

When Ann returned, she found her lover on his knees. "Don't be embarrassed." Ann saw Ralph rise quickly. "I believe in prayer," he said rather sheepishly.

"What did you talk about in the car?" he wanted to know.

"Not much," Ann related. "We talked mostly about you and your dog." She moved closer to his chair. "I thank God, too, that Zack Willis took our case." The man next to her was falling asleep.

Good to his word, Zack Willis located Dr. Bob Benson, who had decided to live above his office. He had dropped all thoughts of opening a practice in Roseville. In fact, maybe Las Vegas would be worthy of his craft, cosmetic surgery.

It was the next day before Ralph remembered his calls stacked up on his answering phone.

First to call was the Indiana farmer. "You can count on us. We would still like to buy your trailer and would give you a good price."

The second call was the pair he rescued in the rain. "We'll be there at once if you think we can help. Say hello to that dog."

Third to call was the motor court prostitute. "Count on me, Doc. A man that loves his dog is my kind of guy."

Fourth was Jim Willis. "You and my dad are two of the most decent men I've even known. Call and I'll be there overnight."

When the voices were played back to Zack Willis, the lawyer was impressed. The media was trying to profile him as a monster. The locals would like to run him out of town, including his own brother and their girlfriends.

Zack asked Ralph to allow him to see his mother's will. After reading it, the lawyer said, "Ralph and Ann, you have given me what I needed." When asked what he meant, the handsome lawyer shook his head in silence.

"By the way, Ella Benson was not pregnant. Her mother called me and said she spoke to Ella when she went to New York for artificial insemination treatment. Incidentally, it didn't work. And Bob ordered cremation at once and no funeral." The lawyer informed, "This is the second time I've handled a bout with brothers, women, and money."

"No, I no longer lust for Ella, no matter what my brother has to say. I cared for her like a big brother. I thought I loved her and carried that in my heart for two years. But when I saw her again after that time, I saw her in a different light altogether." Dr. Ralph continued, "I'm glad she wasn't pregnant. I had concern for her. I knew how frightened she was. I went out in the storm to calm her fears and my poor dog. When did you talk to her mother? Ella never told me about her other than to say her mother lived in Arizona," Ralph questioned. "Is this woman on the up and up or is it someone after Ella's estate?"

"She called me for several reasons. First, her second husband was a friend, an attorney with my firm. She knew about their troubled marriage. Also, she has all the money she can spend."

"I never met her. Sounds nice," commented Ralph.

"She is and charming, too," Zack stated.

"Did my brother know?"

"No, he didn't. I asked," was Zack Willis' reply. "By the way, this could take a long time to go to court. Would you mind if I looked around on your behalf?" the lawyer asked Dr. Ralph. "Because, I smell a rat and it is getting fatter every-day."

No one had wondered why Dr. Bob's car had been parked behind the garage where Ella was killed that night. "How did your brother get home the next morning?" Zack Willis asked. "He had one car, right? I'm sure he didn't walk from Roseville to Four Corners."

"I never thought of it. He has friends, probably bummed a ride. I know country people are like that," Dr. Ralph thought. Zack passed it off but not Ann. Oh no, not Ann.

"Okay, let's sit at the table and make plans." The handsome 60-year-old lawyer started. "First doctor, you stay in the R.V. I'll take your car. I need a car. Ann, can you be at my beck and call? I'll send my wife home because I'm going to be too busy. She will understand."

Ann nodded and Ralph asked, "What about me?"

"You will be fine with books, TV, and that dog. No one will bother you."

"What if crowds gather?" Ann was worried. "They won't. I'll have deputies here twenty-four hours."

"What about me?" Ann asked.

"You can visit him as much as you want but not overnight. We can't add problems." They all agreed and Zack, the famous, left for the Pennsylvania Hotel in Harrisburg in the doctor's new Caddie.

Ann, being Ann, had ideas of her own. She, too, wearing high boots, decided to take Heinze over the same tracks the doctor had taken. Her hope was to rein-force the scent of the murder. By this time, the creek had returned to its banks but the mud was deep and slippery. Heinze, limping along with the cast on his broken leg, and still recovering from his severe wounds, refused to follow her. He took another route because he had picked up a scent he was never to forget.

"Heinze," Ann called. "Did you find something?" The dog returned her call with three loud barks and his tail was whacking at the tall weeds of thistle, causing one wound to bleed. The lion trim, which possibly saved his life, had him tangled in bush and brier at the moment.

Meanwhile, Zack Willis drove over to where Lu was staying.

Lu claimed she had left Dr. Bob's car because when she arrived to pick up the records Bob wanted, she heard a loud argument between Ralph and Ella. She said she knew it was Dr. Ralph's car because she had seen it before. Besides, she heard loud barking and he was the only one that had a dog. "I didn't want any part of a family fight," she told the papers. "She didn't want the two of them to know she had overheard them." So, instead of starting the car or turning the car lights on, she ran home in a raging storm.

Now Zack Willis asked, "Did you call Dr. Bob Benson?"

"I used my cell phone," Lu answered.

"What happened to the records you were sent to get?" the attorney wanted to know.

"Never got to them," was her reply.

"Why didn't you park the car in front of the house or on the driveway in the storm, instead of at the back of the house?"

Lu was obviously nervous. "Because, he told me to park in the back. I had a key to the garage door. But, I never got near the garage, damn it."

"So you had a key, ummm." Zack Willis had her scared.

"You can't talk to me like that. This is not a courtroom."

"Did you get all of that?" he called down a darkened hallway, as if he had others recording or taking notes.

"Get out, get out, damn you! This is my house. You are here under false pretenses and I'm going to have you arrested. I thought you were here from T.V."

He laughed a hearty laugh when he related his story to Dr. Ralph.

"You mean you didn't have anyone down the hall and she thinks everything is on tape? Zack, that's bad."

"I don't like that girl. My gut feeling is in her direction." The lawyer started to say more then changed his mind.

"She's okay, just a little hard. Bob and Lu have been friends for years." Dr. Ralph was still sticking up for brother Bob.

"Are you for real?" the lawyer asked. "He is about to stick a knife in you."

"Not really," was Ralph's reply.

Ann and Heinze returned to the R.V. with news. "Darling," she related her story, "Heinze and I found the real trail the killer had left behind, not where the whole town had tramped." And to prove it, she produced Heinze's collar, tags and all. The dog was trying to pull the collar out of her hands. Both woman and dog were a sight, covered with mud and scratches. But, they looked beautiful to Dr. Ralph, as he praised his dog and kissed his girl.

"Don't handle it, Ralph, whatever you do," said Ann. "We don't want your prints on the collar."

CHAPTER 21

▼

"I'll call Zack right away." The doctor reached for the phone. "Please drop whatever you are doing Zack. This is Ralph. We have something hot!"

The lawyer returned driving Ralph's new Cadillac. He didn't have to knock on the trailer screen door. They ran to meet him. "I knew things were ready to break. What happened?" the handsome attorney asked. "Quick, what's up?"

Ann showed Zack the dog's collar on the end of the stick. "Should we handle this?" She told Zack Willis where and how they found it, where only one other person had been that night.

"Tell me," Zack picked a comfortable chair in the van, "Why wouldn't the collar be at the creek bank and the injured dog lying on the murder scene driveway?"

"Don't you see, it was used to drag the body around her neck or both feet?" Ann was disappointed that Zack didn't share their enthusiasm.

"I wish that dog could talk," the lawyer was thinking.

Ann added, "The path was upstream, just before the creek gets fast. That's why the body was caught on a tree limb when first seen."

Meanwhile, at this exact same time Bob and Lu were talking over the situation. They thought no one could see them in Lu's darkened car, but you can't hide under these circumstances. Someone is bound to be watching. "Why in the hell did you leave my car at the crime scene?"

"Because, if you don't marry me as promised, I can tell a different story," Lu threatened.

The night was warm and their car windows were down. Someone was setting rabbit traps and they were heard. It was a young boy about 13 years old, who knew who they were and realized they were talking about a murder. He sat still afraid to move, hoping they would leave first.

"Oh, take me home. You are drunk again or is it your cocaine? Why don't you lay off that stuff?" Lu said with disgust. The kid outside sitting against a tree was getting an earful. Dr. Bob had become addicted to drugs for the past three or four years. That and gambling were the reasons he had connections with the underworld.

Zack Willis was pleased about the dog collar and really pleased that Ann had not fingered it. He knew, of course, that Dr. Bob's prints should be on the collar since it was his dog, but the murderer's prints should be on top of those. He dropped the collar into a plastic bag.

"I'll take this along and see who had it last. If it was used as we think, prints of both hands could be on the collar." Zack had to hold the sack above his head because Heinze wanted his collar. He tried to block the door.

"Sure you don't want to part with this dog? Smartest dog I've ever been around. If we would listen, I think he could solve the case. Hot damn! I've got an idea," said Zack.

Zack Willis was known for being adventurous; even so, he had never lost a case. He could be very expensive to call upon one time. But sometimes he could go pro-bono and refuse a fee. He knew well enough that there was a lot of money waiting for two brothers, especially since the death of Ella. It was not the money that drew him to this case; it was a strong feeling that the doctor couldn't get a fair chance.

Zack asked himself, as he looked out the large hotel window, "What can I do to make sure this case doesn't get to court? He could get the hot seat. I'm not going to let that happen. I know what I'm going to do." Zack said aloud. He walked to the phone and phoned his client and then he phoned his assistant.

All slept well that night. The next day, Dr. Ralph decided it was time to return the phone calls made by real friends. "God knows I don't have many around here except Ann, the lawyer, and Heinze. I think of Ann as more than a friend."

His first call was to Jim Willis and Mary Pat, his best friends in the world. "Jim," he said, trying to hold back the croak in his voice, "Jim, I think you are saving my life. I'm sure you know your dad is here. I'm in a terrible mess and I am not to blame. But, if this works, I'll be on the next plane to Alaska. I love you both."

Jim had let him talk. "We will be at the airport waiting for you. How is Heinze?"

"He is a hero here. He found evidence that could save me."

"We know the man from Roseville will be coming out of this smelling like a rose. By the way, ole buddy, I have a good offer on your former house. Should I sell it?"

The answer was, "No, I'll match that offer."

The reply, "Good!"

"How are you doing with the town you are building?' Ralph asked.

"Booming, our first stage is sold out. You wouldn't have to worry about Jacko if you came back. Someone slit his throat at the Wild and Wooly."

The doctor sat back in his chair. "Everything is coming up roses. God, I just hope Zack has a rabbit in his hat."

Next, he called the farmer and his wife. Amy answered. "God bless you, Dr. Ralph. We pray for you everyday. Do you still have the Winnebago? You're famous. You are in the papers out here," she laughed.

The farmer took the phone from his wife. "Amy would talk to you all day and this is prime time. Give the guy a break."

"That's what I need is a break. How are you both?"

"Okay, but you? Did Amy tell you we pray for you? We know in our hearts you did not do this terrible crime. My God, you would never hurt your dog."

"Well," the doctor started, "I wanted to thank you for your call and prayers. Things are bad but not entirely shot. By the way, I'll sell you the R.V."

"We will be there in 24 hours," was the farmer's reply. "Amy has never gotten over how wonderful it would be to have."

His next call was to Ann. "If all goes well, Ann darling, will you marry me?" Dr. Ralph proposed and quickly added, "I love you."

"I've got the gown already. You know I will. I love you, Ralph, and I know something good is going to happen." Ann was almost in tears and she didn't cry easily.

"I might as well tell you everything," Ralph hesitated.

"What?"

"I sold the R.V. and bought back my Georgian-type home in Alaska."

"You did what? Tell me again."

And the good doctor man told her once more.

"This has always been my home here in Roseville."

But she, too, had to plan. "I've never gotten back what I put into the town. So, I'm like Ruth in the Bible. I love you and where you go, I go!"

His next call was to the prostitute, who had given him back his manhood. She was easily traced through the motor court receipt he had kept.

"Hi there, this is Ralph, the man with the lion-trimmed dog."

"How are you, sweetheart? How's the mutt and what are you doing out of jail?" she laughed.

"No laughing matter, kid. I just wanted to thank you for the encouraging call you made. Sorry I wasn't here to get the call, but I've been busy."

"I'll bet you have been busy." The call girl spoke seriously. "How could I forget you, Doc? You have the biggest equipment I've ever seen. I could hardly walk right for a week."

"Funny," the doctor laughed. "Ann has never complained. Who is kidding who?" The doctor started to laugh and was still laughing, as he hung up the phone.

The phone rang. It was Ann. "Been trying to reach you but your phone was busy. Why don't you use your cell phone?" Her tone was bossy and the doctor caught her attitude. He said nothing and just listened.

"When is the sale of the R.V. going to take place?" Ann inquired.

"In a day or two. They are on their way," Ralph told Ann.

"Are they taking over at the sale time?"

"Yes!"

"And where are you going to live? Not with me." Ann tried to sound firm. "No way, unless we are married."

"What's wrong with that?" he asked.

"Okay," Ann announced. "I'll call the preacher. You call Zack. We can be married immediately."

"But, I need a haircut." he teased, and then wondered why he said that right after having his hair cut not too long ago. "The mind does funny things," he told himself.

He called Ann back. "You know, you are a very determined woman. Just who is going to be the boss?" he wanted to know.

The answer came easily, "Heinze, of course."

And as fate and Ann would have it, they were married at 4:00 p.m. in Ann's living room. The two lawyers, two deputies, and Heinze were witnesses. The groom needing a haircut and wearing an unpressed shirt held the handsome Ann in a well-pressed suit in his arms. The dog barked and barked. The doctor had given the florist the wrong idea. The flowers arrived in a funeral basket. It made the doctor a little nervous to look at the flowers. "Could that be a bad sign?" he asked.

"Forget it," Zack kidded. "You are not Irish." The champagne flowed and the wedding cake was homemade and delicious.

"A toast to the bride and groom and a toast to Heinze. I think he brought them together in the first place," said the assistant lawyer. And they all had another glass.

"I'll add my toast to the bride," the doctor beamed. "I love you with all my heart." Glasses clinked and they all had another round. Each tried to forget the black cloud that hung over them.

"We are going to honeymoon in Alaska." Dr. Ralph said as he wrapped his arm around the back of Ann. He then added, "We just might stay there if my bride likes the place." Everyone had to drink another round of champagne to this idea.

The preacher decided he had better go home. A deputy helped him to his car. Heinze was the only entirely sober wedding guest.

"Call you in the morning," Zack was leaving. He could carry a lot of champagne but his aid needed some air.

"Don't call too early," Ann called after the lawyer. Then she turned to her bridegroom. "We better eat something. What about hot dogs and beans? Will you look at the time?" Ann exclaimed. "Where did the time go?" She was still a little tight. "I'll race you to bed. Remember, I told you I like skin to skin."

Ralph was right behind her and Heinze was right behind him. Not tonight!" And he closed the door in the dog's face.

While the bride and groom slept late, Heinze had his need to go outside. The dog tried to awaken the pair by scratching on their door, gently at first, but now harder along with a bark. It took the ringing of the phone to make them stir.

"Zack here," the voice informed. "I'm here at the R.V. and there is a couple here waiting to see you."

"He must have taken the first plane out of Indianapolis," Ralph mumbled while stuffing his shirt into his pants.

"I want to meet those people, too." Ann wrapped her braided hair in a twist because it had become undone. "I'm a mess. You go ahead, but don't forget to introduce me as Mrs. Benson."

Zack took the doctor aside. "I'm going to need Heinze tomorrow. I've arranged for a line-up. Just an idea."

"Sure," his interest was elsewhere. A child of 10 or 12, fishing pole in hand, was trying to get their attention.

"Go ahead with your people," Zack Willis said. "I'll see what the kid wants."
"Okay, young fellow."

"I know something about that man here. I mean, I know something."

The attorney shook the kid's hand. "I am the man's lawyer. You can talk to me."

"No, my dad said only to talk to the man, sir."

"We are wasting time. He is a busy man. I am a busy man and you look like you have something to do with that fishing pole." The boy turned to leave. Zack was getting annoyed. "Who told you something?"

"I saw something."

"Where can I find your father?" Zack had other fish to fry beside what the kid was hoping to catch.

"That's him." The boy pointed to a figure coming from Ann's construction site.

"That's my boy," the man stated, as offered his hand to the lawyer.

Now the young man was free to re-tell his story and he did, emphasizing the last part, where Lu had said, "If you don't marry me I can always change my story."

"Good boy. Nice kid." Zack told the father. "Can't beat a country kid. He knew who she was. Her name and face had been in the papers."

Zack opened the door for Ann to enter the R.V., as he was leaving. "Got to go. See you later." He was gone in a hurry.

"You sound anxious to sell, Doc. That makes an easy deal," the farmer laughed at his own humor. The sale completed, the newlyweds asked for a couple of hours to clean up the place. "Bachelor pad, you know."

CHAPTER 22

▼

"I have a much better idea" Amy, the farmer's wife suggested. "Ann and I, with some buckets and rags, could start right now. That way, Cosmo and I can sleep here tonight and get started on our trip. We want to do the entire East coast. We plan to take a month to do it."

"How can you take a month off at this time of the year?" Dr. Ralph questioned.

"Remember those kids you saved in the storm?"

"Yes!"

"Well," the farmer added, "he is taking care of the place right now. We will be home for harvest. By the way," the farmer said, "Those kids never forgot you. They named the baby for you."

"I thought it was a girl," the doctor persisted.

"It is Amy for my wife, Benson for you, and Walker for her father."

"That sounds nice, Amy Benson Walker. Maybe she will become a writer," the doctor laughed.

"Out, both of you," Amy ordered.

"Where is the dog?" the farmer asked.

"What happened to Ann?" The doctor looked around. "She must have taken Heinze for a walk."

"No, she went for buckets, soap, and rags. I'm serious. You guys go for a beer or something—out!"

"We can go outside and sit under a tree or walk down and see the wonders Ann has done to the old house. But, I can't leave here. I'm under a sort of house arrest, I'm sorry to say."

"You will be okay," the farmer assured him, as they settled under a tree. "You are in good hands."

"You mean my attorney? He's one of the best in the country." Dr. Ralph tried to feel assured.

"No, you are a fine man and I'm sure the God above is watching."

"I hope so," was the doctor's reply.

Ann, the dog and Zack were at Ann's house, where she had gone to get cleaning supplies. The attorney saw her car and decided it was time to talk. As they talked, Heinze was listening. On certain words, the dog would lift his head, sometimes to the left and other times to the right. If Heinze wasn't happy, he had that funny deep noise in his throat that he would air if he were really upset. When someone was spooking around, Heinze would draw his lips back over his huge teeth and release a growl that would turn into a series of loud, meaningful barks.

Heinze knew words like Ann, Ella, walk, leash, collar and the word he hated most, gun. He also hated anything that shone brightly such as scissors or knives that he associated with the fights and violence he'd seen.

The men under the tree were startled by the young fisherman yelling, "Where is my Dad? The guys are finished working at Ann's house. Look, what I found?" the kid yelled as he approached the seated men.

"My God, he has a knife." Ralph yelled.

"It was under a rock, really stuck under there. I had to move the rock to free my line."

Ann and Heinze were coming up the hill, when Heinze saw the large knife flashing in the sun. In a leap, he was on the boy and the sharp, large weapon got stuck in the tree.

"That just went over my head," the farmer said, while Ann and the doctor were trying to pull Heinze off the boy.

"I'm not getting much done in here," the farmer's wife complained.

"But we are out here." Ann decided it was time to buy Heinze a new collar, something to grab other than his heavy thick coat.

The dog released the boy. The child wasn't hurt, just scared. He recovered enough to say, "I've got first dibs on that knife. It's mine."

"That kid is going to college. Honored if he studies," the doctor remarked.

"And I've got to have that dog," the farmer remarked.

They called Zack to tell him about finding the knife. He wasn't as overjoyed as they were. "You say it isn't a regular butcher's knife? That might be easier to trace. Ann, honey, most of the fingerprints would have been washed off by now.

Now listen to me, both of you. Doctor, you hear me. You cannot live with Ann in her house. You must stay in the R.V. until this case gets settled. Ann can stay with you, but not the other way around," Zack paused, "unless you want to go to jail."

"Oh shit, now what?" It was Ann that protested. "What about the farmer and his wife?"

"Let them stay at your house, Ann. I expect a big change soon," the lawyer predicted.

When they repeated what the lawyer had told them to the farmer and his wife, the two new owners took it better than expected. "Well, Ann." the farmer said, "we will watch you finish that beautiful house."

"Don't worry about your house," Amy added. "I'm a good housekeeper. I'm just glad to get out of a motel."

Ann remembered what Zack had said before he hung up the phone. "Don't forget about tomorrow morning."

Ann replied, "Heinze and I will be there by 10:00 a.m. You have the collar and I'll bring the knife."

Dr. Bob had been ordered to appear for a line up at the police department. He arrived early because he was curious. "You have been asked to take place in a line-up." He was told politely.

"Why? What for?" Bob looked around the police department where there was a lot of action for early morning.

"It's just the usual thing to rule out possible suspects," he was told.

"Why me?"

"You were chosen to do your civic duty. We need six men, five of whom haven't done anything wrong."

Ann arrived with the dog and was quickly told she was too early. "We will call you when needed."

"Piss," said Ann. "I'll wait in the car."

Dr. Bob was lined up with five other men. Then Ann was called in to appear with the dog. Heinze looked the men over, not too closely, but he only recognized one, Bob.

"Okay men, you are dismissed."

The large doors opened and in walked Lu. "What in the hell are you doing here?" She almost spat at her lover.

Bob was just as surprised to see her. "Hey," he called out, "What in hell is going on here?" The dog growled but Bob had not been allowed to see the dog. Bob said angrily, "I'm going to hang around here. I don't like this."

Next, they added Lu to a second line up with women. She wasn't dumb. "I don't like this. I'm not going to stand up here. I know my rights." Heinze had never seen her before, but he remembered the voice, as she slashed his throat and smelled the scent as she sweated.

Ann could no longer hold Heinze back, but two large deputies tried to grab the dog to no avail. He was headed for Lu. She screamed, "I thought that damn dog was dead. Shoot that dog. He is a killer."

"Like you," Zack yelled at her.

"Who the hell are you?" Lu yelled.

"I'm the man that has the collar and the knife. And just for the hell of it, you confess or the dog can settle the case."

"He did it, too. The bastard." She was pointing in Dr. Bob's direction. Lu was trying to fight off the handcuffs, and a large matron had her in a strangle hold. Heinze didn't like the light shining on the handcuffs and sprang, throwing the two men, who were trying to hold him, aside like toothpicks. Someone threw a chair that hit the dog just right. When Heinze recovered, the blonde and the matron were out of the room. The last words out of her mouth were, "I thought that dog was dead."

Dr. Bob watched, as they took Lu off. "That's a break!"

Lu called over her shoulder to Bob, "It was your idea to kill her, you fucking bastard."

Zack went to call Dr. Ralph to give him the good news. "You are a free man," he told him.

Dr. Bob snuck out of the large front doors of the police department building. As he started down the stairs in the front of the building, he heard, "That you Dr. Benson?" A man dressed in black called, "That last time was a warning. This time it's for real."

Two shots rang out and people on the street ran for cover, as Bob's body rolled down the steps. Two men stepped back into a big, black limousine that sped off. Dr. Bob was dead.

THE END

MURDER IN THE GARDEN

By Edna Collins

CHAPTER 1

▼

She was molested at four by a good friend of her grandmother's. She was old enough to know she had been violated, but not old enough to know what to do.

Gramma, who Lisa dearly loved, would slap her over the face and accuse her of lying. She didn't tell her mother because her mother wasn't crazy about Mom Mom, as grandmother was called. Mother would just say, "You can't go over there anymore."

However, when she was ten and he crept up behind her, slapped tape over her mouth, took her to the floor, and raped her, Lisa swore, "One day I'll kill you."

Gramma had gone to the dentist. Jim Cory knew, because he had driven her there and knew it was time to go for her. Jim was an attractive youth of 19 or 20. He had been Mom Mom's kennel boy and she had more or less allowed him the run of the house and the kennel. He was Irish of course, with a name like that, and Mom Mom had made many trips to Ireland. It was the place of her roots and she knew the history of her "old sod." Jim would listen to her stories for hours. Ireland and dogs filled hours of conversation.

The rivalry and hatred started when Lisa was just 14. She had been winning at the 4-H shows with her beautiful English long-nosed black and white Sussex sheep for several years. Now she was aware of her age and wanted to show dogs as her grandmother was doing.

"Mom Mom, do you have time to talk to me?" Lisa asked one lazy summer day.

"Sure Honey, what's on your mind?"

"How do I go about finding a dog good enough to show?"

"Don't buy a bum unless you just want a pet. It takes too long to breed out what you started with. I know," the older woman advised her granddaughter. "Sweetheart, if you really want to get into the dog show game, you have to know what you are doing. It is rough. It can break your heart." She leaned over, took Lisa's chin, and looked into her eyes. "I've been in it for 40 years. I still like most of the people who show dogs, but not all."

"It takes money and it takes time. First, you buy the best bitch you can afford."

"No, Mom Mom, I don't want to take that long. I want something to show now."

"If you really want a winner, how much money do you have?" the grandmother asked with a smile.

Lisa said, "I have fifty dollars."

"I might have known," the older woman laughed. "What breed are you interested in?"

"Standard Poodles," Lisa replied, hoping Mom Mom would buy it for her. Mom Mom had a kennel on ten acres of beautiful land right in the heart of Pennsylvania. The view of the mountains and the Susquehanna River as seen from the upstairs windows of the old farmhouse could take one's breath away.

"Come on upstairs." Mom Mom called to Lisa.

Up the stairs Lisa came, as only a 14-year-old could fly. "Find something?" she asked.

"Yes." Mom Mom had a phone number in her hand. "Do you remember Jim Cory?" she asked Lisa.

"I sure do, Mom Mom. I don't like that man." Lisa was quick to change the subject. She had never told anyone that he had molested her because she was so ashamed. She remembered the bastard.

"I remember him. You and he used to have long talks about Ireland, as well as dogs. I remember the story you told about going to Ireland and the plane circled and circled."

"They couldn't get the wheels on the plane down and the pilot or co-pilot came right beside my seat," the grandmother took over. "He ripped up the carpet, then he got down on his belly and with the longest pliers I've ever seen, that hero of a man, physically pulled the wheel down." Mom Mom was short of breath, as she retold the tale.

Lisa finished the story she had heard so many times. "And the airport at Shannon had ambulances and fire trucks all over the place. Your luggage was still in New York."

"And I had to sit in the airport the rest of the day for the next flight to get my luggage." They both laughed. "It was some day," Mom Mom added, "and that wasn't all. It was a night flight and my seat was broken. I had to try to sleep like that because it was a full flight. The trip was worth it, though. I bought the most beautiful little Yorkie."

"How did you get it back in the states?" Lisa asked.

"Shush," her grandmother put her finger to her lips. "I also bought a very large purse," she laughed. "Now, back to what you are interested in. I'm going to call Jim." She dialed but there was no answer. "I'll call him later. Want to stay for supper?" Mom Mom asked.

"Sure, I love your cooking." Lisa hugged her Mom Mom and followed her out to the kennel. The high school boys, who acted as kennel help after school, were also on their way up to the kennel.

"Nothing's sweeter than a 17-year-old boy," she continued. "He has his dreams and ideals."

"And then what happens?" asked Lisa.

"Ask the girls," was Mom Mom's answer.

"Show me the Yorkie you smuggled out of Ireland," asked Lisa. "Point her out."

"She smothered in my large purse." Mom Mom was not that stupid. She had connections.

Boys were cleaning dog runs. Others were mixing the dog food and the dogs were jumping and yapping. Lisa was filling the water pans. Music was playing on the radio inside the kennel. Mom Mom said the dogs liked the music. It was a good thing that she did not have close neighbors. It was like feeding time at the zoo. You could hardly hear yourself talk.

The dogs came first, and once taken care of, then they returned to the lovely old house. Grandmother and child sat on the porch that went all the way around the house. Both were snapping green beans fresh from the garden when Lisa asked, "Why do you go to Ireland so much?"

"It's my roots sweetheart. I am Kitty McGovern from County Caven, the most beautiful place in the world."

Lisa's mother, Ruth, had a small kennel, but it was for boarding dogs. No dog shows for her. Ruth, Lisa, and Mom Mom would laugh and tease about her attitude. Ruth was sure all dog shows were crooked because as a child she had been dragged around to help Mom Mom at shows where, to her, only the handlers did all the winning. This love of dogs had been transferred to Lisa, who had to have a dog of her own. In addition, she could start her own strain of winning dogs.

Dinner and dishes over, Mom Mom reached for the phone. "Let's see if the son of a bitch is home now." She dialed Jim Cory's number.

Finding her mother not interested in what she wanted to do, Lisa had turned to Mom Mom. They became very close.

Lisa was not the average child. She was a winner. She wanted to be head cheerleader in middle school. She was head cheerleader. She was very smart, a straight A student. If she wanted to be the queen in the Veterans Day Parade, there she was on top of the float among all the flowers. Lisa had drive, even push. At her early age, some people despised her. Others wanted to stand in her shadow. On top of everything, Lisa was beautiful without trying. She could pull her long black hair into a ponytail, slap on a baseball cap, and show those gleaming white teeth. She was something and she knew it, too.

Her father, Mom Mom's only son, was a handsome black Irishman, who went to Ireland when he was 39 and never returned. Lisa had his black hair, his flashing teeth, but not his blue piercing eyes. Hers were dark brown.

Mom Mom was on the phone with all the polite chitchat. Lisa, who was listening in on the bedroom phone heard Mom Mom tell the reason for the call. "You're crazy Kitty! What makes you think I'd let a 14-year-old drag one of my dogs around the show ring?"

"I just don't believe it," the grandmother wiped a tear. "So that's how a hot-shot acts. He didn't have a pot to piss in before I took him in. I'll never forgive him." She blew her nose on her apron.

"Neither will I," Lisa thought.

"He didn't have a dime till he went into the Army. After that, he met 'Miss Hootsie Tootsie.' She was and is as homely as the bulldogs she shows. But she is stinking rich. Her father owns some big soap company. That woman is so homely that they threw the wrong stuff away when she was born!"

"Mom Mom, stop," said Lisa. "You are getting yourself and me upset. But I'll mark this day. He will get his one day. I promise!"

"He practically lived here, the son of a bitch." She hit the table with her fist. Mom Mom was mad and hurt.

Lisa remembered Jim Cory only too well. How he would sneak around saying, "Let's play hide and seek." When he found her, his hands would try to get into her pants. He would say, "Don't move, I have a piece of candy for you."

When she was ten, he came back from the service and tried the same thing. She picked up the fireplace poker and demanded, "You stay away from me, or I'll kill you!"

At 14, Lisa was fully developed and could have passed for 20. "I don't want one of his dogs," Lisa promised herself. "One of these days will be pay-up time for that louse." She never forgot his face or name and he would come to rue the day he first laid hands on her.

The grandmother had two famous dog handlers, one for her Cocker Spaniels and the other for her Miniature Poodles. They showed Lisa how to trim a Standard Poodle show-style, how to pose the large dog, how to care for their coat, and how to win.

CHAPTER 2

▼

Lisa never had a handler. She learned to show a dog to Best in Show, not once but repeatedly. Lisa loved to look at pedigrees with her beloved Mom Mom, who taught her many things, like to look to a dog's grandparents instead of parents.

"When breeding, watch a ball player. Get your sweater," she told the girl.

"Where are we going?" Lisa wanted to know.

"To the ball game. It is easier to show instead of trying to tell." Most of the seats were empty, so they were able to get seats right behind home plate. "Now watch and listen to me," Mom Mom wiped off the dirty seat. "Right there, that's what I mean."

"What?"

"He's on first. We have to wait. Look, he's going to steal."

"Steal what? What am I looking for?"

"Oh Lisa, I'll explain first and then someone might run. The jackass didn't make second."

Lisa had no idea of anything but she gradually learned.

"Check the bite. Never buy a dog that shows the whites of its eyes—temper. You don't even want temper in a large dog. There's an old saying but it is true. If it's a bitch, you want head and shoulders like a lady and the behind of a cook. If it's a male, he should look like a male with type, balance, quiet spirit and a look like he has something to give to his breed."

"I want a female," Lisa told Mom Mom. "I want a white one and of a famous line."

Time passed and she was finally able to get a dog, and she settled for a male. I've been going to some famous kennels now that I'm 16 and can drive. Mom

Mom, there are two breeders of famous dogs, who have been wonderful to me. Mrs. Wendell Gordon is one. She has the Willow Grove Kennels. And Mrs. Knowles of Fox Fire Kennels. They are so nice."

"I know them both," Mom Mom approved.

"I've been working for Mrs. Gordon at some of the shows. I'm going to show one of her pups next week and he is beautiful at eight months. His name is Fox Fire Rumble."

"Remember this darling, always act like a lady and pick your best pup at birth. Then confirm this at three months."

Mom Mom did not live long after that talk and Lisa was on her own. Mom Mom had left Lisa enough money to buy a five-year old ranch house in the heart of Lancaster County, Pennsylvania. The rest of the estate, and it was sizable, went to County Caven, Ireland.

Mrs. Gordon attended the grandmother's funeral but Jim Cory did not. As Mrs. Gordon was leaving, she asked Lisa to have dinner with her at the hotel where she was staying. At first, Lisa did not want to eat anything, but instead of refusing, she managed to accept. At the hotel, Mrs. Gordon opened the bathroom door and out came a breeding dog. "You finish Rumble to his championship and he is yours." The dog knew Lisa and was glad to see her. "I'll see you next week at the Harrisburg Dog Show. There are 15 standard males entered. It's a five-point show, so get him ready."

Lisa left with her beautiful snow-white poodle. "I wish I had bred you, young man," she told the dog seated next to her in the car. "We'll get a female because of you that will carry my kennel name." Lisa would finish Rumble as promised and demand for him a stud fee of $500.00. That kept both dog and girl in food and the niceties of life for a little while.

The ranch house had two bedrooms, two baths and a double garage. Lisa gradually re-made the house as she finished high school and took leave of her mother to live independently. It didn't take Lisa long to reason that the car could stay out all the time and if she knocked out some garage walls and bought some kennel wire, she had her kennel. The place was about five miles from the city of Lancaster. The second bedroom and bath were automatically assigned as puppy space. Good, good pups brought a fine price of $3,000.00 to $5,000.00, especially if they were house-broken and ready for new homes at 3 ½ months. Remembering what Mom Mom had told her, "Pick at birth and decide if you are right in three months."

Lisa needed three things: An Amish carpenter to turn the garage into kennels on the inside and dog exercise runs on the outside, a good brood bitch, and an Amish girl to take care of the house. Lisa would take care of the dogs.

When the Amish carpenter arrived he asked, "Where is your man? I don't do business with women."

"What?" Lisa didn't believe her ears.

The Amish girl, called Greta, arrived right out of the eighth grade. She had wanted to go to high school, but she had to go to work. That was their way. No Amish husband wanted a wife smarter than he.

Where could she find a good brood bitch? That was easy. She called upon Willis Gun, one of Mom Mom's handlers, who had befriended her. He knew just the dog. He would try to get it for her, but it would be pricey.

"God bless you, Willis!" Lisa exclaimed when the bitch arrived. She was white and was three-years-old. She had a litter of six, three males and three females. Every one of those pups had finished their championship. Lisa paid $5,000.00 for this prize. Now, at the ripe old age of 20, Lisa was out to fulfill her dream, to breed the most beautiful Standard Poodles in the country.

A local carpenter had completed the kennel and Rumble was waiting for his turn. Lisa took the best of life wherever she found it. Four years later, and at the age of 24, she was disliked. Lisa had found her mark. The young woman had 26 Standard Poodles to her credit, all shown and finished by herself.

Best of all, Lisa managed to beat Jim Cory any time he ever entered her ring. Years after she had vowed to kill him, she was killing him at dog shows. She would glare at him, push ahead of him, and point out to the dog show judge the mistake in breeding of Jim's dogs, simply by stroking her dogs' beautiful shoulders. The judge would look at Lisa's dog and realize Jim's dog was coarse in that area. There were tricks and Lisa knew them all.

Jim told a friend, "That woman hates me and I don't know why." Jim Cory had a short memory, and had forgotten to associate Lisa with his abuse during her childhood. Lisa remembered well and never forgave.

Lisa was breeding her own dogs now. The stock carried famous kennel names. Now these dogs were three and four generations under her colors and kennel name, "Mom Mom Kennels." With a sire name like that, her dogs were called Mom Mom's Kate or Mom Mom's Jack, etc. The number of letters by the A.K.C. on registration limited the length of the name.

People thought Lisa was reaching for the stars when she decided to be satisfied with the beauty and balance in her dogs. She knew the faults in her breed and she was determined to breed out the faults: hindquarters, bad flat feet, overbite, and a disposition that needed watching.

With a new litter of standards being born in the whelping box next to her bed, Lisa thought about what Mom Mom had said. "This is the time to pick your winner."

As the tenth and final pup arrived, Lisa reached across the back of the mother dog, who was a champion. The litter sire was also a homebred champion. "Good stuff," Lisa said, as she picked one out of the group. "You are just what I'm looking for." He was an entirely snow-white male puppy out of an all black litter. "You little recessive gene!" Lisa squealed. "Mom Mom told me to watch out for two recessive genes popping up out of black." Lisa was talking to the slimy new pup and the mother dog was being distressed. "Just you wait a minute. Take care of your nine babies while I check this one out." Lisa held the baby dog at eye-level and announced, "You will be my next champion, and I name you Mom Mom's Ice."

Dog shows became a way of life for Lisa. There were hundreds like her. Most of the handlers liked and respected Lisa, but many other exhibitors in the game hated her. Then there were those, and they were not a few, who would drive in many miles to a show and see she was setting up under a tent or in a hall. They would sneak in like the baseball player she was shown at an early age, and sneak away to kill the points if it was a major. Because they knew she would beat them in the ring with her looks, her style, and her beautiful top dogs. Dog shows are wonderful and considered a sport, but some of the meanest, nastiest, and most dishonest people are in the dog show game.

The first time Lisa won "Best of Breed," she was told by a *friend* "You heard I am sure, that the judge forgot his glasses." However, Lisa was no ordinary young woman.

She remembered the remark and used it later. Sportsmanship was almost nil in the dog show game.

Lisa overheard a remark like this, "You can tell a breeder that his kid is cross-eyed, but don't try to tell him that his dog is cow-hocked." She watched losers congratulate the winners when they really wanted to trip them, at best. Best friends split over a show win. Lisa witnessed it more than once. She had done her share of winning. She learned early if there was a judge, who could be bought. Lisa would go to the trouble to make sure that if he was political that she would not show under him. For the most part, the judges were very decent people. That was her conclusion.

Lisa loved the dogs and her dogs loved her. She trained her show dogs. They were so beautiful. All of them were snow-white and in perfect condition. When they entered the ring, the audience would come to their feet. When it came time to part with a dog going to a new home, it was hard on both girl and dog. The young and beautiful woman was making tracks hard to follow. She was known everywhere for her beauty and her beautiful dogs. The rich and famous were her customers.

Not all was being overlooked. There was a man, a very rich man, a man twice her age, who had spotted her the year before. At that time, he was married. At 24, Lisa had never had a serious love affair. She had dated and gone out with friends, such as customers or handlers after a show. However, she never had time for a lover or husband. The young woman traveled the country doing one circuit of shows after the other, calling home to make sure everything was okay.

This was her life until, "Hey sweetheart," one of the light shoe-handlers called to her. "I've got a note for you from Bert Taloomas." Everyone knew who he was. Besides being a Greek tycoon, he also was the owner of the Bert Boxer Dogs in the country. O'Donner was the dog's name. Lisa opened the note thinking he was interested in one of her dogs for a lady friend. Instead, it read, "Will you have dinner with me tonight? Bert."

"Oh darn!" She was not sure. "Does he expect an answer right now?" she asked the pretty man staring there like a post.

"What do you think?" the handler laughed.

"Where is he?"

"In the box seats."

"Call me at the hotel. I am at the Hamilton," Lisa wrote. Lisa wasn't rich, but the price of her puppies and show dogs offered her a nice living. She dressed well, and looked like the rich and famous that she had always associated with. She was comfortable with that group ever since her association with Mrs. Ralph Gordon and Mrs. Maxwell Knowles, the women who had befriended her and were partly responsible for her success. However, she always felt scruffy after a dog show. The grooming area at the end of the day was always a man-made mess, akin to a baseball dugout! Pew!

Lisa was heading for a warm shower at her hotel when the phone rang. It was her mother. "Your sister, Nancy, is getting married in June. Can we depend on your being here?" she asked. "It's June 19th."

"I'll be there if I can," was Lisa's answer. "I gotta go. My tub is filling." She took three steps closer to the shower and the phone rang again. Lisa paused. "He can call again," she told the hotel room.

The phone continued to ring and out of curiosity Lisa answered. It was a good thing her tub wasn't filling. "Oh hello," she answered.

"Are you entered in the big Harrisburg show?" he asked.

"Who are you and why do you want to know?" Lisa was disgusted and annoyed.

"If you are, there is no point in me entering."

The voice was familiar. "Who the hell are you?"

"I'm sorry, I'm Jim Cory."

Lisa put her head back and howled.

"What is so funny?" he wanted to know.

"You are, you bastard." She hung up the phone. She would never forget that moment. "I've hated that man for ten years," Lisa told the phone. "What goes around comes around, Mr. Big."

In the shower, Lisa couldn't hear the phone trying to ring off the hook. With no make-up on and her beautiful black hair soaking wet, there was a knock at her hotel door. "Who? What? I didn't order room service." Lisa McHugh opened the door to the handsome Greek hiding behind a large bouquet of roses. "Oh," she groaned. "Come in. Come in and find a place to sit." Lisa took the flowers with her. "I'll be dressed in a moment."

CHAPTER 3

▼

"You look just fine to me." he called after her.

At his time of entrance, Lisa was wrapped in a large hotel towel. Now she was wrapped in a terry-cloth robe and her hair was wrapped turban fashion in a white towel. She knew she looked luscious. "Well, here I am in the raw with no make-up. I know I look terrible, but I didn't want to keep you waiting."

"You are a beautiful woman. Now let's stop playing games. Why didn't you answer the phone?" he said with no accent.

"I didn't hear the phone. I was in the shower," Lisa explained.

"I called and called from the lobby. The line was always busy. Did you take the phone off the hook?" the tone was insulting.

"Okay," Lisa stood up. "There is the door, Bert. I don't think we have anything more to say. I don't play games."

The older man apologized. She relented. They went to dinner and enjoyed each other.

When they returned to Lisa's hotel room, Bert called for champagne. Her dog Ice was closed in the bathroom. It didn't bother him that much because he had gone Best of Breed. At nine months, he somehow knew he was special even if he had been left out of the party in the other room.

Lisa was not used to drinking. She would have a glass of wine if the evening called for it. Even then, she would leave half a glass. Tonight, Lisa was about to have her third glass of Mum's Champagne. As they drank, and got closer on the divan, Bert told Lisa the things all women want to hear. "You are beautiful; your eyes, your lips and your hair. Your coloring is Greek, dark skin, shiny dark eyes and flashing white teeth. God, what a child we could make."

"Make a child!" Lisa was not drunk yet.

After Bert left in the morning, Lisa awoke to find the triple bed messed up all over. She was alone. "My God, what happened? What did I do? Oh, my head." The phone rang. It was Bert. "What happened? What did I do?" Lisa feared the answer.

"Darling, you were a very good girl; just a little drunk. I never take advantage of that situation," Bert consoled. "I just wanted you to know, furthermore, I'd like to see you again. This time we will stay sober. I think I have fallen in love with you," Bert whispered.

Lisa lay back on the messed up bed, Ice in her arms, and thought aloud. "Bert has had three wives, all were Greek. He is twice my age. I wonder if he is any good in bed. I'll find out tonight."

Lisa lifted the nine-month-old Ice to look into his face. "Today belongs to you, young man. Be sure you make me proud." It was his debut into the dog show ring. Thinking of herself in the shower, "It's okay at 24. It's time to try for keeps. I'm not getting any younger."

Lisa's dogs were equal to the finest racehorses or top ball players. People fought for her dogs. Sometimes a whole litter of pups at huge prices was sold before they were born. She was very decent in that she didn't show all over the country at the same time, not using traveling handlers, and showing her dogs herself. She gave other people a chance, but when she did show up, the other Standard breeders hoped against hope. Ice was her *crème de la crème*. Lisa couldn't fault him and she knew Standard Poodles.

Some people forgave her because she did nice things such as showing kids how to handle their dogs in children's handling classes, and even offered her well-trained dogs to kids at the shows. Lisa never forgot where she came from or the things Mom Mom and the other two women had taught her. She also never forgot Jim Cory.

She might run into him today. "I know he isn't judging, but I think he lives in Atlanta, the bastard!"

"I'll stay over another day to see what happens," Lisa told herself, as she took the nine-month-old pup off his bench and stacked him on the grooming table. "You look good to me." She looked around at the other dogs. This was a specialty show that followed the All Breed Show of the previous day when Ice had gone Best of Winner for five points toward his championship, giving him a total of ten points. Today was also a five-point show, so if he wins, and competition is tough, he will have finished his championship before a year old. His two littermates were leaving for their new home.

"Are you sure Ice isn't for sale?" one customer had asked at the show.

Lisa looked at her prize, white as snow and still in puppy trim. "Mom Mom, I wish you could see him. I think he is perfect. I can't fault him. If he wins, I'm going to hide him. I'll keep that first sperm for his kennel. Then, I'll bring him out for the Golden. I expect big things. God has been good to me." It was almost a prayer.

The specialty show was in Atlanta. Her hotel was close by where she would spend one more night. Then, she would pick up her 35-foot R.V. and head for the beach, where Ice and she could spend a few days before going on to the Harrisburg, Pennsylvania, dog show.

Ten or twelve people had kept the Harrisburg Dog Show alive during the Second World War. Today, it was one of the largest and most successful of all shows. Mom Mom had been one of them. Therefore, Lisa never missed the show. Ice was entered, but if he wins in Atlanta, she thought, it's go-home time for the dog.

In Lisa's early days, she drove a second-hand Volkswagen, like a lot of hippies drove. She was not a hippie, no way, but she would stay at the bash, any beach that was handy. She had been chased away from the best of them. It didn't take long until she knew where she could stay. Lisa would sleep there, cook there, exercise with her dogs, and play in the sand. At that point, she bought a gun for personal safety, which she kept close by. She still carried the gun in her car. It was registered and had never been used. It was antique but she figured it really worked.

Lisa and Ice entered the Atlanta show into the breeders, exhibitions, and handler's area, a section set aside for grooming and gossip. "Whatcha got there?" Norman Buxton, a top handler and friend, asked Lisa, as they arrived.

"Should I show him Ice or keep the dog in his crate?" she wondered. "I'd like to keep it a mystery."

"Come on Lisa," a competitor teased. "Let's see him."

"It's just a pup." Lisa replied, as she set up her grooming space. The others went on with their own jobs, for which Lisa was glad. "I'd hate to take him out of his crate. These guys will be all over him. He still has to be groomed, puppy clip or not."

Lisa reached into the crate and lifted the sleeping dog very gently, placed Ice on the grooming table and watched for the influx. No one seemed to notice, all were doing their own thing.

One handler, whose back was to her, turned to ask, "Where did you get the white pup? Some of Polaris' breeding?"

Lisa ignored the handler until Bert arrived. Bert drew attention wherever he showed up. All the show people knew him and his famous Boxers. "Where is the black one you showed yesterday?" Bert wanted to know.

"That one is on her way to her new home," she replied without looking up, as she clipped a white hair, one here, and one there.

"What did you get for her?" It was none of his business, but she loved to tell him.

"Five thousand and they promised to finish her. I picked the stud and got six pups out of her first litter."

"My God, you are rough! Keep it up and I'll sell out when we get married," he laughed.

That got attention from all over the area. The ones who had not heard it asked, "What did he say?"

He knew he had an audience. Bert loved being the center of attention. So in a voice all could hear, he proposed. "Lisa, sweetheart, I'm madly in love with you. Will you marry me? You are everything I want and need."

"Oh, go away!" she shocked the group. "I'm busy." She thought he was trying to be funny. "Bert, get lost," she repeated, scorning him, and he did as asked. He was gone. "Where did he go?" Lisa looked around. He wasn't in sight.

Bert was singing in the men's room. "Oh, I love that woman! She has spunk, looks, class, independence, and just what I've looked for most of my adult life! I'll make her a queen, my queen." When he finished his song, the others in the men's room gave Bert applause. With that, he walked off to watch the poodles shown at the specialty show.

Someone called, "Puppy dog, nine to twelve months, in the ring."

"Where you going with that pup?" her best friend in dogs asked.

"Just you wait, Carter," she told the handler, who had helped her many times in the past. He followed Lisa and the pup to ring-side.

"What a beautiful gait on a little guy." Lisa was proud to hear him say so because Carter knew his dogs.

CHAPTER 4

▼

"Did you hear that jerk in the men's room singing the virtues of Lisa?" Jim Cory had been there. "The damn fool is twice her age. She is just a girl."

"What about when she was just a child of four?"

"Puppy class, nine to twelve." There were only three contestants. When the female judge handed Lisa the blue ribbon, she said, "What a beautiful puppy."

When Lisa and Ice returned for the Winner's Class and a different judge handed her a purple winning ribbon, he remarked, "You have done it this time." In addition, the amazingly perfect puppy left the ring to the applause of watchers. The dog strutted like a winner to the delight of the ring-side. Everybody likes a winner and they gathered around as if he was a celebrity.

Lisa picked up her dog and held him over her head to get through the crowd. They followed Lisa to the bench, where she opened his crate. She got him out of sight until they called in the champions for Best in Show. He had gone Best of Winners the day before. The judge told Lisa she just could not put a pup over champions.

This time, the judge was a well-known man, who pretended not to know Lisa. He knew her well, but he had never seen the snow-white standard puppy before. This was for Best in Show. There stood this beautiful Standard Poodle challenging for Best in Show. The crowd at ring-side was quiet, as the judge placed his hands over the contender. The crowd and Lisa watched his expression. No sign of what his thoughts were. Lisa's heart was pounding. Ice was aware of the silence.

"Take him around," was the only remark the judge made.

Lisa and Ice started to circle the large ring. Around they paraded, not once but twice. This time, Lisa had Ice on a loose leash to show him at his best. Then the judges called to the toy poodles, the best miniature poodle, the best-corded poodle, all adults, and the best 9-12 month standard. He ordered all to circle for his pick. He ordered them to stop and to the wild cheers of the crowd, he picked Ice.

There were trophies, flowers, hugs, and kisses. One exhibitor was heard to say, "It's okay to be beaten by a dog like that, even if he is a pup."

Bert was at Lisa's side. "I thought you were not going to show any more for awhile?"

"And miss all of this! Did you see him? Did you watch? He showed himself and charmed the judge." Bert smiled, showing exceptionally beautiful flashing white teeth for a man of his age.

"Where do you want to go for dinner?" Bert had his arm around her like, "She is mine!"

"I'm so excited!" Lisa bubbled. "Let's go back to my room and order dinner. Let's make it about 8:00 p.m. I've got a lot to do here."

Bert turned her chin his way and kissed her for all to see. "I'll be there," he said and pinched her behind as he left.

Ice and been fed and cared for. Lisa and Bert had enjoyed their dinner with no champagne. It was dark and all the lights of the city were at their feet as they stepped onto the balcony and the fresh nighttime air. Bert took Lisa in his arms and kissed her, as only a man of the world could kiss. Lisa was thrilled to her knees.

"Whoa, too much in one day." She pushed him gently away. Bert opened a recognizable Tiffany ring box containing a large 7-carat emerald-shaped white diamond ring. It took her breath away. Lisa accepted the 7-carat emerald-cut diamond ring. During the lovemaking that followed, she would turn on the light to admire the ring.

"What the hell are you doing?" Both laughed and got back into action, first class. Not once. The first time he said, "That's a boy! Let's go for a girl!" With the dawn, they could try for quintuplets. "Not bad for a guy twice your age." Bert bragged and hugged his bride to be, as if he had never been so happy.

Breakfast was ordered and Ice was placed in the bathroom. A blue diaper pad was there for his convenience. "Why a baby diaper?" the lover inquired.

"That's the way we travel." Lisa laughed. "He goes and then I dispose."

"Don't lock him up, darling. I want Ice to know me." The dog was glad to be with them and all that wonderful people food. "Do we feed him from the table?" Bert questioned.

"Sure," Lisa responded. "He is family."

"Is he going to sleep with us, too?" He knew the answer.

Lisa looked him in the eye, her eyes sparkling like a figure in a DeGrazia. "You were the one who wanted him out of the bathroom."

Bert grabbed her, held her close, and picked her up, slippers falling off her feet. As he dropped her on the bed, he said, "Here Ice, nice fellow," and he coaxed Ice back into the bathroom. From that day on Bert was a dead duck. Lisa's slightest whim was his command. He wanted it that way. It was his greatest pleasure to be her "genie." Lisa had promised to marry him, if and when, she became pregnant. The young 24-year-old must have conceived the first time they were together.

They spent a delightful ten days at the shore in her Winnebago R.V., where Lisa and Ice went off on their own to romp upon her private beach and play in the surf and sand. It was a Jersey beach she had found years ago. She had never seen another human being there other than herself, so what was this coming out of the water. Her first thought was to run but Ice recognized him and took off to greet Bert. "Oh honey, you scared me. Where did you come from? How did you know where to find me? Did you follow me?"

"You told me about a beach not far from Sea Bridge. I'm not dumb. Stop talking, my dear." He had her in his arms and her back in the sand while the dog seemed to enjoy the semi-private scene, as he chased seagulls and sand crabs.

"We could have gone into the R.V.," Lisa laughed, shaking sand out of her hair and trying to get it out of her mouth. "How did you get here?" she asked.

"It was only ten miles away from where I'm staying," he teased. I walked and I swam and then I saw your coach."

The sun was going down. It was a great big sun like the kind that comes up in Texas. They braced themselves against some rocks and enjoyed the orange, red, and blue sky. "This is a beautiful spot." He hugged her closer. "I wonder if it's for sale."

"You are kidding?" Lisa poked him in the rib with her elbow.

"I don't kid," was his answer.

"Gee, it must be wonderful to be rich," Lisa smirked.

"It is, to be rich and to be in love with the most wonderful girl in the world!" Bert blew a kiss skyward.

Lisa insisted on making a dinner cookout. He wanted to take her to the hotel for dinner and a night of dancing. It was decided, a cookout on the beach, a drink and dancing at the hotel with dessert in his room. Ice was in the Winnebago with his blue diaper.

Nothing lasts forever. It was time to head for the Harrisburg, Pennsylvania, dog show. She had entered Ice in the Open Class. Not too many 9-12 month dogs enter that ring. It would be like a 12 year-old entering a fight ring against Mohammed Ali. The older dogs were going to have to strut to beat Ice and somehow, this beautiful faultless dog knew it. He was no longer a puppy, even if his birth said so or even if the trim on his back said so. It meant nothing to him. Lisa swore she could hear him say, "Come on guys!"

While Ice was strutting at the end of a leash, Lisa was looking around. "Bert said he would be here," she muttered to herself.

Bert was in the enormous Farm Show Building. He was talking to a handler about his Boxers and who the young man planned to show. "What about Buckaroo?" Bert asked. "I left him home today. If it's Best in Show you are looking for, Lisa is here with that pup people say that can't be beat." Bert had never handled his own dogs. Only the best handlers ever took his Boxers in the ring.

"If Ice is as good as people seem to think, he will win regardless."

"Let me take him into the group," one of the handlers begged.

"Look who's going to judge! My God!" Lisa was going to get sick again.

"Call a doctor!"

"I did," someone volunteered.

The doctor arrived and took Lisa aside. "I'm Dr. Ralph Benson." He handed her his card. "I'm really from Alaska, but I had some business here in Harrisburg." Then he continued, "I like dogs, so I thought I'd just take a look. Big show! You are going to be okay," he said, as he got off the hard ring-side chair. "Eat a few crackers. That helps some at first." Dr. Benson smiled and left the show.

The judge was a substitute. Dr. Brook had gotten ill. "Bert," Lisa called, "take Ice in the ring. I couldn't win under him." Jim Cory, the replacement, knew the dog and the owner. Ice won the Non-Sporting Group followed by Best in Show. Lisa felt much better. Someone had overheard the doctor tell her to eat some crackers. The unknown donor left a new pack of crackers that Lisa devoured.

"I'm going in the ring," she told Bert. Under her breath, she said, "This is for you Mom Mom." Lisa looked skyward as she entered the ring under a female judge. The show building burst with thunderous applause. Men whistled, women cried, and others stomped on the floor. Everyone loves to see a pup clobber the big boys.

CHAPTER 5

▼

"What was that look I saw you give Jim Cory? Do you know him?" Lisa asked Bert, after the excitement had calmed down.

"Of course. I know who he is and I'm sure he knows who I am."

Lisa had parked the motor home at Wal-Mart, which was across the street. "What do you want to do?" Lisa asked Bert. "I feel a little woozy." On the way back to the motor home, Ice was on Lisa's lap. The dog kissed her and she kissed the dog in return. She told the dog to settle down and the dog obeyed.

"Did you have any children?" Lisa was interested.

"No," said he.

"Three wives and no kids?" Lisa questioned.

"They didn't want children."

"Why?" she wondered.

"Ask them." Bert laughed. "They are still around. Don't get me wrong; I wanted children. Every man hopes for a son. I respected their wishes and a lot of other desires. So, young lady, that is why I'm not married now."

"What if I'm pregnant?" Lisa looked at Bert.

"It would be non-stop to the courthouse, darling, and I sure hope you are. Seriously, I'd like a formal Greek wedding sometime. Okay?"

"Okay." Lisa replied. "God, is this ring really real?"

"As real as you, my darling."

The next stop was to a doctor, who proved what both really expected.

The wedding was simple. Her bride-to-be sister, Nancy, was Lisa's only attendant.

Bert's best man looked like a man connected to the Mafia. Bruno Cosmos was his name. The man had a way of being around wherever they went or stayed. Lisa didn't like him and said so.

"He's okay," was all Bert ever said. He still gave Lisa shivers.

Ice was no longer being shown. He was Lisa's constant companion, to Bert's annoyance. "Why don't we take Ice back to your kennel in—what do you call that place?"

"Paradise!" Lisa smiled. "The next town is called Intercourse."

"I wouldn't like that. I wouldn't want to live in a town with a name like that. By the way," he asked, "Do you want to continue living in the hotel or would you like a palace somewhere?" Bert crossed the room and placed his arms around the woman he loved. "Or would you like a palace in the sky? I'm your Genie, remember."

"What a great guy. I love you Bert. I've been thinking. I'd like to live in Kentucky."

"Kentucky! My God, why?" Bert was totally surprised.

"Just a whim," she smiled and looked so beautiful. The world was hers.

"Ya'll! I can learn to say that," he kidded as he affected a southern drawl.

"Hand me my purse. It's right beside you. I want to make a call."

"My God, that's a heavy purse. What are you carrying in that thing besides money?" He dumped the purse in her lap and the gun fell out. "What in the world is that thing? Is it a gun?" Bert picked it up.

"Yes, it's a gun? It's a 'knuckle buster,' a thing of beauty and service. I bought it years ago at an antique show. See," Lisa demonstrated, "it's solid brass and it just fits right into your hand. The brass knuckles fit right over your knuckles. So, if you don't want to kill someone, you can knock him out."

"What are you doing with anything like that?" Bert wanted to know and know right away.

"It intrigued me. It has no bullets. I wouldn't know where to find any. I thought it was protection without having to kill anyone."

"Give me that thing. You will never need a gun. I'll see to that." The gun exchanged hands. Bert looked at it and turned it over in his hand. "It must have belonged to an Irishman, someone who liked to use his fists. This thing would never shoot."

Lisa called her house in Paradise, Pennsylvania, to talk to Greta, the Amish girl, who had been staying there. There were no dogs, as Lisa had sold the last two litter mated of Ice for fabulous prices. Those dogs carried the same genes that Ice had. They were suddenly worth twice as much since Ice had finished his Championship so fast.

"Greta, honey, I'm going to put the place up for sale. Would you like to join my husband and me? We are going to live in Kentucky."

"Where? Oh, no!"

The house sold quickly. It was in the heart of tourist country. An antique dealer by the name of Bette Schultz was the buyer. Lisa did not ask for a profit because the new owner would have to make a few costly changes.

There were no more shows for Ice. Lisa wanted time for Ice to come to his full growth and time for his coat to get ready for the adult show. Then he would be ready for the Garden.

Lisa became the "lady in waiting!" She was waited upon hand and foot.

"Where is your diamond, dear? You are not wearing it," Bert asked.

"My ring finger swells sometimes," she answered.

"What? For God's sake, what does that mean?" He waited.

"It means that the ring gets tight. That's what it means." Lisa turned to leave the room.

"You sure?" Bert was on his feet. "I'm calling the doctor."

"If you do, it will be the third time this week. I'm fine." They had just discovered it was a boy.

"Lisa, my dear, I have the opportunity to buy an apartment here in New York. Would you like that or do you still want to go to Kentucky?" Bert was always at her side.

"I'd rather have a beautiful home and farm in Kentucky with rolling hills, white fences and a really beautiful kennel just like Mom Mom had."

"What's with this Mom Mom stuff?" Bert was disappointed. "How could you prefer Kentucky to New York City?" After a thoughtful moment, Bert decided, "The mother of my son can have it all. What about me?" This was Bert's silent thought. "But, I love her so much."

Bert heaped luxury upon Lisa. Some things she really did not want, like the 7-carat diamond she was expected to wear all the time. Together they looked for land and a beautiful plantation home. Things like that are not too hard to find if your purse contains millions. The perfect place was found; not too far out of town sprawled out over 100 acres with a man-made lake and out-buildings.

The out-buildings were torn down. The lake was drained for a golf course and a large kennel was built for Boxers and a smaller one for Poodles. Bert found two experienced Japanese girls to run his kennel while Lisa planned to take care of her kennel herself. Although there was only one Poodle and he was her constant companion, no one else was permitted to comb a hair on his body.

It was a happy time for both, although Bert managed to go to Atlanta from time to time for business reasons, he said. Lisa wondered about that also since he had decided "no sex" until the baby came. She assumed that was some kind of Greek custom.

Ice had been called the perfect dog; the only such animal anyone had ever heard of. Now, the dog's beautiful white coat was to give Lisa trouble. Dry spots, not many, but several had begun to appear. Hair refused to grow. Lisa and the vet were unable to coax the leathery skin to absorb any medication. Then, she remembered her grandmother had used sulfur and bacon fat that were mixed into a paste and applied. If the dog could reach the spots, he would lick them dry. Neither she, nor the vet, nor Mom Mom knew the problem for sure. Was it from inside or outside? However, the mix did the trick.

When Bert heard about it and saw the results he remarked, "Someone could make a million. Think of all the bald heads out there and how this could help them."

Lisa guarded the dog like gold. Bert was beginning to resent the dog. "Why don't you sleep with the damn dog?" he asked. His tone indicated what was meant. Lisa realized she was devoting too much time to Ice. Looking in the mirror as she brushed her long black shining hair, she decided to give Ice a wonderful run in the blue grass, shower, and then head for town. Bert had been in New York for a few days. He would be back the next day.

Lisa was beginning to show her intended motherhood. It was time to indulge in some glamour. The leading beauty parlor was expecting her and the red carpet and cash register were waiting. "Give me the works," she ordered, and they did. They cut her hair and added a few blonde streaks. Lisa was pleased. It looked so New York she thought. It was a bad choice.

CHAPTER 6

▼

Lisa knew where to find the best shops. She managed to spend $3,000.00 without buying too many things. That was a mistake. After the dinner that she and Ice had together, Lisa looked in the paper to find the most expensive and best address of a place to dine. That was stupid, too.

Bert was getting too hard to please. "What the hell did you do to your hair?" he asked as he swore in Greek before he kissed her or removed his scarf or coat. "Now you don't look Greek." He pushed past the dog.

"Please don't upset me, dear," she pleaded.

"Why not?" He shot back. "You have upset me. Don't you know what you have done? Why do you want to look like everyone else?" he demanded.

"I had planned a nice dinner tonight. I thought we'd dress and go to Ivan's." She was fighting back the tears.

"Why would I want to do that? Christ, I just got home!"

"Rat fink!" Lisa yelled after him, as he was leaving the room.

"That's more like it," Bert laughed. "That's my girl." That night, they slept together for the first time in three months.

In the morning, Lisa had the blond streaks removed from her hair. Bert was pleased and apologized once more, adding that he liked her much better. "I love you as you are." Bert planted a kiss. "Well, now, I'm off to Atlanta. I wish you'd travel with me once." Ice got the dirty look. "Try to get some help. That dinner, if you could call it, was lousy."

"Just a minute," Lisa stopped him at the door. "After the baby, I promise to travel with you, all three and no dog." He kissed her again. The chauffeur was waiting at the limo. Lisa closed the door singing aloud, "Only a bird in a gilded cage. Right now, I hate myself. How did I let myself get caught in this kind of life? Bad thought! Bad thought!"

The baby thought so, too. She felt her first baby kick. Lisa watched out the large living room windows, as the limo sped away. "I wonder what draws him to Atlanta all the time. I saw Cosmos was seated in the back seat. I don't care for that man. He smells of garlic."

The dry spots on the back of Ice were clearing up and hair was appearing. The vet had told Lisa the dog needed carrots. "He should stick to horses or rabbits." Lisa laughed, as she and Ice ran through the field of blue wildflowers.

Seated on the large patio in the rear of the mansion, Lisa realized she needed a female friend, someone to talk to. She was alone too much. "I will look up the local Kennel Club and find out when and where they meet. Next, I'll see if they have a Daughters of the American Revolution or Daughters of the American Colonists here in Lexington. Or, better still, maybe I should buy a race horse if I want to be a part of this place of Southern Belles." Lisa watched Ice chase a butterfly.

"You know," she said to herself, proof that she needed female friends, "I could pick a good horse. I'd be looking for all the things Mom Mom taught me about selecting a good dog."

Bert is going to have a surprise when he gets home. "Did he say when he'd be back?" Lisa couldn't remember. "Maybe there is a note in his office." She started to root around through his address book. That's how Lisa found out about Kitty. Bert had her phone number in his file. Lisa didn't remove the note. She did write down Kitty's phone number and placed it in her phone book. At the moment, she found the number, her baby kicked again. Lisa didn't know why she wasn't surprised. "I'll bet she is a hang over from his other wives."

Why wasn't she heartbroken? She just had a dead feeling like all the fun and games were over.

Lisa looked through the ads in the paper. She wanted someone to build her a small barn or stable. There was one ad that read: Sommers—Father & Son, one horse or more, bonded and licensed.

The ad looked good to her. She did all the things that she had learned to do. First, she called the Better Business Bureau. Lisa was informed that there were no reported grievances. That was what she wanted to hear. "Good enough." The senior Sommers told Lisa that his son, Gordon, would be out the next day.

Right on time, there stood the son looking like an Adonis. He was tanned from the sun with eyes as blue as the sky and teeth like a dentist was in his pocket. "I'm Gordon Sommers," he smiled. "I understand you need a stable or two?"

"I hope you can't read my mind," Lisa blushed. She didn't ask him into the house. Instead she suggested the lovely late fall morning was too nice too reject. "Please sit here." Lisa pointed to a white wicker rocker. She sat on a matching one across from him. "Beautiful morning, I just love it here. By the way, I'm Mrs. Bert Taloomas." She extended her hand.

"Everybody knows who you are, lady, a nice brave Yankee." Gordon laughed.

"Are people still like that here? Really?"

"Some people, not everybody." He tapped his straw hat on her knee. "People are the same everywhere. Look at the Irish."

"The Irish have reason, for God's sake," Lisa blurted."

"Some think here, we were invaded, too."

"The idea of the North and South still makes me sick. I'll bet half of the people right here in Lexington are direct descendents of carpetbaggers."

He laughed, put his head back, and with a wide grin asked, "Are we going to build a barn? How many paddocks do you want?"

"One, no make it two. I want nice living quarters attached. I'll need help. I know nothing about horses. I had a horse once, though we lived on a small farm with one house and four pigs. The pigs all had names like Mary, Jane, Jill, and Florence. I could tell it was her. I'd call and she would leave the others and come over to the fence, where I'd feed her corn."

"Do you have a way with animals?" he asked.

"I think I do." Lisa decided not to tell him about her prize sheep or the barn would never get built.

"Would you like a glass of sweet tea or a cup of coffee?" Lisa offered. "I haven't found a maid but I'd be glad to make it for you." She was a hostess Lisa arrived with a pitcher of sweet tea and two tall glasses, along with a couple of store-bought cookies. "I was thinking," she paused, "that maybe I should have four or five stalls. What do you think? I have lots of land. Maybe my husband rides." Lisa sought advice.

"Call me Gordon. It's easier to work that way. Do you mind?"

Lisa must have had a change in her expression. "Okay, but I'm still Mrs. Taloomas."

"I understand." It was getting warmer on the porch and the sun had shifted. Then a breeze appeared from somewhere. His plans for the barn were overlapping and the large sheets of paper were hard to handle.

"Come on inside, we can use the kitchen table." Her hospitality pleased the young man.

"Is it okay if I call you Ma'am?" he asked.

Lisa studied him for a second. "Whatever," she responded. "Details, details; I hate details. I want you to build a nice-looking barn with four to six stalls, living quarters and a bath, a space of five acres within a white fence, and a window box on the window of the living quarters."

"And shutters on the windows?" he was teasing.

"Of course! When can you start?" She stood up to indicate he should get busy.

"Tomorrow. We have a great crew of Amish men. They can build this barn in three days. They do it all the time in these parts."

Gordon made her heart race, as he looked straight into her black-brown eyes. "Aren't you too young to be married?" he asked.

"Watch it, buster!" Lisa didn't smile, but she had a lump in her throat. "My God, he is gorgeous." She thought as he left.

"I want the barn underway by the time my husband gets back from Atlanta," Lisa called after the tall, handsome figure in jeans and blue gingham shirt. "That son of a bitch even knows just what to wear," she thought and she had not over-looked his cowboy boots either.

He stopped at the foot of the porch stairs, turned shyly, and flashed a smile. "I was hoping you were not married when I saw you downtown one day. That son of a bitch, I've got to stay away from him." Lisa's heart leaped into her throat and this time the baby had nothing to do with it.

"Come, come." Lisa was tugging at Bert's hand. He had hardly gotten through the door. "Wait, you will be excited, too. It's good news."

"Great, did Ice run away?" he laughed.

"Don't spoil it, please. I'm so excited. Sorry, or did I say that before?"

"I'm tired. Lisa, you pick the damndest times for your games."

Lisa suppressed a tear and tried to regain some of her enthusiasm. "Just take a look outside. You'll see a difference." She walked away. They hadn't even kissed in greeting.

Sex does strange things to people, the young mother-to-be thought, as she heard his voice.

"My God, Lisa, haven't you hired any help yet? I'm not eating another pizza." Bert knew he was acting like an ass, but the trip to Atlanta hadn't gone as expected. "Sweetheart, I have something for you. Where is your ring?"

"In the bedroom. It's there for the duration. I'll wear it after the baby. We had better decide on a name. You are kidding, I hope."

"He will have my name, Bertram Arturus Taloomas. That's that."

"Of course," Lisa obeyed.

"He can sleep alone tonight," she decided. "He has really rained on my parade. How could things fall apart so suddenly?" Now she was ready for the phone number. Her small voice said, "Wait."

CHAPTER 7

▼

So, Lisa waited but she smoldered.

"Did you buy a horse?" Bert snarled.

"That will be your job." Lisa was sickeningly sweet.

"What do I know about horses? You can't ride in your condition." Lisa knew this was going downstream and she didn't want to fight. So, she walked off to him, not in defeat, but to make peace.

Lisa walked over to Bert and said, "I missed you so much."

Bert melted. "And, I love you so much." Lisa led Bert out on the terrace, where she had two drinks waiting. The evening was beautiful and stars lit up the late September sky. Bert held her in his arms.

"No one should argue with you. You are a pro. What sort of horse would you like?" he whispered.

"One with four legs; just a horse I could ride. Let's go in. It is getting cool."

Bert asked Lisa if she would like a fire in the fireplace in the large "gathering room." With no other light lit, the flames in the massive stone hearth sent shadows across the ceiling and walls.

At this point, Bert announced that he had found a housekeeper and a houseman. "Her name is Lahr and his name is Moses. They are both good at what they do. I found them highly recommended when I was in Atlanta. They will be here in the morning." He did not mention that they had worked for Kitty.

Lisa thought she was playing a game. Bert was playing a larger one with higher stakes. Lisa cuddled. "It's all your fault that I want a stable and a horse."

"How so?"

"You told me to find something to do besides Ice."

"I meant find a girlfriend," Bert argued.

"Like you did?" Lisa tossed it right back.

"What do you mean?" He was off his chair. Lisa handed Bert the name and the phone number.

"Where did—how did—" He planned to leave the room but Lisa dared him.

"Welcome home!"

"God damn! That was one of the reasons I went to Atlanta, to call it off and to tell her everything was over."

"It took three days to tell her that?" Lisa's voice was toneless. "What if I told you that I have someone when you go away?"

"I'd kill him!" Bert threw the gift, box and all, across the room. It came close to her head.

"Is it really over with Kitty?" Lisa waited for an answer.

"I said it was." Lisa noticed he didn't seem to be too happy about it.

What Bert did not say was, "She is a friend, probably the best one I had ever had." Kitty stepped out of the picture, but did not mention that she, too, was pregnant.

Bert found Lisa opening the gift, an 18-karat, 2-inch wide cuff bracelet. "You are so thoughtful." Lisa put her arms around Bert's neck and with the heel of her shoe; she closed the door in the dog's face.

"I do love you Lisa, but sometimes you are very hard to live with. I want to be a good husband and father. It will be new to me but I'm going to try." Bert meant every word at the time.

"Darling, let's work at the stables. I'd like to see what money could buy."

As they walked hand in hand, Bert asked, "Have you been looking around?"

"No," was all she said at the time.

"Come to think of it, that was a pretty good dinner you cooked, but I want it to be your last, okay?"

"Okay," came out of the darkness.

The new barn smelled of new wood. She found the light switch. It was so nice that even Bert was pleased with the construction.

"Lisa, this is beautiful work." Bert ran his hand over a wooden sill. "It looks hand-sanded."

"It is. Two whole families worked in here. They got it all done in three days."

"Like in the Bible?" he teased.

"Yeah!" Lisa was happy again.

As they walked back to the large house, both were making plans.

"Do you realize it's after midnight? Let's get that baby of ours to bed. It's been a long day."

They lay in bed, neither able to sleep. Ice was at the foot of the bed. He could sleep. In fact, he was snoring so loud that Lisa slipped out of bed and put him in the bathroom. Lisa said softly, "All we want will take a lot of money."

Bert whispered, as if there were a third person in the bathroom. "When money is concerned, of course, I can always sell the yacht!" he joked.

"And I could hock the ring!" Lisa teased.

"You make me feel so young, you 'young shrew.' I thought I was too tired and too mad for the thought that is stirring in my groin."

Lisa pulled off her gown and tossed it on the floor. "Skin to skin!" Bert followed suit, birthing suit. All thoughts of others disappeared in their embrace.

The next morning after coffee, there was not much else. The two, hand in hand, went out to size up the new barn and the white-fenced pasture. It was all anyone should wish for.

"I'm going to have to have my barn. The beauty of this whole place is so staggering. Honey, I've been around, but this takes the cake."

"You want a barn, too?" Lisa questioned. "I only want one or two to ride and get in with the 'horsy' crowd. You could have the other stalls."

"That's what you want?"

"I want a winning race horse. I'll need my own racing stable. We will find the best for you and the best for me."

"I'll get you an Arabian horse."

Funny how Burt can settle things his way in just a couple of minutes. Maybe that's why he is rich and maybe that's why he has no friends. Lisa sighed and wished he were different.

"I'll have to make sure Ice never wanders into the barns or the pastures. He could be killed. I can see it now, land, more and more land, all enclosed with beautiful white fences with mares, colts and beautiful thoroughbreds all gleaming in the bright sunlight. I'm glad he has loads of money."

Then she thought, "With the baby coming, I must ask him about his insurance. That won't go down well. If he wants a church wedding, that will be my trade off." Lisa sat far back in her chair. Her pregnancy was starting to show. She rubbed her tummy and said aloud, with no one to hear, "It sure is a boy. I didn't need to be told. This kid is a mover and a shaker. I must tell Ice about the blessed event. I wonder how he will take it when the baby is born. Some dogs become jealous."

She mused, "The baby is due in late March. The Garden show is February 12th. No one else is going to show Ice but me." Lisa realized she would have a fight on her hands. Regardless, that was the way it was going to be. "I'll just keep my mouth shut." Lisa drew her forefinger across her lips. "Silence, she promised herself.

"Up, up!" Bert called to Lisa, as he tightened his belt. "If you want to go with me, I'll give you 20 minutes. I'm not going to wait around. We can get a cup of coffee down the street." Bert was in charge, as usual. "Come on Lisa, we have lots to do today."

Lisa yawned a big slow yawn just to irritate Bert. "You know, it isn't good for an expectant mother to just jump out of bed."

"Then stay right where you are, damn it." He was mad as hell and said so.

"I'm up, I'm up! Throw me that pair of jeans on the chair. Give me ten minutes." She was ready. Ready for what?

Bert seldom drove himself, so Lisa was at the wheel of her red two-door sports car. "Where? To Copleir?" She selected the beanery at the corner.

"Lisa, what did you eat while I was gone? There isn't even any coffee that I could find." Bert grumbled.

CHAPTER 8

▼

"I've been up for hours." Bert told her as she sped along. "I know you need your sleep and it was pretty late last night till we got to sleep." He gave her a smile and a wink.

Lisa was thinking "He reminds me of the old adage of the carrot and the horse. He gives me just enough to keep me. I'm talking about personal affection."

"Are you talking to yourself?" Bert wanted to know. "I can see your lips moving.

"No, I was singing a tune to myself." She didn't look at him.

"Anyway, I called the bank and got the president. I told him what we wanted to do. I also talked to the guy who built your horse barn. Watson, at the bank, told me they were three-generation Kentuckians. They are good people to know. Aside from their horse barns, they know horses and people. George Watson is the name of the banker. He was very friendly."

He should be, Lisa thought. "When are they going to start your barn?" Lisa asked, after they had eaten at the beanery.

"I was told right away. Over there, pull over, that's their place—J. B. Sommers and Son—Builders of Fine Horse Barns. It was just like the ad in the paper. Here comes the guy right now."

Lisa's heart sank a bit when she turned toward her husband. The builder was in overalls and his face wore a white beard. Lisa hissed "damn it" under her breath. Be careful, she warned herself, Bert is no fool. Lisa loved action and so did Ice. They looked, they watched and they snooped. They tried to stay out of the way of the builders. Ice found the smell of new lumber very interesting. He lifted his leg again. He was marking his territory. Ice was out of place. This barn belonged to Mr. Sommers, who really didn't like Ice too much.

"Watch those wives," an Amish man warned. Funny, Lisa thought, he is a master electrician here, but he wouldn't have electric in his barn. I'm afraid I wouldn't want kerosene lanterns in my barn full of hay. Lisa and Bert were rank novices at what they were trying to do. They asked for advice and they got a lot of free help.

They were informed that horses do not come cheap, not good ones and especially racehorses. With racehorses, you are talking big bucks. Bert was so excited; his fine Boxer dogs were all but forgotten.

"Lisa, sweetheart, I want you to have a three-year-old Arabian mare, something beautiful but not a large horse. I want something to compare with your beauty when you ride."

"Hot dog! That guy sure has a line of bull, but I love it." Lisa laughed and went to answer the door. There stood the new housekeeper and butler. "Bert," she called, your friends are here." They did not look like too much to her. Lisa left the job of showing the house and their room to Bert. It was obvious that Bert knew them. "I'll bet they worked for his friend, Kitty."

"Lisa," Bert called. "Lahr wants to talk to you about the kitchen."

"Yes," Lisa addressed Lahr, and there was hostility from the word go.

"You will have to get help. I can't take care of a house this size and cook three meals a day and grocery shop, too."

"What is he supposed to do?" Lisa pointed to the man holding her suitcase.

"He'll look after Mr. Bert and answer the door."

"Okay, I'll see if I can get someone to help." Lisa turned to leave the kitchen.

"That's not all." Lahr stopped Lisa in her tracks. "I want full control of the grocery money." Lahr was even rude.

"That's fine. I'll set up a credit line with the store of my choice. That way, you won't have to worry about house money. Do I make myself clear?" Lisa was just as rude. Bert must be paying them well or she would have left. She walked to the study, red-faced and looking for a fight.

"Sommers," said Bert, "our builder, tells me there are good horse auctions held right here. I want to race a good challenging thoroughbred. Can't you see us in the box? The race is on and we are the favorite. He's coming down the stretch."

"And you wet your pants." Lisa interrupted.

"I get what I want. Just look around at my beautiful wife who is carrying my beautiful son. Gaze at our surrounding, the house, the land, and our health. God Bless!" Bert kissed two fingers of his own and raised them to the sky.

"Yes, we are lucky," she thought, too lucky. Something is bound to happen, seems like it always does. Lisa felt out of place. Ice was at her side. Lisa reached down to stroke his head. He will be ready for the Garden show. The babe inside reminded them both. Her hand left the dog and as Lisa placed her hand on her stomach, the baby kicked.

"We will have a party to meet our neighbors and make new friends." Bert was making plans. "Should we wait till everything is finished, horses and all, or should it be an outside barbecue? It isn't too cool, just a real good time of the year. There is nice color in the trees. October is a beautiful time of the year." He was talking to the room because he most certainly was not asking Lisa. Both she and Ice had left the room.

Bert found Lisa and Ice sitting on the patio. She was watching the setting sun. The sky was covered with rainbow colors. "You know, I'm sure that half of everything here is mine or are you forgetting that?"

"Of course, you are my wife," he conceded. "But you have not given your half." Bert made it clear that something wasn't right.

"What the hell did that mean?" Lisa asked herself. "I'll figure that later."

"I'm a patient man," Bert told himself. He was about to say so and decided against it. Instead, he said, "Let's go to the club."

Lisa could be disagreeable. If she got too much out of line, she would blame her condition. "My opinion, for what it's worth," Lisa sounded cold. "The barbecue is the best idea. That way, we can feel our way around here."

"That's ridiculous!" he slapped the magazine, *Horseman's Horses*, down on the table. "That was over a hundred years ago."

"Do you want to bet," was her reply. "Don't forget, we are Yankees." Bert had bought his way into the country club when he deposited a fortune in the favorite bank in town. He had simply asked the bank president to sponsor him.

"We will make the barbecue an event, like the brunch. This will be an event like no one has ever attended. We will have a grand opening of the stables, or better. I have an idea," which he did not share.

"We'll keep the party country, like a ho-down. We will get a chef to make large pots of 'country goulash.'"

"What's country goulash?"

"It's a lot of stuff together in a pot. The cook will know."

"You mean chili?"

"No, I don't mean chili. Whatever it is, it will be good."

"I'll get Gordon to build a temporary dance floor out on the patio. I'm in a party mood." Bert slapped the sides of his slacks.

"Who is Gordon?" Lisa yawned.

"He is the son of the building contractor. You know the one who built your barn." Bert took his cell phone from his shirt pocket.

"Was he talking about Gordon? Is Sommers the last name, Gordon Sommers? I see trouble." Lisa warned herself and the baby inside kicked again. "I can see it now, rough, loud, and vulgar. These people will have nothing to do with his 'barn party.'"

"Smarty, smarty, thought he'd have a party!" she sang off key to herself.

The party was a huge success. They came, much to Lisa's surprise. They ate hot dogs, beans and the best of all was Bert's goulash. They drank kegs of beer and the best liquor in the house. At 2:00 a.m., dancing was still underway. Everyone claimed they had a wonderful time. A voice saddled up close to Lisa's ear. "Don't try this as a formal affair, like at a club. They won't come, and don't look to be invited to their parties." Lisa knew from the warm breath on her neck, who was giving advice.

"Oh, hello, Gordon. I wondered if you were coming." Lisa smiled and flashed her eyes.

"You knew damn well I'd be here. Let's dance." The baby kicked once more.

The house was closed up tight. Lahr and Moses were helping, along with a lot of temporary help, to keep the party rolling. The washrooms in Lisa's barn were marked "Gals" and "Guys."

Ice was watching the brightly lighted party from a bedroom window. The light in the bedroom made Ice visible to the crowd, when some guest pointed, "That's the dog, and I've read about him! Go get the dog and bring him down. We all want to see the super dog." One who was a little drunk said, "Come on Bert. Be a good guy. We want to see this great show dog."

Bert, wanting to be a perfect host and a little drunk himself, was thinking about doing so when Lisa took charge. "No way!" she shouted at the small group, who were still there. "And, don't anyone else ask! The answer is NO!" That broke up the party and Lisa left to return to her dog.

"Those bastards! They will eat our food and drink our booze, but we are not good enough to enter their homes," Lisa reflected on her way to bed. Bert was already in bed asleep. But she continued, "Most of them are descendants of carpetbaggers. They think of us as Yankee trash." Bert stirred and so did Ice.

"What you talking about? Wasn't it a great party? Come give me a kiss." Lisa sat at the side of the bed and watched her husband fall back to sleep. Her thoughts fell to Gordon and the baby inside her kicked.

In the morning, Bert asked, "Honey, what happened last night? Why did they all leave at once?"

"Beats me," was Lisa's reply. Lisa was remembering how close Gordon held her as they danced. "Why can't I be satisfied with all I have?" She removed her 7-carat ring. "It's like an anchor," Lisa thought.

The social life didn't bother Lisa. It was the crust of these people that burned her. "I'm probably more Southern than most of them. My Revolutionary ancestor was a Virginia hero and I'm a Daughter of the American Revolution because of him." Lisa, now showing her "coming event," set out to prove a point. She discovered who was president of the Daughters of the American Revolution in her territory.

CHAPTER 9

▼

"And furthermore, I am a member of the Daughters of the American Colonists. That's the big one. Those people owned property before the American Revolution and if I want to be a real snot, I can prove I'm a Daughter of the American Confederacy. So, let them stick their noses down at me and I'll stick their noses in their own manure! It was my great, great, great grandfather who died at Gettysburg. All of this was on my mother's side, not the Irish side. They arrived much later." It made her think of Mom Mom, who liked to say, "I'm Kitty McGovern from County Coven, Ireland." Lisa's snobbery could match theirs anytime anywhere. She joined, paid her membership, and never attended a meeting. She just wanted her name on their books.

Lisa loved to shop and spend money. She wasn't buying for herself in her condition. She was shopping for the nursery. Lisa was decorating in yellow instead of blue. It upset Bert and she knew it would.

Lisa and Lahr were about to hang a criss-cross organdy curtain at the one large nursery window. Lahr spoke, "Don't you get up on that ladder. Mr. Bert isn't going to like this girly curtain. You need planter's shutters in all these windows across the back of this house. That's the way it's done in the South."

Lisa wanted to slap Lahr across the mouth. "How dare her." There had been respect, but no affection between the two women ever since she had taken over the beautiful home. Lisa knew she would be lost without Lahr. She also knew Bert would not allow friction on Lisa's part because Lisa was no cook or housekeeper. Things were going well, so dirty looks were as far as she went. When Lahr left the room, Lisa hung the curtain by herself and the baby inside kicked. While

Lisa was fooling with the curtain tiebacks, Lisa and Ice looked out the window just in time to see a horse van backing up to her barn.

Lisa, Lahr and the "house man," whom Lisa refused to call the "butler," all went running toward the action. Ice was not allowed to go because of his coat.

Out of the truck walked the most beautiful thing in all of "Horsedom." It was a three-year-old Arabian mare, a priceless horse. She shone and gleamed in the sunlight, like black satin. This creature had a mane that swished across her shoulders as she walked with a man attending her. The gate to the pasture was opened. Her action of grace and beauty showed, as she seemed to float in fairy tale movement. This brought out a cheer from Lisa. "Oh, my God." The horse hesitated a moment, turned and looked at Lisa. The baby inside her kicked. Lisa stretched out her hand and the lovely animal came to the fence.

"Oh Missy Lisa, look at them big soft eyes. How she gonna stand up on those skinny legs?" Lahr observed.

Bert was standing behind Lisa taking in the beautiful sight. The gorgeous October blue sky, the green, green grass of the pasture, all the white fencing and his beautiful wife excited with pleasure.

Lisa turned to Bert and snuggled in his arms, as he whispered, "She is all yours; beauty to beauty." In a louder voice he added, "She cost me a fortune. Her name is Jett, with two t's, to remind you I expect 'tender treatment.'" He laughed and kissed Lisa in front of everyone. "That's hers," he pointed to the free flowing horse, as she seemed to be chasing a butterfly. "But this one is mine," he hugged Lisa once more.

Out from behind the horse trailer came Gordon. "Ohhh," Lisa caught herself. "Where did you come from?" Lisa asked and at the same time, she felt Bert's eyes upon her. This time, the baby really kicked.

"I was part of the team." He smiled and shot her stare right into her eyes and let it linger there. Unbeknown to Lisa, but not to Bert, Gordon found reason to drive by the farm. He would stop and each time he would run into Bert. "Have the painters finished the barn?" Gordon asked. "Just checking."

"No," was the abrupt answer.

"Have your ordered the hay?"

"Yes," was all he would say. "That's twice," Bert thought. "Is he being helpful or looking for a piece of ass, my ass! Another time on a drop by."

"If you plant wheat now, the straw will be ready for winter," Gordon advised.

"Thanks," was Bert's answer.

Then there was the time that Bert was fed up with it when Gordon stopped at the barn and asked, "Have you decided to use wood chips? They are much nicer in the stalls. Oh hello, Mrs. Taloomas." Lisa happened to be there. Lisa blushed and Bert was watching.

Lisa was shopping for an English saddle when they ran into each other again. Sparks flew. People in the store sensed something was going on. "I'll show you what you should have." Gordon made a quick turn to be out of sight. He placed her hand on his crotch. It was hard and gnawing. They kissed for the first time. "You are driving me crazy." He panted. Gordon knew the store well. Holding Lisa in one arm, he rushed behind them and opened a closet door.

Big as a woman can get at six months did not stop him, either. "Lock the door," Lisa whispered.

Gordon's hands were all over her body, reaching for her enlarged breasts and sliding his lips and hands over the tight round tummy, he found what he was craving for.

"I'm going crazy for you." He whispered. "You have got to leave him, for your sake as well as mine. I see how he treats you. You are just another possession. I love you and I want you." His zipper was open and in a standing position, he tried to enter her body.

"No!" She drew back, but Gordon buried his tongue in her mouth and entry was heaven for both.

"He will kill us both." Lisa regretted her sin but only for a moment. "God, that was wonderful." She smiled as she tried to pull up her slacks. "When you open that door, make sure no one is out there," Lisa cautioned.

"It's okay," he said. And she slipped out the back door.

Lisa knew what she must look like. She combed her black hair with her fingers and found her car. No saddle was bought that day. Sex standing up was new to her. "Next time, we can try it covered with straw. I'm a sinner, that I know, but what a wonderful way to sin. Yes," she laughed. "I'm looking forward to a good 'roll in the hay.'"

Arriving home, bathed and dressed, Lisa and Bert had dinner at home. Lahr watched as the pair ate in silence. "How was your day?" Bert asked.

"I realize now I'm going to need help to select an English saddle." I looked today, but I didn't know what to look for." Lisa hardly looked at Bert.

"I saw you." He sipped his coffee and peered over the edge of its cup.

"When did you see me?" Lisa was terrified.

"You were in front of the dress shop. You were talking to a cop."

Lisa laughed in relief. "I talked him out of a parking ticket. I had overstayed my time."

"What did you buy?" Bert was making conversation.

"Nothing, I'll have to wait till I'm a size ten once more."

Thus ended the evening. Lisa went to the barn to see her horse. Bert made some long distance phone calls and one local one. On the local one, the detective informed, "She has been alone all day."

Lisa and her beautiful mare were becoming friends. Jett would take an apple from her hand. Jett allowed Lisa to groom and brush her long luscious mane and tail. Jett wasn't a tall horse. She was about 14 hands. She had such a beautiful concave face. The large soft eyes were placed just right. Her ears were small, while her muzzle tapered to the size of an apple. It was moonlight, not quite dark, when she entered Jett's stall.

"What you gonna do with that horse, missy?" Lahr had followed her.

"You frightened me." Lisa stomped her foot. "You frightened the horse, too.

"Now, let me tell you something." There was no accent. "You in your condition can be trampled by a jealous mare. She knows you are pregnant."

"Who are you to give me advice?" Lisa was trying to soothe horse.

"Another thing, missy, you smelled like Clorox when you came home today and I know you're not doing housecleaning."

"Lahr, you have got to go!"

"Before I go, Mr. Bert and I will have to have a talk!"

Lahr ruled the house after that. Her accent was restored.

Jett's mane was magnificent, as was her funny tail. Her grace was like that of a dancer. Lisa loved to stand at the fence and watch Jett dance and play all by herself. The sun was setting through the trees. There was just enough crispness in the air to make Lisa ashamed of herself. This is heaven on earth. She hugged the fence. "Why can't I be satisfied?" The baby kicked twice.

Each evening, after a good dinner that Lahr cooked, while Bert was on the phone, Lisa would go out to her barn to talk to her horse. Lisa loved the way her barn smelled of hay, oats, and straw over wood chips. What a fire hazard it could be if anyone smoked. Lisa didn't and neither did Bert.

One beautiful October day, Lisa and Ice were standing at the white fence. The horse came to Lisa and whinnied. She shook her beautiful black head and took off in a walk. She invited Lisa to follow her. Lisa had an apple in her hand. Jett seemed to float, as she returned to the fence. Without a thought, Lisa mounted the horse bareback, grabbing onto his mane for a way up, just as she had ridden her horse when a child at Mom Mom's. The unexpected event startled the horse enough to make her shy and Lisa found herself on the ground. The baby no longer kicked.

The "house man" had seen Lisa leave for the barn and noticed that she had not returned. Now it was dark. Moses, his name, called to Lahr. The two of them walked out to the covered swimming pool, where Ice was running back and forth barking and barking. Moses was frightened. He decided to notify Mr. Taloomas. Lahr took off on foot for the barn.

One tall and handsome man entered the hospital room. His face was hidden behind a large bouquet of flowers. "Stay only a minute." Lisa's nurse advised the visitor. The place was covered with flowers. Gordon looked around for a place to set his.

"I thought you didn't have any friends?"

CHAPTER 10

▼

"His friends and my family."

Gordon bent over and kissed Lisa very gently, as if he were afraid she would break. She had many bruises and a whopping black eye.

"Tell me you didn't do that stupid thing," Gordon scolded.

"I did." Lisa started to cry.

"Why, and in your condition?"

"It was a terrible mistake." Lisa turned her head away. She was crying as the nurse returned.

"Someone is waiting to see you."

"Who," Lisa asked. "Bert is in Atlanta."

The nurse handed her a card. "James Cory" it read.

"My God, what is he doing here? Yes, I'll see him."

Jim arrived with flowers also. "Lisa, I was coming here to see you. I know nothing about this." He referred to the hospital and her problem. "I've been asked to judge the Best in Show at the Garden." He tried to look sincere.

"And?"

"I know that would make things uncomfortable for both of us." Jim tried to feel her out.

"Not me." Lisa looked Jim dead in the eyes. "I hope you didn't make this trip to ask me to stay home."

"I'm in a spot, don't you see?" he almost pleaded.

"I'm coming. I'll be there. If it's a problem, it's your problem and not mine." Lisa rang for the nurse.

"I can see you are still a son of a bitch," Lisa called after him. The show of shows for the country was four months away. Nothing would stop her from being there with Ice in topcoat.

Bert was her third visitor that day. He reeked of liquor. "How could you do this to me?" He laid his head on her hospital bed and cried. Lisa cried also. They had lost their son. "I'm going to shoot that rotten horse," Bert sobbed.

"Shoot me Bert, but please don't blame Jett. I frightened her.

"I wanted to tell you that I'm leaving for Ireland."

"Wonderful," Lisa choked on a sob. "This time I can go with you."

"Not a chance, this is all business and you aren't ready to travel. I'll leave right after I get you home."

"No, I want to go. Please, I know you will be looking for a race horse. I want to go." Bert never denied her before, but this time, no meant no.

"Then you give me back my gun," Lisa pouted.

"I sold that thing. That was just a toy."

Lisa lay back in the bed. She rang for her nurse. "I need something to stop the milk coming into my breasts."

With that, Bert said, "Milk for my dead son!" Bert left the room without kissing her goodbye and she knew he had been to Atlanta for comfort.

"I know he saw Kitty." Lisa cried again.

Lisa reached for the phone. "Gordon," she asked.

"Yes, dear."

"Is anyone taking care of Jett?" she asked.

"I am. I'm not there all the day but I'm there by 4:00," Gordon explained.

"Get help. I'll call Bert and tell him I've hired a man to look after Jett till I get out of here." Lisa didn't tell Gordon she feared the worst because Bert had guns, lots of guns.

Lisa's night nurse was taking up her station. "I just saw your husband at the livery store. He was buying lots and lots of heavy rope," she told her patient.

"You don't need lots and lots of rope to hang yourself," she thought. "I wonder what Bert is up to? Maybe it's for the Boxers, who knows?" Lisa turned and fell asleep.

Lisa was scheduled to go home the next morning. She had called Lahr to have her remove and pack away all the things in the nursery. "Call the store and ask them to pick up the unused crib and chest of drawers. And take down the damn curtain. I'll order planter shutters for across the back of the house."

As it turned out, Lahr had nothing to do with the nursery. Bert had a huge fire going out back, so large that the fire department was called. The firefighters stood by and understood that the nursery was empty so the furniture was being burned. "My son and heir," one firefighter heard him say as he threw toys upon the fire.

Gordon understood and stayed away as long as Jett wasn't there. Bert had stashed Jett elsewhere.

Bert kept throwing things onto the fire. He was so drunk that a firefighter kept a close watch. Only Bert knew about the really long rope that was soaking in kerosene. He had hidden it in a corner of the basement of the beautiful old plantation home. Bert was filled with animosity and hate. He loathed Lisa, life and himself. Bert felt he had given, or offered Lisa, everything she ever wished for and in return, Lisa had given him nothing.

He returned to the house in a drunken state to call Kitty. "Stick by me Kitty, cause I have plans."

"You are drunk!" was Kitty's reply.

Lisa called Bert to come and get her. She was being released from the hospital. Lahr answered the phone. "He is not here, Miss Lisa. He left when the fireman decided it was safe to leave. I'll send Moses," her maid offered.

"No thanks, I'll call someone else."

Lisa was about to hang up when she heard, "There will be talk, missy," Lahr warned.

"Talk if I come home in a cab?" Lisa asked.

"No!" Lahr conceded.

However, she did call Gordon. He was more than pleased to take his lady home. "If that bastard shows up, he will get a piece of my mind," was Gordon's wish.

Bert didn't show up that day, or the next three days. He had taken his need for comfort to Atlanta to be with Kitty. Gordon and Lisa sat on the front porch swing and hugged and kissed, much to Lahr's disgust. The two walked hand in hand to Lisa's barn. "When are you going to bring Jett back here? I miss her so much."

"Maybe tomorrow? Don't forget, you are not completely well." Gordon had his arm around her.

"I won't ride her." Lisa put her arm around Gordon.

"What was that? I heard something." Gordon moved to the small windows in the barn.

"What are you doing?" Lisa asked anxiously.

"I swear I saw something move," Gordon replied. "Who in the hell put that stack of hay this close to the barn?" Gordon left her side and removed the hay.

Lisa followed Gordon. "I think we are being watched," she whispered.

"From now on, I think it best if we meet somewhere else." Gordon and Lisa were inside the empty barn.

Lisa agreed. "Servants talk and people love gossip."

"I love you darling." Gordon returned to her side. "I think I shall leave. I'll walk you back to the house."

Gordon didn't see the figure that saw him. And the long rope continued to soak in the kerosene.

Lisa walked through the tall white gate that separated the house from the barn and fields. She looked around. All she could think of was New York and the Garden. "First will be Thanksgiving. Nancy, my sister, wants me there. Then there will be Christmas. I don't want to think about Christmas; not without the family here. But," she smiled, "after Christmas, only six weeks to the Garden and Ice never looked better."

"Where did Bert go without a note or call? I hope he is okay." She worried for a minute.

Later, Lisa walked into the empty nursery, as she often did. Bert had torn off parts of the baby wallpaper. Lisa stood there tearing off the remaining strips. Tears rolled down her cheeks. "Why did Bert think he was the only one disappointed? Why were we not the perfect family? We had everything, but in reality, we had so little. He and his whore and I with a lover. Maybe Bert, Junior was not meant to be."

As Lisa turned to leave the nursery, she saw a spurt of orange color and wild red flames. In a second, her barn was encased in flames. Gordon appeared from nowhere. "They are on their way." The sound of fire engines clanging and screaming on their mission filled the air. Of course, it was no use. Everything was gone in minutes.

"Thank God, Jett wasn't here." Black smoke was splitting the evening blue sky.

Nothing gathers people together faster than a fire, especially a barn and the thought of horses within. A blazing fire throws the fear of God into the hearts of men.

The next day, volunteers, Gordon, and his friends came to clear the rubble. Gordon discovered some burnt rope. The rope gave him something to follow. He trailed the rope right up to a timer. "Who would have done this?" Gordon remembered the figure he saw before Lisa had tried to ride her horse.

Lisa was in bed unable to sleep when the bedside phone rang. It was Bert calling from Paris, France. "I'm glad you are okay," he said. "It was the horse I was after!"

"Bert, is this you? Paris, what are you doing in Paris?" Her head cleared. Now she was fully awake.

"Lisa, let me talk. Go to the bank. The key to the box is on my desk. Kitty and I are on our way to Greece. She tells me she is pregnant and it's a boy. So, my life isn't over yet and Kitty is Greek. I wish you the best at the Garden. I'll be there. Goodbye."

"What about his Boxers? I'm not going to take care of them. He really is a bastard."

"This is not my favorite breed of dogs," Lisa told Gordon as they walked toward Bert's kennels on the opposite side of the house.

"I think Boxers are handsome," Gordon offered his opinion.

"Not I. I think they look so naked."

Bert's kennels were locked, so they looked through the small highly placed windows. Lisa could not see, but Gordon, at 6'2", could tell her. "Everything is empty," he reported.

"Any sign of the kennel girls?"

"No dogs and no kennel maids. Everything is cleaned out. Looks like it was never used."

"I can't believe it. Bert must have planned his get away while I was in the hospital. What a rotten thing to do."

"He had to have help," Gordon reasoned. "This place is clean!"

"When you have his kind of money, everything is easy. Money talks, they say." Lisa quoted bitterly.

CHAPTER 11

▼

"What kind of business is he in?" Gordon had wondered many times.

"I really don't know. I asked more than once. His answer was standard," Lisa shrugged her shoulders.

"Like what?" Gordon persisted.

"Like in a conglomerate. He had many companies with many things and many places around the globe. Not too long ago, he was going to Ireland. I begged to go, but he claimed it was business. I'll bet he was trying to find a race horse."

No one mentioned the rope. "Let the insurance company find it," Gordon advised.

When Lisa and Gordon entered the big house through the back door, there stood Lahr.

"Whatcha wonna me do witch the kerosene and bucket? I found it in the basement." There was no accent on the last part of her question, and Lahr also knew that someone had set the fire.

"I think I can stand one more shock. I'm going to the bank in the morning. I want to empty the security bank box."

"I'll go with you, honey." Gordon invited himself.

"This I can handle. I'll give you a call tomorrow, Gordon." Somehow, he wasn't as attractive now.

The first thing Lisa picked up as she opened the safety deposit box was a note addressed to her and read:

I want that 18-karat bracelet returned, the one I never saw you wear. Send it to The Grand Hotel, Paris, France. I will have it picked up there. That expensive piece of jewelry is for the woman who can bear me a son.

There were other papers. Most of them were in Greek. At the bottom of the stash lay a large yellow envelope. Lisa reached into the envelope, which was addressed to her. Hand-written across the front he had written, "Open carefully. This is what I owe you." Inside, on a singe piece of white paper was written, "Nothing!"

As Lisa separated things in the box, she found something she could read. It was another envelope, half the size of the first. She was half-afraid to open it. Inside were the words, "See my lawyer, Lisa."

She sat down hard on the chair in the small room that the bank had for their customers while they placed things into their safety deposit boxes, or for their comfort and privacy, if they wanted to remove papers, jewelry, or items that they treasured. Lisa laughed and cried at the same time. "What am I going to do? I have very little money, just what I got for the sale of the house in Paradise, Pennsylvania."

Adding to her day, as she arrived home, there stood Lahr and Moses. They were dressed and packed. With pleasure, they announced, "We are leaving. We is gonna get married." Lahr announced in her fake accent she liked to use to annoy Lisa, that wasn't all. "Mr. Bert gave us ten thousand dollars to tell him what we saw around here." Moses told her with pride.

It was a bad day all around. "I wonder what lies that pair cooked up. I really don't care," Lisa added.

Ice crossed the room and placed his cold nose in Lisa's lap, as if to say, "I love you." Lisa sighed a soulful sigh, as she patted her dog. "What is going to happen next?" The dog was trying to comfort her. He licked Lisa's fingers and moved a little closer. "Thanks to flowers of sulfur and bacon drippings," she muttered.

Her hand ran through his beautiful coat. "Not a sign of a dry spot. Maybe," Lisa addressed the dog, "I should look up a chemist. You may have an important cure in your hair. Maybe all the bald-headed men could use some for posterity. I don't want to be poor. I like being rich."

The dog saw an improvement in Lisa's manner. He wagged his tail and gave a bark. "It's not too far away, dear old dog. You and I are going to make dog history in the show game." She knew her dog.

Lisa wondered about everything around her. All their possessions were in both names she thought. Her eyes fell on the 7-carat diamond ring on her finger. "I'd be lucky to get half of what he paid for this rock. The house and land will bring a very good price, but selling might take awhile. Then, there is Jett. No, that horse stays with me. I don't know much about horses. I sure do know dogs. But they are put together in much the same manner. Things aren't too bad. I have my youth and health. I did it before. I met Bert and I'll do it again." Lisa was seated alone in the large colonial mansion. She reached for the phone just as the doorbell rang.

Gordon entered smiling from ear to ear. "I want you to apply for a divorce immediately."

"What do you know? I just had a whole hour by myself without being told what to do. What's on your mind?" Lisa asked resentfully.

"Now, be nice." Gordon gave her the peace sign. "I know something is wrong. Should I come back?" he questioned.

"I have been left without a sou." Lisa was mad. "The bastard has left the country. He is on his way to Greece." Then she added, "and he has that woman with him."

"I thought he was the one who set the fire," he added. "It wasn't you, was it?"

There were no brownie points for Gordon after that remark. "Go away. Go home!" Lisa turned and left the parlor.

"What about Jett?" Gordon called after her.

"She will have to stay where she is for awhile. That is, till I know what I'm doing."

Later, she thought of taking Jett to her sister's small farm in Pennsylvania. Lisa knew that there was a beautiful empty back barn on her property. Lisa called and asked for help.

"Of course," was her sister's reply, "we would love to have you. You will have to take care of the horse yourself. We know not a thing about a horse. Now don't misunderstand." Ann was serious. "We would love to have you. You know, we have plenty of room for you and your horse. What about the dog?" Ann asked. "We have three dogs in the house now, plus the cat."

"I love you, Ann. Give my best to Harry. I'll try to think of something else. Bye dear." Lisa bit her lip.

"Are you off the phone?" Gordon asked.

"Yes!" The phone rang almost immediately. "Hi," Lisa spoke. It was Bert calling from Greece.

"Things are better this way," Bert tried to console. "My attorney is John Holt. He is downtown in the Holt Building. See him. I have filed for divorce and the attorney has a packet for you. Have a good life and I'll see you at the Garden in February." Bert hung up the phone without another word.

"What the hell are you doing?" Gordon was annoyed. "You are on the phone all the time!"

"It was Bert," was all she furnished.

Gordon's blue eyes were jealous slits. "What are the two of you cooking up?"

"I'm to see a lawyer; a John Holt," she informed quite briskly.

"That crook!" Without a goodbye, Gordon left the room. Lisa waited to hear the front door close. Gordon slammed it.

"At this point, I have nothing to lose," Lisa advised herself.

At first light, Lisa was up out of bed and set for a good run with Ice. The dog loved the air in the early morning. It was fresh, crisp, and exciting. Both of them romped and played. Lisa stopped to look at the burned out hole that once was her barn. "What am I going to do about Jett? Just when she started to know me and I her. Damn it! I will hate to give her up." Lisa laughed a cold laugh. "Hell, I might not even be able to live here."

"Today I'll call for an appointment to see the lawyer. Maybe Bert was kind, but I doubt it after those two stupid yellow envelopes he cast my way. He really is a son of a bitch. But I hope he was kind." Lisa lay on the soft damp grass and watched the sun create a new day.

It was a new day and a new life, as things turned out. Lisa could keep the house and all that it contained, along with all the land and $20,000.00 a month for life if she did not remarry. His note to her, "Why make some other son of a bitch suffer as I did." He added, "If you insist on marrying, go right ahead but make sure he has a dime because, sweetheart, it all ends here."

This was okay with Lisa. At this point, another husband was out of her mind. He was still trying to control her. "Men!" She looked further at the agreement and it said Bert and would pay all taxes and all maintenance for the house and grounds. There was nothing for horses and dogs.

John Holt, Bert's lawyer, or Jack, as he asked Lisa to call him, said, "You are aware your husband has applied for divorce."

"Yes, I know." Lisa was pleased with the terms. "He could have done a lot worse," the young woman thought.

Jack inquired, "Are you going to contest the divorce?'

"No way!" Lisa smiled.

"I love to see a woman who isn't afraid to wear color." Jack was on the make. He reached for her hand in a handshake. It was a dismissal. Lisa knew she looked good in red with her shiny black hair and eyes to match.

"One thing?" Lisa stopped at the office door. "When or where do I pick up my first monthly check?"

"It's set up with the Milton Bank."

"I need it now." Lisa wasn't kidding.

"Wait a moment. I'll see what I can do," the lawyer offered.

Lisa settled down on a very comfortable chair. Looking around at the luxurious office, Lisa thought, "I wonder if he is the main man here." She could see other offices behind glass.

CHAPTER 12

▼

"It's all set," said the man in the French cuffs and tailored grey suit as he made his move. "I'm going your way. Let's have lunch and get acquainted." The two went to the oldest country club in Lexington for a very long lunch.

Lisa was noticed for her beauty and as the wife of the rich Greek. Others had heard of her love of animals; in particular, her Arabian mare that someone they knew had been pressured to sell. She was not being overlooked. Lisa knew it and so did Jack. He loved the looks and stares. The gossip was so evident you could read their lips. "What is she doing here? Is Jack out for another? I thought she was married to some gangster? God, I hope she isn't trying to get into our club." Their husbands were looking, too. They were not talking; just enjoying the beautiful young woman in the red suit.

"My dear Mrs. Taloomas," he reached for her hand. One of the wives at another table took notice. She was so upset she had to leave the club dining room and headed for the ladies room. "Mrs. Taloomas," he continued, "What was your maiden name?"

"McHugh," she responded.

"I'll bet you will assume that instead of Taloomas?"

"I'm not sure what I'll do."

Jack decided to forget that approach. They talked about other things. Lisa found out a lot more about her area than she really wanted to know. The rumors and tales were interesting. The men, who knew full well that they would be talking about her to "their crowd," were especially telling these tales.

"Honey," Jack was getting cozy after his second drink. "I hope you know you could be asking for twice as much. He is a very rich man. He wants the divorce as quickly as possible. He wants to get married."

"Get me another ten thousand per month and then I could afford to stay here in style."

"I was hoping you planned to stay here." Jack squeezed the hand he was holding.

"He's no better than I am," Lisa thought, as she pulled her hand away. "Thirty thousand a month; close to half a million a year. Hot dog!"

When Lisa returned home, she found Lahr encased in the largest, softest, most comfortable chair on the front porch. "What the hell are you doing here?" Lisa approached her, as though she was going to pull her out of her spot of comfort.

"I's want my job back," the woman of color stated in a matter of fact way.

"You want what? Do you think I'm crazy?" Lisa had had a drink or two. She wasn't used to drinking. "Get off my porch!" she demanded. With outstretched arms, she went for Lahr's throat. She managed to upset the chair and with a heavy foot, she kicked Lahr off the porch. "And stay away or I'll call the police!" Lisa looked down and saw that Lahr had ripped off her pocket on her lovely red suit. That didn't help matters. At that point, Lahr would have settled for the police. Instead, she got up and decked Lisa in the front yard. Lisa was shaken. She hoped no one had witnessed the scramble.

While she was shaking off fall leaves and grass, a voice behind her said, "I'm staying!"

"Where did you learn that trick?" Lisa faced her.

"I got more than one, missy. I know who burned down the stable," the former maid stated boldly.

"Who?"

"You!" Lahr shouted.

"What, you she witch!" Lisa shoved her.

Recovering her balance, Lahr shook her finger. "I saw that rope soaking in the kerosene. You done it. It was you missy!"

"I'm calling the police. This is blackmail!"

"You call the police and I'm really going to stick it to you." The accent was gone again, but the threat was still there. Lahr followed Lisa into the house. "Missy, let's not fight. I need a job and a place to stay. Moses didn't marry me. He left town with the money. I'm a good woman. It was that I wanted to get married. I like Ice," Lahr continued. "Ice likes me. You won't be sorry," Lahr promised.

"Jail is where you belong. I'll give you one week." Lisa didn't believe her own ears. "Why am I doing this?"

Now Lahr wanted to get in solid. "Mr. Bert set the fire."

"How do you know?"

"I's knows!"

"Cut out that accent crap!" Lisa couldn't believe Bert wanted to kill Jett!

"Mr. Bert had Moses buy the kerosene and I saw him drop the rope into the tub."

Lisa wanted more proof, as she trailed after Lahr to the maid's former bedroom. Lahr was making herself at home, as she hung her clothes in the closet. Lisa was braced against the bedroom doorframe. "Can you prove what you have said?"

"Yes, I can, but I won't," was Lahr's pronouncement.

"That rat!" Lisa started down the stairs.

Lahr hung over the banister. "That's why he gave us money. He knew I saw him drop the rope."

"What did you think he was going to do with the rope?"

"Just what he did," was Lahr's reply.

"All this is too much for me. You do one thing that I don't like, you are out. You understand?" Lisa meant it.

Lisa thought, "I can use her, but I don't know if I can put up with that woman. I'm going to need help getting to New York." Lisa reached for the phone to call Gordon.

"What do you want for dinner?" Lahr entered the large family room to ask.

Lisa put her hand over the phone. "Anything will do. I had a large lunch."

"I know," Lahr snickered. "My brother is a waiter at the country club."

Lisa told Gordon the story. "The police knew it was set. But, there were no prints to be found. The police thought it was Moses because he skipped town."

"I can't believe you took that woman back." Gordon shook his head. "That was a stupid thing to do," he continued. "You don't need her help for the Garden show. I was planning to go with you."

"No overnights with me. I'm not ready for that," was her answer.

"Well, fuck you! What about in the livery store closet?" Gordon was burning.

"That was not for all to see and know. Gordon, get lost! I don't want any more fights today."

Lisa sat before the fire eating a light supper. The flames from the fire flickered and made shadows in her favorite room. Her thoughts flowed back to her lunch and Jack Holt. "I'm sure he is a scoundrel." The thought made her smile. "Why do women like bad boys?"

Ice was given a little bit from her plate. Ice pushed her knee with his paw. It was his way of saying, "More, one more morsel."

Lisa kept watch on Lahr and Lahr kept watch on Lisa. It was an unusual truce.

Gordon arrived early the next morning. He apologized and asked her how she had made out at the bank. "I hope you will take this in the manner I'm offering it. Do you need money?" Gordon was about to make an offer.

"Thank you, darling. I'm going to be all right. I'll be fine." She crossed the room and took his hand. "I'm sorry; also I have a short fuse."

"You're telling me!" Gordon took the independent beauty in his arms and kissed her, not once but twice. Guess who was looking, Lahr and Ice. Both were jealous. "Tell me all that happened." Gordon pulled up a chair closer to Lisa.

Her inner voice called for caution. "He took me to lunch and gave me some free advice."

"Like what?" Gordon moved closer.

"I can keep the farm and I can afford to replace the barn. Bert wants a divorce. That's the first of it."

"Good, all the way around." Gordon suggested they take a walk. The night air was crispy, brisk, and refreshing. Signs of Christmas were at hand.

"I love Christmas." Lisa squeezed his hand. Gordon placed both of their hands into a large, warm pocket in his parka. "What do you want for Christmas?" Lisa asked trying to keep up with his long stride.

"You and only you!" Gordon pulled her close. "I love you, my pet. I have never loved before." Gordon picked Lisa up in his arms and they sat on a bench reserved for bus riders.

"I'm waiting." he whispered, but Lisa didn't answer. Gordon got the message. He changed the subject. "I heard you created quite a stir at the club."

"Like what?"

"It seems you turned a few heads."

"Who said?" Lisa wanted details.

"My mother said. She was there playing bridge."

They walked in silence. The moon in the late harvest sky shone huge and bright. No one was holding hands. Gordon left her at the door without a kiss or remark.

Days passed without a word from Gordon.

Lisa noticed the humble talk and accent were disappearing from Lahr when she spoke. "What is going on here?" she asked Lahr. "Are you watching me?"

"No, that was Moses. I don't spy," Lahr lied.

Lisa pretended to accept her word. "Be careful!" she warned herself. "I am not comfortable. Could it be Bert or even Gordon? Who knows, maybe Jack Holt. I'm sure there is mischief about!" It was none of those she had suspected. Jim Cory was the culprit. Jim, the dog show judge, who had molested her at four and raped her at ten. He was a first-rate snake in the grass. He had befriended Lahr and had come to the house when Lisa was in the hospital and while Bert was away.

CHAPTER 13

▼

Jim Cory and Lahr had worked out a deal. Money had changed hands.

Lisa tried to shake off her feelings of distrust by being busy with Christmas. "It's the little girl in me," she told Lahr. "This is the most wonderful time of the year. I'm going to need your help. I want to buy toys for children and take them to the hospital.

"There are groups that do that; Toys for Tots or something like that. You don't have to bother. Just give them a big check." Lahr pulled the rug out from under Lisa.

"Oh damn! You ruin even Christmas!" Lisa threw a sofa pillow at Lahr. Christmas was not just a Holy time. She wanted to decorate the house inside and outside, as well. Lisa would place Christmas wreaths and electric candles at all the windows.

"You can hire someone to do all that," Lahr advised. "It's better than falling off a ladder."

"Oh shut up, you scrooge!" Lisa was ready to drop a wreath over Lahr's head. "Go, get out of my sight!"

Lisa found that she was being invited to Christmas parties. Gordon escorted her to the club dance and Jack Holt waltzed her around. The divorce was over and now she had been accepted, as she had hoped from the beginning.

All this glitz and glow had to be left behind, as she had promised her mother that she would be home for Christmas. The young woman told Jack Holt that she would be back from Pennsylvania for the big gala New Years Eve dance at the club. Her gift to Lahr was a ½-inch 18-karat gold necklace with the promise she would stay and take care of the place until she returned.

Her red sports car, packed to the top with gifts, Lisa and Ice were on their way. She had not heard from Gordon for days. "Who cares?" Lisa tossed the thought off her shoulders. "Jack is more fun."

After the first hour of traveling north, it began to snow. The roads were wet, glossy, and slippery. The car was fairly new and it held the road.

"Ice, look! Isn't it beautiful?" She turned the head of Ice, who was seated next to her. "Look!" Lisa repeated. The world around them was becoming a fairyland. Ice decided to move around and bark at the large floating snowflakes. Lisa started to look for a place to spend the night. They would reach her "childhood" home the next day. "Oh, I just love Christmas." Lisa hugged her gorgeous white dog.

The motel was decorated for Christmas. Colored lights shone against the diamond-like gifts from the sky. Artificial snowmen were being covered by the real thing. Green wreaths and electric candles were at every window.

Lisa took snow off the windshield to make a snowball and threw it at the head of Ice. Lisa slipped and fell. She lay laughing while Ice, the dog, licked the tears away. "Let me help you to your feet." He said, "You are covered with snow." The man was Gordon. He had followed her the entire way, always trying to be at least two cars behind. Lisa had never recognized him or his car.

Lahr had told him she was going to Carlisle, Pennsylvania for Christmas, "fer a fee." She also called him when Lisa left with Christmas presents loaded in the car. "I don't know how she will be able to drive and see." That was the remark that helped Gordon make up his mind to follow, that and one more thing.

Lisa was glad to see him. She was in such a Christmas mood. Once on her feet, she threw her arms around him shouting, "Merry Christmas!" After registering and paying extra for Ice, Lisa asked Gordon, "How did you know how to find me?"

"I followed you," he laughed his wonderful laugh.

"You didn't. Why?" she asked.

"I have your Christmas gift."

"You are crazy, but I love you." Lisa had not planned to say that. "I'm sorry; I didn't plan to say that." Lisa bit her lip.

"To say what?" he kidded.

"That I love you," she repeated.

"I heard you the first time. I wanted to hear it again."

"You didn't let me finish." She wasn't able to say anymore because Gordon had covered her mouth with his lips.

176 DOG MYSTERIES

"I've taken the adjoining room. Ice can have this one tonight." Gordon had plans. "I'm sure you know by now that I've fallen in love with you, sweetheart." Gordon's room was connected, so there was no need to go out into the weather. It was 4:00pm and he reached for the phone and ordered dinner for 6:00 o'clock.

Cuddled up with all the pillows of both rooms, their heads together on a single bed, Lisa asked, "What is my Christmas present?"

"This," he answered, as he ran his hand up and under her sweater. He kissed her between her round soft breasts. "I love you." Gordon whispered trying to hold his passion. "Why can't you love me?"

"But I do, I really do, darling. The timing isn't right." Lisa lifted his head and kissed him softly at first. They embraced and all time was forgotten. It was almost 6:00 p.m. when there was a rap at the door.

"I should have made it 8:00 o'clock." The tall handsome young man laughed, as Lisa grabbed her clothes and ran for the adjoining room.

It was still snowing late into the evening when Lisa suggested, "Let's turn off the lights and watch the large falling snowflakes." They glistened and shone like diamonds in the moonlight. The trees and decorations were covered with the white stuff and the little girl in Lisa wanted to go outside and play.

Ice thought it a wonderful idea, too. Gordon stood in disbelief as Lisa tossed him his jacket and opened the front door. "Last one out, is out," she called as Ice followed her out into the night. Gordon tossed a snowball that hit Lisa at the center of her back. Lisa lay back in the snow and made an angel by moving her arms back and forth. Gordon picked her up and stuffed some snow down her neck. Lisa didn't like that and neither did Ice. Together, they had him down and covered with snow.

Back in the warm room, they all shook off snow. Gordon suggested, "It's time for a drink."

"That was wonderful." Lisa was rosy from the cold and a drink sounded good, but only one. She remembered another time when she was a little drunk. They clicked their glasses and Lisa asked, "Now tell me, what is my Christmas present?"

"You just had it," he teased.

"The roll in the snow or the roll in the hay?" she laughed.

"Take your pick." He wasn't teasing now, as he made himself another drink. The ring he had for her was still in his pocket.

When they awoke the next morning, the world was covered with ice. It looked like a fairyland. Every twig, every bush, and every blade of grass was frozen in place. The sight was strikingly beautiful. Gordon walked outside. The roads were clear, but they were covered with black ice, the kind that makes a car slide out of control. Gordon was dressing. Lisa covered her head in complete satisfaction. "I don't want to move," she mumbled from under the sheet."

"Okay, there is a coffee maker here in the room. I'll walk over to the restaurant and get some Danish or donuts? Can Ice eat a donut?"

"No, I'll get his food. It's in my car."

Dressed and ready to leave, Gordon warned her of the dangerous roads ahead. "The sun is out and everything is melting. The cinder trucks are out, but be careful and call me when you get there. Promise?"

"I thought you were going on to Carlisle with me?"

"No, sweetheart, you have Christmas with your family. I'll see you when you get back. Remember, I love you." He kissed her for the last time. The ring was still in his pocket. They parted. Gordon went south and Lisa went north.

The sun was very bright and the glistening ice-covered trees and shrubs along the roadside made it hard to watch the road. Dark glasses helped, but not too much in the blinding sunlight. Lisa was beginning to wish she had remained at the motel one more day.

Gordon, after all the sound advice he had given Lisa, found himself in the same position. "Careful, careful!" He just tapped the brake on a wide curve ahead to be confronted by a large R.V. lying on its side. It covered the entire width of the road and was directly in front of him. Gordon was dead with the diamond ring still in his pocket. He was a beautiful young man, a terrible loss.

When Lisa reached her mother's house, she was greeted with, "Someone has been calling for you. He has been calling all day."

"Probably Gordon, a friend of mine. I'll call later."

Lisa was loaded down with gaily-wrapped packages. Her mother helped to place the many gifts under the huge Christmas tree. The tree was the showplace of the room. It was covered with treasures from an earlier time.

After greeting all, Lisa made the phone call. Lisa swayed and almost fell. "No, no, it can't be!" Lisa was told that Gordon was dead.

"The dearest friend I ever had has been killed in a highway accident." Lisa sobbed. "I can't believe it. I saw him only last night. I have to go back," she wept. Ice sensed the tragedy and came to her side. "Only last night the three of us were playing in the snow."

"Three?"

"He, the dog, and I." At this point, her mother took over. She held Lisa in her arms and encouraged her to cry.

"Spend the night and we will talk in the morning." Her mother led Lisa into the kitchen of the big farmhouse. "You must eat something." She brought Lisa a hot cup of coffee. "Drink," she ordered, "While I fix something." The mother's hand was shaking as she made a sandwich and added several homemade Christmas cookies to the plate. "Now tell me about this," her mother encouraged.

"I" sob "think" sob "that he was going to ask me to marry him but I wasn't ready." She blew her nose on the paper napkin.

"I understand that. You needed some freedom. You were newly divorced, probably confused."

The mother was trying hard not to let this spoil Christmas for the others, who were already in the house. At the same time, she felt sorry for her youngest daughter.

There were four girls, Nancy, Mary, Rose, and Lisa. They had never been close because they all had different interests. Lisa was the only one that ever gave her trouble. Lisa was the baby.

CHAPTER 14

▼

It was a large country kitchen; very familiar to Lisa with its pale yellow walls and crisp white curtains. It had never changed with the times. Her mother didn't have a dishwasher because she didn't want one. She liked to look out her window along the sink. She enjoyed her lovely garden in summer, spring, and fall. In addition, this day, with melting snow the Blue Jays and Cardinals were out there feeding on the peanuts she had provided.

There was a clothes washer in the basement, but no dryer because she loved to hang her sheets and clothes in the fresh air, even in winter when the towels froze stiff. Out they went. If it was raining, she hung them in the basement. Monday was washday. On Tuesday, she ironed, Wednesday she house cleaned, Thursday she shopped, and on Friday, she played bridge with the girls. Saturday was a movie or a lunch and Sunday was church. This is how she lived. Mary still lived at home. She was a schoolteacher; not an exciting life, but it was a good one. Mother's name was Ruth.

Ruth was not an old woman, not yet 50 years old. She had been without a man ever since her husband and Lisa's father had gone to Ireland at the age of 39. His body was shipped home and was buried nearby. Ruth knew why he had gone, not alone but with other Irish men, who were mostly kin. A list of their names was in the hearts of the people they left behind. This list was not written down.

Lisa woke from a troubled night. "Why didn't I insist he follow me? Was it because I didn't want him? I swear I cared. I just wasn't ready for marriage. I had the Garden on my mind. Damn the Garden! It has been my albatross."

She reached over and hugged her companion, who had shared her bed. She started to cry again. Her salty tears were wiped away by a long, red tongue. "I love you, Ice." She wept and buried her head into the dog's massive front and shoulder coat, a trim ready for the show ring. "What should I do?" she asked the dog.

Ice had the answer. He jumped off the bed and tugged at her pajama leg. "Let's go home." He wagged his pompom tail.

Breakfast was as festive and happy as her mother would allow when she saw the sleepless red eyes of her daughter. "I don't want any food." Lisa looked terrible.

"We had a meeting this morning." Mary, the eldest daughter, announced. "When you are ready to leave, I'm going with you."

"Why?" Lisa wiped her eyes and blew her nose. "Why would you miss Christmas here?"

"Because, we all love you." Mary replied.

They all got up from the table and gathered around Lisa. Lisa broke down once more. The sisters were surprised to see her so distraught. She never cried when they were kids. "It must have something to do with the loss of the baby." Her mother whispered to Mary, "Be gentle to her."

The back seat and trunk of the car was free of Christmas boxes. This gave Ice the whole back seat. The white dog leaning against the cream-colored leather in Lisa's two-door Lexus made Lisa laugh for the first time in the past 24 hours.

Her sister, Mary, looked like a spinster schoolteacher. She was very tall, almost 6 feet. Her glasses were thick-rimmed and the worst. Her large brown eyes were nice and her natural rich auburn hair was very nice. Her hair was pulled back into a tight twist. Lisa took a good look and decided there would be a few changes.

"I'll drive, give me the keys." Mary took over and it was okay with Lisa. Even Ice noticed the new boss and decided to behave. Once underway, Mary informed, "We will take Route 81 south to Natural Bridge, Virginia. It will be a good while. Try to relax, even take a nap. We had a good breakfast, so we won't need to stop. Mother packed some food for us."

Lisa wasn't listening. She had fallen asleep, a sleep she needed.

When they left the road in Virginia, Mary turned onto Route 64 going west. There she stopped for gas and the keys to the restroom. Even then, Lisa had to be awakened. Ice needed a rest stop, too. "Potty stop for three," Mary told them. "I'll make reservations for tonight." Mary had always wanted to stay at the hotel at White Sulfur Springs, West Virginia. She had seen pictures and friends had told her about the place. "No motel for him tonight. If they won't take dogs, he can stay in the car."

When Lisa was sure no one was around, she walked Ice over to some grass. The dog was much relieved and so was Lisa. "I couldn't use that filthy toilet." Mary handed the garage man his restroom keys with a lecture on sanitation.

"I'll take the wheel for awhile." Lisa tried to get into the driver's seat.

"Oh, no." Mary took over the car. "You can drive tomorrow."

"Not tomorrow. I want to drive straight through," Lisa pouted like a child.

"Tomorrow is your day." The schoolteacher took off, as all heads bounced, including the dogs. "I never had a chance to drive a car like this one." What she wanted to say was, "You are not in any shape to drive, Lisa." Lisa did not have much to say. In no time, she was back to sleep.

The large sign at the side of the road read: "Welcome to Wild and Beautiful West Virginia." The sign said it all. The roads were completely clear, but the trees and bushes along the side of the highway were still covered by a lot of snow. It was a wonderful world of beauty. Mary realized she had missed so much of life by teaching first grade for years. "I've never had a boyfriend. Maybe that's why I look so sour." She thought of many things as she covered the miles alone. Lisa was snoring and so was Ice.

As Mary approached the town she was looking for, she found herself stuck in 4:00 o'clock traffic. People were hurrying along the street; most loaded down with packages. Men, women, and kids waved to each other. Mary heard "Merry Christmas" everywhere because her car window was open. Mary, to her own amazement, called "Merry Christmas" to the traffic cop she drove past.

The hotel was all Mary could wish for. The outside was a dream of loveliness. There were tall trees covered with lights, huge wreaths on all the large outside windows and a red carpet up the front walk-up of the stairs and into the lobby of this beautiful white hotel. It didn't matter where you looked; it was Christmas in total splendor. "Awesome," was all that this 28-year-old woman, who still lived at home with her mother, could say.

Mary told Lisa to stay in the car and that she would register. As she approached the desk, she saw a choral group gathering. They were boys dressed in red and white, like altar boys. At the first note, Mary lost it. It was her turn to cry.

When Mary started to register, her eyes caught a small formal sign that said, "No Dogs." That didn't stop her. Mary registered.

The doorman had called for help. The bags were on their way and Lisa, with Ice, paraded to the elevator. People smiled and made room for the elegant dog, as they rode to Floor 12.

They bathed, ordered dinner, and admired the view from the large decorated windows. There was a Christmas tree and a fire glowing from the fireplace. Mary had ordered a suite.

"Great balls!" Mary slapped her hip. "This is the most wonderful Christmas since Dad was home and I was a kid."

"Do you remember him? I was a baby."

"Not very well, but I do remember when the Irish Republican Army returned his passport."

"That would mean he was dead?" It was a question.

"I would think so. Mother never talked about it." Mary changed the subject.

The next day, they were home.

"Your room is next to mine," Lisa told her sister. "I'm getting a bath and we can go to the club for supper. Look around and make yourself at home. Looks like the maid took her Christmas bonus and left town. She was supposed to stay here and look after things. Can't turn your back with her." Lisa was fussing and unpacking.

There was a knock on the door. Mary didn't wait for an invitation to enter the bedroom. She was in. "What the hell is that sun-tanned witch doing in the kitchen? She looked and me and demanded, 'Who yous? Whatcha wan?' Then, she reached for a butcher's knife. I swear it was 2 feet long."

"Oh, come on, that is Lahr. She is the self-appointed maid. Someone told her we were back."

"I don't like her," Mary stated.

"That's nothing. I don't like her either." Lisa left the room to the amazement of Mary.

"When we go downstairs, I'll announce that I want to call Mother," Mary suggested. "I'll bet you dinner Lahr will be on another phone listening." Mary was ruffled. Lahr met them as they came down the stairs.

"I want you to meet my sister, Miss Mary Mc Hugh."

"I figured. I'm sorry about your boyfriend, Missy."

"He was only a good friend," Lisa was firm.

"Not what I know!"

"What do you know?" Lisa was aware her sister was taking it all in. "If you know so damn much, what are you trying to say?" Lisa was losing it.

"They found a diamond ring in his pocket. It was marked, 'Lisa 04 Gordon.'" Lahr announced with satisfaction.

"How do you know this?" Lisa grabbed her arm and spun Lahr around.

"We maids could write a book," Lahr laughed in Lisa's face.

Mary was horrified!

CHAPTER 15

━━━━━━━━━━━ ▼ ━━━━━━━━━━━

The sisters returned upstairs. Lisa called to Lahr, "We will eat out tonight. Maids have had a system of communication since slavery," Lisa explained.

"That woman isn't African. I'll bet she is from Port au Prince. She has blue eyes and when she forgets, she has no accent. What do you know about her?" Mary was afraid for her sister.

"Could she be Greek?" Lisa asked.

"Could be but I'd guess Gypsy." Mary had Lisa shook up.

"My God, I've read where some of those people eat dogs. I'll get rid of her in the morning."

"No!" Mary played older sister. "Get rid of her right now!"

"If you don't want the job, I'll be glad to do it!" Off she went to the kitchen.

Lisa stayed in her room. Mary stood over Lahr as she packed her things.

"Here," Mary stuffed money that Lisa had given her. "This will take care of you for a day or two." When Lahr opened her purse, it was stuffed with money and a 7-carat diamond ring.

Lahr saw Mary spot the ring, so she swallowed it on her way out to the cab Lisa had hired.

Lahr was gone for good or so they thought.

"How could I have been so stupid? I don't give a damn about the 7-carat ring. I was glad not to have to wear the gaudy thing," Lisa continued. "She won't be able to sell it. No jeweler would take a chance."

"But, a fence would," Mary offered.

After a day or two, Lisa managed to get her brain together. "Why didn't she hear anything from Gordon's family?" She decided to call. She did and was told it was a family matter. "I should have stayed in Carlisle with my family," she thought.

She called several funeral parlors and found the one who had attended the body. Yes, he had taken care of things. The body was cremated and it was a family affair. "Who wants to know?" Lisa hung up.

Lisa called the local jeweler. She identified herself and told him of the loss of her 7-carat diamond ring. She also asked, "Have you seen a diamond ring with an engraving 'Lisa 04 Gordon?'"

"Yes!" was his answer. "It's here right now."

Lisa decided to try to forget the past, even the bastard Jim Cory. "Tomorrow is another day." Since no one other than Lahr and Mary knew about the love affair between Gordon and herself, she felt safe in asking Gordon's father to rebuild her barn. "Wait till you see this happen." Lisa told her sister. "The Amish, like back home, will build a beautiful barn in three days."

After everything was finished, she sent for Jett, her beautiful Arabian mare. And then she introduced Jett to Mary. It was love at first sight.

Christmas was festive due to Mary's insistence. They had a tree, presents, and a turkey. Lisa invited her lawyer friend to join them for Christmas dinner. After a drink or two, the three had a Merry Christmas. Lisa didn't mention Gordon and asked her sister to refrain. Before he left the lovely home, Jack spoke. "I must congratulate the two beautiful ladies. Your dinner was delicious. Did you really cook the wonderful meal by yourselves?"

"Pennsylvania style!" Mary bowed.

"Don't forget New Years. I'll be here for both of you at 8:00 p.m." He returned Mary's bow and stepped out into the freezing night. Lisa smiled and Mary giggled.

"What a catch!"

"New Years! Did you bring a smashing dress?" Lisa wanted to know.

"Like what?'

"Beads and stuff?"

"You know I wouldn't wear that confetti."

Mary had never been asked out and had no need for anything but teacher's clothes. "You will be stepping high that night. Let me take you shopping." Lisa called her favorite shop.

They found the perfect dress. It was long and black with most of the back missing. It was just right for Mary's figure that she had always hidden.

Jack Holt called earlier on the "special day." "One of my friends just hit town. May I bring him along tonight?"

"Great!" Lisa smiled a wide grin and then both girls giggled.

"I should feel guilty so soon after Gordon, but I don't. Shame on me."

They were like two teenagers as they walked to the barn. Jett whinnied at the sight of them.

"And who are you I might ask?" Lisa was surprised and alarmed to see a stranger on her property.

"I'm Tom," the young man answered. "I'm the one who took care of Jett at the boarding farm."

"Why are you here?" Lisa was not pleased.

"I was told you needed help." Tom continued, "You would not make a mistake if you hired me. I can do anything when it comes to horses; and I love Jett."

Lisa thought he sounded a bit slow. "Come inside the barn." She wanted more information. Jett recognized Tom. The mare came to the man. In the better light, Lisa saw the large blue birthmark on this side of his face.

Mary stepped forward. "Tell us something about yourself."

"I have my M.B.A. from North Carolina State. That was for my Mother and Dad. It was not for me. My life is horses. I paint them, I write about them and I live with them. Horses treat me like a man. No one else does." His statement was not bitter.

"You are hired!" Lisa returned to the house to try to figure what to offer.

She thought, "He can stay here if he wants. There are brand new quarters. He would be free to come and go. Jett likes him. Maybe I should offer him respect and have him tell me what *he* wants. I'll see to it tomorrow."

They had fun getting dressed for the New Year's dance.

When Mary slipped on her black bias-cut dress that followed every curve in front and was backless to her waist, she was no longer, "Mary the teacher." Lisa grabbed a handful of auburn hair and piled it high on her sister's head. "My God, you are gorgeous! Give me those glasses."

Mary complained, "I can't see."

"Tonight, I'll guide you." Lisa laughed and put Mary's glasses in her purse just in case.

"This is an amazing dress." Mary was looking at herself in a full glass mirror. "I have nothing on underneath, not even panties because I don't want the panty line to show."

"Don't worry, you are safe enough. Expensive clothes have the underside well taken care of. Nothing will fall off or out," Lisa reassured with a laugh.

Jack Holt was pleased to introduce the beautiful woman to his friend. Mary tried to have a good time. Jack's friend, Major Ron Williams, was dashing in uniform. He was flattered by his friend's choice for the evening. But, there was something wrong. Mary drank more than Lisa expected.

The reason for her behavior was understandable. She would have much rather been with the handsome half-faced man at the barn. "Poor Tom," Mary sighed to herself.

"Happy New Year!" Lisa called through Mary's door. "Remember, we have to have pork, sauerkraut, mashed potatoes, and applesauce today." There was no answer. Lisa peeked. The bed was still made.

"Now where in hell has she gone?" Lisa walked to the window. Mary was watching Tom exercise Jett. Lisa was about to join them when the phone rang.

"Do you really mean pork and sauerkraut?"

"Yes, it's traditional for good luck the year through, although I've thought other reasons." Lisa laughed, she knew it was Jack.

"Down here, we have black eyed peas," Jack continued.

"What are they?"

"You'll see." Jack Holt laughed.

Later there was an argument. "I don't care if he is a groom or stable boy. My God, you make him sound like Heath cliff. I have asked him to come to dinner."

"Mary, Mary, don't spoil my day." Lisa was unhappy.

When Lisa explained things to Jack, he was delighted to have dinner alone with Lisa. He started to play footsie halfway through dinner. At dessert, he had her in his arms.

"Don't play with me." He warned. "I'm not just a boy, but a man of deep passion."

"I'd better put Ice away and I'll see you in my bedroom. It's the first one at the top of the stairs."

He was ready and waiting, stark naked with the largest, roundest and hardest penis she had ever seen. "My God!" Lisa stared. "What are you going to do with that thing?"

"First you wait." He walked over and locked the bedroom door. He didn't want Mary walking in on them.

Meanwhile, Mary was getting her first roll in the hay, so neither sister was missed.

"Happy New Year!" Mary shouted on her return to the house.

Lisa wasn't going to be the pan that called the kettle black. She didn't inquire about the lost afternoon but curiosity got the better of her. "Are you still planning to leave tomorrow? When does your school start?"

Mary tossed off the question, turned and went back to the barn.

At dinner, Jack told Lisa that Tom had come from a wonderful family. "No carpetbaggers there. His family were the first in the valley, pre-Revolutionary, lots of money, old money and very social. So, treat him right or you will really be dead wood around here. Furthermore, he is not slow."

CHAPTER 16

▼

"But, she has never even had a boyfriend." Lisa argued. "I really hope this isn't serious. She doesn't know him. It's only been a week. She will get over it, I'm sure."

The next day the front door burst open. Mary and Tom entered. "Look, look!" Mary flashed her ring at Lisa. "We just got married."

If Lisa had been the fainting type, she would have been on the floor. Instead, her only comment was, "How is the horse?" It didn't matter. Lisa was wordless.

Mary went on and on. When she would stop for breath, Tom would take over. "And I don't have to teach school one more day!" Mary shouted and pretended to fall into Tom's arms.

"Why wasn't I asked or why wasn't I told?" There was disapproval in her voice.

"Because that's why. Listen to your voice." Mary was Mary again.

"Where do you plan to live? Not here!" Lisa was cold and disappointed. "And you?" she glared at Tom. "You better look for a job. You two can't live on a stable boys' salary."

"If you want to break in with that horsy crowd, you will have to do it through me," Mary boasted.

Lisa put her head in her lap and laughed. "That's the funniest thing I've heard all day!" Mary left the crowd and they continued to discuss the strange circumstances of the wedding.

The phone rang. "Jack calling. What do you think?

"About what?"

"The wedding," he teased.

"How did you find out?" she questioned. "I only heard an hour ago."

"I've been with them all morning working out some details. I know one thing. Mary has married a rich young man. His family owns one of the largest remaining plantations in the South."

"Larger than mine?" Lisa asked.

"Don't make me laugh!" and he did.

"Heck!" Lisa declared. "I guess I lost my stable boy."

The phone rang once more.

"Now whatcha tink about dat?" It was Lahr. "I's got a fine job at the plantation." Lahr hung up.

"That female witch!"

"Who?"

"Lahr, who else!"

The phone rang again. This time it was Mary.

"We are going to the airport to get Mother, Nancy, and Rose. Do you want to come along?"

"Might as well. We can use my car," Lisa offered.

"No," Mary stated. "Yours is not large enough. We will take my car. Wait till you see my wedding present."

Lisa stood in the middle of the family room and screamed! Poor Ice came running to her aid. She hugged the dog and started to cry. "Thank God for you. I have no one else. Why didn't she trust me?"

A small voice inside of Lisa said, "Because you would have tried to ruin things."

They all knew about the wedding. Apparently, they knew from the first plans, such hugging and kissing. "Not me, I'm still mad. I'm hurt. I feel like a fool."

"There will be a large party at the club tomorrow. Where do they all expect to sleep?" Lisa gritted her teeth. Lisa's family lived well, but not like she did. So, one and all roamed from room to room exclaiming "ooh's" and "ah's" as they added, "Lisa, you always seemed to know how to live."

Mary didn't make many points with her sister as she gushed, "Wait till you see the plans for my house!"

"My God, they sure have been busy between Christmas and the New Year!" "That's one week! And, no one told me! Their party, reception or introduce the bride, whatever they want to call the damn thing, I'm not going! Second thought, maybe I'm not even invited!"

"You will be there," her mother made it a fact. "Why are you walking around here slamming doors? You can't even lay a magazine down without making it clear that you are angry."

"Mother!"

"Are you jealous of your sister's happiness?" the mother asked.

"Not jealous," was Lisa's reply. "Just hurt."

The best of the best in the area and surroundings were invited to the reception. After all, Tom's disfigurement made no difference. His family represented pre-Civil War South, not a carpetbagger in any generation. To this day, not money, but birth counts. Lisa didn't have to be told that. Tom's parents were gracious, old money, and they were delighted to have Mary join the family, even if she was a Yankee.

"You belong in the reception line," a voice just behind her ear whispered.

"Not me; besides no one asked me to join." She turned expecting Jack but it was the handsome Major Ron Williams.

"Let's dance."

He could dance like a pro. "Were you invited or did you crash the party?" Lisa blurted.

"I'm from here. We have known each other since childhood." He waltzed Lisa in a large circle.

"When did you begin to dance like a cloud?" Someone cut into the cloud, someone she didn't know.

"I did not know Mary had such a lovely sister." It was Tom's brother. "They call me Mike."

Lisa thought, "When the Major had said, 'I'm from here,' it rang a bell. That is why I've had a hard time to make friends. In Mary's case, it was automatic. Now she is a lady of the South through marriage. I better take a better look at the man they call Mike. He was a little older, probably 40. Lisa was still "sore." The money didn't impress them. We just didn't belong. Lisa was going home. She had driven herself and, with her hand on the door, she was stopped.

"Where are you going?" Jack asked. He had spent time at the bar. "We haven't danced." He took her wrap and escorted her back to the party.

Lisa took another look at the beautifully decorated country club with everyone in formal attire. Everything was beautiful, the flowers, the candles, the white, white linens, gleaming silver and china. This couldn't have been accomplished by Mary. Her mother-in-law knew just what and how to accomplish a short notice jubilee. Lisa realized that Jack was no place around. "What happened to Jack?" she asked the Major.

"He had to go to New York on sudden business. He asked me to look after you."

After being married to a man twice her age, these young vibrant bachelors her age, or a little older, were more exciting than expected. Ron offered Lisa a cigarette. She refused. "Shame on you, and a military man. Tish! Tish! You should know better." Lisa was flirting.

"I only smoke if I'm in an area out of my control," he teased in return.

"God, he is handsome; red hair and all," she thought. He was in uniform, so he stood out against the men in tuxes.

Lisa refused to look at the wedding table, where she knew Mary was smiling from ear to ear. Instead, she danced and flirted with the men who asked her to dance. She took special delight in playing "Scarlett" when she danced with Tom's older brother, Mike. Even the older men were good dancers. And the oldest, probably 80, asked for a dance. It seemed the older they were, the more eager they wanted to dance with the beautiful woman who was deliberately stealing the picture from her sister, Mary.

"I could strangle her," the bride whispered to her mother.

"Why wasn't she invited to the bridal table?" the mother scolded.

"Because, I didn't want her here." Mary stood up, tossed her napkin on her plate and went to the ladies room and cried.

"Too bad the groom is mis-marked," Nancy whispered to her mother.

"Don't ever use that term again," Ruth, her mother, whispered.

The next morning, her sister Rose rapped on Lisa's bedroom door. "Get up lazy bones. There are men here to see you."

"What time is it anyway?" She looked at the clock. It was 10:00 a.m. She had gotten home at 2:00 a.m. She imagined three or four of her dance partners waiting at the foot of the stairs hold vast bouquets of roses. "What to wear?" she rifled through her clothes in her closet.

There was another knock and Rose was in the room. "Grab a pair of jeans. The guys have gone to the barn."

What a let down. "What did those men want?"

"What? Is this about my house?" Lisa jumped into jeans and a shirt. She looked for her boots in the huge closet that was filled with things to wear.

Mother said Tom and Mary were going on an extended honeymoon. "He must have hired another groom for Jett. But why three men?" She could see ahead of her at the barn. At first sight, she recognized Tom's brother, Mike, then his father and two other men.

"What's up?" she called. "Good morning, what is going on here?" Lisa wanted to know. She had never seen the other two men before.

"We wanted to look at your horse. Tom talked about her all the time. He asked me to take a look at her. She could be ready to be bred."

Tom's father stepped forward. "I'm sorry, Mrs. Taloomas, this is Burke Pollock, and I want you to meet Dr. Morton, President of the Kentucky Arabian Horse Club."

They knew a lot more about Jett that Lisa did. Jett had been a wonderful gift. The young woman knew dogs not horses. The club was well known for its Arabian horse shows and racing. Lisa was aware that these people could teach her, so she remained in the barn with the horse and four knowledgeable horsemen. While they talked about bloodlines, Lisa quietly listened.

As far as Lisa could tell from what they said, Jett was in full bloom and ready to be bred. The horse's jet-black fur glistened in the morning sun. Her mane was longer and even more magnificent, as she shook it over her shoulders. Lisa thought about Jett as she floated toward her. Jett wagged her beautiful tail and lifted her head looking for the apple, which Lisa forgot to bring.

"I will offer you my stallion at stud if you will agree that I have first choice at the foal."

"Watch me stop on toes," Lisa said to herself. "As all of you know, I'm a novice at this. First, Dr. Morton, I mean no offense. Tell me about your stallion. What is his name?"

"We call him Ebony. Like yours, he is completely black with no white star on his forehead. I do have a coal black one with a white star on his head. We call him Star."

"I think you would be wise to stay with coal back. You have to steer clear of that white recessive gene. What is your stud fee?" Lisa asked like a pro.

"I said in lieu of the fee for a foal." The doctor tried to make that clear.

I asked, "How much is your stud fee?"

"Twenty-five thousand."

"I'll pay that and keep the foal." Lisa left the barn to get her checkbook. She still had the money from the Pennsylvania house.

"You didn't tell me that could happen," the doctor told the others.

"We didn't know." Tom's father shook his head. "You really socked her with that price."

"Oh, he is worth every penny," Lisa said as she returned holding the check.

"I have the best dog and I'm going to have the best horse; maybe not the first generation, but just you wait. I'm young and I have time."

Unbeknownst to others, Lisa had acquired a library of books on Arabian horses. And when the doctor mentioned a name, it was a name she had come across many times in her reading. Her check was worded at the bottom, "Full payment for stud fee." She asked the doctor to sign right under it. He looked like a carpetbagger. She was thinking, "I'll wind up forced to sell my best horse. Twenty-five thousand dollar stud fee, I must be crazy."

Lisa commanded, "Now, bring your stallion over. I want to see him."

"No," she was told, "that isn't the way it is done."

Jett must go with the men. "You wouldn't want to be near a mating stallion. It would not be safe for a woman," Tom's father interfered.

"Do you know the stallion?" Lisa asked Tom's father.

"Tom picked him out for Jett and he would never steer you wrong." Mike told her.

Lisa let the men take her beloved Jett away with no contract, only a handshake. It's still done that way in some circles.

"I wish I could talk to Mom Mom." Mom Mom had been raised on a very large farm, not far outside Washington D.C. On her 16th birthday, her father presented her with a Tennessee walking horse. She named it "Macfonso."

Lisa had seen pictures of Mom Mom as a young girl placed sidesaddle on her horse. "That's the way I'll ride Jett. I'll bring back the fashion. I really will," Lisa laughed at herself. "As soon as the Garden is over, I'll find a mate for Ice."

Mary and Tom had left on their honeymoon. "I wonder where the rest of the family is staying or did they all go home?" Lisa returned to the large house alone until Ice spotted her. She was greeted with barks and a wagging tail. Ice led the way to the front door. Lisa could see through the windows. Her mother, Nancy and Rose were seated on the front porch.

"We spent the night at Tom's parents' place."

"Funny," Lisa thought that Mike or Tom's father had not mentioned it. "Is it a nice place?" Lisa knew better but she asked.

"Beautiful!" they all raved. "Just what you would expect, a real plantation."

"This house is old South." Lisa spoke up.

"But you didn't ask us to stay, you know," It was her sister Rose. Lisa never liked her much and at the moment, it seemed like the same old thing. "Lisa, we would like to spend some time with you."

"You know you are welcome." Lisa opened her arms to her mother. The others followed suit. "I don't have a maid. Mary got rid of her, so I ask, let's keep it easy. Follow me and I'll show you your rooms."

The nursery was empty, no bed. "Mother, take my room. Here's a room for Nancy and one for Rose." Lisa took the bedroom that Lahr used. It was on the first floor and at the back of the house.

As the women scattered, she saw Tom's brother, Mike, his father, and Mr. Marlowe, the president of the bank. "May we join you nice ladies?" Mike asked.

As far as Lisa knew, no one had eaten breakfast or lunch. "Oh, heck!" she said to herself, "I can't cook but my mother can." That made her feel better. So, as the perfect hostess, Lisa invited, "I hope you will all stay for lunch."

Mike's father said, "It is too bad you had to let Lahr go. She is doing a good job for us."

"I hope she doesn't poison all of you! I'll bet Mary doesn't know she's there."

CHAPTER 17

───────────▼───────────

"I'm about to make brunch. I hope you all will stay." Lisa didn't mean a word of it.

"Thank the Lord," Lisa's mother spoke up. "I'm not Southern but I can make a good brunch." Now everyone was back on the porch. "Food will be ready in 30 minutes."

Lisa and her sister, Nancy, joined her and pans began to fly. They made fried apples, bacon, eggs, biscuits, and lots of black coffee. Everyone ate and praised the cooks.

"What does Ice have in his mouth?" Rose took a hand-written envelope out of the dog's mouth. But Ice wanted to play.

"Who is Jim Cory?" Ice was about to tear the envelope up.

At the name, Lisa was on her feet. "Give!" She commanded Ice and he did. Lisa excused herself and left the table, while the others wondered who the new boyfriend might be.

The letter read: Lisa, if you had a hand in my removal from the Garden judging roster, I'll sue you for every penny you have. J.C.—P.S. I could kill you.

"That asshole! To think, I was going to forgive and forget. I wonder if it could be Lahr. It sounds like her. I'll keep the letter and ask John what to do."

"You missed doing the dishes," Nancy pointed out. "Got another boyfriend?"

Lisa ignored the remark. "Nancy, why don't you take Mother and the girls on a tour of the place?"

"So, you can talk to the men?" Rose smirked.

"I have the nicest sisters." Lisa turned to the men who were discussing Arabian Horses.

"May I join the ladies? I'd love to look around." He almost ran to catch up and take her mother's arm. It was the banker, George Marlowe. Lisa saw a glint in his eyes.

"Hot dog!" Lisa thought. "He isn't too bad for being fat and forty." What she had not noticed was Mike, trying to get a look at her mother before she disappeared out of his sight.

While Mother and family toured the place, Lisa, Mike and Mike Sr., talked Arabian Horses. "I know so little about Arabians, in fact, horses in particular. But, I'm a quick learner. I hope you people will help."

"Dear Lady," the elder Mike, Sr. began, "You own a very fine pure-bred Arabian Mare. Tom has spent his time with horses rather than meet the world face on, if you know what I am saying. My son, and now your brother-in-law, knew her blood lines and helped you agree on the stud. Tom was the one who contacted Dr. Watson. My dear," the older man addressed Lisa, "once you own a mare like that, you don't have to know much. You already have what others strive for. Tom will be back by the time Jett is returned to you."

"I was worried about that," Lisa stated. "That's good to hear."

"Enjoy your classic beauty. She is the envy of all the Arabian horsemen in the area. I'm glad you paid the stud fee."

Mike interrupted. "Lisa, may we see your Garden hopeful?"

Lisa looked from father to son. "There is something different about these men. Is it because they are Southern? They really are gentlemen." Lisa returned with Ice. Ice was social but distant.

"Just like a lady," Mike smiled. "She has to win, beauty plus beauty." He stared at Lisa for a moment and then let his eyes return to the dog. As the two men were leaving, the younger one hesitated. "May I call you?"

Lisa felt a blush rush to her face. That had never happened before.

The older man remarked, "My thanks to your lovely mother."

In an hour or two, the phone rang. "So soon?"

Lisa rolled her eyes. She was expecting a call from Mike. But it was Jack, the attorney. "Where have you been?" Lisa inquired.

"Had to get to New York." He did not explain.

"Why, you missed all the doings." Lisa wanted him to know.

"Yes, I understand there was a big wedding reception at the club. It did not take her too long to snag the big bucks."

"Shame on you. They seem to be very much in love," Lisa defended her sister, Mary.

"He is a lucky guy. Your sister is a very nice lady and too good-looking for him," Jack stated.

She wanted to ask him if he were jealous, but dropped the thought.

"What about you, my dear, do you miss me?" he questioned with a laugh. "You still love me? I heard from the Major. He wanted permission to fall in love with you."

"Go on!" Lisa teased. Jack was taking up too much time. Lisa wanted the line clear in case Mike might call. She interrupted his conversation with, "I have a houseful of company. Glad you are back."

"What about tonight?" Jack asked.

"Come here for barbecue," Lisa invited.

"Barbecue in winter? You Yankees sure have different ways."

"Be here by 6:00 p.m. We will eat at 8:00 p.m. Bye bye."

Lisa put the phone in its place. Mike didn't call that day, or the following day.

The honeymoon couple was back and Lisa still had a houseful of company. So, the barbecue idea worked out fine. It wasn't too cold for the last of January. In fact, there were a few signs of spring here and there. The barbecue was more work than Lisa expected, especially since her sisters considered themselves company. So again, Mother, Jack, Mike, and Tom took over. They had a bonfire going where everyone gathered with their sandwiches and beer.

Jack came over to Lisa. "Let's take a walk." Hand in hand, they left the group.

"I want to talk to you." Lisa spoke first.

"No, me first," he laughed.

Mike watched them leave the party. Then he watched Ruth, the mother, dance to real county music. She was in the arms of the short, fat banker. Tom decided to cut in. "Save your dancing for me, will you?"

Mother Ruth's face and eyes were shining from the heat of the fire and the fun of the dance. "My God, you are a beautiful woman. Where have you been all my life? Ruth was at least 15 years Mike's senior. She thought she was a little drunk from the cider she had been drinking. No one had ever said anything like that to her before, not even her beloved husband. Ruth was embarrassed.

Jack was having his say as they walked. "I have an apartment on Central Park East. I keep it for a number of reasons. In the first place, it is a tax write-off and the second; it becomes handy time and again. Would you like to stay there while you are at the dog show?"

"Oh, boy, would I. Only today, I was afraid I had waited too long to get a hotel room. Some people make arrangements a year ahead. Thank you, thank you!"

Lisa reached up and gave Jack a kiss, which he expanded to a soul kiss. "This has been a long time coming." He kissed her again and this time, he pulled her rump into position. His hand was inside her coat. It found its way to her breast. "I'll be in New York at the same time," he whispered and kissed her exposed breast.

As they got closer to the house, it sounded like an Irish bar at midnight. The house was packed with people; some she didn't even know. Tom's parents heard that the honeymooners were back so they joined the crowd. Mike was still there. Lisa didn't realize that her lipstick was smudged, but Mike didn't miss the smear. Lisa felt like a stranger in her own house. She said goodnight to Jack and went up to her own bedroom only to find her mother, Mary, and Ice waiting.

"I thought you were downstairs?" Lisa really kicked off her shoes. They landed across the room. Dogs are funny. Ice felt her dissatisfaction. He came over and offered a paw. "It is too much, too much. I'm not used to all this. It's too much. There is too much booze and so much noise. I just hate to think what my place is going to look like in the morning." Lisa was upset.

Her mother understood. "Think how I feel. I'm a small-town woman. Listen to all this racket." She opened the bedroom door. "It's 2:00 a.m. I'm getting too old."

"Old, my God, you are only 50! If life begins at 40, think how great it could be at 50. Aren't you tired of living alone? I've seen the banker looking you over and what about Mike? He has his eyes on you, too."

Her mother's heart jumped into her throat. "Stay Mother, stay two more days. I want to take you to town just like I did Mary."

"That was a waste of money," Mary scoffed.

"Forget it; men only want the young ones. Look at you, your husband was older than I." The 15 years between Ruth and Mike would never work out, she was sure.

"Watch her, Mother." Mary warned. "She will try to make you over and you won't like yourself."

Off they went anyhow, beauty parlor first. Mother's blonde hair was highlighted and the perm cut off. She was given an easy casual style that took ten years off her face. Mother Ruth was delighted with the cut. Off the two of them headed to the most expensive casual clothing store in town. She looked wonderful in blue denim. Next, for a tailored suit and blouse. Last, a long black chiffon skirt and a white lace top. They had more boxes and shopping bags that they could handle.

"Were you following us?" Lisa saw Jack coming toward them at the same time that she was dropping a shoebox in the street.

"You can always depend on Jack," he smiled those flashing teeth.

"Are you going to the club tonight? All of us will be there."

"That was a sideways invite. Sure, I'll be there." Then Jack turned to Ruth. "Save the first dance for me." He was gone after all the packages were in the trunk of Lisa's car.

Everyone was pleased with the change on Mother. "She looks 30!" Nancy exclaimed.

"But she doesn't look like Mother." Mary wasn't sure how she felt.

When they went to the club for dinner, Ruth was the most beautiful woman at the table. Every man she had met, and a few more, asked her to dance. "What have you done to Mother?" Mary scolded Lisa. "She is not the same. I never saw her drink champagne before. In fact, I think she is a little drunk." Ruth lit up the room.

"I heard a man say once; a woman can't be beautiful until she is forty. Before that, she is just a girl. Maybe 50 is even better," Lisa told the sourpuss, Mary. "A teacher is a teacher!"

Nancy, expecting her first child got into the car with her husband's assistance. She called to her mother, "Don't forget, you are about to become a grandmother. Are you sure you don't want to go home?"

Mary interrupted, "We will keep an eye on her. Tom and I will keep her busy. Love ya!" All waved as Nancy and her husband, Todd, drove to the airport in a rental car.

Lisa turned to Tom. "I've got to get another groom. Jett will be coming back."

"Lisa," said Tom, "I never had a sister. Will you be my sister?" he dared. "You have a stable boy. I never quit. We could get a couple of Arabians. If Jett is in foal, we would have a colt. I can take care of four or five horses. You'll have to expand the barn. If I need help, Mary loves Jett."

"Like hell!" Lisa thought. "Jett belongs to me!"

Tom continued. "It is what I want to do. It's what I love and it is what I'm good at. You, Lisa, Mary, and I could develop a stable with our own colors."

It sounded too good to be true. Mary entered the discussion. "One thing, we want an acre of land to build our new home. Tom and I can stay in the quarters at the barn. The quarters are brand new and very nice."

"Don't do that to me," Lisa objected. "You can live here. I have a lot of space."

CHAPTER 18

▼

"No," Mary stated. "You can have the fruits of his labor by day, but at night he is all mine."

"There is something about an older sister. She is so bossy. Maybe it's the teacher in her. Or is it me?" Lisa wondered. "I'm glad they won't be staying here.

The Garden was finally in view and Ice never looked better. Lisa was never more excited. She had made plans to leave three days before the show. Mother had been to New York on a tour bus, but she had never seen New York as Lisa planned to show her. The two had never been close in spite of being mother and daughter. It was always Mom Mom Lisa clung to. Her mother resented the bond.

Jack Holt dropped by to give Lisa directions to his apartment. "Be careful, it isn't easy to drive in New York, he advised, as he handed Lisa the keys. When he saw the transition in her mother, he shook his head and rolled his eyes. "I see where Lisa got her beauty, a rare compliment for both mother and daughter.

Lisa's mother was tall, like Mary. Her figure had improved with each child because she had been married to a man who insisted on nothing else. Lisa was proud of her mother. Mary took Lisa aside. "Don't you try any funny business with Mother."

"Like what?"

"Like trying to fix her up or something dumb," Mary warned.

"I think that acre of ground she wants to build her home upon better be over the hill, just not too close." Lisa decided.

After Mary's remark, Jack took a second look at Ruth McHugh. "She is a classic, a true beauty, not the same type. Lisa could tan easily and Ruth would have to stay out of the sun. Why don't you change your name back to McHugh?"

He was talking to Lisa. "You are not a Taloomas. You can do it legally I'll show you how. Of course if you'd be interested in trading it for Holt, I would not stand in the way."

There was total silence in the room until Ice barked at the mail coming through the slot in the huge door.

"That reminds me," Lisa said as she recalled the letter from Jim Cory. She had set it aside to show him, but had put it out of her mind.

Jack read it. "Does your mother know about this?" he asked.

"No!"

"Come see me this afternoon. I have a good map for New York City." He put the envelope in his pocket and left.

Mother and daughter went shopping for last minute things and then went on to lunch. "I'm going to drop you off and see if Jack can see me." Her mother tried to ask, but Lisa reached for the cell phone and made the call. "Fine, I'll see you in ten minutes." The phone went back into her Coach purse.

Tell me about the letter," she asked as they spun along in Lisa's small red sports car.

"I'll tell you when Jack tells me if it is anything to worry about, okay?" The mother was dropped off at Lisa's house. The ten minutes had grown to thirty minutes by the time she parked the car in front of Jack's office.

"This," he dropped the letter on the large, polished table in his office, "is dangerous. He is a dangerous man from any point of view. Lahr got a note like this," he said.

"It figures," responded Lisa. "He was paying her to keep an eye on me."

"You knew?" he seemed surprised.

"Yes, what should I do?" Lisa wanted to be sure she was safe.

"He has been on a list for a long time. Wanted, if you know what I mean. He is a dirty dog regardless of your persuasion. I have said enough. Do you have a gun?"

"I had one but Bert took it from me." Lisa didn't know she was being set up as she took his handgun and put in her purse. Lisa knew how to handle a gun from the days when she was 17 and 18; when she had slept in her van on sandy beaches, rest stops, and Wal-Mart parking lots with her show dogs in order to save money. The thought of those days sent shivers up her back. "I'll never be poor again," Lisa promised herself.

Her mother was waiting at the door. "What is this all about?" she asked.

"Nothing, really. Some man thought I gave him a bad reference, but I didn't. Jack is going to write him a letter, okay?"

"I was worried. No, I was scared for you, like a mother."

"Let's forget it. I want to have a good luck party right here."

"That's work. We have no help," her mother cried.

"Okay, the club then. But, I want it semi-formal."

"Let's see. I'll invite Mary and Tom, Tom's parents and Mike, Jack, the major, you and me, the banker. I'll need another formal," Lisa counted on her fingers. "We won't ask the funny little banker, that way it's okay. Jack said he'd be away. Let's keep it simple, Mary and Tom, you and I, the major and Mike. That's six. That's enough." Her mother seemed satisfied.

"What about the banker?" To Lisa's amazement, Ruth replied, "Just six?"

"And who am I stuck with?" Lisa asked.

"Guess?" Ruth laughed. "Mike is mine."

"You hussy! Welcome to him." Lisa was astonished. "I've noticed that all these dear, sweet, and handsome men were not as attentive. Could it be because of my mother?"

"I'll give a small party at the club, just six of us. That would be fun and I wouldn't have to get in since we would be leaving for New York the next morning. Let's see, Mary and Tom, Mike and Mother, the major and me. Jack told me he would see me in New York. It will be our Good Luck Dinner."

It was a dinner party for six. On weekdays, the club closed at 9:00 p.m., so there wasn't too much dancing, but all seemed to enjoy the evening. Next, it was rush, rush to pack all the things Ice needed. They were on their way by 10:00 a.m. This was what Lisa had waited a year to be a part of.

"Mother, my dear, have you ever stayed at the cool Bramble Inn in West Virginia?"

"No!"

"Well, sweetheart, be prepared for something special. That's where Mary and I stayed before Christmas. I'm sure that is where Tom and Mary spent their honeymoon. Mary is so quiet." Her mother knew Mary.

"Just a very good guess." Lisa noticed the road was very wet.

"Will this place take dogs?" Ruth inquired.

"They did the last time. Maybe I should keep the name Taloomas. It opens many more doors than McHugh." The snow was getting thicker. The bushes and trees along the road were changing colors. It had been a beautiful morning when they left home. Now, the sky was grey and the clouds hung low. "I believe we better think of stopping pretty soon. The road is getting slick." Her thoughts were of Gordon and how he was killed. Now the snow and wind were causing small drifts along the road.

"About how far away is the hotel?" Her mother was disappointed.

Lisa, driving with her headlights on, came upon a huge machine with bright lights all over it. It was the snowplow. "Thank goodness! I'm going to follow him. Maybe this way we can make it to the Bramble."

"Thank God!" Ruth was pleased all the way around.

Lisa cut her speed considerably, and turned on the car radio. They were playing big band songs. Her mother, Ruth, knew all the words and sang aloud. She had a nice voice. "You constantly surprise me. One thing after another amazes me. I didn't know you could dance and had such a nice voice."

"I know, Mom Mom was always more interesting." Ruth looked at Lisa with caution. It was time to be said she thought.

"Don't say that Mother, please. I was just thinking how much this trip to the Garden would have meant to her."

"See what I mean." The older woman was hurt.

"How old is this hotel? It looks like the South a hundred years ago. What a snooty looking bunch of people." Inside the hotel, her mother was looking around. "All this splendor and I'll bet there are hungry people in those hills over there."

"Hush, Mother, people are looking." Lisa was trying to register and hide the full-grown poodle behind her.

"Good evening, Mrs. Taloomas. We have been expecting you. Your suite is on the top floor. It is ready and waiting. It is a terrible day. Can we help you with anything? Your luggage will be put in the room."

Lisa turned to her mother and stuck out the tip of her tongue, as if to say, "See, money talks!"

The suite was even more beautiful than the one Lisa had shared with sister Mary. There were flowers everywhere.

"Who? How?" Her mother ran past the flowers to inspect every aspect of the lush surroundings. "There is a Jacuzzi for four in the main bathroom!" Then she turned her attention to the flowers. "Who are they from?" she asked.

The flowers read, "Good luck in New York. My best to your mother." The card was from the bank president. There were flowers from Mary and Tom, the major, Mike, but none from Jack. "He is a strange man." Lisa thought, "I like him, but I really don't know much about him. I think Jack is interested one minute and then I remember Bert said he was a crook. He sure goes to New York a lot," Lisa reflected.

"How late do they serve dinner in the dining room?" asked Ruth.

"Why, I thought we'd have dinner in the room."

"That's okay." Lisa saw her mother looking out one of the huge windows. "I just wanted to see what the rich ate. Besides, it is still snowing."

"Still snowing? For Pete's sake," was Lisa's remark. "Let's order dinner and get to bed."

"I won't be able to sleep. The place smells like a funeral parlor." Ruth remarked on her way to bed. "By the way, is the banker married?" she tried to be casual.

"Never has been and he is loaded! Is that what you wanted to know?" Lisa stopped and looked at her mother.

"What about Mike?" Ruth wanted to know.

"For God's sake, act your age!" Lisa walked away. This time, her mother stuck out her tongue.

Before she closed her bedroom door, Lisa let her have it. "People say Mike is gay."

This time, the mother said, "Shit!"

It had snowed all night. The surrounding beauty was spectacular, but not what the women wanted to drive into. Lisa said she would leave her car at the hotel. "We are not far from Frederick, Maryland, and a good airport. We will get a plane to New York. Thank God, I planned to leave early. Those three days in New York could be a God send."

Lisa called the desk and told of her plight. "We will arrange everything, Mrs. Taloomas." She asked that her crate for the dog be included. It was. With a sigh of relief, the two ladies went to the main dining room to watch the rich and famous eat their breakfast. There was a call. The waiter brought the phone to their table.

"Sweetheart!" It was Jack. "New York is a mess. The storm is all up and down the coast. When you get in and get your luggage, call my number. It will take me at least an hour to get to the airport. Allow that time. I'll see you soon, lots of love. I'll be in all day. Don't worry, I'll be there."

Later, when Lisa's mother saw the wings of the plane being sprawled to drive them, Ruth balked. She didn't want to board the plane. She did, swearing she would never fly again in the winter.

The airport was a mad house. There was no way Lisa could get to a phone to call Jack. Her wet phone was in the car. They went outside to hail a limo. Most dog people travel in cabs, but they were always filled. They made their way across the street with their luggage, collapsible dog pen and a beautiful white dog covered with salt, slush, and real ice. Ice recognized the tosser, but Lisa and her mother never saw the person who had thrown the street slop all over Ice.

CHAPTER 19

▼

New York was cold with a driving wind coming from the east. There were people, people, dogs, dogs, and more dogs. Lisa hurried toward the waiting limo. She heard a splash in the dirty melting snow. Ruth had tripped over her own luggage and had fallen feet first in the street. It was a zoo. As the limo pulled away from the curb, Lisa spotted Jack trying to find space to park his car. "Oh my God, he will be so mad at me. I'm so sorry, but I left my cell phone in my car."

Her mother had no use for one of those things. "This is the worst day of my life." Ruth complained.

"Hush, for God's sake, at least we are heading for a good warm tub."

"I hate this place!"

"It's pretty nice when the sun is shining. You will see," added Lisa. Ice was another thing. He could not be wetter or dirtier, but he wasn't complaining. At least he was warm, if not dry. As they rolled along in the slush and freezing rain, Lisa tried to make things better. "Look, Mother, look how the lights glisten through the snowy rain. Look at the lighted trees along the sidewalk. Read the signs on the store fronts. Some of these shops you can't find anywhere else.

"I should have gone home. This is terrible!" Traffic was stalled. They were moving three cars at a time.

"Shut up! Shut up! Can't you see I'm trying to make the best of this?" Lisa pulled at the cuff of her mother's cloth coat. The sleek black limo finally rolled to the curb of Jack's apartment, where a doorman with an umbrella was waiting to take care of the two women.

Once in Jack's apartment, they kicked off their shoes and looked in the fridge for something to eat. The phone was ringing. It was Jack. "Glad you made it. I was there. I saw you get into the limo. I hope you like Chinese. I'm bringing supper. Jack was in the apartment elevator at just the time Lisa became ill. No time was lost.

"Do you like Chinese, Mother?" Lisa asked and didn't know why she had bothered.

"Yuck, pure cat or even rat!"

"Mother, for God's sake, behave yourself. Jack has had a bad time, too. He is bringing dinner."

"Why didn't he stop at McHeeley's? They have good hamburgers and fries." Her mother was stopped by a rap on the door. "I'll eat the rice," Ruth mumbled.

The next morning, the sun was shining brightly. A knock at the door produced a bouquet of roses and a card that read: "Leave your room unlocked tonight." It was payback time, Lisa thought.

"Who are the flowers from?" asked Ruth.

"Jack! See if you can make some coffee. I'm going to bathe Ice in the Jacuzzi."

"All I hope is that he knows which bed to crawl into," commented Ruth as she read the card.

Lisa shook her head and rolled her eyes. "No wonder we never got along."

The dog was magnificent once more. The task, at the hands of a pro, took until noon. "All that road salt almost ruined his coat. All's fine that ends fine," Lisa made up her own quote.

"Get ready Mother. I'm starving. We will find some place to eat."

"I noticed a New York deli not far. I saw it last night." Ruth was ready to go.

"It's amazing that today has no resemblance to last night," Ruth remarked, as they were leaving the deli. "Let's go shopping. I'd like to buy you something nice. I want to make up for yesterday. I was so scared. Remember, I'm just a country girl. By the way, I got a phone call last night. I thought I'd better answer. Your door was closed."

"Jack again?" Lisa asked.

"No, it was for me."

"Really, who?"

"The banker."

"How would he know where we were?" Ruth wondered.

"I think they all know each other in some sort of mystery. Bert was right in the middle of it, but I never knew what."

Lisa had a large foot and she loved shoes. So, the first stop was for shoes. She bought six pairs, alike but in different colors.

While Lisa was busy, her mother got lost in the store. Her gift for her daughter was a three-ounce bottle of Joy perfume. When she turned around in the large department store, Ruth had no idea of which way to turn to find her daughter.

In the meantime, Lisa left the shoe department searching for her mother. Suddenly, a hand reached out from behind her. It was Jim Cory. Lisa pulled her wrist free and glared at him. "What do you want?" she stepped back.

Her mother came out of nowhere. "Oh, Jim, how nice to see you again." She shook his hand. "It's been ages since we sat in my kitchen and talked."

"My God, come on Mother!" Lisa almost pulled her off her feet.

"Why, that was rude." Ruth was shaking herself free.

"I'll tell you. First, let's get out of here." Lisa was shaken.

When they returned to the apartment, her mother forgot about the past scene because at the door was another vase of flowers.

"Could they be from Jim, who had a funny sense of humor?" Reading the card, Lisa began to laugh. "They are not for me. They are for you, Mother, dear."

The card said: "Lovely Lady Ruth, I hope we meet again."

"You made that up."

"No, I didn't. It's right here. Ha ha, it's old fat belly himself, Rob Marlowe." Lisa made fun.

"I think Rob is a little sweet on me. Is he rich?" She looked interested.

"Does a dog have fleas," was Lisa's reply.

Mother and Ice were sound asleep when Jack found his way into Lisa's bed. "My God, you scared the heck out of me!"

Jack covered her mouth with his. "It's only me."

"I was asleep," she whispered in the darkness of the room.

"Take off that little piece of silk you are wearing. I want your body close to mine." Jack began to make love to Lisa.

Lisa woke to the odor of coffee. Jack was gone.

"Didn't your friend show up last night?" Mother inquired.

"What friend?" Lisa yawned.

They drank coffee and took in the view. They were looking over treetops at the high rises all around. The sun was brilliant, for 10:00 a.m. The roadways were clear of the ugly gray and black slush and snow. It was a Saturday in mid-February and the streets were filled with people. The city had come alive. "See," Lisa pointed. "Look, this is what I mean by New York. There is no other place like it in all the world." From their vantage point, they could see people scattering, running, and walking their dogs in the park. "Good idea," Lisa exclaimed. "We could take Ice for a walk before I have to get him ready for the show next week."

"Is it safe?"

"Of course, it is safe. Mother, you should get out more often. You act like an old lady. Are you listening to me?"

"No!" This was her way to avoid an argument.

Children were sailing toy ships in the unfrozen lake. The trees were bare with just a suggestion of spring. As the three walked in the sunshine, there was a sudden jolt. A kid of 15 or so jolted both women. He had their purses by the straps, as he whizzed down the street on rollerblades. Their purses were gone and so was Ice. In a minute, Ice had the kid flat on his face on the sidewalk. A crowd was gathering.

"What's up? What did the kid do? Is that beautiful dog his or was he attacked?" Lisa called for Ice but he didn't return. Instead, he was looking under bushes and trees.

"That brat stole our purses!" Lisa reported to the park police, as the officer appeared. The boy was in a seated position, wiping the blood from his forehead.

"Ladies, he has no purses. Where is that dog of yours? He caused this. Why wasn't he on a leash?" the police officer charged.

Lisa looked down at her hand. Ice had thrown his collar and leash to go after the thief. By this time, the crowd was becoming a larger crowd.

"You see why I don't like New York? Look at these nosey people, just a bunch of hippies," Ruth lamented.

People turned to look at the woman who was being insulting. She went on, "You smell," she told the man standing next to her.

A second police officer appeared. "Who owns this dog?" The Irish brogue was still in his voice. Ice was standing next to the cop with two shoulder bags hanging from his mouth. "This dog pulled them out of a kid's hands before he could get into a waiting car. This kid on the sidewalk is one of them. They were a team." The second cop told the people to leave. As they were dispersing, people were remarking about a wonder dog. Many people in the group had cameras; so many pictures were taken of the dog. Pictures appeared in the paper and on the news. When it was discovered that Ice was a contender for Best in Show at the Garden, Ice became a celebrity.

"They are not going to like this publicity at the show," Lisa remarked to the empty room. Her mother had gone to lie down. "I'll have to give the credit to the breed. They are a very smart group of dogs."

The phone never stopped ringing. "Your dog is to be honored on the morning TV show."

The police called. "We want to honor your dog. We have been looking for that 'Fagan' for months, the three-way purse snatching trio. Can you bring him down to the station sometime today?"

"Yes!" Lisa said with pride. "I'll grab a cab." She left a note for her mother.

The police gathered around the beautiful, friendly dog. Someone placed a police cap on the animal's head. The dog picked up on the excitement, but didn't know why.

One man started to speak; "We have tried to catch that 'Fagan' for weeks. He has been operating all over town. He has had a three-way team. One kid works the street at a designated spot. Another kid picks up the purse, while the first kid is on the run. Then, with the cell phone, the second calls the driver for pick-up. Thanks to this dog, those thieves are off the streets of New York." Pictures were being taken from all around.

Lisa and Ice were leaving when she heard that Irish brogue again. "Let me get that door. Can I get you a cab, or better yet, will you let me drive you home!" He smiled and God, what a smile! It lit up his entire face. He was not handsome. He was beautiful. Then she saw the gold band on his finger.

"The phone has been driving me crazy," Ruth said as she greeted Lisa at the door. "You are to call ABC, CBS and XYZ TV stations. You are supposed to call them first thing."

"Oh, crap!" Lisa breathed. "I knew about being interviewed for the dog show, but that was just NBC. I wonder what the others want."

The dog show was being covered by this human-interest story entitled, "The smart wonder dog—a real hero." One woman gushed to the reporter, "He and he alone, broke up a three-way robbery ring. The police couldn't do it." She added, "I've been afraid to go into the park for months. I happen to live right across from the park."

Ice and Lisa were from one studio to the next. Funny, people like a good story with a happy ending.

On her arrival back at the apartment, Lisa removed her long woolen scarf and tossed her coat on a chair. "Mother," Lisa called, "I don't feel very good." The vision of her mother began to sway and spin. So did Lisa. She hit the floor.

Ruth didn't call 9-1-1; instead, she found Jack's phone number and called. Jack was in the apartment elevator at just the time Lisa became ill. No time was lost. He carried the limp Lisa to the bed. She had come to but didn't seem to understand what was going on around her. "I'm so sick at my stomach." She pulled herself up to head for the toilet.

"It's no wonder," her mother explained. "She hasn't had a decent meal since we got here."

Lisa was frightened. She had missed her second period. "What to do? What should I do?" When she returned to bed, Jack showed her the newspaper headlines. They read, "Best in Show Contender Sends Fagan Three to Jail." Ice had his picture in all the papers. All the news stations had covered the story. Everybody loves to hear about good deeds a beautiful dog can fulfill. The inquiring reporters asked Lisa to fill in the story.

"Enough is enough," she said. Lisa could not make all the media requests because the show was the next day and she was not feeling well.

"I could go," her mother offered. "I was there. I could tell the story."

Lisa gave her mother a look that made it clear what she thought of her idea. "I have been waiting for this event for an entire year." Lisa sucked in her breath to ward off the tears. "I want this for the dog, as well as myself. I know he is a very fine show example and if I'm too sick to show, there is one handler there I'd ask to show Ice."

Ice had won 20 Best in Shows across the country as a puppy. Now Ice was to be shown as an adult and trimmed as such. The dog had won his Championship many months ago. Now he was to be shown against champions of his breed and then the non-sporting group. Best in Show will follow that. Ice has to win his one showing and the second one to contend for Best in Show. Lisa had no doubt. Ice was the perfect dog.

Lisa had always shown her own dogs. She had been smart enough to make friends with the handlers. Some liked Lisa and they even admired her. Even the ones who felt her abrasive and bold gave her due credit. Her Standard Poodles were owned all over the world. The young woman had a natural eye for beauty, gait, balance and a love for all animals. She could pick her winner at birth, as she'd been taught.

Now the day to strut their stuff was at hand. Ice was as high as an ace from all the attention. Lisa was sick with worry concerning the show and her condition.

Lisa heard the call for the non-sporting winners. "This is the Garden and we are here." She patted Ice on his shoulder. Into the ring they went. The announcer announced the Best Chow, the Best German Shepherd, the Best Dalmatian and her Ice, the Best Standard Poodle. Around the ring they went.

Lisa saw nothing else, because seated in his box, was Bert, her ex, his pregnant wife and Lahr.

Lisa and Ice had won the first hurdle.

Lisa was a pro. She looked every inch a lady in her $500.00 suit; skirt length just right with shoes to match with moderate heels. As she accepted the winner's trophy, the losers congratulated her. They shook her hand and gave her kisses. All this was going on by the ones who really hated to see her come through a dog show door because she had become unbeatable.

Lisa didn't remember anything except that Bert was there. "That son of a bitch is here for some rotten business." Her thoughts were right. It was Lahr who disturbed her.

"May the best dog win." She could feel his warm breath at her ear. It was Bert.

"What are you doing here?" That was a stupid question. When she saw him, she should have realized he had one of his Boxer champions entered. Lisa benched Ice and ran to the ring where they were showing the working group of dogs. No question, Bert's dog won that group. His dog was a famous dog and his handler was one of the best in the county.

Next, all of the first place winners from each group arrived one at a time in the Winner's Circle. However, the judge was missing. They called for him over the loudspeaker, as each handler looked worried.

CHAPTER 20

▼

The woman standing next to Lisa whispered, "I saw him enter the men's room. He can't hear the call in there."

Lisa gave Ice to the woman next to her. The men's room was next to the ladies' room. Lisa pushed open the door. There lay a man face down, dead as a crock in stone. Two men were standing over the body. "Call the police. I've got to get back in the ring." To Lisa's shock, they had found the judge and judging was underway.

Excited and almost out of breath, she ran to the steward's desk. "There has been a murder. I've got to get my dog. Please wait."

There was no dog. The dog had left the building with someone he knew well. The show had to go on because of the National television stations that were covering the event.

"I feel like I'm running in a dream." Lisa burst into hysterical sobs. "Where is my mother?" Lisa sobbed. Matters were getting worse. Bert's Boxer went Best in Show at the Garden. Lisa slipped to the floor and cried in consuming sobs. "Where is my dog?" She sounded like a little girl.

A police officer, with an Irish brogue, stepped forward. "We are looking for the dog." He tried to comfort her.

Bert stepped forward and helped her to her feet. "Now we are even!" he whispered. The smell of bourbon encircled him.

The crowd was leaving the show building. Only a few knew about the murder, which seemed to be a suicide. One man, who had found the body, asked Lisa if she knew who it was. The man's body was lying flat on his face. As they entered the men's room, someone turned him over with the toe of his shoe. It was Jim

Cory with her knuckle buster gun in his right hand. "That's my gun. How did he get my gun?" She reached for the gun.

"Don't touch that gun." He reached out to steady Lisa. The brogue was familiar.

"Do you know this man?" Pat, the officer asked.

"I've known that man since I was a child. And, he was left-handed. That was no suicide. This is a set up. This man was murdered." She turned toward the officer. "Do you know where my dog could be; or did someone kill him, also?" Lisa could sound cold and humorless.

She turned and right in front of her stood Bert. Without hesitation, Lisa kicked Bert right in his balls. Bert bent over in pain and then she kicked his head so hard that his head and balls rolled over the floor. "You damn fool! Did you think that gun that belonged to me could kill without bullets? Bullets to fit that gun went out of sight a hundred years ago. Oh, my poor dog."

The thought of being the Garden dog's Best in Show had gone out of her head. "That gun and my dog go hand in glove. Whoever killed Jim knew me and I know who it points to." Lisa looked around for the first two men she had seen in the men's room. They were no longer there.

Lisa had not paid too much attention to her mother, who had isolated herself. Ruth was the one who had handed the dog over to the woman, the woman who said, "Give me the dog." The dog knew her.

"I thought she was a friend," Ruth said. She didn't have to tell Lisa who the woman was. Lisa knew.

She was far more distressed over the loss of the dog. "Jim probably deserved what happened." Lisa was stiff, like self-frozen, and in a state of disbelief. "Too much," she kept repeating, "Too much. I'm worried about my dog. The tears rolled down her face.

Pat handed Lisa a fresh snow-white handkerchief. She sniffed and blew her nose. "This has been a terrible day. I waited a whole year for this day."

"What did happen?" Pat urged.

Between chokes and sobs, Lisa told what had happened. She also told him about the encounter with Bert.

Lisa's mother asked if she needed to stay any longer. It was dark, damp, and getting colder.

Pat stepped up. "There is no reason to stay here any longer." The body had been removed and just a few police officers remained with them. Pat offered to drive them home and to take them to dinner. Lisa and her mother declined.

Ruth went straight to bed, but Lisa was too hungry and tired to sleep. A glass of milk and some crackers took care of the hole in her stomach. Lisa crawled into bed without the love of her life, Ice. The phone interrupted her deep sleep. It was Officer Pat Sheldon. "Would you be willing to answer a few questions?"

"When," was her sleepy reply?

"About 10:00 a.m."

"Okay." She liked the sound of his accent.

"I'll pick you up," he offered.

To Lisa's surprise, she felt rested. Then she looked at the clock. No wonder, it was 9:00 a.m. After a trip to the bathroom, Lisa came out singing. It wasn't because she was about to meet Pat. She had discovered she was no longer pregnant. "Thank God!" She blessed herself. "I sure didn't want to have to make that decision."

On the way to the police station, Pat inquired, "Have you seen the morning papers?"

"No!" she replied.

"Here." He handed her some headline clippings, which read, "Wonder Dog on the Lam? No Dog Show for Ice. Dog on the Town." There were more, but no mention of the death during the dog show.

"You know, it isn't funny. Someone has been murdered over this." She held back the tears. "I'm sure I know who is in back of all this."

"Who?" Pat wanted to know. "Maybe you had better stay out of this, as best you can until we know more about that Jim guy."

"I know!" she added. "I'm not ready to say, but it all falls together like a pattern."

Pat eyed the pretty girl beside him, as he pulled to the curb in front of New York City Police Station, Number 36.

As she entered, there were smiles. It was nice to work with a looker once in a while.

"We will find your dog. Boy, I'd sure like a dog like him," one of the friendly policemen offered.

"Me, too," came from another.

While Lisa was gone, an intruder rang the apartment doorbell and rapped at the same time, like someone was in a hurry. A woman Lisa would have recognized at once was standing in the hall with a dirty, forlorn dog that looked like a Standard Poodle. "Where is Mrs. Taloomas?" she asked Ruth abruptly.

"Can that dog be Ice?" The dog wagged his tail at the sound of his name. Ruth gasped, "Come in!"

"Thanks, but no. I found him running through traffic on Madison Avenue."

Ruth took the dog and said, "Haven't we met somewhere before? Does Lisa know you?"

Lisa would have been at the woman's throat. It was Lahr! She left as quickly as she came.

Lisa's mother had gone for her purse to reward the woman, but the hallway was empty. Ice was at his dish in the kitchen drinking much needed water. Ruth opened the door a peek to see if the half-way familiar woman had left. The paper was at her feet. According to the headlines, Jim Cory had a flawless background. He had married well and had been considered an honest dog show judge. "Then why did they cancel his assignment to do Best in Show?" Ruth knew that much about his last day.

"We can't find anything. Apparently, the man led an ideal life; not even a parking ticket." the sergeant laughed. "That's better than most of us."

"Evidently, he has covered his tracks well." Lisa wished she had kept her mouth shut in the first place.

"You seem to think our assumptions are wrong?" another officer intruded.

"I can't tell you why Jim Cory was murdered or by whom, but I can tell you what kind of man he was."

"Tell us," the second in command pulled up a more comfortable chair.

"He never worked an honest day in his adult life. He lived off rich and famous women and one day he married one. There have been enough jealous husbands over the years. One of those could have been your assassin. I've known this man since I was four years old."

"Was he involved with your life?" Pat asked.

"In what way?" she asked.

"Were you involved with him?" Pat wanted to know.

"Heaven's no! He was old enough to be my father."

"So was your husband." Pat got a dirty look from Lisa.

She knew she was making a mistake asking them to stop worrying about a dead man and search for an animal but she changed the subject. "I dread the thought that dog of mine, the stolen poodle, could be dead. He is a very special dog and means the world to me. Please find him. I must go before I start crying again." Lisa turned to Pat. "Take me home." It was almost a plea. "I've got to try and find my dog, if he isn't in Greece by this time."

The sergeant had been listening. "Who? What? Greece?"

"See if you can find him with my ex, the Greek tycoon, Bert Taloomas."

Pat pulled into the No Parking zone in front of the apartment. "Would you want me to take you inside?" Pat invited himself.

"No, I have a lot to talk to my mother about. Call me later." She added. Lisa all but leaped out of the car. She thought she knew the figure leaving the apartment. She turned suddenly to face Pat. She saw recognition on Pat's face. He knew the disappearing figure. "Who was that?" Lisa asked the doorman.

"I make a point of not knowing who comes or who goes," he said in a snooty way.

"Thanks a lot!" Lisa was mad. "This is a three-ring circus. It's like a nightmare. What do all these people have in common? There is something going on. Woman's instinct. Hell, it's easy to see. But what? They can't all be murderers."

Lisa put the key in the apartment door. Ruth opened it. Ice met Lisa full face and knocked her to the floor. She tried twice to get on her feet, but Ice was licking her tear-stained face and wouldn't let her get away. The boy on the elevator and her mother came to the rescue. He pulled Ice off her and her mother was able to get Lisa back on her feet. The dog was dirty and smelled awful. He certainly didn't look like a prize. "Oh, Mother, I'm so grateful. How did you find him? Where was he? He sure needs a bath. Mother, I'm so glad."

Her mother was trying to explain to Lisa, but the dog was all over his master. The young woman tried to make her way to the phone to call the police. "This is Lisa McHugh. My dog has been found."

"Good, lady! So it was just another run away," the man laughed.

"Down! Damn it!" Lisa demanded and Ice responded. Then, he licked her hand.

"Lisa," her mother began, "you should have seen this strange looking woman who brought the dog home. She had grayish-brown skin and ice blue eyes with lots of white around the eyes, just like a bad horse. She was spooky but seemed a little familiar."

"Oh, I should have known!" Lisa gasped. "I know who she is. She was my maid once. I'll say she is spooky. Remember, you met her because she went to work at Tom and Mary's house later."

There was a knock at the door and a key turned the lock. Jack seemed surprised to find all three still in his apartment.

"Look at my dog," Lisa pointed to her dirty, ratty-looking, former Best in Show contender. "Lahr was behind this."

"Yes, I know." Jack surprised her.

"How do you know?"

"I saw her just now out front trying to hail a cab." Jack quickly changed the subject. "Haven't you packed your bags? President's Day weekend is coming up and I have people coming here."

"Do you rent the apartment out?" Lisa wondered.

"No, dear, they are other guests and they won't have a filthy dog."

"We are on our way." Lisa headed for her bedroom. "I'm sorry we over-stayed," she called as she tossed her luggage on the bed.

"There's something else." Jack followed her into the bedroom. "I've just been to the hospital. Your ex is in bad shape. Why in the hell did you kick the 'Golden Goose' for both of us so hard?"

"Oh, both of us! Ha!" She thought Jack was ripping off Bert.

"What you did was stupid." Jack had never talked to her like that before. "He, your ex, wants me to find a way to cut you off entirely!"

"Come back at 6:00 p.m. We will be gone. Men! Hurry, Mother. We don't have much time."

"Why didn't you say 8:00 p.m.? You can't take that dog into any decent hotel."

Lisa reached for the phone. She called the York West Hotel and asked for a suite with a rear door entrance. They readily agreed when she gave her name.

"Okay, let's finish and get out of here," she told both her mother and the dog.

"Was Jack still in the place?" She had not heard the door close. At that point, she heard the door. "Oh, no, he knows where we will be!"

When they left the elevator, a cab with roses was waiting and the driver knew where to take them. "Remind me to call the Bramble Inn to pick us up tomor-row." Lisa smelled the roses.

CHAPTER 21

▼

"That no good S.O.B. knows Lahr!"

Lisa said it so loud that the New York cabbie said, "You must be talking about my wife!" It was good for a laugh.

The suite was very nice. It had two bedrooms, a living room with a balcony overlooking the park plus a Jacuzzi tub. "Like the grasshopper, live for today." Lisa laughed, as she and the dirty dog danced around in the lovely room.

"I'm getting into that fancy tub before you give Ice a bath in it." Lisa heard her mother take care of that item.

Lisa had another idea. She found the telephone book and made a list of the phone numbers of New York hospitals. The first one that sounded right to her was Manhattan General. Lisa called. Luck was kind. "Hello, I'm Mrs. Bertram Taloomas. How is my husband?"

"Just a moment. I'll put you through to his room." The voice answered. Lisa hung up. Now she knew where he was.

She quickly ate, bathed, and dressed. Lisa looked at her watch. "I'll have to get there before 6:00 p.m. I know Jack is a go-between. Damn these lawyers! Their hearts are in their wallets."

"I'll go with you," her mother offered, as Lisa reached for her purse.

"No, Mother, this is a course I have to take alone. I won't be gone too long." Lisa was rehearsing a speck, as she rode in the cab.

"Did you say something?" the cabbie asked.

"Just talking to myself. I do that now and then," Lisa laughed.

"I do that, too. Is the front entrance to the hospital okay?"

"Sure thing," was her answer. The fare was honest so she tipped the man well. "Why do they say these cabbies are terrible? I sure don't think so," she thought.

Lisa introduced herself at the front desk and was given Bert's room number. "Visiting hours are over at 8:00 p.m.," said the clerk.

Private room number 1240 was easily found, but there was a patrol officer stationed at his door. Bert could see the corridor. He watched as Lisa tried to get past the man. "I'm Mrs. Taloomas!" She announced, as she entered the room. "Darling, I'd have brought flowers but I just found out you were here. Why the police?"

"To keep you out!" he was thinking. "What a good-looking broad you are. Why did you want to hurt me so bad?" He patted the bed beside him. "Sit, Mrs. Taloomas. Are you going to keep my name?"

"It's a good name. It opens doors."

Bert remarked with a smile, "Be careful around Jack. He's a two-faced bastard. I warned you about him before. Do you still love me?" he asked.

"You are a liar, you know."

"It's okay. Kitty will always love me and my beautiful son. It will be enough."

"Are you thinking of retiring?" Lisa asked.

"I still love you, sweetheart and I'm going to prove it." He patted her hand. "What brought you here? Were you afraid I would die and leave you nothing? I'm not so easy to get rid of!"

"What is this all about? Jack tells me you want to cut me out of our agreement."

"I don't like dealing with him," her former husband stated. "Honey, I really do feel rotten about the way I treated you." Bert took her hand. "No ring?"

"You know what happened to that ring. Your cohort stole it from me." Lisa looked at her bare hand.

"I paid her to do that." Bert laughed. "You know, she was in the pay of your friend, Jim Cory, and Jack uses her for information. Anyway, I'm glad Jack told you I wanted to see you."

Lisa held her tongue. "What is Jack's game?" she wondered.

"I want to go back to my country and hold my newborn son in my arms. I don't want to be trying to find out where you are because I'm taking my money out of Jack's hands. I've always been 'legit' and I don't trust Jack. I'd like to write a check for sixteen million dollars if you would consider that a lifetime settlement."

"My God, no strings? The house and land are mine?"

"Of course!" Bert replied. "I'm still sorry about the Garden. You know that Cory guy had quite a history."

"Don't I know! Who killed him? Was it you?"

"Lady, you scare me! Where did you get that idea?" Bert sat up in bed, rested on one arm and looked into her eyes. "You are not serious are you?"

"One thing I'm sure of is Jim didn't kill himself," Lisa believed.

"Here is your check. Sorry it wasn't to be. I still love you."

"Me, too, especially now!" Lisa laughed, walked over, gave him a kiss, and was on her way home to wash a dog.

The next morning, Lisa was waiting for the bank to open. "I don't want to lose this check. He could change his mind. Life plays dirty tricks on you. To lose out at the Garden was heartbreaking, but this check will make up for his rotten behavior. Only a month ago, I was afraid I was losing everything. Now, this will change my life."

The president of the bank entered his office. "My dear Mrs. Taloomas, please have a cup of coffee. It's a beautiful morning. What can I do for you?" His teeth needed attention, as he gave her a false smile. Then, she handed him the check. You could see him counting the zeros.

"I wish to deposit this amount in my bank in Lexington, Kentucky."

"All of it?" The banker thought she needed advice. "Surely, you are going to invest part of the money."

"Is there any way I could talk to my bank president, George Marlowe?"

"Oh, I know George. He is a nice man," the banker grinned.

"See a dentist," Lisa said under her breath.

"I have George on the phone." The man in charge handed her the instrument.

"May I speak to Mr. Marlowe alone?"

"Of course." The banker left the room.

"Mr. Marlowe, Lisa Taloomas here. I've arranged for a large check to be deposited in my name."

"Yes!" he waited.

"This transaction must be very confidential, you hear?" Lisa was business like.

He heard. "By the way, Lisa, how is your mother? She is a very charming lady."

"What about that?" Lisa thought on her way out of the bank. "He's an old coot. Now I have to get a certified investor to help me. I hope he is honest. I'm beginning to feel like I'm surrounded by strange people."

Back at the hotel, her mother wanted to know when they were leaving. "I'm anxious to get home," she complained. "What about the airport?"

She was stopped when Lisa announced that she had torn the airplane tickets to shreds. "I'll send you home first-class tomorrow. I'd like to stay here for a couple of days. I want to become better acquainted with an Irish cop I've met." Lisa patted her cleaned-up dog and smiled a knowing smile.

"Stop that!" Ruth scolded. "I didn't raise you to be a hussy, you know."

"Mother," Lisa replied, "when you have sixteen million dollars, they don't call you a hussy! You are called, 'that interesting Mrs. Taloomas!' Ha!"

"And, I hope you drop that name!"

"Which one?" Lisa teased. "No one ever called Jackie K. a hussy!"

"What are you going to do about that dog? That dog isn't covered with street dirt." Ruth continued, "Someone emptied a vacuum cleaner bag all over him. I can smell it and it's making me choke," the mother laughed.

"First, lunch. Where do you want to go? Then, the three of us will get into the Jacuzzi; you, me and Ice."

The dog was being brushed and dried with a hair dryer when the two females, dressed only in terry cloth robes, heard a hard knock on their door. Their heads turbaned in towels matched their white robes. They yelled, "Who is it?" There was no answer. Another knock bellowed out; this one much louder. "What in the hell do you want? Who are you?" Lisa was annoyed. She opened the door just a peek.

Outside in the hall was a large entourage of hotel employees, maids, workmen and the hotel manager. Lisa recognized Tom's brother.

"What is going on? What is the matter?" the younger woman asked.

"Mrs. Taloomas, there has been a complaint."

"This gentleman, pointing to Mike, complains that water is dripping from his ceiling onto his bed."

"May we take a look?" the manager of the hotel asked.

Lisa looked at her mother. "I didn't know how to turn off the Jacuzzi. I forgot to tell you."

"I thought you knew the system."

There to be expected, the bathroom floor was covered with water and more was flowing over the sides of the tub. The employees came in with towels, mops, buckets, and went to work while the non-workers watched.

"You women will have to move. Here are the keys to Room 1244." The manager's eyes were on the dog. "After you are settled, I'd like to see you in my office." He gave Lisa a look.

"It's just down the hall." Mike addressed them. "Get your stuff and I'll help you move. I've got to get another room. My bed is soaked. What were the two of you trying to do?"

"How was I to know that you pushed the same damn button for on and for off! I sure don't want anything like that in my house." Ruth stomped the floor with her slippered foot.

"That manager looked like a 'prissy sissy.'" Lisa remarked. "We were having so much fun; three in a tub! He can't make us pay for the mess. That's why the hotel has insurance."

Mike was still in their new rooms. He was talking to Lisa's mother. "Mike, are you the complaining type?" Lisa asked. "What are you doing in New York?"

"I just got here and tried to take a nap. This is an old hotel. There is probably damage," Mike reflected. "But then so is the White House, yet they keep after the place."

"Why and how long are you going to be in New York?" Lisa wanted to know. She looked around in her new surroundings. She noticed that he had a tub and shower but no Jacuzzi.

"I'm here on family business. It will take a day or two."

"How are Mary and Tom?" Ruth asked about her daughter and new son-in-law.

"They are fine. Tom says Mary is expecting!" the older brother announced. "Everyone is happy about it."

"That didn't take long." Lisa could be a pain in the ass at times.

"What about dinner?" Mike asked. "The three of us, of course." He really wished it could have been Lisa and him. He found Lisa damned attractive.

"Sorry about the dog. That was too bad. The family was watching for you on TV at the dog show." Those were Mike's parting words. Lisa imagined a circle of Mike, Tom, Mary, and his parents watching the television.

Lisa looked around. "We don't have a balcony off this room. I'm gonna remember this place; all because of a little water."

"Mike didn't think it was a small matter," her mother interrupted.

Lisa seemed to be thinking, "Oh, well, damn him!"

"Him who?"

Both Lisa and her mother laughed and let it pass.

Lisa walked to the phone in the room. She called the police station where Pat was stationed. "This is Lisa Taloomas. Is there anything new about the murder in the Garden?" she inquired.

"What?" someone asked.

"Is Pat Sheldon there?"

"No, he is out of town. Who did you say was calling?" the voice at the other end asked.

Lisa hung up. "Rats!" was her only comment.

"Look, Mrs. McHugh," she addressed her mother. "I know you want to get out of here. Why don't I buy you a new car and we can drive back to Carlisle?"

CHAPTER 22

▼

Ruth wanted to resist. But how could she with an '87 Ford with almost 100,000 miles on the odometer? "Mike said he wasn't staying here too long. Maybe he would go back with us if we drove," said Ruth.

"We had better get dressed. Mike said he'd pick us up for dinner at 7:00 p.m. It's 5:30 now." Lisa looked at her watch. "If you do my hair, Mother, I'll do yours." Lisa walked to the large hotel window to take a look. "Oh, I forgot, I'm supposed to see that sour-faced manager." Instead, she called him.

"My dear Mrs. Taloomas, I only wanted to make sure you were comfortable since the hotel is sold out for the holiday."

"I can't believe it is the same person," she turned to her mother. "Butter would melt in his voice. Money talks. Maybe I will keep that name."

"Lisa, are you talking to yourself?"

"I guess I've been alone too long. I talk to the dog, to the horse, to the television and to myself."

"There is a cure for that. Come live with me," her mother suggested. "I'm alone since Mary left."

"What? No way!"

At dinner, Mike surprised the older woman. "Would you care to dance?"

"Oh, I'd love to dance," she smiled. Lisa watched as the two of them waltzed around the floor of the beautiful ballroom.

"I had no idea my mother could dance like that." Ruth and Mike made a handsome couple and they were being noticed. "Holy cow!" Lisa thought. "He is at least forty, why should ten years surprise me? Bert was twice my age. That was okay. Why should I be shocked?" Lisa wasn't shocked. She was jealous.

"Your mother is a beautiful dancer," Mike remarked, as he seated the blushing Ruth.

"I'll be darned," Lisa thought.

That night, as her mother was getting ready for bed, Lisa opened her door. "I know I'm not invited." Lisa was stopped in her tracks. Her mother was talking and laughing on the phone. Somehow, it seemed immoral. "I thought he was interested in me!"

"Lisa," her mother called. "Did you want something?"

"No, go to bed." Lisa felt like the parent.

Lisa lay in bed staring at the ceiling. She was thoroughly annoyed. "He really should have asked me to dance at least once. She is too old for him. I don't want him, except it would be an easy way to get into 'the crowd.' Maybe I should change my name. My family makes me sick." She pounded the pillow. "First, it is Mary into my crowd. Then, it's Nancy having the first grandchild. I should have had the first."

A slit of light shone under her bedroom door. "Are you all right?" her mother asked like only a mother can ask. Mrs. Ruth McHugh slid into the bed beside her daughter. "He wanted to show me New York in the morning." She whispered and Lisa stiffened. "I told him no. I hate that place." Lisa felt her warmth and snuggled closer. She fell asleep.

Now, Ruth lay awake. "He made me feel young again."

"Mother, give Mike a call. I want to see if I can locate Pat before we leave." Mike was a little more than pleased at her call. He asked Ruth to go to breakfast, only Ruth. "That so and so," came out of Lisa. "Oh, well, Mother is still a nice looking woman."

Lisa located Pat and planned to have lunch; her treat in the hotel coffee shop. When he agreed, the smile returned to her face. Pat arrived with those blue, blue eyes and those flashing white teeth. "Whew!" There was a look of Jack Kennedy about him. "Where have you been?" Lisa greeted him.

"Out of town. How have you been?"

"I think I missed you a little bit," he smiled a warm grin.

Lisa's heart skipped a beat. "All is okay now." She reached for his hand in greeting. "Come in."

"What is going on? Am I being seduced?" Pat added, "I hope."

"Not with that ring on your left hand." She didn't have to point.

"That, my dear, was my mother's wedding band and it's an old Irish custom to wear your mother's band for a year after she is gone."

"I'm relieved," Lisa flirted.

"Why?" the twinkle was in his eye and smile.

"Because, I don't do married men." Lisa returned the flirt. "I hate to disturb the moment," she teased, "but I have to get home. I wanted to be sure that I am not needed here any longer by the police."

"Why would you?" he didn't understand.

"Because of the murder in the Garden."

"You are free to leave," he walked toward her.

"Why is everything so quiet? The papers have it on a back page or not at all and TV is nil."

"The police like it that way. It is easier to trace. In fact, I'm part of the job. What do you know about him? He, the Cory guy, seemed to be a friend of yours." At this point, Pat was all cop.

"He was no friend. I knew him many years. I despised the man. I had no respect for him."

"But, how well did you know the man? What about his life?" Pat insisted.

"He was such a phony. I think he was an honest dog show judge. He was such an ass kisser. I made him my private target. For eight of the ten years, I knew who and what he was. I made a point of beating him at any show where he would show up and I did!" Lisa was on a roll. "I'm like my grandmother; just don't tread on me because I don't forget." Lisa's lips were pulled tight at the thought.

"Did you kill him?" Pat asked seriously.

"No!" Lisa said in disbelief.

"Do you want to tell me what he did to you?" Pat inquired.

"No!" Lisa repeated.

Pat thought for a minute, "In any event, James Paul Cory was in deep trouble. The F.B.I. is taking over. Tell me about your grandmother." Pat was curious.

Lisa loved to talk about Mom Mom. "Well, she loved to tell everyone that her name had been Kitty McGovern from County Caven, Ireland. She loved Ireland. She loved America, but she loved Ireland more."

She saw Pat was taking notes. "Have you been to Ireland?" Lisa questioned and decided not to say anymore.

"I was born in Ireland," he smiled. "Where did you think I got this brogue? Tell me about your father," Pat urged.

"First, I know very little about him. He died at 39." Lisa reached for Pat's hand. "I'm not a fool." She warned.

"I'm not just a cop," was his reply.

"You bastard!" Lisa called after him. "What happened to your Irish brogue?" Lisa had been told that some I.R.A. personnel were hidden in the New York

Police Department. "Now I know I'm going home. Where in hell is my mother now?"

Lisa picked up the newspaper that Pat had carried in on his arrival. The headlines read, "One of the World's Richest Babies Born to Mr. and Mrs. Bertram Taloomas at a Private Hospital in Paris."

"Why wasn't the baby born in Greece?" Lisa wondered.

Waiting for her mother's return, Lisa sat thinking of what Pat seemed to suggest. "I remember Mom Mom telling me that the part of Ireland where she was born was shaped like a three-pointed star. They had even made three-pointed stars out of paper to show where they could give a good jump and land in Northern Ireland. I've got to talk to Mother and see what she knows. How has my mother survived and raised four girls? We were never on relief that I know of. My father wouldn't have left a lot of insurance or cash. Why did Jack ask about Mom Mom? I'll bet that feisty, old broad was into something," Lisa laughed aloud. "The money, her money, we all knew a lot of it went to Ireland; at least that is what we thought."

Lisa looked at her watch. "I'm going to get a taxi and ride around the town. I won't leave a note. Let her wonder where I've gone!"

It was a beautiful day in New York. There had been an early morning Spring-like rain. It looked washed and fresh. The sky was blue, blue; like his eyes.

"Where to?" asked the cabbie.

"Around the park and then to Chinatown." Lisa was trying to find comfort in the broken seat of the taxi.

The cab driver had his window down. He noticed that she enjoyed the fresh air. "I'll put it up if you like, but it smells so good right now. In an hour from now, New York will start to stink."

Lisa laughed and returned to her thoughts. "What was Jim Cory up to? Was he working money, buying guns or sending money to the I.R.A.? Lisa wondered if so and whose side he had been on. Did those long talks about Ireland get him involved? I know she hated the English and the terrible way they treated the Irish poor, who lived in Northern Ireland; the part that the English stole."

"Are you enjoying the ride?" the cabbie asked.

"Yes, very nice. You can skip Chinatown. I think I'm ready to go back." She wanted to see if her mother had returned. "I want to talk to her while all this stuff is fresh in my mind."

"Did you say something?" the man with the cap on his head asked.

"The only thing Mom Mom ever told me about Ireland was its beauty and its soul. I knew she went there at least five or six times for extended periods of time.

I thought she always went alone. I know she still had family there. Pat is looking for information of some kind, but he has gotten all he is getting from me. I hope I haven't said too much, as it is. I remember the notes he was taking and I'm sure he wrote what I said about Mom Mom's background."

This time when he called, the lovely brogue was in place. "I'm leaving town for a few days."

"Are you going to Ireland?" Lisa interrupted.

"Yes, my dear, and you keep your mouth shut from now on, okay?"

"Why?" The phone went dead. "I'm so mad I can't see straight!" She threw the phone across the room. "What have I done?" she cried.

The door opened. "Are you alone?" It was her mother.

"I thought you had left town." Lisa was angry. She was mad at Pat, her mother, and mostly at herself.

"Mother, sit. We have to talk." She told of the afternoon, of what she had said and of her fears. Then the questions began. "Why didn't you ever tell me why Dad went to Ireland? I knew that he was dead but I never knew why."

Ruth began, "Conditions were so bad for the Irish in the north around Belfast and near. The British were determined to make them suffer by giving them lousy jobs and high taxes. They were being spit upon and it drove your father crazy. There were twelve men who left at different times. To date, ten passports have been returned. There are still two there. We are sure they are there. They would be I.R.A., I'm sure."

"Who were they?" Lisa asked.

"I don't know and I don't want to know either." Her mother suggested that Pat could have bugged the room.

"He didn't have time," Lisa laughed. "I all but pushed him out the door. Did my father have a lot of insurance?"

"No, just what he had through the Union. I think it was twelve thousand."

"You didn't raise us on that!" Lisa knew that was impossible.

"Let's not talk anymore. I'm getting upset." Her mother looked around, even underneath the bed. "You can't be too sure. Grandma wouldn't have had any connection with 'outlaws.' Her mother offered quietly. She still had family with long memories."

CHAPTER 23

▼

They didn't spend the night. Mother and daughter were on the plane. Ice was being shipped to Harrisburg, Pennsylvania.

"How did we live?" Lisa had to know.

"I'll tell you everything in the sanctuary of my kitchen at home." First class or not, both women took mental notes of all their fellow passengers. "I don't think we have to fear the one in the turban," her mother laughed.

"Why not? He could be one of the bombers." Both snickered.

"Once home, your father told me nothing. One night, bag in hand, he kissed me goodbye and in the black of night, he drove off in someone's car. Then, five years later, I received his passport stamped 'deceased.' So, what else do you want to know?"

"How did we go on? Were we on relief?" Lisa wanted every drop; the good and the bad.

"Mom Mom paid the bills. I got a check every month from a third party and that made everything possible. Satisfied?"

"For now, but who sent the checks?" Lisa asked.

"Over my dead body, sweetheart." her mother made it clear.

"What a story? Why didn't you tell me before?" she asked her mother.

"You were always at Mom Mom's. Get it?" Her mother was resentful.

Lisa had rented a car at the Harrisburg Airport to drive her mother to Carlisle. Now that she had heard the rest of the story, she and Ice planned to drive to West Virginia and pick up her car. Without even a cup of hot tea, both women were glad to say goodbye to each other. Neither woman had mentioned Mike. Lisa promised to call her mother when she got home.

After Lisa exercised the dog, she gave him water and food. Lisa then headed for a hot tub. After that, she crawled into bed and pulled the covers over her head. She had forgotten to call her mother.

She was awakened early in the morning by a persistent phone ringing. "I know, Mother. I forgot."

"I'm not your mother, sweetheart. What town in County Caven?" Pat asked. Lisa slammed the phone in place. The phone rang again. Lisa refused to answer. An hour later, as she showered, the phone continued to ring. She ignored it. Then, a message on her cell phone read, "Your mother is in danger. Pat."

"This is too much! Damn him!" The phone rang and rang. She could hear the ring clear to the stable. Jett was as beautiful as when Lisa had left the treasured horse.

Tom, her new brother-in-law, popped up. "Gee, you are back." He seemed serious. Tom was serious. "There have been two men asking about you. They wanted to know when you'd be back. I didn't know and told them so. If they come back, you call me right away. I didn't like their looks, okay?"

Lisa promised and went into her stable to feed Jett an apple. She stroked the beautiful horse and she could see that Jett was with colt. An hour or two later, the phone rang. Without thinking, Lisa answered.

"Lisa, for God's sake, you really had me worried." It was her mother. "I found something." She sounded intrigued. "I found a name of Billy McGovern; he was Mom Mom's brother. I found his address."

"Stop! Not another word. You are scaring me to death. Pat called for information this morning. Listen to me, Mother. Burn that name and address. Do it right away. Your phone could be tapped right now. I'm not sure that I'm not under surveillance."

"My God!" Her mother promised.

"Take this seriously, Mother. I am." Lisa remembered Pat's voice saying, "Your mother is in danger."

"I can see it now. They are trying to find the two men who have escaped them. Who are they? Are they Irish or English?" Lisa felt sweat on the palm of her hands.

Her mother followed orders. With a barnburner match, she burned Billy's name. There was a name on the back of the slip of paper, another name. She didn't mention that to Lisa. In the same box, she noticed a check that was uncashed. It had been made out to the second name and signed by Kitty McGovern McHugh.

"Now, what does all this mean?" she muttered. Ruth considered burning the check also. While she wondered what to do, there was a knock at the door. She jumped. Two men were standing on her porch. Ruth opened the door a crack. She stuck her toe in the opening to block a forced entry. "What do you want?" She didn't like their looks.

"Is your daughter here?" one man asked.

"I have no daughter." She slammed the door. She wanted to be sure they left. Her heart was racing with fear. Ruth was on the phone once more, but Lisa was back in her small barn talking to Tom.

"Were those men who were here, did they look like twins?" Lisa asked.

"Could be," Tom reflected.

Lisa remembered the two men who found Jim Cory's body. They looked like very somber twins. "Now what is their game?" she pondered.

After asking about her sister, Lisa asked Tom if he could help her with what had been Bert's Boxer Dog Kennels. "I want to get back into breeding Standard Poodles. Ice is more than ready to help. I have always taken care of my own dogs. I know where there is just the right bitch to start a new breeding program." On the way back to the house, with Ice by her side, she told the dog to expect a bride. "I miss puppies. Time to start over."

"They saw me coming," Lisa explained to Ice. "I had to pay five thousand for your mate. She is almost as beautiful as you are. Her background is entirely white for generations. She is a proven bitch. Her name, sweetheart, is Snow. She has been bred once. Hey dog, I'm talking to you about your bride." Ice wasn't interested. The car seat next to Lisa was comfortable and it had been a long trip.

Once home, with nothing in the house to eat, Lisa decided she was forced to go to the store. There was something familiar about the car driving up to the house. Out stepped the Major carrying a bouquet of flowers. She was trapped. "Maybe I can get him to take me to dinner!"

The big brass doorknocker was used instead of the doorbell. Lisa hesitated and then decided that she had better be nice. She was running out of escorts.

"What a nice surprise on such a beautiful day. I was hoping you were home. I heard you were back. I tried to call. He held the flowers high. Will you have dinner with me tonight?"

"The flowers are beautiful and the invitation accepted. You will have to give me time to dress." Lisa looked down at the boots and jeans she was wearing.

"I'll be back at 7:00 p.m. to get you." He reached for the door.

"It will be a pleasure." Lisa was at her "Scarlett" best.

The Major almost clicked his heels and then bowed slightly. "He really is handsome in the military uniform," she thought, as she ran for the stairs, tub, and her best dress.

That evening, Lisa invited the Major to come in and have a nightcap. The Major didn't need another drink. He had had a couple at the club. He accepted the offer, nonetheless. "I'll have a coke or a ginger ale." He surprised her. "May I escort you to the barbecue?"

"Where? Who is having a party?" Lisa sat closer. She had had a drink or two, also. "I just got home from New York, so I don't know anything about a barbecue," Lisa blocked a yawn.

"I know. I didn't want to waste any time. You are always in such demand. I hope we can get better acquainted. I find you such a tantalizing woman."

"That's the first time anyone has ever called me that," Lisa thought.

"One ice cube or two?" Lisa laughed and invited the Major to join her in the large, handsome family room. He followed her like a puppy dog.

"We have so much in common," he announced, as he picked the most comfortable leather chair in the room.

"In what way?" They had nothing in common unless he was hiding something not yet known to her.

"First, we are both Yankees," he said. Lisa was fighting a yawn.

The Major finished his coke and wondered if he dare try to kiss her goodnight. "The evening has been most enjoyable. I hope we can do it again." He took her hand and she squeezed his. A smile flashed across his face. He took her in his arms and squeezed her back.

"That was different," Lisa reflected, as she locked the door behind him. "Come along," she told Ice. "I'd rather sleep with you. He is so boring. On the day of the barbecue, I must take a nap in the afternoon or I'll fall asleep right in front of him."

It was raining and raining very hard in Carlisle, Pennsylvania. Even so, it was Monday and on Monday, you did the wash. Therefore, Mrs. Ruth McHugh was working under the rule of rain before 7:00 a.m. and clear by 11:00 a.m. In her house, the washer, no dryer, was in the basement. It had always been there. She didn't want the washer anywhere else because it could flood. She had never had a clothes dryer. Ruth checked outside. It was really raining. She started to run the clothes lines inside just in case she would have to hang the wash inside. At the moment, Ruth thought she could hear voices above her head. She stopped the washer and listened. "I must have left the TV on."

Before she could turn the washer back on, she heard footsteps. There were at least two people in her house. Whoever they were, they were intruders. Her first thoughts were of the two men who had been on her porch in search of Lisa. Then, Ruth heard a loud thud, like a piece of furniture had been turned over.

She turned off the lights in the basement and headed for the fruit cellar. She locked the door from the inside and sat down on a bench. Her heart was thumping in her chest. "What do they want?" She questioned herself and then she remembered the slip of paper with the names of two whose passports had not been returned. They would be in their early 50's and probably causing trouble for the cause.

Her cell phone was in her apron pocket. She had brought it along because she had planned to call a friend or two between her laundry loads.

Very quietly, she rang 9-1-1. "This is Ruth McHugh at 1141 West Jones. Some one or two have broken into my house."

"Where are you? Are you safe?" the voice at the other end asked. "Help is on the way. Where are you?"

"I'm hiding in my fruit cellar in the basement."

"Stay there. We will identify ourselves before you come out, okay? Help is on its way." She could hear the sirens approaching her home within three minutes.

About the same time, at Lisa's house, one of two men reached for Lisa's doorknocker. The huge double windowless doors made it difficult to see who was outside. The peephole wasn't worth much.

"May we come in?" the one twin asked.

"No, get off my porch!" Ice was right by her side barking and jumping at the doors. "I'll set my dog on you!" She screamed.

"You are about to be charged with murder," they yelled back at her.

"Who would do that?"

"We will."

"Oh, my God!" Lisa ran for Tom. She didn't have to go far. Tom had recognized their car.

"Oh Tom, I've been set up." She told her story of finding Jim Cory's body and the two men standing over his body. Jim had had her gun in his hand.

Meanwhile, back at Ruth's house, she waited and waited for the promised release. Ruth opened the door and peeked into total darkness. She was afraid to turn on a light. She felt her way in darkness. Once, upon the stairs up to the kitchen, she crept a step at a time into her house where furniture had been overturned. "I've got to get a dog!" she thought.

Back at Lisa's at the same time, Tom advised, "Call the police! Do you know them? What did they want? Please don't upset Mary."

"I'll call the police and you get up to the house. I'll keep the dog."

Tom was trying to be helpful but would he be helpful enough.

CHAPTER 24

▼

"Give me Ice. I'm not going to let the dog out of my sight."

The police were there in moments. They heard her story. The officer who acted like he knew what he was doing, asked, "You didn't invite them into the house, did you?" He picked up one of the two unfinished drinks.

"No, I had a guest before the two men arrived. It had to be after 8:00 o'clock, as it was dark."

Up the steps and into the house stood Tom's older brother, Mike. "What the hell is going on?" Mike inquired. "There are cops all over the place. I just talked to your mother and she had a houseful of cops because someone broke into her place."

The phone rang. "Probably nosey neighbors," she said as one policeman seemed amused.

"Answer the phone," another police officer ordered Lisa.

She did and she recognized the fake brogue. "Don't say a word. Keep your mouth shut. You are being watched." Lisa dropped the phone.

A police officer picked it up. "Who is it?" he asked.

"I've just been threatened." Lisa fought off the shakes to no avail. She had to be helped to a chair.

"What is going on around here?" The Chief of Police had just arrived. People were gathering outside. Tom was worried about Mary.

A handsome, tall figure approached Lisa. "What in God's name are the two of you mixed up in?" It was Mike, Tom's older brother. "Your mother called and she is very upset. I'm on my way over there now. Pack a few things and come along." He could see she wanted to get away.

The police interfered. "You have questions to answer." The chief had taken charge.

"There is someone trying to blackmail me. I am afraid and want to be with my mother. She has these people harassing her, too. I want to be with her." It seemed reasonable.

Lisa was allowed to leave since she wasn't bringing any charges. Most of the things she wanted to take were still packed in her luggage. Off the three of them went to Carlisle; Mike, Lisa and Ice. This was the thing to do. Lisa agreed as they drove at top speed through the beautiful and wild West Virginia.

"Over there at the Bramble Inn is where Mother and I stayed on our way to New York."

"Over there is where your mother and I were going to meet this weekend," Mike shook Lisa in disbelief.

"Not my mother."

"What did I hear about Washington?" Lisa asked. Mike was silent. She asked again.

"I told the big guy that I had just called Washington. That's all." Mike was driving faster and faster.

Lisa decided to be quiet. "Why would he call Washington? Who would he call? Not the President!" All of this was said to herself, as she kept an eye on the speedometer.

"You are going to need a lawyer and not the crooked one you have." Mike had cooled off and the car was losing speed.

"Bert said he was crooked, too," Lisa told him. "I've had a settlement with Bert. I hope my check made it to the bank and Jack didn't get his hands on it. I'm not sure I trust Marlowe. Jack has been a good friend, but I get the feeling he is two different people."

They drove on. "What time is it?" Lisa was waking. "I'm sorry I fell asleep. Let me take over. I don't mind driving at night." Lisa rubbed her eyes.

"No, I've set a pace and we are almost there. Tell me, for God's sake, what is all this thriller stuff all about?" Mike didn't take his eyes off the road as they were running into early morning fog.

"This I know," Lisa explained. "I think my mother knows more. Twelve men left for Ireland. All but two were killed. Someone wants to know who they were. I don't know why because I'm sure they never used their real names. They were likely mixed up in the Irish Republican Army. That group is still trying to make peace with England. They are probably in the opposition."

"Why would they want to have peace with England? They would never keep a bargain they never had," added Mike.

"Ireland has joined a European business group and Ireland is booming right now. I think they are trying to locate some older hold-outs. I'll never believe that. My dad died for what he believed was wrong and two wrongs don't make a right."

"I hope Ruth has a better understanding." Mike shook his head, as the sun was peeking over the horizon.

"When they find them, they will kill them. I'm sure that is why Jim Cory died." Lisa slumped in her seat and crossed her arms. "I'm getting hungry." Then Lisa asked, "Are you Irish?"

"No," and he laughed, "Not every Mike is Irish."

The lovely, lush landscape of Pennsylvania was appearing. Gettysburg was the next exit. Lisa commented, "It's just the same old, same old, all over again; just like the war of 1864."

"People will die for what they believe in," Mike added.

Lisa knew the way up the long driveway to the limestone house that had been built by an Irishman in 1806. Her mother ran to meet them. She was brushing her blonde hair from her face and holding onto the clothespins in her apron pocket. Mike, with wide-open arms, embraced Ruth. He held her so close and kissed her so tenderly that when they broke apart; both had to suck for air.

"Should I take a walk or pick some daisies?" Lisa smiled. She was pleased at what she had witnessed, but she still didn't want to be overheard.

The charming house was immaculate with the sun streaming through the sparkling clean windows of the huge country kitchen. Mike felt at home from the moment he entered the place.

Out on the back porch laid the largest German shepherd dog anyone had ever seen. The animal got up and walked to the screen door. He took time to size things up. There was not a sound out of him until he saw Ice. "He's on loan and I'm so glad." Ruth gushed with her eye on Mike. "The police left him here to protect me. He is trained, they told me."

"Where did Ice go?" Lisa had just missed him. Ice was no fool. He knew when he had been beaten.

CHAPTER 25

▼

Mike, Ruth, and Lisa were all relaxing and sitting around the large kitchen table drinking coffee and eating homemade doughnuts. Mike pushed back his chair and walked over to the window. The women watched in silence as he turned and put his finger to his mouth. Mike then retrieved a small, black box that was hidden in the left-hand corner of the window and placed just behind the curtain valance. This box could only have been seen from Mike's seated position. The women stared, while he wrote a note on the tablecloth that said, "We are wired. Don't talk. Let's get in the car."

The three, plus the police dog, almost tiptoed out of the house. It was too cold and damp in the early evening air, so the car was the best place to talk. Mike opened the doors for the ladies but stopped suddenly. "Oh my God, look what they've done to my car!"

The leather of his new car was slashed and stripped. "I didn't lock the car." Mike blamed himself. The trunk of the car had been pried open with a tire iron. The luggage was gone. "They will be back," Mike warned.

Mike had his cell phone on his belt. He called 9-1-1. "Please notify the State Police that the home of Mrs. Ruth McHugh at 144 W. Cedar Drive has been robbed and vandalized."

"Again?"

"Please call the State Police. I don't know the number. This is serious and dangerous. We expect them to return."

"When?" the dispatcher asked.

"When, who knows?" Mike was in charge and he wished he were in China. He had no idea of what to expect.

"Where is the police dog?" Lisa wanted to know.

They began to look for the dog in earnest. No police dog was to be found. "Get in the car, ladies. We must try to find him. He could be poisoned or stolen."

"I was told to keep him in out on the back porch." Ruth tried to defend the loss. An hour later, there lay the exhausted Romeo. Ice was back on the porch.

"You can't fight sex," Lisa laughed.

A neighbor telephoned to scold Ruth. "You keep that dog locked up. It's the second time he has been in my yard and mated to my beagle dog. She is even chained to a dog house. Keep him home," the woman banged down the phone.

"I'll take care of it in the morning," Mike said, hearing the neighbor's complaint.

"Maybe we should tell him to 'stay'." The others laughed.

"Well," Ruth explained, "if he is trained, he will know what 'stay' means."

"You ladies sleep together tonight. Where are the police for Christ's sake?" Mike threw his arms up in the air.

"I'll stay downstairs with that police dog and you keep Ice with you. That way, we will have plenty of warning."

"Do you have a gun?" Ruth asked Mike.

"No, why would I have a gun?"

They looked out the window and two State Police cars were approaching. "Thank God!" They all said at once.

It had gotten quite dark and no one had turned on a light. So when there was a knock on the front door, the three jumped in spite of seeing the police arrive. That was nothing compared to what the dogs did. They seemed to roar and show lots of teeth. No one could hold them back.

The State cop yelled through the door. "Put the dogs away." One dog was pushed through the entrance to the cellar and the other was sent outside. The police dog rounded the house after being put out. The trooper called 'stay!' The dog, who expected a piece of behind, stopped in his tracks.

"We thought we were at the wrong place until we looked in the car. You left your lights on. Who did that knife job to your car seats?"

"Oh my God, said Mike. We know that somebody isn't playing with a full deck. This chasing us around has got to stop."

The second trooper said, "Why doesn't Mrs. McHugh file a charge of harassment? This is the third time we have been here."

"No, that's not true. We think it's someone else. We have been away."

"She called twice in October and this is the third time," said the trooper.

"Mother, is that true?" Lisa was annoyed.

"I heard things other times, too. Once was right after Dad died." Ruth felt all their eyes upon her. "I don't make things up. I don't know who is doing it because I hide when I hear strong male voices in or around the house."

"How old is your mother?" the first trooper inquired.

"Fifty-one or two."

Ruth watched Mike's expression. Now he knew the difference in their ages. Ruth started to cry. "That's not old," she sniffled. "And, I still know what I'm doing." Now the tears were gone.

Mike stepped forward and put his arm around Ruth. It really comforted her. "Ruth, a woman isn't truly beautiful until she is forty. Before that, she is only a girl and at fifty she glorifies that beauty."

Lisa saw the first patrol officer writing in a notebook. "What was that last part?" he asked. "Boy, will my stock go up when I get home!"

"Back to business." The second trooper broke up the humor.

Mike spoke to the troopers. "You can't file a claim if you don't see who has forced entry. You have been here before. Didn't you see the disruption before?"

"It was as neat as a pin," the trooper stated.

"Of course, I cleaned it up each time before I called the police. I fixed the turned-over furniture, the dumped drawers, and the tracks on the floor," said Ruth.

Mike didn't want to call Ruth stupid, but he said, "Next time, please let everything be." The officers agreed.

Mike stopped them, as they were about to leave. "That should be enough to make a charge."

"I'll have the car picked up." The trooper made a note.

After the State Police left, Ruth suggested, "Let's go down in the fruit cellar. I have recalled something."

"You know, Pat, the one in New York?" her mother asked Lisa.

"Yes, go on," Lisa pushed.

"I've been thinking of something," she said.

"Well?" Both Mike and Lisa listened.

"I didn't think anything about it at the time. He said Lisa was known to the police. I thought it was when Ice dropped that kid who tried to snatch our purses."

"Dropped a kid? What kid?" Mike wanted to know.

"Pat knows more than we thought. Anyway, listen to this. I had forgotten something Mom Mom told me and made me swear never to speak of it again. There is a list of the ten men who didn't return. Mom Mom had the list."

"Who is Mom Mom?" Mike interrupted.

"My grandmother. Go on." Lisa wanted to try to piece the parts together.

"Well, Mom had this list of names. She never revealed their names. Anyway, Mom thought they were entitled to a decent burial. Those men would have been first generation to leave these shores to fight for Ireland. I've always thought Mom had a hand in all this and I know for sure, most of her fortune was sent to Ireland."

"Get back to the story, Ruth." Mike was very interested.

"She told me she put all their names in a tin box. She asked her priest to bless the contents and then she herself dug a hole in the ground and buried the can of names. One of the names was her only son, my husband, and Lisa's father. After she did that, she had a cement slab poured and built her kennel right on top of it. They will never find those names."

"Why would they want them?" Mike asked.

"Who knows?" She paused and looked at Lisa, who was dewy-eyed. "Those men could have fathered sons before leaving. It could be revenge or they are after the two they can't account for."

"Could Jim Cory be one of them?" Lisa wondered.

"Possibly." Her mother wiped a tear. "Mike, are you Irish?" Ruth asked.

"No, I was named for the angel." He tried to laugh.

Ruth continued. "The Irish are great storytellers. They sit and smoke their pipes, but they remember just like I'm telling you now. They have very long memories. They learn to write and read early in life. The mothers are the great teachers. They teach the love of music, the love of family, the love of poetry, history, and reading. The fathers taught their sons to hate the invading English who came into their beautiful land. Together, they taught their children their own faith. And, most beautiful, they taught them respect of women and love of the land. Do you think the police have been ordered to find that list?" Ruth asked.

"No," Lisa replied, "but I do think we are dealing with heroes or saboteurs, depending where your passion lies."

"On that list could be the names of sons or grandsons who have had their history lessons taught at home," Ruth related. "I'm English, but after being married to Joe, I'm a born-again Irish."

"I'm not sure what I am." Mike got off the hard wooden bench in the one bulb-lighted fruit cellar. "Did you do all this?" Mike referred to the shelves of canned peaches, pears, and tomatoes. "They look too good to eat." Mike stretched his arms, and then wrapped them around the woman he loved.

"Right here, in front of your daughter," he turned to Ruth, "I'm asking, will you marry me?"

It was a nice sight to be shared by all of them.

CHAPTER 26

▼

Lisa walked quietly away. Through the cellar window, she could see Mike's car being taken away, but not by the police. They were men who were wearing knitted ski masks. Lisa, in horror, opened the door to the fruit cellar within the basement. "You could have knocked!" Ruth screamed, as she scrambled for cover. Mike wrapped his shirt around his naked waist. "I refuse to be embarrassed. What in hell do you want?" Mike was not happy.

Lisa turned away in shock. "I wanted to tell you that your car is gone. The police did not take it." She stated boldly. "I saw three masked men get into your car and drive off. That's why I didn't knock!" Lisa walked to the cellar stairs. Tears were in her eyes. "I could just die! Why did I have to see that?"

She didn't want to think her mother could be loved that way. That was okay for everybody else; not her mother. She was saddened and embarrassed. The masked men were much less stressful.

The next morning, the police had questions and asked Lisa to come to the station to talk with them. Lisa went into detail to describe what she had seen under these strange and moving circumstances. "You say there were three people in ski masks?" The sergeant was writing as she spoke. "How could you be sure one was a woman?" The sergeant inquired.

"I could tell by her small, but thin ankle. I'll bet these are Irish rogues and I bet I know her name," Lisa added.

"What do you know about the Irish rogues?" He inquired and waited for an answer.

"Nothing," Lisa replied. "I only know what I've said that there were two men and one woman terrorist. There seems to be two teams working here. There has been a woman who appears in my life every now and again. She is a thorn in my side; to put it mildly. It could be her."

"Are you talking about Lahr?" the sergeant asked.

"I don't believe it," Lisa was open-mouthed.

"She has been involved for at least ten years. She works for the F.B.C."

"Are you sure her name is Lahr? I found her to be a thief, a liar, and an arsonist. I could go on and I'll bet you can't trust her. I'll bet she works for both sides for the highest dollar." Lisa was excited. "I know one thing, she dog-napped my entry into the Garden show. She ruined a life-long dream of mine."

"It's possible she has done you a big, big favor," the officer said.

"That's a lot of bull!" Lisa stood up, planning to leave. "I don't want to be found in the same room with that witch. You police seem to have some strange ideas and even stranger friends."

"You must be Irish," the sergeant replied. "Irish blood? Tisk! Tisk! You have a friend waiting in the outer office."

"It better not be her," Lisa flashed.

The officer led the way. There stood Pat. Lisa turned to the sergeant, who had escorted her into the large hallway.

"And, now you have really ruined my day!" she said as she saw him. "What do you want?" Lisa asked with blazing eyes. "What side are you on, double-crosser!" Pat reached for her arm.

"I've known nothing but pain and misery since I met you, so don't touch me!" Lisa blurted out.

The handsome Irishman backed away as Lisa paraded past him. Pat turned to the officer next to him. "Thank you."

"For what? That lady doesn't like you," the police officer kidded.

Lisa was standing at the top of the stairs in the police station. "I have no way home. No volunteers? Oh, darn, I'll have to call a cab."

"No way home! Tisk! Tisk!" The voice was familiar as he approached her.

Lisa turned away. "I'd rather walk," she glared.

"Who asked or offered?" Pat grinned, as he walked past her.

"Mrs. Taloomas?" a man in uniform called, "I'll be glad to take you home." His brogue was real. She took him up on his offer.

The car was there when Lisa returned.

"Pat called here," her mother advised, as Lisa entered the kitchen.

"What did he want?" Lisa picked up a fresh baked cookie. "I could care less."

"He said the car was searched for fingerprints. All the damage is covered by insurance," her mother said. Then Ruth turned to Lisa. "When are you going to buy me the car you promised?"

"As soon as I'm sure my money is really and truly in my account." Lisa reached for the phone to call Lexington.

"Mrs. Taloomas here. May I speak to Mr. Marlowe?"

"Sorry, Lisa, he is out to lunch. Banker's hours, you know."

"Who is this?" Lisa wanted to know.

"His secretary," she replied boldly. "What can I do for you? I can tell you what your balance is, if you want to know."

"Thank you, no."

Lisa returned to her room to pack some clothes. "Did Pat ask for me?" Lisa called from the bedroom.

"Yes and no," her mother recalled. "He said to tell you that George Marlowe, your banker, has just been arrested."

"My God, I've got to get home! My money could get tied up. Let's go. Mike, did you hear about the bank?"

"I don't bank there. I never did like Marlowe." Mike was in no hurry.

Lisa and Ice were standing at the front door. "Come on please. Kiss Mom goodbye and let's scram!" Standing on the porch, as she waited, Lisa ran over a few things in her head.

"Jim Cory was assassinated, that I know. My dog was stolen, that I know. Pat was in Ireland, that I know. But why? That I sure don't know. I think we are mixed up in something big," she thought.

"Come on Mike, unless you want to take me to the airport. I've got to get home, please. The police did it." Mike had her luggage in hand.

Ruth had two pillows. "Sit on these, dear. That torn leather can't be comfortable." They kissed all around, while Ice jumped into the car.

Lisa laughed. "Ice acts like he knows cake and candy await his arrival."

"At least the 'who' filled the gas tank and didn't stick the motor. Listen to my car purr." Mike was pleased.

"Just so it doesn't explode," was Lisa's reply.

Mike was all smiles, as he thought of his "bride to be." "You know, kid, I'm going to be your step-father and also your brother-in-law's brother. Does that make us cousins?" He laughed at the frown on Lisa's face.

Lisa felt they could speak freely as they sped down the road. She was mistaken. As the young woman continued to talk, unbeknownst to both of them, the car was bugged. Lisa commented, "The things Mother talked about like the list of Irish names was just what the anti-Irish had been looking for."

There were three people leaving Washington for Carlisle. "This country is sick and tired of terrorists and murder," the one twin said to the others. "I still don't like killing a woman."

"I'll take care of that," the woman volunteered.

Mike turned the speeding car on two wheels. "I will not leave Ruth alone." Alarm rose in his voice, as he pointed to a very small box stuck under the dash.

Lisa opened her mouth in surprise, but Mike put his finger to his lips. Mike pulled the car off the highway and removed the piece. He placed it under the car wheel and fought his way back into the fast moving traffic, making sure the car drove over the box to destroy it. Even so, Mike was not sure that was the only one in the car. "Keep talking," Mike whispered. "Otherwise they might get wise to us. There could be another one under your feet."

Lisa jerked up her feet. He laughed and Ice barked.

Looking out her kitchen window, Ruth spotted a slow-moving orange-colored car that looked like an armored truck. She turned off her light and watched the vehicle approach her house. It was getting closer. "Oh, no!" Ruth cried. She dropped her dishcloth and headed for the basement. She was stopped by a hooded figure with a female voice. "How did you get into my house?" Ruth tried to be brave. The woman flashed a revolver.

"Come with me!" the woman demanded.

Ruth had no choice but to cry and that she did very well. With tears streaming down her face and prayer on her lips, Ruth followed the masked woman toward the woods. Lisa's mother noticed the sod under her feet was soft from spring rains. She stomped along trying to make footprints that would lead to being found dead or alive. The female terrorist fired her revolver into the night air. Ruth dropped to the ground. She thought she had been shot.

"Get into the woods," the woman snarled. "Lie down here at my feet. Take my jacket and wrap yourself. I'm not going to kill you, but the others might, so stay still. Don't move. I'll be back." With that and a parting shot, the woman was gone.

Ruth lay as still as dead. She could see the light from her house, as the invaders went from room to room. They were searching for the list of names. It was as dark as midnight. The bare tree limbs against the moonlight were terrifying. She could feel animal movement upon the earth. "Please God, make it a deer." She thought of everything, about her husband leaving her with three children because he had to go. She thought of Mike and Lisa and thanked the Lord that they had gotten away.

Mike and Lisa were arriving in time to see three figures jump into the Hummer. "Quick, get my gun. It's in the glove compartment." It was loaded and Mike was quick enough to put a bullet in the rear tire. A second shot hit his aim. A woman's voice cried out in pain. Two of the men looked back as they drove off on the sagging tire. Mike's gun had four bullets left.

Lisa ran to the house and looked for her mother and her father's shotgun. Fortunately, the neighbors were calling the police and 9-1-1. Lisa called over her shoulder thinking her mother might hear her. The gun case was locked. Lisa was about to smack the glass front of the gun case with an iron frying pan.

"Don't bother." Mike took the frying pan out of her hands. "They are gone. Where is Ruth?"

"I can't find her." Lisa looked around and called her mother's name.

Ice was barking and jumping trying to help. The German shepherd lay dead on the back porch. Lisa looked at Mike. "What should we do?"

CHAPTER 27

▼

Mike grabbed Ruth's apron and rubbed Ice's nose in it. "Come on, boy. Make yourself useful, as well as beautiful." The two left the front porch. Mike had a large flashlight. Ice smelled the ground.

Police were everywhere. One touched Lisa's shoulder. It was Pat. Without thinking, Lisa dropped into his arms. "That terrible woman has been shot. I'm sure it is Lahr. I don't know where my mother has gone. That witch probably does!"

Pat lifted her chin. "We will talk later." He crawled into the orange-colored van to speak to Lahr. The police were holding back the increasingly curious.

"What is that light in the woods?" one officer asked Lisa.

"I don't know. I didn't see it. It looks like a flashlight. I assure you that it isn't for me." Lisa spun around at the distant sound of Ice. Bark! Bark! It was loud and meaningful. "That's my dog! Lisa yelled between joy and tears. "He has found something! He has found something!" Lisa repeated and ran at top speed for the woods. Someone joined her in the darkness. It was Pat.

Not far away, Ruth had been found. "Don't shoot, please don't shoot! I don't know anything," Ruth begged. Ice licked her face and ran circles around her. The dog thought it was a game. Ice and Mike had separated in search and it was the dog, who found her. "Thank God! Thank God! Ice, you scared me so much. I heard you approaching. I heard twigs snapping and footsteps. I kept my eyes closed." She sat up and hugged the dog. She was covered with earth and leaves and so was Ice.

At that point, she saw the flashlight again. Fearfully, she lay down again and Ice followed suit. "Shush!" Ruth whispered in the dog's ear and held onto him, as he struggled to be released. He knew the scent approaching was Lisa. The bright light from Mike's large flashlight found Ruth and Ice.

"Oh, my God, Ruth, are you okay?" The voice was familiar. At that point, Ruth opened her eyes. "Mike, Mike, I thought I would never see you again." Ruth had tried to cover herself with leaves, grass, and twigs. Mike lifted her to her feet.

"Oh, Mother!" Lisa sobbed as she ran up. There were hugs and kisses.

"I was so afraid, but some woman, maybe Lahr, helped me hide," Ruth said, as she sobbed and held onto Mike.

"I was never so scared," Mike laughed through his tears. "Ruth, I'm never leaving your side again."

"In that case, I'm glad that I didn't burn up the thirty thousand dollar check."

"What check?" Lisa asked.

"Billy McGovern, Mom Mom's brother, left it here. He must have known Dad wasn't coming back. He had endorsed it and left it here. Boy, there were lots of times I could have used that money. I found it in an old teapot when I was trying to hide something else.

"What else?" Lisa leaned forward. "Mother, were you in this, too?"

"Not me, I'm from the generation that was willing to let their husbands take care of things."

"Hear, hear!" Mike clapped in approval.

"I'm out of here at first light," said Lisa. "Ice and I still have a date back in Lexington."

Mike asked the police about burying the German shepherd. "He is dead on the back porch. I hope I can bury him here. I'm sure he has been a hero and he died with a hunk of someone's pants in his teeth."

"That could contain DNA. That would take care of one of them."

Everyone was ready for bed. No one had eaten dinner and no one was hungry. Mother and Mike took off with one another. Neither had a moment's hesitation.

"I thought that was my generation." Lisa resented their co-habitation. "I'm really going to be able to sleep tonight." Lisa dropped her clothes beside the bed. The sheets felt cool and clean against her naked body.

A voice in the darkness asked, "Would you like company?" It was Pat with that fake brogue!

Without a word, Lisa lifted the blanket and sheet. Pat, stripped off his clothes and just as bare, climbed in. "You have no idea how many times I've dreamed of this moment," Pat whispered passionately.

Lisa snuggled closer. She trailed her fingers over his hairy chest. She whispered, "Why was Jim Cory killed?" Pat was out of bed in a shot, as if hurt that her mind was on something else. Lisa jumped out on her side. She picked up her clothes and held them close to her. She was easily seen in the moonlight. He began to melt again.

"Please don't go." She really wanted him to stay. They surrendered in each other's arms and her clothes fell back onto the floor.

Pat held Lisa close and kissed her like she had never been kissed before. When she came up for air, Lisa drew him back to her bed.

Before daybreak, Pat was gone. He left as he had arrived. He slid down the balcony post, the same one he had climbed earlier to reach Lisa's bedroom. When she awoke and found herself alone, she stretched and smiled. "Love and hate are akin," Lisa told herself. "I think I've loved that damn Irishman for some time." The young, naked woman reached for the pillow he had slept on. Lisa hugged the soft contents close to her bare breasts.

"My brother, Tom, just called." Mike greeted the still-smiling daughter of the woman he loved. "Breakfast—and I'm the cook?"

"What did Tom have to say?" Lisa asked. "I hope everything is okay." She waited for Mike to speak.

He said, "You have got to get Ice home or your chances of puppies are out the window. He also said that Snow, that's what you call your new dog.

"You mean my new bitch?"

"I hate that word." Mike made a face. "But I know that's what you dog breeders say."

"Did he say it was too late?" Lisa dreaded the reply.

"He said she is ready, okay?"

"Thank goodness. I'll get a flight as soon as possible. I want puppies. I miss puppies. That's my life; dogs and horses." Her mother had entered the kitchen.

"What about men?" Ruth had a grin on her face.

"I'll fit them in from time to time," Lisa laughed. Lisa was packed. She had two suitcases, a large dog crate, and the dog.

"What are you all smiles about?" Mike asked. He acted like he knew something.

"Can't I smile?" Lisa smiled.

After a moment's delay, Mike added, "Pat could have been shot last night."

"How? Why?" The smile was gone from her face.

"He tried to open our bedroom balcony door. I think he is some kind of a secret agent. I watched him leave at 5:00 a.m. in the darkness. He just disappeared without a sound."

They dropped Lisa and Ice off at the heavily secured airport curb. Mike was only allowed to drop her and her belongings off. Mother and Mike were blowing kisses as they drove away.

Lisa looked for a "red cap," but there were none. She almost fell over her own luggage, as Ice circled her with an entangled leash. A military man was coming her way.

"A lady in distress; what a lucky discovery. You angel, and how are you, you handsome dog?" She was going to get some assistance.

"What a beautiful dog." The major admired Ice. "Beauty to the beauty!" He was so gallant. "Let me help you before they wipe you off the sidewalk in this mad traffic."

In what seemed like seconds, the Major had Lisa's luggage, the crated dog, and they were on their way. He discovered that they were on the same plane going to the same place. Then, he turned to Lisa. "There is a pretty decent restaurant here in the airport. Let me buy brunch because they won't serve a meal, even on first class, as the flight is so short."

"Thank you for your help." Lisa flashed her white teeth and dark brown eyes. "Where is your luggage?" She was looking around.

"I have been transferred to the War College in Carlisle. Let's get a seat and catch up."

"Great!" She slipped her arm in his and let him lead the way. Once seated, they both began to talk at the same time. Lisa put her finger in the air, "Me first." She took a deep breath. "Since I saw you last, I could write a book."

CHAPTER 28

▼

Lisa told the Major her story of New York and about the action she had just been through.

"This is making sense to me." The Major studied for a moment. "You know, my friend, John Holt, is being detained. I'm sure he will be indicted."

"What for?" Lisa urged.

"I'm not sure of the details, but money laundering is at the base of things," the young man informed.

Lisa, in turn, added, "Bert warned me about him. I thought he was my friend."

"Lawyers are a rotten lot." The Major was venting his opinion.

Lisa was in deep thought. "They say follow the money." She was serious.

"I hope it isn't the money. Lisa, he isn't to be trusted."

Lisa was thinking, "Isn't this a strange way for a man to talk to a woman."

They had no assigned seats so they scrambled to be seated together. "Lisa, there has been some talk and I think Jack was responsible for the talk. He was half bombed at the club one night when he told all who would listen that you had been involved in a murder. You!"

"I won't say I was involved. I wasn't, but I did find someone I knew dead. But, there were witnesses who saw that I arrived after the man was dead."

The Major changed the subject. "Looks like an early spring."

"I hope so." Lisa also changed the subject. "I'm looking forward to the birth of an Arabian foal."

"I've heard." He reached for Lisa's hand. She gave him a sideway glance. The Major removed his hand and adjusted his seatbelt. He wondered what he had said or done to make Lisa turn cold.

He offered to drive Lisa home. She thanked him for his help, but she had to hire a car. She wanted to retrieve her car that she had had to leave at the Bramble Inn in the snowstorm. That seemed like such a long time ago.

Once home with the people she loved and trusted, Lisa suggested they sit outside while she related her story and told of her fears. She wanted to talk about the things she knew and about her suspicions that there was a huge conspiracy. She felt a lot of big shots were involved. "I know there is a lot of money involved. I'm sure that my money has been messed with. First thing in the morning, I'm going to the bank."

"Marlowe is in jail," Tom informed.

Tom, with an M.B.A. degree he might be of value, she thought. He offered to look at her account if she did not mind.

They decided not to wait. The next day would be one more chance for some skullduggery. The bank was one of the most beautiful banks in Lexington. It was made of glass, marble, and brass. When she and Tom asked to see her holdings and records, two bank investigators stepped forward. She was told the bank was closing. Someone or more were on the move to bring things out in the open.

Tom stepped forward. "I'd like to see proof that you are what you say." The strangers' mouths dropped open in disbelief.

Lisa took over. "I'm Mrs. Bertram Taloomas. I've just made a very large deposit and I want to know that I've been credited properly."

"Mrs. Taloomas," the bank man groaned, "you have no idea what you are getting into. Go home, please, Mrs. Taloomas. Go home. Read the papers."

As they were leaving the bank, police were arriving, along with men with F.B.I. printed on their jackets. Booking auditors also arrived dressed in three-piece suits. The bank was closed to everyone else.

When they returned home, Mary met them at the door. "Listen to the TV. I think Bert Taloomas has just shot himself or been shot but he didn't die. He has been living in Paris too afraid to go home."

Lisa burst into tears. "I can't stand one more thing!" She turned to Tom. "Take Ice to Snow. Let's not miss that."

They charged Bert as the major gunrunner to Ireland. He was classified as the worst of all the culprits. The gunrunner, with lots of help, kept the hatred in Ireland alive while he sat and played with his child, making millions and millions of dollars.

It's the fault of many people who just can't forgive each other. The man was Greek, not an American citizen. He carried a lot of grief. Police didn't know why he tried to kill himself.

Lahr had slipped back into Port au Prince. When she was asked why she chose such a dangerous game, she laughed. "I only answer to the top dollar! I work for money, different people, and many nations." But some, like Ruth who was saved in the woods, knew that even Lahr had her principles.

"But, who killed Jim Cory?" Lisa wondered. "I can't believe I was under suspicion. With friends like that, I'll take the enemy!"

Lisa started to wonder about Pat. "Was he a double agent? I'm almost afraid to trust him. Where is Pat now? I want to know what is going on. I might need his help." Lisa was also thinking about her sixteen million dollars that Bert gave her.

The Major called to remind her she had a date with him for the Full Moon Barbecue. "Oh darn it!" she thought, "I'd so much rather be home."

Tom interrupted her thoughts. He called from the new kennel. "There has been a tie." He announced. "It was at least thirty minutes. You are going to have pups."

"You better get this kennel finished. You know Standards have ten to twelve pups at a time. Whoopee!" Lisa squealed with pleasure.

"By the way, while you were away, Dr. Morton stopped by. He told me to tell you that he wants the foal. Male or female, his offer is one million bucks!"

"No way!" Lisa declared. "I'll eat beans if I have to, but this is my life, my home, my dogs and my horses."

"Think about it, Lisa. What you want costs lots of bucks."

"Especially if my sixteen million dollars are confiscated. I'm sorry Bert got shot. Maybe he didn't shoot himself. Maybe Lahr shot him."

A voice behind her said, "You'll do okay, Lisa. You are a tough lady. Shut up and get a new lawyer." It was Pat.

"Where did you come from?" Lisa wanted to know.

"I've been out in the kennel helping Tom with an interested bitch. There are at least two around here! The first one had curly white hair. But, like all females, a few kind words and she relaxed. At first, I was afraid she was really going after him. Tom said we had waited too long."

"We?" Lisa lifted her head.

"I've been to London, not to visit the queen, but to make sure you are not under suspicion. You were, you know?"

"So, I've heard. I can't see why."

"Don't take it lightly. There were witnesses who were going to swear they saw you kill. So many people knew how much you hated Jim Cory. If they could nail you, it would have been a payback because of your grandmother. She had been sending money to groups for years."

"Poor Mom Mom." Lisa was saddened. "I know how she felt. Those were different times. Ireland is no longer the impoverished nation she once was. The I.R.A. wants to make peace."

Pat said, "I lived it, too, as a boy, but when Ireland joined the European Trade Agreement, their world changed. The young of Ireland are staying home. The average age is under thirty. Now their people, who were forced to leave for parts of the world making other nations rich, are taking care of their people right at home."

Lisa pushed a footstool his direction. "Do you need a soap box?"

"You didn't hear a word, did you?" Pat asked her. "You are something else." Pat continued, "For some reason, I know I love you. You'd make a hell of a wife and a damn good mother to my ten children!"

"Did I hear a proposal?" Lisa was on her feet.

"No, just a suggestion," he smiled.

"Who killed Jim Cory?" Lisa had to know.

"The twins. There was a hundred thousand on Jim's head. The twins decided to take the bounty money instead of sticking it on to you."

"But, why did they kill Jim? Why won't you tell me?" Lisa stomped her foot.

"Okay. For years and years, he was Ireland's top promoter. He sold Ireland wherever he went, especially among the rich Irish. For every two dollars he sent to Ireland for the cause, Jim kept one. Now I'm talking about millions over the past years starting with your grandmother. Then her brother, then his friends, etc."

"So, Jim was one of the two they were looking for?" she questioned. "And who is the second man, you?"

There was a rap at the door. "Oh my God, my date!"

"Your what?" He had never thought of her belonging to anyone else. "Who?"

"You answer the door. Please tell him I'll be ready in a minute." Lisa took off on the run. When she returned, her date was nowhere to be found. "Where did the Major go?" she asked.

"I told him you were busy, because we were getting married tonight!"

While the bridegroom was proving his prowess, Lisa's million-dollar foal was being born.

THE END

About the Author

Edna (Eddie) Collins wrote her first murder mystery at the age of twenty-six. She had no plans to write another. It had been a challenge but once done, she was satisfied.

She married and raised a family. She dabbled in many areas such as antiques, raising and showing purebred dogs, and traveling the world.

These mysteries with dogs as central characters kept buzzing around in her head for years. One day, much later, she decided to put pen to paper and here is the final result, with more already on the drawing board.

She located an editor, Dr. Diane Holloway, author and co-author of non-fiction books such as *The Mind of Oswald, Dallas and the Jack Ruby Trial, Jacuzzi, Before You Say 'I Quit'* and *Who Killed New Orleans?*

Edna then selected iUniverse.com to publish her work and make it available everywhere.

Eddie's motto is: "You're never too old to start writing!"

978-0-595-42168-8
0-595-42168-7

Printed in the United States
71949LV00004B/151-189

9 780595 421688